MIRROR, MIRROR

Jessica Jesinghaus

Kathleen~
I really hope you
enjoy & don't think
I'm too crazy when
you're done -
JJesinghaus

Mirror, Mirror
Jessica Jesinghaus
Paperback Edition, Copyright 2016
Published via Kindle Direct Press

ISBN 151906991X

To my husband, for your ever-patient love & support.

I couldn't have done this without you.

Table of Contents

I am the dark knight.

As I avenge a history that I cannot change,

I seek hope for a tomorrow of silence

From the bats inside my head.

Screaming to fight the wrongs I cannot right.

If I were to complete this task would I be done?

-Anonymous-

Batman said
this. →

Chapter One

"Hey Samantha," Tony called from his desk, the phone receiver pressed to his shoulder, "There's a pileup out on the highway. Some idiot with a freighter lost it and caused a five-car mess. Two dead on the scene. Just your speed! You want it?"

"I'm already out the door," she called back, pausing just long enough to grab her coat and purse, the latter always containing her pen and notepad. "Where exactly?"

"Highway 26, westbound, marker sixty-five," her editor replied. "Take a camera."

"It's in the car."

"Spoken like a pro."

It took her twenty minutes to get to the accident site, but she could see it well before she was upon it. In the twilight the flashing lights of emergency vehicles gave the sunset an eerie strobe effect and a stream of smoke cut the sky in a giant black gash. So, she thought, we've had a fire? That always made for a great picture. Front page maybe? The readers always went for stuff like that, and so did her editor.

As she rolled up on the scene she instinctively pulled her Oregon Tribune press pass from the glove compartment and attached it to the lapel of her jacket. She parked behind one of the police cruisers, did a quick check of her makeup in the rearview mirror, and hopped out into the slow-falling rain.

"Hey Sam, back again?" She turned around and was greeted by a familiar, smiling face.

"Sergeant Torrance. How are you doing this fine evening?"

"Well, as you can see," he said, sweeping his arm across the panorama before them, "it could be better."

"So what have you got for me?" Sam quickly snapped a couple photos of the crash before the wreckers could get a chance to clear it away.

"Well cutie, freighter lost its cargo all over the highway and the five cars behind him couldn't stop fast enough on the wet road. Got two dead here. Five injured, a couple of 'em serious."

"Any names?" she asked, pushing a damp, wayward curl from her face as she jotted down the info Joe was providing. "Just on the injuries. Got a John and Jane Doe in the car up there. Can't get to them, what with the fire and all, but the crew's almost got the flames out. You know I can't give you those names until we find next of kin."

"You and your rules Torrance. You'll get me those names as soon as possible, right?"

"Sugar, you're always on the top of my list."

"Great. Got any objections to me asking a few questions?"

"It's all yours darling. Just stay clear out of the way. You know me and my rules."

"Thanks. I'll talk to you later, when you've got a little less on your hands."

"Promise?"

This was their standard routine. A little harmless banter was all it was, something to lessen the gravity of their meetings. Torrance was a good man, not a unique specimen as far as his looks were concerned, but he was a family man with two little girls and a wife at home. He'd shown her pictures of them once and Sam couldn't help but notice the beaming smile of pride that had covered his face.

"I promise."

Sam watched Sergeant Torrance trot toward the still smoldering sedan to lend a helping hand. She could see the outlines of the two bodies inside. Oddly, she felt no twinge of emotion at the sight. After only six months on the crime beat for the Tribune she was shocked at how hardened she'd already become.

Sam set her sights on a young lady about her own age sitting on an ambulance gurney. She'd already been tended to by the medics, as the square of gauze taped upon her forehead evidenced. Sam made her way over, trying to establish eye contact, but the woman wouldn't look up. She just sat there with her head in her hands, her blunt-cut red hair forming a type of canopy around her face.

"Hello," she said to the woman once she was within range. "My name is Samantha Williams. I'm with the Tribune. I was wondering if I could ask you a few questions about what happened here tonight?"

"Hey Sam," the woman stated, looking up, not at all surprised to see her friend standing before her. "I was wondering how long it would take you to get here. You're a regular vulture, you know?"

"Oh, good God! Jen? Are you all right? Are you hurt?"

"Nope, I checked out okay. I'll probably have one hell of a headache in the morning. I may have whiplash too, but it could be worse." Jen unknowingly mimicked Sergeant Torrance's action earlier and spanned her arm across the accident scene.

Sam sat down beside her roommate. "What happened?"

"Well, after work I was on my way home from the grocery and I got stuck behind this damn truck hauling chickens. Chickens! Feathers were flying everywhere, just flying. It was actually kinda funny, like you'd see in a cartoon. But then one of the tie lines snapped, I guess, and all these crates came tumbling out into the road. The damn idiot driving slammed his brakes and somebody rear-ended him. The car on fire, that's the one. Anyway, I swerved right, trying to miss it all and ended up off the road. I think I caught the gravel ditch there, and I flipped. Just once I think. Dinner's all over the road." Jen let loose a nervous jitter of laughter. "God. It all happened so fast. It was horrible. The car that hit the truck, I heard it explode." Jen began to sob heavily. "Sam, did they get out? The people in that car? Did they get them out?"

"No honey," Sam said gently. "They didn't make it."

Just then Sergeant Torrance approached them. "Sugar?" he said, "Can I see you for a moment?"

"Not a good time Joe. This is my roommate, Jen. She was in the red Civic, the one in the ditch. Jen, this is Sergeant Torrance."

"Yeah, nice to finally meet you Sergeant. Sam talks about you a lot."

"Look, Samantha, this is really important. It's about our John and Jane…"

"You've got names for me already? Mister, you're good."

"Samantha, honey, it's not that. I think you should come with me."

"What is it Joe? Whatever it is, Jen can hear it too. It's not like she'll try and beat me to the story."

"All right." Joe took a moment to collect himself. "The boys thought I should be the one to talk to you… Angel, we got 'em out of the car and we've got some identification off the bodies. Driver's licenses." He stopped and took Sam's hands. "Damn, this is hard." Joe paused again and swallowed hard, "Samantha, I need to know your folks' names."

"What? Wh-why?" Sam stammered, the reality of what Joe was asking beginning to sink in.

"I think you know why."

Jen spoke up when she saw Sam was incapable of responding. "Jeff and Susan. Their names are Jeff and Susan Williams."

4

Joe lowered his head so no one could see the tears forming in his eyes. "That's them. Samantha, I'm so sorry." He squeezed her hand lightly and cast an imploring look at Jen. "Look honey, I've got to go. Jen's gonna look after you for now. I'll swing by your apartment later to check on you, okay?" Joe Torrance turned to leave, but stopped. "I'll take good care of your folks."

"I know you will Joe."

~ ~ ~

The rest of that rainy Tuesday night was a blur. There was no story, and certainly no front page picture. Sam and Jen stayed at the crash site until they'd pulled the Williamses completely out and quenched the last of the flames licking over their charred Mercury. Sam pushed her way through police lines and curious onlookers until she could catch a glimpse of her parents' burned, unrecognizable bodies. When one of the officers tried to pull her back, she shrugged him off vehemently.

"Those are my parents, God damn it!" Every head in the crowd turned momentarily to stare at her in pity. A flash bulb lit the night for a second as a reporter from a rival paper snapped a picture of her; a beautiful, distraught young woman, drenched by the rain, her press pass clearly visible on the front of her charcoal suit. His photo caption would later read "Tragedy Hits Home for Local Reporter."

"Sorry," the officer mumbled.

"Sam," Jen said softly, "Come on, I'll drive you home."

"No, you're hurt," Sam stated as she turned away from the charred corpses. "I'll drive."

Jen was awed, and a bit repulsed, by Sam's lack of emotion. *She's in shock,* Jen thought. *Wouldn't you be if you rolled up on a standard story to find your best friend involved and both your parents dead?*

By the time they reached Sam's car, though, Jen could see a definite shift in her friend's demeanor. Her face had fallen from its usually composed state into one of utter despair and confusion. Sitting in the driver's seat, her white shuddering hands in a death grip on the wheel, Jen thought she looked like a frightened, pitiful child.

"Sam... Hon, are you sure you don't want me to drive?"

"No." Sam turned the key in the ignition and eased her car into the single lane of traffic skirting the chaos. She took one last look at the crash site in her rearview mirror and found herself unable to pull her gaze from the wet feathers spread all over the road.

~ ~ ~

After riding in silence for several minutes, Sam spoke up. "I need to make one stop before we go home." She glanced at Jen's confused face. "The paper. I need to make sure Tony knows he's not getting a story on this one."

"Can't you let me call him for you?" Jen offered, but one look at the determination on Sam's face told her it wasn't an option.

Sam was admirably calm by the time they reached the Tribune's offices. By now, the May twelfth morning edition had been sent to the printers. Tony hadn't waited for Sam's story after all, so Jen guessed he must have heard the news already.

Almost in confirmation of Jen's hunch, Tony stood from a nearby desk. He'd stayed late, knowing surely Sam would drop by. "Samantha..." he started, "God, I'm so sorry! Sergeant Torrance called to make sure I didn't bug you about the story. He's worried about you. And to tell you the truth, so am I."

"I'll be fine Tony, thanks."

"Is there anything I can do?" Tony asked.

"Yes. Let me handle their obits."

"Sam, are you sure you want to do that?" Jen asked as she stepped forward and placed a hand on Sam's arm.

"Yeah, Randy can handle it for you tomorrow," Tony assured his crime reporter. "I'm sure he'll handle them special, if that's what you're worried about."

"No, that's not it Tony. Just let me do this!" Sam snapped.

Tony stared at Sam with an obvious look of confusion. "Sure. I mean, anything you want."

"I'll be at my desk."

Jen sat beside her friend as she clicked out a short obituary on her computer keyboard. Tears trickled down Sam's cheeks the whole time, but she never made a sound. It broke Jen's heart to see her best friend so distraught, but she knew there was nothing she could do.

With the declaration of her parents' deaths finished and printed, Sam dropped it onto Randy's desk. "Let's go home."

~ ~ ~

Jen saw Sam to bed that night and sat with her until she drifted off to sleep. She watched over her for a little while, her hand unconsciously stroking Sam's dark, curly hair. Then she padded down the hall into the living room. Their apartment was small and old; cozy and quaint if you wanted to put it nicely, but it fit their needs well. They had found it after their college graduation. They'd had a little money saved to tide them over until they found their dream jobs and this little place fit the budget nicely. Once they had found those dream jobs, it just seemed too much hassle to move. So they had stayed for two whole years, simple as that.

Jen had just settled onto the couch with a glass of milk when she heard a light knock on the door. Remembering Joe Torrance's promise to drop by, she opened the door with no hesitations.

"This late at night, you should really be more careful," Joe scolded her.

"Hi Joe," she said, smiling for the first time since the crash. "Who's your friend?"

"This is Patrick Logan. We were on our way back to the station."

"Nice to meet you," the stranger remarked. He was tall and, Jen noted, ruggedly handsome with darkly tanned skin and short, curling hair.

"Likewise," she replied, "and thanks for stopping by. This will mean a lot to Sam when she's able to look back on it."

"How's she doing?" Joe asked.

"Well, I just got her into bed. She's sleeping now."

"That's good. I don't want to wake her, so I'll call in the morning."

"Look, would you two like to come in for a cup of coffee? You've had a rough night too."

"Thanks, but we really should get back," Patrick replied.

"You'll tell Sam I stopped by?"

"Of course, Joe."

"Take care of our girl." Joe dropped her a friendly wink, and with that he and Patrick headed back to their cruiser.

~ ~ ~

Jen awoke the next morning to the ringing of the telephone. She was not at all surprised to find she had fallen asleep on the living room sofa. As she reached for the phone she grimaced in pain. There was a terrible kink in her neck. *That'll teach me to sleep on the damn couch,* she thought.

"Hello?"

"Jen? It's Joe. I'm calling to check on our Angel."

"Well, to tell the truth, I don't know. I just woke up. But do you want to hang on and... Wait a second, here she comes."

Sam staggered down the hallway just then. "Who's that?"

"It's Joe. He's worried about you."

"Mind if I take this alone?" Sam asked as she took the phone.

"Not at all. I'll be in my room when you're done if you need to talk."

From her room Jen could overhear Sam's muffled conversation with Joe. From time to time she could hear the distinctive sounds of crying. Jen sat in front of the mirror in her room brushing her hair. Then she carefully began to inspect last night's injury. Gingerly she peeled away the surgical tape and gauze so she could get a look at what was beneath. She began to sob when she saw the angry red gash and its contrasting black stitches. One of her amber colored eyes was swollen nearly shut, bruising lightly. The paramedics had warned her it wouldn't be a pretty sight and that the cut may scar, but actually seeing herself like this was too much. She'd have to call in sick today; there was no way she could leave Sam alone.

Oh, that's noble, she scolded herself. *Let's be honest... You don't want anyone to see this ugly thing on your forehead!*

Quietly, so as not to disturb Sam, Jen tiptoed to the bathroom to get fresh bandages and to snag a quick shower. As she let the hot water cascade down her naked and bruised body she was hit by the gravity of all that had happened in the last twelve hours. Soon she was sitting on the floor of the tub shaking and crying, the shower still pelting her with water. *Just let it out*, she thought, *you've got to grieve in order to heal.* She began to giggle then, tears still coursing down her cheeks. Her interior psychobabble was just too silly. But what else would you expect from a counselor? Once she had her emotions back in check, she grabbed her cell phone and went about the business of calling out sick at work.

"Kennedy Middle School, this is Megan."

"Hey Meg, it's Jen. Look, I'm not going to be able to come to work today."

"Are you sick?"

9

"No. But did you hear about that wreck out on the twenty-six last night?"

"Yeah."

"I was in it."

"No way!" Meg exclaimed.

"Yeah. I've got a nasty gash on my forehead, but I'm gonna be all right. But here's the kicker. You remember my roommate Samantha, right?"

"The reporter? Sure."

"She was covering the story, so she was out on the scene, and it turns out her parents were involved too."

"No way," Meg repeated.

"They didn't make it."

"Oh my God! Tell her I'm sorry."

"I will, but I think I'm going to need a couple days off. For both of us."

"Oh, absolutely. I'll take care of it. Take as many as you need, we'll get around it. I'll have Perry call if he's got any questions, but I think we can handle it."

"Thanks Megan. I'm sure I'll be back by Monday, Tuesday at the latest. I'll call you and let you know for sure."

"Okay. Take care."

"Bye."

Still in her bathrobe, Jen rapped gently on Sam's open bedroom door. "Mind if I come in?"

"Sure. How are you feeling?"

"Pretty well. This cut on my forehead isn't a pretty sight, but I'm sure I'll survive. How about you? Are you hanging in there?"

"I've got a great support system," Sam said, smiling just a little.

"Yeah, well I'm not sure what you'll think of me after this," Jen muttered, sitting beside her on the bed. "Is there anyone we should call? About your parents? Family, friends?" Sam began to sob again. "Sam, I'm sorry. I know this is tough, but they need to know. If you want, you can just give me a list and I'll make all the phone calls," Jen offered.

Sam sprang forward and hugged her faithful friend. "They should hear it from me," she said between sobs.

"I'll stay with you if you'd like."

"I think it would be helpful."

So for the next three and a half hours Jen sat beside her friend at the kitchen table, stroking her hand in reassurance, while Sam broke the news to her family and their friends. She must've heard Sam recount the events of the last night five or six times, and each time it upset her just as much. Then, with her calls complete, Sam announced she was going to lie down for a while.

"Do you mind if I borrow your car then?" Jen inquired. "We have no food in the fridge and I'm getting hungry."

"You sure you're ready to drive?"

"Yeah, I'll be fine." Sam nodded her approval and tossed Jen her keys from off the kitchen counter on her way out of the room.

~ ~ ~

When Sam woke up next it was seven o'clock on Thursday morning. She'd slept almost a whole day! Rolling out of bed she staggered down the hallway and threw herself into the shower. Her head was pounding with memories of her parents. Vividly as a Hollywood movie, images of childhood picnics and school recitals flashed through her mind. And in every picture her parents were together, smiling happily. It was more than she could bear, and for what seemed like the hundredth time, she broke down into tears.

Finally, half an hour later, she emerged from the steamy bathroom, her damp curls wrapped tightly in a bath towel. Sam followed the smell of pancakes into the kitchen where she encountered a smiling Jen.

"Hello sleepyhead. I thought maybe you'd pulled a Rip Van Winkle on me."

"Good morning to you too." Sam was glad to see Jen in a better mood. The bandage was still taped to her forehead, but she looked well rested. "Did you save any for me? I'm starved."

"I figured you would be," Jen said, producing a whole heap of pancakes from the oven where she'd been keeping them warm. "Here you go."

"You're a peach!" Sam exclaimed, surprising Jen with a genuine sparkle in her pale blue eyes. "So, when do you head back to work?" she inquired, stuffing a mouthful of flapjacks into her mouth.

"I told them I'd be back Monday or Tuesday," Jen replied. "But get this, I called my insurance company yesterday about my car, and it turns out the freight company is going to cover everything. I mean, my car is totaled. It's not worth repairing, but with the insurance money I can get an even better one."

"You mean, one that won't break down three times a week?" Sam cracked.

"Well, it won't be anything special, but it's got to be better than Grant." 'Grant' was Jen's car's name. She and Sam had named it on a whim over a year ago when Jen's parents surprised her with it on her birthday.

"I've got enough in savings for a down payment, and the insurance company faxed me a settlement estimate for financing. So," she offered, "do you want to get out of this house and go car shopping with me?"

"I don't really have a choice now, do I?"

"What do you mean?"

"Well, somebody's got to drive you there."

Chapter Two

"Oh Sam! This is perfect!" Jen exclaimed. She was referring to Sam's new house. Almost six months had passed since that fateful crash. In that time, Sam had found herself with a cash settlement from the freighter company to avoid a civil action lawsuit. Sam was astounded they had thought she would sue them, but upon Jen's advice she let them continue to think so. In the end, she had just over a million dollars in her bank account. It was a lot of money, more than Sam really knew how to wrap her mind around, but it would never be enough to compensate for the loss of her parents.

She'd spent many sleepless nights talking to Jen about what she should do with the money. She knew she wanted to put most of it somewhere safe, but she also wanted to do something immediate, something her parents would have liked for her. That's when Jen suggested she get a home of her own. The idea was perfect. Two days later Sam was out with an agent looking at homes. And now she'd found one.

This was the first time Jen had seen it. Sam had wanted it to be a surprise, and she was pleased it was going so well. The house was spacious compared to their apartment, but modest by most standards, with a great front and back yard. It was a respectable little blue two story with matching dormer windows on each of the upstairs bedrooms. Jen was instantly enamored with it, just as Sam had been.

"You mean to tell me this is all yours?" Jen asked, still incredulous. "I can't believe how fast you put this together!"

"Yeah, it's amazing. The paperwork was finalized this morning. And I owe it all to you for helping me figure this out. I really do feel like Mom and Dad are proud of me right now. I owe you one."

"How about you just promise me you still need a roommate and we'll call it even. I'd hate to end up homeless all because I gave you this great idea."

"Homeless? Are you kidding? Your home is with me for as long as you want. You're like family and I honestly don't know what I'd do without you." Sam captured her friend in a warm embrace. "So, when do you want to move in?" she inquired.

"When can we start?"

"Any time we want, the house is ours." Sam smiled, "And I hope you don't mind, but I gave notice at our apartment as soon as I knew things were concrete with the house."

"Of course I don't mind!" Jen reassured her. "Let's do this."

"I was hoping you'd say that."

The two rented a U-Haul van the very next day. The entire afternoon was spent boxing, packing, and loading the van. Joe called at one point and Sam told him their wonderful news. He informed her he was off duty soon, and since his wife and daughters were down south visiting his mother-in-law, he had a whole evening to help them if they wanted. Sam gratefully accepted his offer.

By six o'clock they had most of their apartment cleared. Only the larger items remained. So Sam and Jen bundled up against the cold October winds and took a trip to their new house and unloaded the boxes, jumbling them haphazardly into the middle of the living room floor.

"We'd better hurry back," Sam announced. "Joe said he'd drop by about any time now. I'd hate to keep him waiting out in this cold." Waiting, they discovered, was exactly what he was doing. As the girls approached their apartment door they saw Joe and someone Sam didn't recognize sitting against it.

"Where were you two?" Joe asked as he stood, a friendly twinkle in his eyes. "I was beginning to think you didn't want our help after all."

"Sorry," they apologized in unison. "We took a van-load of boxes over to the new house," Sam continued.

"Likely story Angel," Joe laughed. "Anyway, Sam, I'd like you to meet my new partner, Patrick Logan. Jen, I think you two have met."

"Yeah, night of the accident," Patrick offered.

"He wasn't doing anything tonight either," Joe explained, "so I brought him along."

"Jesus, Joe! You make me sound like a charity case!" Patrick laughed heartily.

Sam had a tough time pulling her gaze from Patrick's chiseled face. She informed the men the only things left to move were the big items: couch, table, beds, and dressers. "You were busy kids," Joe marveled. "Well, let's get you two finished."

It only took them one more trip to move all the large items, including a quick stop at the Goodwill to drop of their old, beat-up couch. Sam wanted to get a new one. "Besides, this is where we got the damn thing," she laughed.

A few hours and several sore muscles later, the four of them stood in the new kitchen amid the clutter of boxes, sipping coffee. "Sugar, you've done well," Joe reported. "Your parents would be pleased, I know."

"That's what I'm hoping," Sam sighed. "I really do feel good about this."

"Well, I hate to break things up, but I've really got to get going," Patrick announced.

"That's my cue," Joe chuckled.

The girls thanked their badge-toting knights, sending them on their way. "Once we get settled, we owe you both a big, home cooked meal," Jen offered.

"Sounds nice." Joe hugged his favorite reporter and gave Jen a friendly smile.

"Be sure to tell your wife I said hello."

Four sweaty hours later, and well into the next morning, Sam and Jen lay collapsed in the middle of the living room floor, surrounded by empty boxes and crumpled packing paper. They had successfully packed, moved, and unpacked all their worldly possessions in a mere day. Looking around their new home, Sam was shocked by how much space they still had. She found it almost pathetic how hollow the house looked, sparse, even with all their affects.

Suddenly Jen spoke up. "I don't know about your parents, but I'm sure proud of you." Sam smiled silently. "And it's not just this house. It's how well you're doing at the paper, and how much I've seen you grow these past months." Jen paused to give her friend a hug. "I'm really proud."

~ ~ ~

The next night as she lay silently staring up at the ceiling of her new bedroom, Sam thought about how far she'd really come. Not just since her parents' deaths, but before that. In the play of light and shadow upon the walls of her newest sanctuary Sam felt sure she was able to see those she'd loved in childhood. Great shadowy monsters leapt from the gloom to devour the shimmering faces of her mother and father as they traveled across the wall in the beams of a passing car's headlights. Then, in an empty corner, Sam saw a great looming shadow and she knew instinctively who the shadow was. It was the biggest shadow in her family's history. It was the monster responsible for the murder of her cousin.

Fifteen years ago, when Sam was only ten, her cousin Emily was brutally murdered. Sam didn't know much about what really happened, she'd been so young at the time. As she grew old enough to understand she could never bring herself to ask, knowing how painful it would be for her family to re-live. What she did know was that one blustery March night her Aunt and Uncle left their sixteen-year-old daughter, Emily, at home while Phil treated Carmen to an elegant night out celebrating their twentieth wedding anniversary.

When they returned home, well after midnight, and found the front door unlocked, they were not alarmed. To lock doors in their rural neighborhood outside Portland, Oregon was almost unheard of. It was quiet, so they assumed Emily was in her room sleeping. It wasn't until the next morning when she didn't answer her mother's call for breakfast that Carmen thought something might be amiss. She asked her husband to check and see if Emily was feeling all right, while she continued to mind the stove.

What Phil saw, exactly, when he pushed open his daughter's door, Sam would never know. But according to the few news stories she had looked up covering the case, her cousin had been tied up, bound at the wrists to the headboard of her bed. She had been raped and then stabbed to death with a knife from her mother's kitchen. In a show of modesty, before he left, the killer covered Emily's body with the blue comforter from her bed.

Now, lying beneath her own blue bedspread in the darkness of her strange, new room, Sam closed her eyes. She felt momentarily vulnerable to the shadow monster on the wall, but as the images began to play upon the back of her eyelids, she forgot all about it.

In the cinema of her imagination, Sam saw her Uncle walk into Emily's room. The look on his face conveyed the fact that he didn't know what to make of the two pale hands he saw jutting from beneath the coverlet. Hands with pink polish on the fingernails. Hands which were still tied to the bed with simple, white rope. She thought he must have screamed, maybe he even vomited. She could imagine Carmen running into the room while her husband swooned over the cold, bloody body of their only child. Sam's mind was filled with the high-pitched screams of her Aunt as she drifted into a restless sleep.

Chapter Three

The next morning, as Sam drove to work, she reflected upon her late night visions. She became determined to discover all she could about the murder of her cousin. Once at the office, Sam sat at her desk and pulled up file after file from her computer's extensive database, printing a copy of each to review at her leisure. The newspaper stories spanned from March 18th, the day after Emily's body was discovered, until late November of the same year. Coverage of the story dried up as the police investigators ran out of leads.

According to reports, the police didn't have much to go on. The autopsy showed none of the usual evidence accompanying a rape. The rapist had apparently used a condom so as to leave no trace of his identity behind. No unusual fingerprints were found, and there was no forced entry since the front door had been left unlocked. The murder weapon led them nowhere as well, since the killer used a knife from the house.

It was conjectured the killer had watched the house from a safe distance after Phil and Carmen had left. Sam's imagination kicked in again. She imagined him as he continued to scrutinize Emily's every move until she headed upstairs and crawled, unknowingly, into her bed.

From there it was a simple matter to slip quietly into the house and upstairs. In the sliver of light which fell through her bedroom door, he could probably see her sleeping peacefully. Sam began to tremble as she thought about the cousin she never really knew and about her frightening final moments.

Just then the phone at her desk rang, startling her back to the present. "Oregon Tribune, crime desk, Samantha speaking."

"Hello darling."

"Oh, hi Grandma."

"I'm sorry to bother you at work dear, but I was just wondering how your first night at the new house went?"

"Fine Grandma. It went just fine."

"That's wonderful darling."

"Yeah. Now all I've got to do is fill the place up. The furniture from my apartment just isn't enough. You'd be surprised by how empty the house looks."

"Well, that's good," her grandmother stated dryly.

Laughing, Sam asked, "What do you mean?"

"Well, that's my reason for calling, dear. My basement is full of things you may find useful, not to mention many of your parents' things. What do you say you bring Jennifer by this weekend? The two of you can sort through it all and take what you like."

"Really? Thanks. It would mean a lot to have some of Mom and Dad's things."

"Yes. That's why I kept them. So, can I expect you Saturday?"

"Absolutely. We'll be there around ten?"

"Sounds wonderful, dear. Take care."

~ ~ ~

Sam had another hour to look into the newspaper coverage of her cousin's murder investigation before she was called out to cover a story. Some shoplifters had been apprehended at one of the department stores downtown. The Tribune didn't usually cover shoplifting, but these were more than petty thieves. According to her editor, video surveillance at the store had footage of these suspects spanning several months. There were also rumors one of the store's own employees was facilitating the entire operation. Early estimates put the total value of stolen merchandise well over five thousand dollars and the Tribune wanted a story. Grudgingly, Sam left her amateur sleuthing and headed for the downtown shopping district.

Parking in a nearby garage, Sam hoofed it the three blocks to her story. She spotted a police cruiser parked in front of Robinson's and headed inside. "Excuse me, Miss," Sam asked the nearest clerk, flashing her press ID, "could you please tell me where your security offices are located?"

"This floor, near the elevators. You'll see a hallway off to your right. It's the door at the end of the hall."

"Thank you."

Sam made her way to the security offices and knocked politely only after she'd found the door was locked. A faint voice from the other side inquired, "Yes?"

"Samantha Williams, Oregon Tribune. May I ask you a few questions?"

"Not right now," replied the voice.

She knocked again. "This won't take long."

The door opened and Sam was a bit surprised to see Patrick's face peering out at her. "Hey Patrick. Fancy meeting you here."

"Hello Samantha." Patrick dropped his voice to a husky whisper. "Do me a favor... Could you make it Sergeant Logan? This is my first call as an investigator. I want to make a good impression."

"You've got it Sarge." She dropped him a playful wink and a miniature salute. "While we're talking favors, do you have time to give me a statement?"

"Joe warned me about this," he smiled. "Look, I'm a little busy at the moment, but we're almost done here. How about I call another car out here to make the pick up, and I'll meet you in about half an hour at Rosie's Grill. We can talk there, okay?"

"Sure. Half an hour." With that, the door closed.

Sam asked a few questions of the employees she passed on her way out and then headed over to Rosie's. She ordered herself a Pepsi and asked the waitress if she could have two club sandwiches at the table in about twenty-five minutes.

"Sure hon," the harried-looking redhead replied as she headed off to check on some of her other customers.

As it turned out, Patrick was late. Sam cast him an accusatory glance when he strolled through the door. "No need to look at me like that," he smiled. "You're lucky I agreed to meet with you."

"Is that so?"

"Absolutely. Is this for me?" He gestured toward the sandwich on the table. Sam nodded. "But Joe likes you," he continued, "so I've got to treat you well or I'll go off making a bad impression with my new partner."

"He's that protective of me?" Sam smiled slyly.

"He talks about you like you're part of his family." Patrick saw a flash of pain cross her face, fast as a flicker of lightning in the sky, and immediately apologized.

"There's no need to apologize. It's just… sometimes I forget they're really gone. It's like, maybe they're just on a long vacation and they'll be home next week. And then an innocent comment reminds me. Silly, isn't it?" They ate in silence for several awkward minutes until Sam spoke up again. "What can you tell me about this shoplifting case? My editors want a catchy story for the morning edition."

"Well," he began, "we've got one employee involved, along with two outside accomplices. Close to five thousand dollars of stolen merchandise. We're talking designer clothing, small electronics, and cash primarily. Looks like their favorite method was to lift the merchandise and then return it for cash. The two outsiders would try to process most of the returns with their buddy inside, using fake names and information. They were running rings around store security with all the false info. Each time they'd flag a name in the computer system, these guys would come up with another."

"Sounds like they were familiar with the store's security procedures?"

"Looks like it. The inside guy had worked for another department store a few years back in their security offices. He would have known all the basic methods and what this particular security team would be looking for."

"What about video? I saw camera bulbs in the ceiling. Why didn't they just pick these guys out on tape?"

"Do you know how many cameras Robinson's has?" Sam looked blankly back at him in response. "About ten on each floor," he answered for her. "That's somewhere around sixty cameras. They've got twelve video monitors in the office, but they really only cue in on someone if they get a call from one of their officers on patrol on the sales floor, or if a salesperson calls them about a suspicious customer. They've got our guys on a couple tapes so far, but it'll take some time to watch all the old footage. These guys were good. Really good."

"So what happened? If they were so good, how did they get caught?"

"Mainly it was ego. Looks like they had a planned return this afternoon, but when our two boys showed up their buddy wasn't around to take the return. Security had an idea he might be involved. There was nothing solid, just his employee number on a majority of the return transactions in question. It was pure coincidence that he was up in their office when it all went down." He paused for a bite of his sandwich. "Anyway, the other two thought they could handle the return even without their friend. But the gal they picked, they underestimated her."

"How so?"

"Turns out, she's the store's leading tipster. She puts in an average of three calls a day about customers she thinks are up to something. Initially, security thought she was over-zealous, but then they realized she was right a good deal of the time. Now they take all of her calls seriously."

"And her name?"

"Nice try."

"Oh, come on. One little name? That's all I ask."

"Nope. Now, do you want me to finish or not?"

"Finish," she pouted. Sam wasn't used to this kind of refusal. *I'm going to have to work on this one*, she mused.

"Anyway, security got her call at the same time they had their employee up there. Now, the security office is only one room, with the video monitors along one wall. When they zoomed in on his buddies he thought he'd been nailed for sure and started to panic. Downstairs, the other two were trying to charm their way through the return, but the sales gal wouldn't do it without taking a look at their identification. I guess they were feeling pretty sure of themselves, because rather than give up and try it another time, they handed over a driver's license. When she punched in the name on her terminal, it cued one of the flags in security and they had them."

"Nice and neat." Sam tapped the side of her Pepsi glass with her pen for punctuation.

"Yeah, but get this... Security brings the two into the office and they see their buddy sitting there and assume he ratted on them. You couldn't shut them up. They were all talking so fast trying to bury each other and clear themselves. I've seen it before, but never anything quite like it."

"That's honor among thieves for you." Sam took another bite of her sandwich and continued, "Can I ask you a question?"

"Sure. But what were the last fifteen minutes about if not questions?"

"All right, smart ass. Are you a recent promotion?"

"Yes. Three weeks. How did you know?"

"Just something you said back at the store. You said it was your first call as an investigator, that's all."

Patrick stood up smiling. "Can you excuse me for a moment, Sherlock?" Sam watched as he strode up to the small counter, conversed with the waitress, then returned.

"What was that about?"

"I paid for lunch. Look, I've got to be getting back to the station. I trust you'll keep my name out of your story?" She smiled and nodded. "Great. I'll be seeing you."

Sam watched him leave, the smile still lingering on her face. There was something about this guy she couldn't quite put a finger on. But it was something she liked. As she gathered up her pen and note pad, stuffing them into her handbag, she noticed the waitress standing at the table.

"The guy you were with? He asked me to give you this," she said, exchanging a small scrap of paper for the empty plates and glasses, then walked away. Sam's smile widened when she saw what was scribbled on it.

~ ~ ~

"He just gave you her name?" Jen asked, amazed.

"Well, yeah. But he made like we were going to have to play hardball first. He was driving me crazy. I mean, with Joe it's always, 'Now, Sugar, you didn't hear it from me, but blah, blah, blah...'" Sam laughed out loud at how aggravated Patrick had left her that afternoon. "He really had me going."

"You like him, don't you?" Jen accused, delighted by the look of capture that fell across Sam's face.

"I do not," she tried feebly, and then gave up. "What makes you say that?"

"Oh, I don't know. The way you talk about him, for starters. I mean, the last hour you've spent more time talking about him than about your story."

"My exclusive story," Sam beamed.

"With an exclusive eyewitness interview," Jen added.

The story itself wasn't such a big deal, but her editors were extremely pleased. Sam whooped in delight as she bounded into the kitchen and grabbed a Corona and a lime out of the refrigerator. She called back to the living room, "Want a beer?" as she sliced into the little green fruit. Jen grunted an affirmative, so Sam grabbed a second beer as she replaced the rest of the lime.

"Here's to a great story," Jen saluted.

Sam raised her beer to the toast and moved it straight to her lips, chugging half of it down immediately. "You know," she sighed, "I really owe Patrick a thanks." Jen watched, amused, as Sam made her way to the phone. Jen began to giggle like a grade-schooler as Sam dialed the phone, and Sam waved a hand at her to shut up.

"Joe," she spoke into the receiver, "it's Sam. Look, I have a little favor to ask you." There was a pause, and then Sam continued. "Do you have Patrick's number? I need to talk to- No! Joe, wait! Joe...?" Sam looked to Jen in a panic. "He's there! Joe's going to put him on!"

The look on Sam's face was more than Jen could handle and she burst into hysterics, a little beer sloshing out the top of the bottle she held as she slid out of her chair onto the floor. "This is too perfect!" Jen giggled. "Hmm!" she exclaimed as she gulped down a mouthful of Corona. "Invite him over!"

"No!" Sam snapped, and then turned her attention back to the phone. "Patrick, hello." There was a pause. "No, I was just calling to get your number from Joe. I wanted to thank you." Another pause filled with Jen's giggles. "You know, I owe you for lunch... Yeah, well

Jen and I just cracked open a couple beers and I was planning to order a pizza. Would you like me to make it enough for three?"

Jen's laughter was now loud enough for her to feel compelled to leave the room. "Sure," Sam continued. "See you in a while." And with that she hung up the phone. "Jennifer!"

"What?" Jen emerged from the kitchen, two fresh beers in hand, her laughter finally suppressed.

"I will get even with you later," Sam pointed an admonishing finger at her friend, smiling in glee, "but for now, we're going to have company!"

~ ~ ~

About an hour later, Sam, Jen, and Patrick sat cross-legged on the floor, an open pizza delivery box set before them on the coffee table. The girls hadn't had a chance to replace their old couch yet, but their guest assured them he didn't mind the floor.

"Who wants the last piece?" Sam asked.

"Go for it," Jen replied. "I'm stuffed."

Sam caught Patrick eyeing the slice. "I can tell you want some. Shall we split it?"

"No. Go ahead. Joe and Lisa had already fed me before I came over here. I really didn't need to eat what I did. You take it."

"Thanks." Sam grabbed up the last slice, devouring it quickly.

"Well," Jen announced as she stood, gathering the six empty beer bottles, "I'm gonna hit the hay. Patrick, it was good to see you again."

"Likewise."

"Good night Jen." Sam and Patrick watched in silence until Jen had completely disappeared up the stairs. "Want to go for a walk?" Sam asked suddenly.

"What?" Patrick was incredulous. "It's freezing outside."

"You've got a coat, right?"

"Of course, but..."

"Great, let's go!"

"Samantha," he groaned in protest.

"Okay," she interrupted, "First, call me Sam. My grandmother and my editor are the only ones who call me Samantha. And even then, it's only when I'm in trouble. And second, I'm going for a walk, so get a move on."

"Oh, all right." As Patrick pulled on his thick-soled work boots, Sam found herself examining him, unable to pull her eyes away. He wore a simple pair of Levis and a thick, oatmeal-colored wool sweater. It was the kind of look she'd seen on hundreds of men during the cold and rainy Northwest winters. But something about this man held her rapt. Perhaps it was his tanned skin, despite the sunless winter? Or was it the sexy, dark hair, cut short to control the unruly curls? Whatever it was that drew her to him, Sam was eager to find out more.

"Come on slow poke," she teased.

"Hold on. Do you think I'm actually looking forward to catching cold?"

"Just come on!" Sam grabbed his hand, tugging him up off the floor and toward the door. They shrugged into their coats as Sam shut and locked the front door.

"Well... Where to?" Patrick inquired.

"Just around the block."

"Do you do this often?" He caught the puzzled look on Sam's face. "Go for walks in the middle of the night in the freezing cold?"

"Oh. Only when I need to think," she confessed, "or if I've been drinking. I do this to clear my head."

"So what is it tonight?"

"A little of both."

They started down the block in silence, Sam marveling at the warmth she could feel just by walking alongside Patrick. Something about being near him made her feel, somehow, different. Sam looked over to find Patrick staring at her, unashamed.

"Can I ask you something?" he asked, his voice barely a whisper. Sam nodded. "Why did you invite me over tonight?"

"To thank you for helping me with my story this afternoon."

"Don't mess with me Samantha. Why did you *really* ask me over?"

"Really... I wanted to thank you. And..." Sam broke off, shifting her gaze to the cracked sidewalk, embarrassed by what she was about to say.

"And what?" Patrick cupped her chin in his slightly calloused palm, pulling her eyes back to his handsome face.

"I... I wanted to get to know you better," she stammered, feeling the heat rise in her frozen cheeks.

"Really?"

"Yes." Sam moved away from him and turned the corner, proceeding around the block. She could hear Patrick's heavy footsteps as he jogged a few steps to catch up. "I find you interesting," she heard herself saying. She was amazed by her own words, and slightly nervous just saying them.

Whenever she became anxious, Sam found herself quite talkative. She would babble on about anything she could think of just to remove attention from whatever it was causing her nervousness. Tonight, she did just that. As she watched little puffs of freezing breath escape her mouth with every spoken word, Sam heard herself rambling on about the afternoon's case and her story. She was talking just to talk.

Patrick took hold of her arm suddenly, turning her toward him. "You talk too much," he stated, smiling as he covered her mouth with his in a quick, soft kiss. He pulled away, leaving Sam stunned. "Now, can we hurry up and get back inside where it's warm?" Sam just nodded. "Great. C'mon."

Patrick took her by the hand, tugging gently to hurry her along. He led the way around the rest of the block, his mind racing, thinking about what he'd just done with a grin lingering upon his face. Once back at her door, he turned to look at her again and began to laugh out loud. Sam still looked stunned, as if the cold had frozen the look of surprise on her face. "Sam? Are you all right?" he asked.

"Uh-huh. Yeah." This seemed to break her shocked stupor. Fishing her keys out of her coat pocket she admitted, "You just caught me by surprise, that's all."

"Must've been some surprise."

"Don't flatter yourself," Sam quipped, pushing past a laughing Patrick to get through the open door. She glanced back at him as she hung her coat in the closet and saw him shiver just a little. "Would you like some coffee? To warm up?" she offered.

"Scurrying for a reason for me to stay?"

"Hardly!" She looked momentarily indignant. "You know, I didn't give you permission to kiss me."

"Yes. Well, I didn't hear you complaining." Patrick stepped closer to her, dropping his coat in the corner.

"You didn't give me a chance," Sam responded, moving in toward him as well.

"Did you want to complain?" He wrapped one arm about her waist, draping the other casually over her shoulder and around her neck.

"No." Sam allowed herself to be drawn into his warm, beautifully masculine body. She couldn't believe she was permitting this to happen, but she wasn't about to make herself draw away. Her voice plunged to a whisper and she confessed, "I rather enjoyed it, actually."

"I'm glad to hear that." Once again their lips met.

"Am I interrupting something?" Jen stepped quietly from the kitchen.

Sam pulled away from Patrick with a quick jump. "Jen! Um, no. We were just..." Sam trailed off, too startled to know exactly what to say.

"We were just getting to know one another," Patrick finished for her, a cunning and mischievous smile dancing upon his lips.

"Well, don't let me stop you," Jen giggled, taking a sip of the water she'd come down for, then heading back upstairs to her room. "Don't stay up too late kids," she called back. "We've all got early mornings tomorrow." And with that they were alone again.

"She's right," Patrick sighed, picking up Sam's hand. "I do have an early morning. I should probably get going."

"Sure." She couldn't explain it, but Sam was positive she could feel herself tumbling off the cloud she'd been on as she walked him to the door.

"I'll call you tomorrow?"

"That's what they all say."

"Yes, but has anyone said it like this?" He quickly pulled her into him, assaulting her lips with a deep, hard kiss. Sam could feel her legs begin to quake in a blissful unsteadiness. As the shiver traveled through her entire frame she allowed herself to collapse against Patrick's muscular body. His fingers twined within the soft curls of her hair, pressing her mouth more forcefully against his own before pulling away.

"I've got to go," he growled, his voice husky with the desire he felt for her. As she nodded her head in agreement, Sam could feel the evidence of that desire pressing solidly against her hip. Suddenly she realized she didn't want him to leave. A lightning fast vision of Patrick, naked and passionate, lying with her in bed flashed through her mind. Rationally, she pushed the thought aside.

"I really will call," he reassured her.

"No you won't," she teased. There was a note of regret in her voice, wishing he didn't have to leave. Sam scolded herself for entertaining such thoughts. After all, she'd known him less than a week. It was bad enough she'd allowed him to kiss her so intimately. And repeatedly.

Patrick just smiled his knee-melting smile and slipped out the door. As he unlocked his truck and climbed into the cab he wondered what would've come about if he'd told Sam he wanted to stay? If he told her he wanted nothing more than to innocently hold her body against his in a sleepy embrace until the sun cleared the horizon?

He sat quietly in the driver's seat of his Ford for a few moments, still wrapped in that imaginary embrace. Finally, reluctantly, he turned the key in the ignition but nothing happened. There was the unmistakable 'click-click-click' of a dead battery. Glancing down he saw why.

"Damn it," he cursed, before realizing the up side. With this simple mistake of leaving his lights on, he'd inadvertently given himself an opportunity to linger here with Sam. His winning smile began to dance its way across his face again, from his commanding mouth up to his chestnut eyes.

Inside, Sam was almost to her bedroom when she heard a faint knocking at the front door. She abruptly retraced her way through the living room, all the while her brain criticizing her heart's hopefulness. As she opened the door it was her brain, not her heart, which was disappointed.

"I must've left my lights on," Patrick stated as he easily pressed his way inside. "I'll need a jump."

"Jen's got a set of cables," she offered half-heartedly.

"Good."

"But," she continued, "it would be a shame to wake her." Sam didn't mention she knew exactly where the jumper cables were, hanging quite openly just inside the garage door.

"Yes," he agreed, "a shame." And Patrick didn't mention he could still hear Jen moving about upstairs, obviously still awake. "I guess I'm out of luck."

"You're welcome to stay." Sam berated herself for such foolishness, but it was too late. The words had already escaped.

"I don't mind, if you're okay with it."

"Fine," she assured him. "But we, uh, don't have a couch, so..." Sam's voice trailed away as her eyes flickered unmistakably to her bedroom door and back again to Patrick.

"Look, Sam," he began, suddenly feeling guilty for his presence and for her veiled invitation. "I don't want you to regret anything," he stressed, "but I would like to stay."

His smile weakened when she didn't respond, but he gave it another shot. "I'd like to stay with you," he paused, unable to breathe, "to hold you, if you'll let me."

He let out a shaky sigh of relief when she nodded her head in silent acceptance of his offer. As Sam re-locked the front door and led the way to her room, her better judgment conceded defeat. He was staying. The fight was lost. Sam smiled, confused by the fact she'd just invited a mere acquaintance into her bed, but happy nonetheless.

Sam heard her bedroom door click shut behind her and turned to face her guest. "Make yourself at home," she managed to say. "Do you... need something to sleep in? There may be a pair of my father's pajamas in one of the boxes in my closet."

"That would be nice." As she disappeared into her walk-in closet, Patrick continued, "Joe may raise an eyebrow at me wearing the same clothes tomorrow, but wrinkled and slept in? I'd never hear the end of it."

Sam emerged from the closet laughing. "Lucky for you I kept these then." She offered up a neatly folded pair of cotton pajama pants and its button-up mate. "Give me a minute while I change, then the bathroom's all yours." Sam tugged open her top dresser drawer and pulled out her pj's and shut herself in the adjoining bathroom.

When they had first moved in, Sam had wanted one of the rooms upstairs, near Jen, like always. But Jen had objected. "You're not going to let that huge, beautiful room go to waste! Besides, it'll be your own space. And just think... no more sharing a bathroom." Apparently that had been the major issue for Jen, given Sam's penchant for excessively long, steamy showers. Smiling broadly, Sam silently thanked Jen for her foresight. She thought about how awkward it would be, taking Patrick upstairs, with Jen just one door down. Suddenly she appreciated her privacy more than ever.

Shrugging out of her clothes, Sam couldn't help but let her thoughts wander to the man waiting just beyond the door. What were his intentions, she wondered? Had he really meant it when he'd said he just wanted to hold her? Or was it merely feigned innocence to earn her trust? Sam laughed a little when she realized it really didn't matter. She knew by the way her body reacted to his touch and his kiss that if he wanted more from her she wouldn't refuse him. She couldn't.

Once she'd changed, Sam opened the door. "Come on in. I think I've got an extra toothbrush around here somewhere if you..." But she was unable to finish. Her heart's giddy patter stopped abruptly at the sight before her.

Patrick had, she saw, already changed. Sam had seen her father in those pj's before, they were his favorite pair, but Sam couldn't imagine them ever looking quite this good on her dear old dad. The loose blue pants sat low and comfortably on his hips, the shirt on but left unbuttoned with the sleeves rolled up and pushed to his elbows. Sam could openly admire the deep tan of his skin and the taut muscles it covered. No, they'd never looked this sexy, she was sure of it.

As he moved toward her, he was aware of her appraising gaze and smiled. Performing an appraisal of his own, Patrick was nearly blown away by Sam's simple, innocent beauty. She stood there before him in a similar pair of gray cotton pants and a heather tank top, her hair free about her shoulders. The slight chill in the room gave Patrick a cheap thrill as her nipples strained against only the thin blue cotton of her tank.

She saw Patrick's smile as he approached and, following his gaze, Sam saw exactly why he was smiling. Flushed and embarrassed, she hastily folded her arms across her chest to cover her breasts. "Uh.. Where was I?" she giggled.

"Toothbrush," he prompted.

"Oh! Yeah, hang on." Sam turned, kneeling to rummage through the bottom drawer near the sink. "Here you go." She stood and tossed him a toothbrush, still in its wrapper.

"You're prepared," he teased.

"What? Look, I don't do this sort of thing," she retorted vehemently.

Regretting his jest, Patrick apologized. "I didn't mean it that way. I was only kidding."

Sam giggled a little, realizing she'd overreacted, and tossed him the tube of toothpaste. "I know, I just don't want you to think... Well, you know."

Patrick smiled. "Yeah, I know... and I don't think that." He brushed his teeth and then returned to the bedroom while Sam washed her face. Unsure exactly as to how 'at home' he should be, he settled for sitting upon the edge of the bed as he waited for her to finish. He could see the hesitation in her step as she approached. But as she turned back the blankets and crawled beneath them, Patrick saw the worry drain away. Sam reached for the alarm clock on the nightstand, setting it for 5:30. She glanced his way and he nodded that yes, that was good. Sam set down the alarm and turned off the light. Then, without a word, she patted the bed with her open palm, unmistakably inviting him to her side.

As he slipped between the cool sheets beside her, Sam could feel a gentle tingle course through her entire body. It was as if every nerve in her body was pleasantly electrified. Sam waited quietly and patiently for him to settle into a comfortable position lying upon his back. Then she expertly fit herself against him, nestling her head into the little hollow where his chest and shoulder met. She heard his sharp intake of breath when she draped one of her legs over his, entwining their limbs in an intimate embrace.

For several minutes they remained like that, silent and motionless. Then Sam felt the muscles in Patrick's body unclench and relax. He reached out in the dark and his hand found the soft, feminine curve of her hip and settled there. Turning his head slightly to the side, he nuzzled contentedly against her forehead. Sam was amazed by how right it felt, how perfect their innocent coupling.

"Comfy?" she whispered. He answered in a purring mumble and a light squeeze. He muttered something about sleeping well, kissed the tip of her nose, and he was out like a light. "Good night," she whispered as she drifted off to join him.

Chapter Four

"Samantha? Are you with us?"

"Huh?" Sam lifted her head from the desktop, rubbing at her eyes with a fist.

"Rough night?" Tony asked.

"No. I just didn't sleep well, that's all," she lied.

"You must be really tired, then. Your phone was ringing off the hook, but you just kept on snoozing." Sam noticed Tony was holding out the phone receiver to her.

She took the phone, shooing him off. "Oregon Tribune crime desk, Samantha Williams speaking."

"Hey Sam." Her face lit up at the sound of Patrick's voice on the line. "Who was that?"

"My editor, Tony."

"I didn't get you into trouble, did I? He sounded kinda pissed."

"Well, he did catch me napping, but he always sounds like that. He's really a pushover." Glancing down, Sam saw the incoming call light on her hone was blinking. "Patrick, can I put you on hold for a sec? I have another call coming in."

With his go ahead, Sam clicked over to the second line only to hear her grandmother's voice interrupt her greeting litany. "No use making you say all that when it's only me," Sally laughed.

"Oh, hi Grandma. Can I call you back? I'm on the other line."

Again, Sam was interrupted. "This will only take a second, dear. I wanted to know if I should still expect you tomorrow?"

"Tomorrow?"

The uncertainty in Sam's voice prompted another ripple of laughter from her grandmother. "I knew you'd forget... You, me, and Jennifer for a little brunch and then I'm turning you two loose on a scavenger hunt in my basement. So to speak."

"Oh, yes! We'll be there." Sam paused, and then added, "Could you make it brunch for four? I have a friend who may come along to help."

"Not a problem. I'll see you tomorrow, dear."

"Bye." Sam shifted back to her conversation with Patrick. "Okay, I'm back. Listen, what are you doing this weekend? Tomorrow, specifically? Jen and I are picking up some furniture from..."

"Sure," he cut in. "I'd love to help."

"Excellent. My grandma is expecting us around ten."

"Wait a second. Family?"

"Yes. My grandma. Is that a problem?"

"No. It just seems strange to meet family when we haven't even been out on our first date."

There was a jovial tone in his voice and Sam met it. "Not having our first date sure didn't stop you from hopping into my bed last night." Several startled glances shot her direction and Sam realized she should have lowered her voice. "Oh shit!" she giggled.

"What?"

"I just started some wheels turning at the old rumor mill, that's all. Listen, I'd better get back to work. Why don't you come by my place tonight around six-thirty? I'll fix you dinner and we can talk then. Okay?"

At home that evening, Sam dropped the groceries off on the kitchen counter and headed straight to her room for a quick shower. As she stood beneath the steaming jets, Sam couldn't help but let her mind wander to its current hot-topic: Patrick. A smile sprang to her face as she shampooed her hair, remembering how Patrick's fingers had twined there as he kissed her the night before. *Perhaps he'll stay again tonight*, she thought, and then giggled aloud.

Suddenly she heard a knock at her bathroom door. "Sam? You decent?"

"I'm in the shower," she called back. "Come on in."

"Are you in a hurry or what?" Jen teased from the dry side of the shower curtain.

"What are you talking about?"

"Are you kidding? All I saw when I walked through the door were your things tossed everywhere! Groceries, gloves, one shoe in the hall, the other in the middle of the living room. What gives?"

"Oh, that. Yeah, I'm kinda rushed. Patrick's coming over for dinner in about an hour, I think... What time is it?"

"Five 'til six."

"Okay, make it half an hour. I'd better hurry."

"Need some help?"

Sam's arm snaked out from behind the curtain to grab her towel. "Could you?" A moment later she emerged wrapped snugly into her towel. "Everything's in the bag on the counter. Maybe you could chop the broccoli? I'm just making a stir-fry."

"Sure."

"Thanks. I'll be out in about five minutes." As Jen headed to the kitchen, Sam tossed her damp hair into a loose pile atop her head. Rummaging through her closet, she pulled out her favorite pair of jeans and a fluffy blue sweater. Heading back to the bathroom one last time, Sam couldn't resist a spray of her favorite perfume, and then she went to join Jen in the kitchen.

"Okay, where are we?"

Jen glanced up from the cutting board for a moment, smiling. "Broccoli's chopped, garlic minced," she announced as she scooped the veggies into a bowl. "Chicken's cut up and in the fridge when you're ready for it."

"You are excellent!" Sam beamed. "I can take it from here. Thanks."

"You sure?"

"Yeah, I've got it covered." Sam dug into the bag on the counter pulling out the rest of the groceries. "I'll have dinner ready in about twenty minutes. You're welcome to join us."

"I won't be intruding?"

"Not at all," she smiled, then recalling her conversation with her grandmother she added, "I almost forgot. Tomorrow we're going out to Gram's for brunch and to pick up some furniture, remember?" Sam dumped onion peel into the garbage disposal.

"*Now* I remember." Jen and Sam erupted with laughter. Once their giggles had subsided Jen asked, "How are we getting stuff home? Do we need to rent another truck?"

"Patrick is going to come with us," Sam explained as she set a pot of water on the stove to boil for the rice, "so we'll have his pick-up. We may have to make a couple trips, we'll see."

"Great. Look, I'm going to go upstairs and change. Might even take a shower, if you didn't use all the hot water, so don't wait for me for dinner."

"I'll keep a plate for you."

"Thanks." Jen disappeared to her room as Sam continued cooking. Just as she tossed the rice into the boiling water, the doorbell rang. Quickly stirring the white grains with a fork and covering the pot, she headed to the door.

"Patrick, come on in," she offered, and as she spoke Patrick swept through the door, capturing her in his warm embrace. He covered her lips with his in a sweet kiss.

"Mmm. I've been waiting to do that all day," he sighed before letting her go. Sam found herself unable to stop smiling as Patrick followed her to the kitchen. "Smells delicious."

"Thanks. Should be ready in a few minutes. Would you help me out and set the table?" Patrick nodded so Sam handed him the stack of plates and silverware she had ready.

"Will Jen be joining us?"

"Maybe," Sam answered. "We'll set a place for her just in case." A few minutes later Sam carried two serving bowls into the adjoining dining room and set them on the table. She could hear the shower running upstairs and announced they should start without Jen.

Dinner was filled with small talk as Sam and Patrick learned more about one another. The more Sam found out about him, the more she found herself falling for him. As she listened she learned about his family. His father had been a cop as well, working in California. His mother was a housewife, preparing, she thought, for a home full of children. This was her measure of a successful, happy life. Luckily for Patrick though, after years of trying, his parents learned they were unable to have children of their own. That was when they looked into adoption, and Patrick was their first child. He had a younger sister, adopted as well. Patrick explained how he had always looked up to his father and the work he did. "He's my hero," Patrick said, unashamed of the emotion in his voice. "I was really lucky to get them for parents."

"Sounds like it." Sam took a sip of her beer and continued, "Do you remember your real parents?"

"No. I was just a baby when Mom and Dad adopted me; I was almost two at the time. I know this is going to sound strange,

41

especially since most adopted kids are always talking about how curious they are about their birth family. But I'm really not. I've got such great parents. I mean, they've given me everything I've ever needed. They are my parents in every possible way."

"That sounds wonderful." Sam looked at Patrick meaningfully, and then added, "You're lucky to have them."

"I know," he replied, catching her double meaning. He reached out atop the table to take Sam's hand and squeezed it comfortingly.

"Any food left for me?" Jen questioned as she entered the dining room.

Patrick slowly released Sam's hand as he stood to greet Jen. "Of course," he laughed, "I saved you at least two bites."

"That's what I was afraid of," she joked back, sliding into her usual spot at the foot of the table. "Sam, this looks fabulous." But as Jen looked to Sam she saw the distress deep in her best friend's eyes. "Sam, what's wrong?"

"Nothing," she insisted. The look on Jen's face betrayed the fact that she didn't believe her. "Really, Jen, it's nothing."

"We were just talking," Patrick explained, "about family." That was all he had to say and Jen understood perfectly. They both knew from experience that given a few minutes Sam's mood would pass. So Jen loaded some food onto her plate, and she and Patrick exchanged useless banter. They both breathed a small sigh of relief when Sam giggled at one of their jokes.

"So," Jen inquired, pushing back from her empty plate, "What time are we heading over to Gram's?"

"She's expecting us around ten for brunch. I figure we should leave here around nine-thirty."

"Sounds great." Jen stood up, gathered her plate, and then took Patrick's and Sam's. "I'll clean up in the kitchen, you two just relax."

Patrick stood. "Are you sure I can't help?"

"Positive. Now, I've got some student evaluations to review, so the sooner I'm done in the kitchen, the sooner I'm upstairs and out of your hair." Jen dropped a wink at her roommate and bustled off into the kitchen.

"What now?" Patrick inquired, moving over to Sam's chair.

"Well, we could watch a movie? Or just some TV? Any suggestions?"

"A movie sounds nice. Something funny."

"Right this way sir," Sam said, donning her best usher's voice, leading Patrick into the living room. "So, I figure you could meet us here around nine tomorrow morning? Have some coffee with us before we head over to my grandma's?" As he settled himself into the oversized chair, Sam noticed the sparkle in his eyes. "What is it?"

"Well, I hope you don't think me too presumptuous, but I have a change of clothes in the truck. I thought maybe it might be more convenient if I just stay here?"

"I was hoping you'd say something like that," she confessed. The two exchanged smiles as she tossed the remote to him and began rattling off movie titles. They settled on a Jackie Chan flick and made themselves comfortable. The big blue chair was large enough to accommodate both of them, so Sam snuggled in against Patrick's warm body.

"Samantha?"

"Hmm?" she purred.

"What are we doing? Is it just me or is this all a little crazy? I mean..."

Raising her gaze to meet his, she smiled. "It is a little crazy. But it feels right, doesn't it?" Patrick nodded. "As long as we both feel the same way, why question it?"

Sam sank back against him, the smile still playing on her lips as the movie began. They barely moved, reveling in the closeness of one another's bodies, the warmth so comforting. When the movie was over, Patrick retrieved his duffel bag from his truck, and then followed Sam to her room for the second time in as many nights.

~ ~ ~

Jen was not at all surprised to hear Patrick's voice as she descended the stairs the next morning. "Good day," she chimed, startling them both as they leaned against the kitchen counter with their coffee. "Did you two sleep well?"

There was a slight blush that rose in Sam's face as Patrick replied, "Like a baby." He took another sip of coffee then excused himself. "I'll go get my things."

"Okay! What is going on with you two?" Jen demanded as soon as the door closed behind him. "Did anything... happen?"

Sam didn't really want to answer, Jen could see that by the look in Sam's eyes, but she piped up anyway. "It was innocent. Nothing happened."

"Yeah, right!" Jen teased, and they erupted into laughter like a couple schoolgirls. When Patrick came back into the room and inquired as to what was so funny, they only laughed harder.

A few minutes later, as they piled into Patrick's truck, Jen whispered into Sam's ear, "You'd better tell me everything."

"Not now!" Sam hissed back.

"What are you two carrying on about? And don't tell me 'nothing.' I know better."

"Really Patrick, it's nothing."

"Yeah," Jen smiled, "she won't tell me a thing. But whatever you're doing, keep it up. I haven't see her this happy in a long time."

"Jen!" Sam exclaimed.

She ignored Sam's admonition and continued, unashamed. "I mean, come on! Check the grin! Obviously, the girl is pleased about something!"

Patrick only smiled and watched as Sam sat, red-faced and embarrassed in the center of the cab. The rest of the trip was quiet, with Sam casting occasional dirty looks at Jen, who was pretending not to notice.

Once they reached Sam's grandmother's though, it was far from quiet. "Good morning!" Sally chirped, bounding nimbly down the porch steps before her young guests could even get out of the truck. "How are you dear? And Jen, you look fantastic! Who's your friend?" Without even giving them a chance to respond, Sally continued, "Oh, never you mind! You kids come in out of this cold. We'll talk inside."

Herding them toward the front door, Sally continued to chatter, firing questions at them without pause. Once inside she led them straight to the dining room to a table covered with serving dishes of eggs, bacon, fresh fruit, and the like. "Dig in." She motioned each of them to a chair then sat down herself.

"So, Patrick, how did you get roped into this?" Sally asked after they'd all settled down with full plates.

"Oh, I'm not roped," he laughed. "Just helping out. Besides, I get a free meal out of the deal."

"I see." Sally looked from Patrick to her granddaughter, dropped a knowing wink, and then laughed heartily.

"Grandma," Sam muttered. "You're almost as bad as Jen." Sam looked apologetically in Patrick's direction and saw him grinning widely.

"What did I do?" Sally feigned innocence, then giggled like a child at the growing look of distress on Sam's face.

"Look at what I have to deal with!" Sam exclaimed, tossing her napkin in the air in mock anger. "From my own Grandmother, even!"

45

For the rest of the meal they all passed light banter back and forth, laughing and having a genuine good time. Patrick was glad he came. Looking across the cozy table at the woman he had grown so fond of, he was pleased with what he saw. Her face was aglow with laughter, the morning sunlight through the window behind her creating a halo of gold through the soft curls of her ebony hair. He thought about the way her hair had looked piled gently on the pillow next to him earlier that morning, and about the smile on her lips after he awakened her with a gentle kiss. All he could think about, it seemed, was her. And all he wanted was to be alone with her, to kiss her and tell her how crazy he was about her.

Patrick was drawn back to the conversation as Sally asked him if he wanted anything else. "Oh, no. Thank you ma'am. I'm stuffed."

"Ma'am?" Sally clucked disapprovingly. "Now that just won't do, young man. You can call me Sally."

"Or 'hot momma,'" Jen interjected, laughing as she stopped to pat Sally on the shoulder. "Let me get that plate from you."

"Oh, I've got it Jen." Sally then turned to her granddaughter. "Look, why don't you and Patrick head on down to the basement and get started. Jen and I can clean up, then we'll join you."

"Are you sure we can't help?" Patrick asked.

"Positive. Now you two get downstairs. Jen and I can take it from here."

Sam knew better than to push the issue. There was no bending Sally's will, so she turned to escort Patrick to the basement. "C'mon. It's down this way." From the end of the hall, before they started down the stairs, she could hear Jen and Sally laughing. She had a hunch what it was about, too. She could only smile dryly, and then led Patrick down the stairs.

"So, what's going on?" Sally asked as she and Jen stood over a sink full of suds.

"I don't really know," Jen grinned. "Sam hasn't really told me yet. But they've been pretty inseparable for the last two days."

"Really?" Sally pursed her lips in thought.

"Yeah. I haven't seen her this happy in a long time."

"He seems like a nice young man," the elder woman said.

"Yes, I think he is."

"And good looking, too."

"Sally!" Jen exclaimed, and then they both burst into riotous laughter. Still racked with giggles, Jen managed to utter, "He is cute though." When their laughter finally subsided, they stood before a rack of clean dishes, dripping dry.

"Well," Sally said, "should we pop on down to the basement and see what our two lovebirds are up to?"

Down in the basement, Patrick and Sam were drawing back a tarp which covered a collection of her parents' furniture and a small pile of boxes. As he lifted his corner to toss it aside, he heard a painful utterance. "What's the matter?"

"I got something in my eye." Already Sam's left eye had taken on a red, angry tint, glassy with tears. "Ouch!"

"Hold still." Patrick moved quickly to her side and cradled her face between his palms. "Let me see."

"Ouch!" Sam winced at his touch.

"Oh, hold still," Patrick laughed. "I haven't even done anything, you big baby." As he looked, Patrick noted a small bit of fuzz, the fragment of a dust bunny, clinging to the corner of her eye. "Ah, got you," and with a deft sweep of his finger it was gone. Still cradling her face tenderly, he asked, "Better?"

Before Sam could answer they heard footsteps on the stairs and Sally's jovial voice exclaiming, "Well, well! Are we interrupting?"

"No. I had something in my eye and..."

"And," Patrick interrupted, dropping a playful wink to Sally and Jen, "she's just so damn irresistible I can't keep my hands off her."

Patrick turned back just in time to see Sam throw her hands up in exasperation and exclaim, "That's it! I can't take it. You're all out to get me!" She plopped herself down onto one of the now uncovered sofas and feigned a faint, much to the delight of her three onlookers. "Now," she said, sitting full upright, "if you're all done harassing me, how about we get to work?"

"You're the boss."

"Well, you kids have fun. My old bones are going to go back upstairs. Sam, take whatever you like. If it's down here, I never use it so just make it disappear." And with that Sally left them alone in the dimly lit basement.

"Where should we start?" Jen inquired, surveying the room around her.

Sam patted the sofa cushion she sat upon. "Right here. These sofas are in good shape. I'd like to take them."

"I guess," Patrick sighed as he sat down next to her. "But next time I stay the night I'll probably have to sleep on one of them."

Jen tried to stifle a giggle as Sam punched him lightly on the shoulder. "Not a chance."

As Patrick cleared a pathway to move the sofas upstairs, the girls began sorting through the boxes. Much of the contents consisted of nick-knacks and family mementos which Patrick added to a small stack near the stairs. As Sam examined the contents of the final box, Jen and Patrick snooped a bit in the darkened corners of the room.

"What are you guys up to?" Sam stood, dusting off the thin film of dirt which had accumulated on her hands.

"Being snoopy," Jen responded.

"Hey," Patrick piped up, "Sam, check this out."

As she approached, Sam saw what he was referring to. It was half concealed in the farthest corner of the basement, the only surfaces not hidden from sight by boxes were covered in a heavy layer of grime, dust, and years. Only a small corner of a mirror was exposed and recognizable.

"Wow. I don't think I've seen it before."

"It didn't belong to your parents?"

"No. Jen, would you grab a couple rags? Grandma keeps a pile in the basket under the stairs. Let's clear it off." Patrick and Sam started moving boxes and soon the three had uncovered and removed a great quantity of dust from a beautiful vanity table.

It sat solemnly in the darkness, the deep cherry wood almost invisible in the gloom. The brass drawer pulls were dull and in need of some elbow grease. Standing before it, Sam saw their reflections in the hazy, streaked mirror.

"I wonder where it came from?"

As if on cue, Sally's voice drifted down the stairs. "How's it going kids?"

"Grandma, where did this vanity table come from?"

"The what? Oh..." Sally's voice cut off when she realized what Sam was referring to. She didn't speak again until she'd joined them in front of the little piece of furniture.

"It belonged to Emily. Your aunt and uncle couldn't bear to keep her things, but I couldn't bear to see it go." Sally paused to take up her granddaughter's hand. "It was so special to her. She used to sit in front of it for hours at a time, ever since she was a little girl playing dress up."

"It was Emily's?" Sam questioned, although she had heard her grandmother quite clearly.

"Yes." Sally ran a hand gently across the tabletop. "And now it's yours."

"Oh, I... I couldn't."

"Sure you can. It's heartbreaking to think of it down here. I would love for you to have it, to enjoy it as Emily did."

"Are you sure?"

Sally smiled and hugged her. "Samantha, you ought to know better than to argue with me."

~ ~ ~

They had to make two trips, placing the large sofa and boxes in the first. Jen stayed behind on the second trip to unpack boxes while Patrick and Sam returned for the vanity and love seat. They struggled a bit getting them loaded, but soon they were off, Sam waving one last time to her grandma through the window of the truck.

"Really Patrick, thank you so much for helping."

"No problem. I rather enjoyed it, actually."

"Anything just to be near me, huh?" she teased.

Patrick took his eyes off the road for a moment to look intently at her. "You have no idea how right you are."

His frank admission took Sam by surprise. She stared at the passing scenery in silence for a moment, and then timidly asked, "Where is this going?"

They had stopped at a traffic light and it turned green, so he pulled through the intersection and turned in the parking lot of a little convenience store. Shifting in his seat to face her, Patrick took up one of her hands. "I don't really know how to... describe this." He spoke haltingly, choosing his words carefully. "You are an amazing woman. And every minute I'm near you I find one more thing about you to..." Patrick stopped to sort his thoughts and continued, "Well... to love."

Sam couldn't stop the laugh welling up inside her, but she apologized quickly. "Patrick, you can't... Well, it's just..."

"Crazy. I know. And I didn't say I was *in* love with you."

"Good. 'Cause then we'd have to get your head checked."

Patrick smiled. "But I think I'm getting there. Sam, you are the most wonderful woman I've ever met. I've never felt even remotely like this about anyone."

"Patrick..."

"No. Let me finish, please. Oh, hell! I don't even know what I'm trying to say. But I don't want to think about spending a single day away from you." He stopped when he saw the big smile on her face. "What?"

Sam laughed. "Shut up and kiss me."

Chapter Five

"So, tell me about her." Sam and Patrick were curled up on her bed even though it was early afternoon. They were exhausted from moving the furniture. Emily's vanity table now occupied its new space in Sam's room. "You don't have to if you don't want," he added, "I'm just curious."

"No. It's okay. Emily was my cousin. She was sixteen. Her parents went out one night and someone slipped into the house. It was right here in town. He raped her, and then stabbed her to death. I was just a kid when it happened."

"My God. Did they get the guy?"

"No. It's still an open case. My family kept me pretty sheltered from it at the time, but I've looked into the old stories on file at the paper. There isn't much to go on."

"I could look into it a bit, if you'd like. She... I mean, you said it happened here?" Sam nodded. "I know a couple of the guys over in homicide. I'm sure they'd let me look at the file. I'll just get some info from you before I go."

"You're leaving?" she interjected.

"Do you want me to stay?"

"Well... don't you want to?"

Patrick grinned. "Okay. How about I run over to my apartment, pick up a few things, and I'll be back in time for dinner?"

"Is that a hint?"

"Hey, a guy's gotta eat."

As Sam walked him to the door she gave Patrick the information about Emily's case he'd need in order to request the file, and told him in no uncertain terms that she'd be interested in seeing what the file contained. As she watched Patrick drive away, Jen descended the stairs. She bounded over and threw herself into their new furniture. "These are so comfortable!" Jen nestled even deeper into the overstuffed cushions, drawing her feet beneath her in a relaxed curl. "So, where did Patrick go?"

"Just back to his apartment for a little while. He'll be back for dinner."

"Okay. Will you explain to me what's going on with you guys?"

Sam sat down next to her friend, the smile she'd been hiding from Patrick ever since their conversation in the truck leaping to her face with a vengeance. "He says he's falling in love with me."

"What?"

"Yeah, I know! And get this, I laughed at him." Sam's faced contracted into a frown of guilt. "I feel so bad! He's sitting there telling me how wonderful I am and how he doesn't want to be away from me and I laughed at him!"

"Well, what about you?" Jen queried, jabbing her friend lightly in the ribs. "Are you falling in love with him?"

"I don't know." Sam laughed nervously, then, "Maybe."

~ ~ ~

Sam passed the time while Patrick was away organizing furniture and accessories in her living room. When she was finally satisfied with her arrangements she moved to her room. Grabbing her mother's old vanity tray and the bottles of perfume from the bathroom, Sam moved them to her cousin's table. She sat onto the little matching stool and ran her fingers across the dark red wood, then pulled them back quickly, startled.

She had felt something. Something unusual, inexplicable. It was as if the tabletop was red hot, or electrified. It didn't hurt to touch it, it was more like a dull ache. Tentatively, she extended her hand to the wood once more, but the sensation was gone. "Weird," she muttered.

She stared at her reflection in the mirror for a while, her mind in another place. What this little piece of furniture must have witnessed! Again, Sam's over-active imagination ran to her family's dark history. The room she saw reflected behind her in the mirror no longer resembled her own. In place of all her belongings she saw unfamiliar things. There was a bed behind her, and someone was sleeping there. The bedroom door opened and a dark figure entered, moving quietly.

"Sam?" She was startled, the trance broken. Her own room jumped back into focus and she saw Patrick in the doorway, a small duffel bag sitting at his feet. "Sam? Are you all right?"

"Yeah, I'm fine." She stood and walked to where he stood, planting a quick kiss on his cheek. "I'm glad you're back."

"Hmm. Me too." He held her tightly to him for a moment. Then, smiling, he asked, "What's for dinner? I'm famished."

Sam laughed. "I don't know. What do you feel like eating?"

"I don't care. I'm just very, very hungry."

"Well, lets go see what we can whip up, shall we?"

In the kitchen, they found Jen with her head inside the refrigerator. "Oh, hey guys. Anybody hungry? I was just getting ready to make some hamburgers."

"You are my new best friend," Patrick quipped, "Just tell me how I can help."

"Everything's out." Jen set a couple condiment bottles on the counter. "I just need to prep everything."

"All right, let's hop to it." Sam clapped her hand enthusiastically as she and Patrick dove into helping Jen with the dinner preparations.

The kitchen was filled with laughter and tantalizing smells as they cooked, then stood casually at the counter to eat their meal. Jen watched Sam and Patrick closely, thinking back to the conversation with her roommate that afternoon. It was obvious she and Patrick had feelings for one another. Jen thought herself a good judge of character, and she felt very comfortable around Patrick; she thought he was a good guy and she hoped all went well for him and her friend.

With their appetites satiated the three pitched in for a quick clean up. Sam excused herself for a few minutes, leaving Jen and Patrick alone. Timidly, Jen broached the subject of his relationship with Sam. "Listen, I know this is really none of my business..."

"Uh-oh. With a preface like that, it can't be good."

"No. It's nothing like that." Jen smiled. "It's just, well, Sam told me about your conversation in the truck today." She paused to be certain Patrick was following. "Well, she probably won't come right out and say it, but I think she feels the same way."

There was an unmistakable light that came into Patrick's eyes. "Really?"

"Yeah. I kind of busted it out of her earlier." Patrick just stood there grinning and Jen nudged him playfully. "Come on. Snap out of it, lover boy."

"Sorry. It's just... Well, you've made my day."

"Good. Because I like you. And you make my best friend a very happy girl." Just then Sam returned and Jen and Patrick tried hard to look innocent. "Well kids, I bid you farewell. Until tomorrow." Jen bowed dramatically and left the room.

"What were you two talking about?" Sam asked, not buying into their charade.

"Nothing," Patrick mocked, then laughed at her frustration. "Now you know how I felt this morning."

Feelings, that reminded her. "Patrick... Look, I really want to apologize for laughing at you earlier. It was... inappropriate. I thought what you said was really sweet."

"There's no need to apologize."

"But I want to."

"Fine. Apology accepted." He paused and his tone grew serious. "I have something to show you." Patrick slipped his arm about her waist and escorted her back to the bedroom. He stooped to retrieve his duffel bag from the floor and dropped it onto the bed. "I called by buddy, Dan, over in homicide and he pulled the file on Emily's murder for me." He removed a thick manila file from the bag and handed it over. "I have to return it Monday."

Sam held the thick file, its reports, photos, and interviews hidden from sight behind the seemingly harmless vanilla cover. She closed her eyes for a brief moment, summoning the strength of will to peek inside. "Well, here goes."

The first thing Sam saw was a crime scene photograph. Emily's body, thankfully, was still concealed beneath her blanket. But Sam was still struck by the stark image of her cousin's hands, exposed and bound to the bed. Struck hard. "I... I need to..." she stammered, unable to finish.

But Patrick could read it in her face. He reached out and closed the file for her. "Come on. Let's go get you something to drink and we'll sit down." Sam nodded and allowed Patrick to take the file from her. Her knees a bit wobbly, Sam let him lead her to the kitchen. Opening the fridge he examined the contents and discovered a few beers in the back.

"Here." He popped the cap off and set it on the counter in front of her. "This ought to take the edge off." He was relieved to see some of the color returning to her face. *Idiot*, he scolded himself. *Why didn't you check the file first? Move the photos so they wouldn't shock her so badly?*

"Feel better?" he asked, then watched as Sam pounded the rest of the bottle.

She sighed and then replied, "I will." She got up and retrieved another beer. "Okay, let me see that again."

"You sure?" Sam nodded and Patrick slid the folder over to her. She took a deep breath and opened the file again.

This time, without the surprise of the photograph, she was much better. Sam picked up the big, glossy picture and held it for a moment, preparing herself for what lay beneath, then continued. The next photo showed her cousin's body, the blanket removed to bare the puncture wounds that riddled her upper body. Sam blinked hard, and then tried to count the crimson holes in Emily's body. At her left shoulder: one. In her abdomen: numbers two and three. Below her right breast: four. Sam felt the bile rising in her throat and forced it back. She quickly set the photograph on the counter, turning it and the rest upside down and out of sight.

Patrick had sat quietly the whole while, but as he watched Sam's trembling hands trying to manipulate the stack of photos, he had to speak up. "Sam, I'm sorry. You don't have to do this."

"Yes I do," she cut in.

"Why?"

"I... I don't know. I just have to!" She threw her hands up in the air, exasperated.

"Okay. It's okay," he said, trying to soothe her. "Just don't make yourself crazy over it, okay? I mean, you look downright sick."

"I feel sick." She rubbed at her eyes furiously, as if trying to erase the images she'd just seen. "That was... horrible. She was so... so..." Sam couldn't find the words.

"I know the feeling." Patrick pulled his chair closer to hers and placed his arms around her, holding on tightly. "My first murder scene," he continued, "was awful. I thought I was prepared, you know? But nothing, *nothing,* can prepare you for that."

"Does it get better?"

"Not really. Not if you're human, anyway. You get to a point where you can control it, but you still feel sick. And you still see the images when you close your eyes."

"Do they ever go away?"

"Sometimes, when the case is solved. But some of them stay with you, even after. I don't know how the guys in Homicide deal with it every day." Sam sank against him and he felt her body begin to tremble as she tried to hold back the tears. "Listen. Why don't we stop for now? We can get a good night's sleep and continue this tomorrow. If you're up for it."

"I'm sorry," she muttered, still fighting the tears.

Patrick just held her tighter. "Don't be sorry. Come on." He led her again across the living room, his arm about her waist, supporting her. As he closed the door behind them, Sam pulled away and made her way to the little vanity table.

When Patrick turned around he saw her sitting on the stool, staring deep into the mirror. Her hands lay flat on the wooden surface, and tears coursed down her face. "Samantha, honey, are you all right?" Her eyes never moved from the mirror as he knelt beside her. Then, suddenly, she turned to face him and the utter grief in her eyes struck him so deeply. "My God, Sam. I'm so sorry! This is all my fault. I thought... Well, you said you wanted to know and I... I guess I didn't think it would affect you like this. I really screwed up."

"No, you didn't. I just didn't realize what I was getting myself into."

Patrick gently brushed away a tear then hugged her once more. "I know enough about you already to be sure you won't back out of this either." Sam laughed a bit in confirmation, despite her tears. "Just know," he continued, pulling back to look her in the eyes, "I'm here for you. For whatever."

His simple and stark concern hit a cord deep within her and Sam knew, at that very moment, she did love him. Whatever complications or problems it brought, she didn't care. "I...," she began, but bit her tongue, afraid to say it for fear of his reaction. Instead, she took his face in her hands and kissed him. It was tender and soft at first, but soon the intensity grew. It built to a fever pitch, Patrick's hands moving against her body and through her hair, until she felt she had to break away just to catch her breath.

She stood, pulling him to his feet as well, then moved to the bed. Sam never moved her gaze as she began to unbutton her shirt, tossing it carelessly to the floor. Then she moved to his, slowly undoing each button until she could move her hands freely across his taut, muscled torso.

"Sam..." he started, but she silenced him with another kiss. As she pressed her body tight against his and down onto the bed, the warmth of her skin sent a tingling sensation coursing through his body. He wanted her.

As her kisses traveled down his neck and across his chest, Sam's hands began to play at his waist, finally centering on his belt. As her kisses moved ever lower, she could hear Patrick's breathless voice whispering her name.

He was trying to get her attention, and when she didn't respond he reached out and stopped her industrious hands. "Sam?" He drew her to him and continued. "Sam, are you sure you want to do this?"

In response she stood, her eyes still locked to his, damp tears still clinging to her cheeks. Sam deftly unbuttoned her jeans, and slowly pushed them to the floor. Moving back onto the bed, she placed one of his hands on her right breast then kissed his mouth once more. "Yes, I'm sure."

"Okay." Patrick allowed Sam to go back to work on his belt, and then laughed as she continued to fumble with it. "Here, let me." Sam giggled a bit nervously, and then she got up and turned out the lights. But the darkness didn't last long. As she lit a candle on her nightstand, the bedroom was filled by a soft, amber glow.

"Do you have any idea how beautiful you are?"

"Hmm," she purred, sliding her half-naked body close against his. "Why don't you tell me?"

Patrick moved his body on top of hers. He kissed the tip of her nose. "Well, to start with, you've got those eyes that just... wow!" His fingers found their way into her hair and he breathed deep. "Then there's your skin." He kissed her neck, moving down to the swell of her breasts, "So soft." He traced a finger under the bottom edge of her bra, delighting in the reaction he got. "Then," he said, moving quickly down the bed, "there are these legs!" He took up her right leg at the ankle. "Incredible!" He began kissing her again, working his way up her leg.

Sam began to giggle. "That tickles."

"Really?" Patrick smiled mischievously, then set to work, fiercely tickling the bottom of her foot. "Ticklish, eh?"

Sam's laughter grew. "Stop!" she pleaded, wresting her foot away.

"I couldn't resist."

"You just wait until I find your weakness," she threatened.

Patrick smiled. "You already have."

For the next hour they explored one another's bodies, kissing, touching, laughing. Soon, the rest of their clothes joined the small pile on the floor. Patrick took a moment to sit back and admire her in the candle light. "How did I ever get so lucky?"

Sam smiled. "It's about to get even better." Sam pulled him down upon her, his penis full and hard against the soft flesh of her legs. "Make love to me," she whispered.

Patrick was happy to oblige. He moved himself between her legs, pressing himself softly against her warmth. Her hips rose against him and they both moaned as he slipped fully inside, filling her completely.

They took their time, enjoying every moment, their bodies moving together in harmony until finally Sam's body clenched and bucked beneath him. It was more than Patrick could take, and as he joined her in orgasm he buried his face against the pillow to muffle his moans.

Spent, he rolled to one side and Sam nestled up against him. "That was..." he started.

"Incredible," Sam finished. Patrick's fingers continued to move through her hair, relaxing her even further until she could barely keep her eyes open.

As Patrick watched her slowly drift off to sleep, he couldn't help but think about what tomorrow morning would bring. He hoped her feelings would match his. Once he was certain she was asleep, he blew out the candle and kissed her forehead. He whispered something to her as he lay down and Sam smiled in the dark. "I love you, too."

Chapter Six

They slept in Sunday morning, curled in one another's arms. Sam was delighted when the first thing she saw upon waking was Patrick's face. She gazed at him in silence for several minutes, reflecting on the pleasures of the preceding night. As he slowly stirred, blinking away the last vestiges of sleep, Sam spoke up.

"Good morning."

Patrick smiled. "Right back at 'ya." He pulled himself to her and gave her a quick kiss.

"So, I guess we should get up," she stated regretfully.

"Do we have to?" Patrick snuggled in against her neck, making it even harder for Sam to pull herself from the warmth of his arms.

"Or… we could stay here a little while longer."

It was about twenty minutes later when they were roused by a light knock on the bedroom door. "Sam?" came Jen's faint voice. "Are you awake?"

"Just a second," Sam called back, moving from the bed to retrieve her bathrobe from a hook just inside her closet. Patrick stayed in bed, covered by the blankets as Sam went to the door. "What's up?"

"I was getting ready to make some breakfast. Do you two want some?"

There was a look of shock that crossed Sam's face and Jen laughed. "I saw Patrick's truck out in the driveway," she confessed.

"Oh," Sam sighed, relieved. She had thought for a moment Jen might have heard the two of them the night before.

"So, are you guys hungry?"

"Sure. Do I have time to grab a shower?"

Jen nodded and Sam shut the door. "So, I'm getting up now?" Patrick asked even as he tossed aside the blankets, revealing his naked, masculine body. "And what did I hear about a shower? Is it a shower for two?"

"It could be."

"Well, let's go then." Patrick jumped playfully from the bed, dragging a blanket away with him. He deftly swept the blanket around his body, and then caught Sam by the arm lightly pulling her into the bathroom with him. He reached out and turned on the tap, then smiled a naughty smile. "Do you like it hot?"

She laughed out loud. "Hot, huh?" She nimbly kissed his lips then tugged at his blanket. Sam stepped out of her robe and into the shower. "Why don't you come on in here and find out?"

Patrick didn't waste any time joining her beneath the steaming jets. He couldn't help but stop and admire her. "My God," he muttered.

"What?"

"Nothing." Patrick slipped his arms around her waist and began kissing her damp skin, at her neck, across the swell of her breasts, centering on one taut, sensitive nipple. He could feel her body pressing hungrily against him, her breath coming in ragged gasps.

"Patrick," she sighed, "we... we shouldn't." He didn't stop right away, and Sam repeated herself. "Jen will be waiting." She didn't really want him to stop though, so when he did, she actually protested.

Patrick laughed and then reached for the shampoo. "There's just no winning with you, is there?"

As they joined Jen in the kitchen a short while later, there was a knowing smile on her face. "So, did you two enjoy your shower?"

~ ~ ~

After breakfast Sam insisted she and Patrick would handle the cleanup, so Jen went to the living room and curled up with a book. Sam had looked positively radiant all morning, and Jen knew instinctively what had gone on between her and Patrick the night before. She felt a little guilty for tormenting her roommate so badly, but Patrick had even joined in a bit. The teasing was irresistible.

Jen didn't mean to be a snoop, but she couldn't help overhearing some of the conversation coming from the kitchen. She was surprised to hear them talking about, of all things, Sam's dead cousin. It sounded like Patrick was trying to talk Sam out of something. But Jen knew her roommate, and Sam couldn't be talked out of a damn thing once she'd set her mind to it.

A few minutes later, they emerged into the living room and Sam sat down on one of the sofas. Patrick proceeded into Sam's bedroom and returned seconds later with a thick file folder. "What is that?" Jen asked.

"The file on my cousin's murder," Sam replied dryly.

"What?" Jen was shocked.

"I can't talk her out of it," Patrick grumbled.

"Of course you can't, but you'll learn that soon enough," Jen joked halfheartedly. "Now, what's this all about?"

"I asked Patrick to help me look into Emily's murder."

"And he agreed?" Jen shot a disapproving look in Patrick's direction.

"Hey, I didn't realize," Patrick cut in, trying to defend himself.

"Oh, both of you cut it out!" Sam snapped. "This is something I've got to know. You can either help me or leave." She didn't mean to sound so brutal, but it got her point across.

Patrick sank dejectedly onto the sofa next to her and placed the file on the coffee table. "I just don't want to see you get hurt."

"Neither do I," Jen apologized, "but if this is what you really want..."

"It is." Sam extended her arm and confidently opened the file. To prove a point to herself and her friends, she went for the photographs again. As she viewed each she took a deep breath to steady herself. She actually made it through the entire stack of photos, and then moved on to the forensic reports and interviews. As she finished each page, Sam handed them over to Patrick and Jen, who read them in turn. Sam found she already knew much more than she thought. There really wasn't much to the case, no real suspects, only a handful of interviews. The kitchen knife and the rope that bound her were the only physical evidence.

Sam read the police interviews done on her aunt and uncle, then on the neighbors. No one had anything much to contribute. Then Sam came across an interview with a young man identified only as "Anthony G." There was no photograph, just the typed interview.

"Patrick?" Sam asked, "Who is this?"

"Let me see." Patrick scanned the document. "A juvenile. Looks like he was her boyfriend."

Sam took back the sheet of paper and began to read it through. Apparently, the young man, Anthony, had gotten a phone call from Emily around seven. It was just after Phil and Carmen had left for dinner. He said he was home all night, and in the pages that followed Sam saw his parents had vouched for him.

Sam passed on those pages and reached for more, finding only two sheets left. One was a photograph, out of order from the rest, clipped to a full sheet of copy paper. It showed the vanity table which now stood in Sam's own room. On it's mirror was taped a piece of paper. The full sheet attached was a copy of this and it showed a raggedly printed motto of sorts.

"Hey guys," Sam piped up. "Listen to this. It was taped to the mirror in her room." She read the note aloud:

I am the dark knight.

"What do you suppose it means?"

"Just some sick calling card," Jen proposed.

"Yeah," Patrick agreed. "It's not uncommon for a killer to leave a token behind."

"It sounds familiar," Sam said, almost to herself. "I've heard this before somewhere."

"Maybe one of your family members talked about it and you overheard?" Jen supposed.

"Maybe." Sam sat back in frustration as Patrick began gathering up the file. "I don't know what that accomplished," she sighed.

"Oh, how about upsetting yourself and giving me material for at least a month's worth of nightmares?" Jen queried. "I will never understand why you torture yourself."

"Me either," Sam confessed. "Look guys, don't take offense, but I need a little time alone, okay?" Sam got up and without another word she disappeared into her room. As the door closed behind her she collapsed onto the floor, trying to hold back the tears. She failed miserably and sat there, silent tears pouring down her face.

When the fit passed, Sam got up and moved to sit on the edge of her bed. She looked at her reflection in the mirror of the little vanity table, saw the tears stubbornly filling her eyes and wiped at them furiously. "Come on girl, get a hold of yourself."

Sam shut her eyes tightly for a moment, and when she opened them again a bizarre sight was before her. The image in the smooth surface of Emily's mirror was different. Sam wasn't looking at her reflection anymore. Instead she saw Emily's room. It was unmistakable, just as Sam remembered it from her childhood.

The image was like looking through a window. Sam could see

almost the entire room. In the middle of the scene stood Emily's bed, and Emily was sitting on it. Sam was frozen, unable to rip her gaze away.

Suddenly, the vision crackled, grew blurry, then snapped back into focus. This time, Emily wasn't alone on the bed. Someone was there with her, over her. Sam could hear Emily's moans; saw Emily's hands tied to the headboard. Pink fingernail polish, white cotton rope, and Emily's voice echoing, "Yes, yes, yes..."

"Sam? Sam!" Patrick stood beside her, shaking her by the shoulders. Jen stood right behind him. There were worried looks on both their faces. "Sam, are you all right?"

"What? What happened?"

"You were screaming," Patrick replied.

"You scared us," Jen added.

"I was screaming?"

"At the top of your lungs."

"She knew him," Sam muttered in disbelief.

"What?" Patrick sat down beside her, pulling her close to his side

"You're going to think I'm nuts," she started, "but I saw something."

"What are you talking about?"

"I was sitting here and the mirror... The mirror was..." Sam collapsed into tears again, unable to stop them.

"It's okay," Patrick cooed, gently rocking her back and forth, stroking her ebony hair.

"I'll go get you some coffee," Jen offered. A minute later, she returned with a steaming cup for Sam. "Here sweetie, drink this. It'll make you feel better."

~ ~ ~

A short while later, Jen and Patrick stood outside Sam's bedroom door. "She'll sleep for a while."

"I can't help but think this is my fault."

"Why?" Jen questioned.

"If I hadn't brought that damn file for her to look at..."

"She would've gotten her hands on it eventually. Somehow. If not from you, then from Joe, or from some one else. That's just Sam, so don't blame yourself."

"What do you think she was talking about?"

"I have no idea." Jen shook her head.

"Whatever it was, it had her pretty freaked."

Sam could hear the two of them talking, she'd only pretended to fall asleep. She needed a moment to sort things out, to try and make order of the racing thoughts inside her head. Was it real? Or had she imagined it? She didn't like the implications of either answer. Something inexplicably scary had just happened to her. Either that, or she was cracking up.

Sam stood shakily in front of the mirror, reaching out hesitantly to touch its surface. Her fingers trembled uncontrollably, and she drew her hand back, afraid suddenly to touch the glass. Afraid it may not be real and afraid it might be at the same time.

"What just happened to me?" she wondered aloud.

Then, in a flash, the smooth pane of glass before her filled with the same image as before. Sam stood mesmerized, watching the scene play out before her again. As she watched, the figure in bed with her cousin rocked atop her in the unmistakable throws of passion. Sam could hear Emily's voice crying out in ecstasy. Then there was that same strange crackle, and the scene jumped forward. Emily's lover now stood by the window, his back to Sam, and Emily was asking him to untie her. But he never moved.

"Come on," Emily was giggling. "Untie me. Please?" Still nothing. "Untie me." Sam could hear the discomfort growing in her cousin's voice with every request.

The scene crackled one more time. This skip brought the vision to its grizzly end. As Sam watched in horror, she saw Emily's lover atop her again, this time wielding a knife. He let out a horrific sound, half laugh and half scream, as Sam watched the knife make its first vicious plunge into her cousin's body. All the while, Emily screamed, and the knife flashed again and again.

Just as suddenly as it began, the vision flickered and disappeared. Sam was utterly astounded by what she had just witnessed. She turned away from the vanity table and quickly strode out into the living room. She must've looked frightened, because as soon as Jen saw her she jumped up from the sofa and rushed to her side.

"Sam? What's the matter? What's happened?"

"The mirror..." Sam started, but Patrick stepped to her side and interrupted.

"Come sit down," he instructed as he led her to the sofa.

"What about the mirror?" Jen prompted.

"I saw Emily." Sam stopped to collect her thoughts and to try to convert them into words her friends would understand. "I was looking in the mirror, and I saw Emily... on... on the night she was murdered..."

"What?" Patrick asked. "Sam, you... that's not possible," he sighed.

"I know what you must be thinking," Sam admitted, "but I did *not* imagine this. It was real."

"Sam, are you hearing yourself?" Jen asked, trying to reason with her friend. "What you're telling us is just impossible."

"Don't you think I know how this must sound? I know it sounds nuts, but I also know what I saw! She knew her killer. He was there, in

69

bed with her." Sam stopped her narration a moment and saw Jen and Patrick exchange worried glances. "Listen, I know you must think I'm nuts, but I'm telling you she *knew* him! She was tied to the bed, they were having sex, and the next thing I saw was him with the knife. And he was stabbing her and she was screaming..." Sam felt hot tears quietly sliding down her face.

"Honey, stop," Patrick cooed, stroking her hair softly. "We can talk about this later. You can get some sleep, you can calm down..." Sam nodded reluctantly.

"How about I run you a nice, hot bath?" Jen offered.

"Okay," Sam relented.

As Jen got up and disappeared into Sam's room, Patrick held onto Sam tightly. "Honey, are you all right? You're scaring me." Sam looked up into Patrick's face and he couldn't miss the terrified look in her eyes.

"You're scared?" Sam managed a half-laugh. "Try being me right now."

"Okay, point taken." They both released a jitter of nervous laughter and when it subsided, Patrick asked, "Feeling better?"

"A little."

"Come on. Let's go check on that bath."

They found Jen in the bathroom, adding some bubbles to the already half full tub. "Hey girl, bath's almost ready."

"Thanks Jen."

"If you need to talk later, I'll be upstairs, all right?" Sam nodded. "Patrick, you got it from here?"

"Yeah. I got it." With Jen gone, Patrick turned to Sam. "Come on, let's get you out of these clothes."

Sam smiled, despite the tears still brimming in her eyes. "Is that all you think about?" she teased, while Patrick helped her out of her T-shirt. As she slipped into the water she asked, "Care to join me?"

"If you'd like," came his reply.

As Sam sank back against Patrick's chest in the hot water, she sighed deeply. After a few minutes of silence, she piped up, "I didn't imagine it."

"I never said you did."

"I need you to believe me. What I'm telling you is real."

"What did you see, exactly?"

"Like I said, I saw Emily." She spoke haltingly. "It was like looking through a window, right into her room. It was the night she died. There was someone with her, in her room. His face was always in shadow. They were in bed together..." Sam's voice trailed off for a moment, and she closed her eyes. Patrick's hands made their way to her hair, his fingers twining there, relaxing her.

Sam continued, "She was tied to the bed, but willingly. Patrick, she knew him. They were lovers... and I... I saw him kill her."

"But honey," he protested.

"I did not imagine it!" Sam sat up and turned to face him.

Patrick cupped her face in his hands. "I believe you. Okay? I believe you saw something." Patrick paused. "But we'd just seen all those pictures. You looked at pictures of your cousin's dead body!" He took her by the shoulders and turned her back around, leaning her against his chest once more.

"Now," he instructed, "Just relax. And try to forget about it for a little while."

Chapter Seven

"Morning Sam."

"Hey Tony. How was your weekend?" Sam had just arrived at work and tossed her handbag onto her desk. It tipped over and a single, unlabeled CD slipped out and onto the floor.

Tony stooped to pick it up. "It was good. Yours?"

"Interesting." Sam took the disk from her editor's outstretched hand. She held it up. "This kept me pretty busy," she said with a hint of sarcasm.

"What is it?"

"An old murder case I'm looking into. A friend got a hold of the file for me, and I was up most of the night last night scanning it onto this disk."

"Got your teeth in a story, eh?"

"Not exactly, Tony. It happened a long time ago."

"Why not? You know those unsolved cases can spark a lot of interest," Tony proffered.

"Not this one Tony. The vic was my cousin."

Tony looked shocked. "I'm sorry Sam, I had no idea."

"That's okay. I haven't mentioned it around the office... for obvious reasons." Sam winked conspiratorially to her editor.

"Now Sam, you know I'd have never asked you to do a story on your own family... Unless you wanted to." He winked back at her and they shared a laugh, then Tony asked, "If it's not too intrusive, care to tell me what happened?"

"Her name was Emily. She was killed while her parents were out one night. She was raped and then murdered. They didn't discover it until the following morning."

There was a hint of recognition on Tony's face. "Did it happen here? Was it somewhere local?"

"Yeah."

"I think I remember that. About fifteen years ago now, right?"

"Yes."

"She was stabbed?"

"Yes, but... how do you know?"

"Sam, I grew up here, remember? It was all over the news. That was my junior year in high school. It was a big deal. I remember a couple kids at my school knew her. Everyone was pretty worked up about it all."

"I never realized you two could have known one another."

"Yeah." Tony looked hungrily at the small disk in Sam's hand. "Look, Sam, do you mind if I take a look at what you've got?"

Sam handed him the disk. "Sure. Let me know if anything jumps out at you."

"Are you sure you don't want to do a story? It could jump start the investigation. Maybe jog some memories?"

"No, Tony. I'm just doing this for my own peace of mind."

"Well, if you change your mind..."

"You'll be the first to know."

Tony headed back to his office. "I'll get you your disk back soon."

Sam sat down at her computer and began to search through the paper's archives. Something from her cousin's case file wouldn't leave her mind at peace. *I am the dark knight.* It kept nagging at her. Sam knew she'd seen it somewhere before. She typed in a search on her computer and in a few minutes, she had returned a handful of articles from a variety of Oregon newspapers.

Opening the first article, Sam read about the murder of a college co-ed. It happened a few years after Emily's death. There were a couple similarities that made Sam's skin crawl. There were no signs of forced entry. She'd been tied up, this time by electrical cords from her room. This woman, however, had been strangled. Sam hit the print key and moved on to the next story. In all, there were four murders over the course of the past eighteen years that bore striking similarities to Emily's murder.

Sam picked up the phone and dialed the police station. "Joe Torrance, please."

"May I tell him who's calling?" the operator asked.

Sam gave her name then waited patiently until she heard the line click over.

"Hey Angel. Patrick's not around."

"Actually, Joe, I called to talk to you. I'm looking into a few old murder cases, and I was wondering if I could use my connections to get a little information?"

"Murders, huh?"

"Yeah. Do you think you can help me out?"

"Well, I don't know. What exactly is it you need?"

Sam gave him the murder victims' names and the dates of the murders from the stories she had collected. "I need to know if there was anything unusual found at the murder scenes."

"Unusual?"

"Like, maybe a note?" she offered. "If so, I need to know what those notes said."

There was hesitation in Joe's voice. "Gee, I don't know."

"Come on Joe. Please? I'll explain later."

"I'll try, Sugar, but no promises."

"And Joe," she paused, "don't tell Patrick, okay? I'll talk to both of you about it later. I just need to know what you find out first."

~ ~ ~

On her drive home that evening Sam's cell phone rang. "Hello?"

"Hey sexy. What're you up to?"

"Heading home. What about you?"

"Just finishing up here at the station, then I'm headed home too."

"Yours or mine?" Sam asked.

"Hmm, good question. I was hoping I hadn't worn out my welcome at your place."

"Never."

"Good. I guess I'll see you in a little while." Patrick paused a moment. "Hey, Joe just walked up. He says he needs to talk with you."

Joe got on the phone. "Hey Sugar. I got the info you needed. You were right. Looks like there was a note at each crime scene."

Sam was shocked, and a bit scared, to learn her hunch had been right. "Joe, you're the best! What did they say?"

"'*I am the dark knight.*'"

"Good God!" she exclaimed, a shiver running down her spine. "All of them?"

"Yeah. Look, I know you said you'd explain this to me, but..."

"Put Patrick back on the phone. You can ask him about it when I hang up. He'll fill you in."

"Okay, Sugar. I'll talk to you later."

Once Patrick was back on the line, Sam asked, "Did you catch that?"

"I think so. What's going on?"

"I had Joe look into four other murders, all within the past fifteen years or so. They seemed similar to Emily's. I found articles about them at work. Now, according to Joe, they all had a note at the crime scene."

"And they all said '*I am the dark knight*,'" Patrick finished.

"It looks like Emily wasn't the only one."

"My God, Sam. Do you have any idea what you've stumbled onto?"

"Joe is going to expect you to fill him in."

"Will do," Patrick assured her. "I'll be home as soon as I can, okay? We'll talk more then."

"Okay."

~ ~ ~

Several hours had passed since Sam's conversation with Patrick and Joe, and Patrick still hadn't arrived home. She was beginning to wonder what the hold up was when the doorbell rang. Sam wasn't at all surprised to see Joe standing on her welcome mat too.

"Come on in guys," she offered. "Joe, you want a cup of coffee?"

"That would be nice."

"Me too?" Patrick asked. Sam nodded and headed into the kitchen while the guys made themselves comfortable in the living room.

When she returned, Joe didn't hesitate to start in with his questions.

"Sam, where did this come from? I mean, how did you put it all together?"

"I saw a photograph of a note in my cousin's file. There was something about the phrase... I knew I'd seen or heard it somewhere before. So I did an archive search at work for murders that bore similarities to Emily's."

"Well," Joe explained, "the boys in Homicide were a bit surprised when we showed 'em the connections."

"What?" Sam was shocked. She had assumed the police must have known the murders were linked.

Patrick saw the shock on Sam's face. "You have to remember, these murders occurred years apart. And they didn't all happen here. First, there was Emily's murder. Then one of the murders was up in Washington, another down in northern California, one here in Portland again. And the last one was down in southern Oregon. And those are just the ones we know about so far."

"They didn't manage to connect *any* of them?" Sam was incredulous.

Joe just shook his head. "Different detectives in different counties."

"And states," Patrick interjected.

Joe continued. "And these murders spanned almost a twenty year period. Now, I know that's no excuse, and so do our guys in Homicide. They were truly embarrassed."

"I'll bet they were," Sam scoffed.

"And," Joe added, "We kinda told them you'd be cool about not including their oversight in any story you may write about this." Joe looked at her meaningfully. "As a favor."

"Although every bone in my body is screaming 'this is one juicy story,' I'm not going to write it. The secret's safe with me," Sam assured them.

"Well, I can tell you one thing," Joe said as he stood up to leave, "This is really going to jump start the whole investigation." He gave Sam a quick pat on the shoulder. "You've done good, Sugar." And with that he headed to the front door. "See you in the morning Patrick."

"Bye Joe," Patrick and Sam replied.

"You know," Sam sighed once they were alone, "I still can't figure out why that phrase rings a bell." She slid across the couch to sit right next to Patrick. "I mean, I've actually seen it somewhere, I'm sure of it."

"Let it go, honey." He smiled at her knowingly. "At least for a little while?"

"I'll try." Patrick leaned in and kissed her lips softly. "Mmm," she sighed, "that makes forgetting things a whole lot easier."

"Does it now?" He kissed her again, harder this time, and she responded in a way that took his breath away. She stood from the couch, grabbed his shirt collar playfully, and without a word led him into the bedroom.

~ ~ ~

In a darkened room, a man sat quietly. Ten photographs were scattered across the desk in front of him. Five were of beautiful, smiling women. The other five were Polaroid shots, and were much more sinister. In those last five photos, the same women appeared, tied in various manners. Vacant, glassy stares occupied their once beautiful countenances. His toe tapped urgently against the floor as he remembered each woman.

The urge was upon him once again. He could feel it creeping in, becoming stronger with each and every day. It had been so long...

Ordinarily, he would have already started looking for a way to get at his next lover, his next victim. But there was a hitch he hadn't anticipated. Someone was looking. Someone was looking at his very first love. If he was discovered, he knew it would be his own fault. He should never have left those notes behind, but he was compelled to. No manner of reasoning could stop him from leaving his little motto behind for all to see.

A noise elsewhere startled him and he quickly swept the pictures into a pile. Pulling open his bottom desk drawer, he removed the false bottom and stowed his most secret treasures safely away. His game would continue, he knew there was no stopping. He was going to have so much more fun...

~ ~ ~

Darkness enveloped her. Sam sat at the foot of her bed, Patrick sleeping soundly behind her. Midnight had come and gone, and Sam still couldn't fall asleep. She stared into the mirror of her cousin's vanity, questions bounding feverishly inside her head. She kept coming back to the note. It was more than just vaguely familiar now. Sam was certain she'd actually seen it written somewhere else before. If she could only remember where...

She got up and moved to the vanity table, sitting on its small wooden stool. In the faint red glow from her digital alarm clock, she could discern the shapes in the room behind her. As she stared through the mirror at Patrick sleeping on her bed, something strange began.

A bright pinpoint of light appeared right in the center of the mirror. As Sam watched in fascination, the point grew, expanding outward over the face of the mirror. It was bright, causing Sam to squint, and illuminating everything in Sam's bedroom. Then, suddenly, the light changed and once again Sam felt as if she were viewing a home movie through her mirror.

She looked in on what appeared to be an office. A man sat with his back to her, everything thickly veiled in shadows. Then, the vision winked out for a moment, only to come back again a second later. This time, Sam felt like she was looking over the man's shoulder onto the desktop. There were pictures there. Pictures of five different women.

Sam cried out for Patrick and as soon as she did, the vision blinked out completely.

Sitting up in bed, Patrick asked, "What is it Sam? Are you all right?"

"Fine. Sorry, I'm fine." Sam decided it was best not to tell Patrick about what she had just seen. He wouldn't believe her anyway. "I didn't mean to wake you. Go back to sleep."

"Are you sure?" Patrick swiped at his eyes groggily.

"Yeah. Go back to sleep."

"Come here." Sam crawled back in bed with him, curling herself against him in a warm embrace. Within minutes Patrick was sleeping again, but not Sam. She lay there in the dark, afraid to take her eyes off the mirror.

One of those women she'd seen was her cousin. She was sure of it.

Chapter Eight

Five weeks had passed and Sam hadn't been plagued with any further visions in her mirror. She was beginning to think she'd never seen anything at all. Patrick still kept his apartment across town, but he no longer spent any real time there. His clothes hung beside Sam's in her closet or were folded neatly in the dresser drawers Sam had cleaned out and surrendered to him. His toothbrush sat next to hers in the holder in her bathroom and other of his belongings were scattered throughout the house.

Sam thought it was rather silly that he still paid rent at a place he was never at, but whenever she brought up the topic of him officially moving in, Patrick would change the subject. Something about the topic made him nervous.

They had just finished one such conversation. Patrick had arrived home from work, carrying a small arm load of belongings from his apartment through the front door. "Why don't you just move in?" Sam asked.

"Honey," he protested, "Why do you do this every time?"

"Do what?" Sam paused and then added sarcastically, "Oh! You mean question why you dump money into an apartment you're never at?" Patrick smiled weakly at her as he continued to walk past her into the bedroom.

"I don't know." It was the only answer he could think of.

"You live *here*," Sam continued, pressing the issue. "I *want* you to live here."

"Let's go out to dinner tonight," Patrick said in a futile attempt to change the subject.

Sam knew what he was doing and wasn't about to fall for it. "Please don't." She shook her head in dismay.

"What?"

"Change the subject like that. Why don't you want to talk about this?"

"I just don't."

"But why?" Sam pressed. She was thoroughly confused by his resistance. She knew how she felt about him and she was sure Patrick felt the same about her.

"Honey, please just drop it."

"Fine." Sam pouted.

She watched Patrick place his things on the bed, and then he turned around and walked back into the living room. "I'm going out for a while," Patrick said dryly. He pulled his truck keys off the rack by the door and was gone.

"Well, that went well!" Sam sighed, sinking down onto her bed. She looked at her reflection in the mirror as tears started to well quietly in her eyes. She lay back and stared at the ceiling. She just couldn't understand why this was such a big deal, why Patrick resisted it so.

She lay there for some time, quietly running their conversation over in her head. Her eyes were closed, arms folded loosely across her stomach. A noise within her bedroom caused her eyes to flick open in an instant.

It was like the sound of salt and pepper static made by a television set when there was no channel to tune in. Sam looked over at the small TV on top of the dresser. It was off. Slowly, tentatively, she allowed her eyesight to scan back across the room to her vanity, instinctively knowing the sound was originating there.

Sure enough, the mirror's surface glowed softly, accompanied by the low static. As Sam slowly sat upright the noise and the light grew in intensity until she could feel the sound reverberating in her head. She narrowed her eyes to a slit against the blinding brightness of the light. In a flash, the noise and white light ceased.

Now, in the face of the mirror, Sam could see a bedroom. It wasn't her own, nor was it her cousin's like she'd seen before. This appeared to be another room, as yet unknown to her. She felt, by the look of the room, that it was a woman's. A bold floral spread lay neatly across the bed, coordinating red pillows piled high at the headboard. A stuffed dog, a childhood memento perhaps, held station on the nightstand near the digital alarm clock. It's face read 9:23pm. A furtive glance at her own clock showed the same time.

As Sam sat mesmerized, she saw two figures enter the room, hot in the frenzy of passion. She felt a sheepish glow creep into her cheeks, a sign of the guilt she felt for watching. She was like an intruder, an uninvited voyeur, yet she could not tear her gaze from the scene before her. The man and woman tumbled onto the bed, knocking pillows haphazardly to the floor.

The woman was petite, a redhead. Her green blouse was open and Sam could see the white lace bra beneath. No sounds accompanied this vision, but Sam could almost hear the woman's sharp intake of breath as the man slipped his hand beneath her bra to tease her nipple, his mouth busy at the nape of her neck. As for the man, he was average in every way. Dark hair, average build and height. There was nothing distinctive about him, yet to Sam there was something vaguely familiar. His face was in shadow and Sam never caught more than a fleeting glimpse of his countenance.

As Sam watched this couple's heated foreplay, she felt a sinking sense of dread. It started in her gut, like a tiny black ice ball, it's fingers quickly reaching out to her every extremity until her entire body was covered in goose flesh. This mirror had shown her cousin's murder in every gruesome detail. What was it showing her now? Sam sat, barely breathing, knowing her question would soon be answered.

~ ~ ~

Sam had no idea how much time had passed. She sat, quietly sobbing, at the edge of her bed. A short time ago, the image in the mirror had been vibrant, lively. Now it was a quiet tableau. Nothing moved. Tears streamed down Sam's cheeks, landing soundlessly on the front of her shirt and on her bedspread. There was nothing she could have done to change what was before her. She had no way of knowing where these events had actually transpired, but Sam felt the guilt none-the-less.

The petite redhead was tied to the bed. She had placed her hands there willingly; trusting her lover as he gently bound her hands to the headboard with a woven satin rope. Sam had yelled a warning to her, knowing it was futile but attempting it anyway. She had watched in horror as the man drove himself feverishly into his victim, moving harder and deeper with every thrust of his pelvis. The woman was beside herself with pleasure, her face contorted in a visage of sheer lust. Her eyes were tightly closed and her mouth open in what was, to Sam, a silent scream.

Suddenly, the woman's eyes popped open wide, her scream instantly changing. Her face became a blank slate for terror and Sam saw the man's hands around her throat, knuckles white as he fiercely closed off her airway. Her feet thrashed and kicked. Sam was sick as she watched him continue to thrust himself deep within the woman even as she lay struggling. He shook in climax as she was dying.

When he was finished and she was dead, the man calmly withdrew, gathered his clothing and left Sam's sight. Now she sat and stared through tear glazed eyes at the pale, naked body on the flowered bedspread. Sam was greatly relieved when the image finally faded and disappeared.

She lurched from the bed, freed from the mirror's enchantment, and headed straight for the toilet. Reaching it just in time, she vomited. She felt so helpless, sitting beside the white porcelain, retching and racked with sobs. Her tears no longer came quietly. Great wails emerged from deep within her, melting the icy terror with heated rage. That man was a monster! One of her hands clenched into a fist and pounded hard on the tile floor, splitting open one of her knuckles.

When the fit had subsided, Sam found her feet and moved to the sink to brush her teeth. As she scrubbed out the bitter taste of bile she started a shower in the hopes the hot water could wash away the memory of what she had just seen. She stood beneath the steaming spray until the water began to cool, and then stepped out into her misty bathroom. She felt a little better... but only a little.

~ ~ ~

Patrick was at the police station. He hadn't known where else to go after leaving Sam's house. Why couldn't she understand the way he felt? Things were almost too good to be true. He loved her with all his heart. But a little voice within him shouted, *Don't ruin it! Don't push your luck!* That small voice told him the minute he moved in things would change, it would be over. Patrick knew this was nonsense. He could see it in Sam's face, could feel it in his heart and soul. But he'd never been in this situation before and it scared him. He hoped in time he'd get over it. And for his own sake, he hoped it was soon.

He'd been there at his desk for several hours, finishing up some long overdue reports and other bureaucratic paperwork. He hated this stuff, it seemed to take forever. When he looked up at the clock on the station house wall, he was shocked to see it was almost midnight. *Sam must be worried... or very mad,* he thought. He picked up the phone to call her, but halted when he heard someone call his name.

"What are you doing here?" the voice continued, even as Patrick turned to face it.

"Hey Dan," he nodded casually. "I'm just wading through my own personal sea of paperwork. How about you?"

"On my way out to a crime scene." Dan looked over his shoulder before continuing. "You might want to come with me."

"What's going on?"

"I think our guy has done it again." The detective paused as if deciding whether or not to continue. "We got a call a little while ago. Gal came home and found her roommate tied up naked in bed. Looks like he strangled this one. Left a note, like before."

Dan was a veteran homicide detective. His salt and pepper gray hair and deeply creased face made him seem older than he really was. But he'd been in this line of work for a long time. Dan, along with the other detectives in Homicide, had felt incredibly sheepish when their oversight had been brought to light all those weeks ago. In the time that had followed, they poured over every page of every case file from all the murders they suspected were linked to this guy. Dan had no doubt they were dealing with a serial killer. Some of the other detectives might frown at him for bringing a beat cop with him to this latest murder scene, but none of them would say a word. It was thanks to Patrick, and his relationship with the reporter who had discovered the connections, this whole mess had remained out of the papers.

"Listen, Patrick, I want you to come with me on this. I could use your help."

"Yeah, sure." Patrick stood to follow Dan. As he did so, his cell phone rang. "Hello?"

"Patrick… He killed her," Sam stated simply. "He's done it again. She's dead." The certainty in Sam's voice was unmistakable.

"What? Who?" There was no way she could know. Patrick was confused. "Listen, honey, we'll talk when I get home. I'm with Dan. We're headed to a crime scene." He looked to Dan and winked conspiratorially. "He needs my help with something."

"She's on a red bedspread. With flowers."

"What did you say?" Patrick stopped dead in his tracks.

"It's a red floral bedspread," Sam repeated. "You'll see when you get there."

"Honey, are you okay?" An icy shiver passed along his spine and

Patrick fought the urge to tell Dan he was going straight home. "Is Jen there?"

"I think she's upstairs sleeping. I'm not sure. I'll be fine. You go with Dan. We'll talk when you get home."

"Are you certain?" Patrick's feet started to move again, and he trotted to catch up with the detective. They climbed into Dan's SUV even as Sam assured him she was going to be fine. Patrick told her he loved her. "I'm sorry we fought," he added stupidly before hanging up.

"Oh, how cute," Dan teased. "Trouble in paradise?"

Patrick smiled. He had to play along, but in his mind he raced back over the things Sam had said. Reason forced him to dismiss her ominous words. There was no way she could know where he was going, or that another woman had been killed. As the car raced through the night to the murder scene Patrick muttered softly, "Absolutely no way."

Minutes later, Dan pulled his rig to a halt across the street from a small apartment building. The entire building was surrounded by police cars, flashers still pulsing in red and blue, their sirens quiet. A uniformed officer was stringing yellow crime scene tape across the front of the yard.

Patrick followed Dan up the sidewalk and into the foyer of the building. "Where are we?" Dan asked of one of the officers heading back outside.

"Apartment 3C," came the reply.

The two men jogged up the flights of stairs and into the narrow hallway of the third floor. It was obvious which apartment they were looking for, as officers and crime scene techs were streaming in and out of the open door. As Patrick stepped into the cozy apartment, he saw the victim's roommate sitting on the sofa against the far wall. She was red-faced, still crying, shaking her head in denial of what had happened to her friend.

Following Dan, knowing instinctively it would be unwise to wander the crime scene by himself, Patrick just listened. He heard Dan speaking with his colleagues and was able to glean that the roommate had come home shortly after 11:30pm. She had borrowed something and wanted to return it. Apparently, the victim had been on a date, so her friend didn't think she would be home yet. She went into the bedroom and found the body.

"Does this man she was seeing have a name?" Dan had inquired.

"Steven. She met him through her work, a bookstore. This was their first date. Roommate can't give us any more information."

"What's her name?" Patrick was met with blank looks. "The victim?"

"Tracy Randolph."

"Let's go take a look," Dan said, tilting his head toward the bedroom.

Patrick followed hesitantly. He stopped at the bedroom door, shocked still by the sight before him. The woman, Tracy, lay atop the bed. Her dead eyes were locked in a glassy stare. Bruising was evident around her delicate white neck. But what caught Patrick's gaze was the bed and its red floral bedspread.

~ ~ ~

It was early morning when Patrick walked back through the front door. He'd have to get up again in a couple hours and head back to work. He was expecting to find Sam curled up in bed asleep, but instead she was sitting in the living room untangling a string of Christmas lights. Two cardboard boxes marked "X-mas" sat near her feet. They had planned on picking up a tree that week.

"Sam? What are you doing up?"

"Couldn't sleep," was her simple reply.

Patrick wanted to ask her a thousand questions, but instead he went to the couch and sat down next to her. He put an arm around her shoulder and pulled her close. "Are you all right?"

Sam was quiet. He waited patiently and after a few minutes of silence he was rewarded. "I saw it happen. I watched him kill her." The hours had worn most of the emotion from Sam's voice. She was tearless as she slowly recounted all that had transpired. She knew Patrick would be doubtful, but it still hurt when he questioned her.

"You couldn't have seen all that. I mean, how? Sam, this is just impossible."

"I know. But answer this: Was she lying on the bed? On a flowered red bedspread?" Patrick hesitated. "Was she?" He nodded. "Then I'm *not* going crazy Patrick! I didn't imagine this. It really happened. I saw everything."

"I believe you, it's just…" Patrick paused, "I just don't understand this."

"Neither do I." Sam let out a heavy sigh. "Come on. Let's go to bed. I might be able to get a quick nap with you here. It's going to be a long day."

Chapter Nine

After a futile attempt at a nap, Sam headed in to work. Except for the death of her parents, she hadn't missed a single day of work since she'd been at the paper. She almost called in this morning. When she saw Tony waiting at her desk, she wished she had. "What do you want Tony? I'm exhausted."

"Good morning to you too!" Tony smiled. "If I didn't know you, I might take that the wrong way."

"All right, all right," Sam forced a weak smile. "Good morning Tony. Now… what do you want?"

"I hear there was a murder last night. Woman was strangled. See what details you can pull together and get a draft on my desk by two." Tony noticed the weary look on Sam's face and asked, "What is it?"

"I was up all night waiting for Patrick to come home. He was out on the scene."

Tony put two and two together. "Hence the foul mood. Well, get cracking on your story and I'll let you go home early." He dropped her a wink and then returned to his office, closing the door.

Normally, Sam would've headed out to the murder scene. Even now there would still be officers there from whom she could elicit a statement. But this time was different. Sam already knew more than she wanted to. Instead she headed directly to the police station. She wanted to talk to one of the detectives. Usually, they'd decline to speak with a reporter, especially at this point in an investigation, but Sam thought she had a slight edge given what she'd discovered about the series of murders and her willingness to keep that juicy tidbit out of the papers.

When she arrived at the police station, she didn't seek out Patrick or Joe, or any other officers she knew. Instead she went straight to the little desk which stood in the main lobby. It served as a reception area. Sam asked the woman there to call over to Homicide and see if Patrick's friend Dan was in.

"May I tell him who's inquiring?" Sam told the woman her name, adding that she was a friend of Sergeant Logan's.

After a short phone call Sam was told to have a seat. "Detective Johnston will be out shortly." Sam nodded a quick thanks then took a seat in one of the hard plastic chairs which lined one wall. After several minutes a man appeared, spoke to the receptionist, then approached Sam.

"Miss Williams?" he inquired.

Sam nodded and stood to shake his outstretched hand. "We haven't met," she began, "but I'm a friend of Patrick Logan's. I believe he and Joe Torrance spoke with you several weeks ago about a series of murders?"

A flash of recognition came across the detective's face. "I thought the name sounded familiar." Dan looked around at all the other officers passing back and forth and thought twice about discussing anything with the reporter, at least not here in the open. "Miss Williams," he began.

"Sam, please," she interrupted.

"Sam," the detective nodded. "If we could hold this conversation elsewhere?" Sam nodded her consent. "Would you follow me?"

She allowed Dan to lead her into a small interrogation room just down the hallway. He motioned for her to have a seat and she obliged, although once she'd sat down onto the hard metal chair she'd wished she had remained standing. "This chair must be part of your interrogation technique," Sam joked.

Dan smiled jovially back at her. "You know it! Can't let anyone get too comfortable in here." He sat down across from her at a small, scuffed metal table and asked, "So what can I do for you?"

Sam laid it straight out. "I know about the murder last night and I have reason to think it is connected to the others." Sam could tell by the look on the detective's face that he understood. There was no need to explain *what* others. "Was there a note?" she asked simply.

"Miss Will…" he caught himself, "Sam. You know I cannot release any information from an ongoing investigation."

"I am aware of that, Detective. My reasons for asking are more personal rather than professional. Patrick and Joe may not have mentioned this to you, but the first victim was my cousin."

"I know," he replied. After a heavy pause, the detective continued. "While I have you here, I would like to thank you for your… tactful handling of the information you discovered."

"I didn't think it would benefit anyone to cause a panic," Sam said. "But, now that he's done it again…" Sam paused.

"You think we need to alert the public?" Dan said. Sam nodded. "I agree," the detective continued. "I had planned to make a statement to the press tomorrow morning."

"Really?"

"Yes."

"How much are you going to disclose?"

"The murders, their dates and locations, and that we have reason to believe they're linked."

"And the notes?"

"The content of the notes needs to remain strictly within the investigation, you understand?"

"Yes."

"Am I safe in my assumption that you'll be covering this story for your paper?"

"Yes, I will." Sam paused for a moment. "I want you to know I intend to keep my word about how it was discovered these cases were connected."

"Thank you. The department will be under fire as it is after we go public with this. Serial killings are very touchy that way. Whatever help I can get, I'll take it at this point."

"What time do you plan to hold your press conference tomorrow?"

"Seven a.m."

"If I get a draft story to you this afternoon for approval, I'd like to run it in our morning edition. Exclusive coverage. It'll hit the stands two hours before your press conference. Unidentified sources, of course."

"I suppose I owe you," the detective sighed.

"Well, I didn't want it to come to that, but if I had to, I was prepared to play that card."

"You don't have to." The detective stood and walked to the door. "Get me a draft of your story. As long as nothing oversteps what I'm prepared to release, you can run it."

Dan held the door open for Sam as she headed out. "I'll be in touch," she said.

~ ~ ~

Back at her office, Sam sat at her desk typing out a draft for Detective Johnston when her editor stopped by to check her progress. "How's it going?"

"The police are issuing a statement to the press tomorrow morning," Sam replied dryly.

"And...?" Tony asked expectantly.

Sam smiled. "And I happen to have some advance information on what the press release will contain."

Tony sank into a chair in mild disbelief. "Care to share?"

"Not just yet," Sam replied. "I struck a deal with the detective in charge. He gets the draft of my story today. Once he approves it, it's a go for the morning edition. Our story will be on the stands before the press conference has even started."

Tony was slack-jawed in disbelief. "Come on, you've got to share. Just a little?"

Sam sighed reluctantly. "If I tell you, will you leave me be? I want to finish this story and go home." Tony nodded. "All right. Last night's murder is connected to several others, including the murder of my cousin, Emily. I have a list of the victims, the dates of their murders, and a note left at each scene that links them."

"Jesus!" Tony muttered. "How did you manage to get...? Never mind. It doesn't matter." Tony stood and started to head back to his office. "Just get that story on my desk."

Almost an hour later, Sam was on the phone with Detective Johnston. "Draft's finished. Do you have a secure fax? Or can I e-mail it to you?"

"I'd prefer the fax." He gave her the number, stating he'd be standing by the machine waiting for her story.

"How soon until I hear from you?"

"No promises, but I'm hoping to get back to you within the hour." Sam gave him her cell phone number, asking him to call her.

"I'm going to get something to eat," Sam said as she poked her head into her editor's office. "Story's done, I'm just waiting to hear back from my detective. You should have it on your desk soon. I've got my cell if you need to get a hold of me." She got a grunt in reply from Tony, so she headed out into the early December sunshine.

Pulling her cell phone out of her purse, she dialed Patrick's number.

It rang several times before he answered. "Hey Patrick, it's me."

"Hi honey. Are you doing okay?"

"Yeah. Just heading out to get something to eat. Have you had lunch yet?"

"Joe and I just ate."

"All right. Listen, Tony gave me the afternoon off, just as soon as I get him the final copy on a story. When are you off?"

"Shift's over around four. I'll come straight home."

"Promise?"

"You know I'll try." Then he added, "I love you."

"Okay. I love you too," Sam said as she turned the corner into a hole-in-the-wall café just up the street from her office.

Approaching the counter, Sam pulled a worn paper menu from the rack near the register. It had been some time since she'd been in here. This used to be a frequent lunch spot for many of the employees at the Tribune. But the owner had sold it and she and her co-workers just didn't seem to come around anymore. That was ages ago. Sam didn't really care about any of that right now, she just wanted a quiet place to sit, eat a little something, and pass the time until Detective Johnston approved her story.

Sam ordered a sandwich and a Pepsi then sat down in a corner booth. There was only a small handful of people in the café and Sam situated herself so she could sit back in her booth and observe them all. Most were businessmen and women hurriedly picking at their lunches while discussing various work issues with their counterparts or talking on their cell phones.

Of the people sitting around her, Sam found herself paying closer attention to the men. She took stock of their builds and their hair color. Then she compared them to the man from her vision the night before. She didn't have much to go on, she knew, but her mind wouldn't let

95

go.

The gentleman two tables over? The one talking so sweetly on the phone with his wife or his lover? Could it be him? Or the man working the cash register? The one who took her order? Her mind was awhirl with irrational conclusions, speculations, and they all started to press in on her at once.

Sam got up swiftly and tried to will herself to walk slowly and calmly to the little bathroom in the back. Her legs were wobbly and she felt like bolting straight out of the café, back to the safety of her office. Out here she felt too vulnerable, but she made it safely to the small commode.

Once inside, Sam turned and locked the door behind her. There was only this one bathroom with a small sink, counter, and a single stall. Sam stooped to ensure no one was inside the toilet stall, and then stepped over to the sink. Splashing her face with cold water, she felt a little better. The fear and anxiety she had felt out there was overwhelming. "You've got to pull yourself together!" she scolded herself.

As she turned to pull a paper towel to dry her face, Sam stopped cold in her tracks. Beads of water still standing on her face, it was all Sam could do to force her trembling fingers to dial her cell phone.

When the other party answered she said, "It's Sam. I think there's something you need to see right away." She gave the name and address of the café and then went numbly back to her booth.

~ ~ ~

"Do you think it's him?"

Detective Johnston shook his head. "No way to know for sure just yet."

The little bathroom held more people at this moment than it probably ever had or ever would again. Detective Johnston had called the station as soon as he arrived and had a crime scene technician sent out. Then he called Patrick. He didn't say it directly, but the tone of Dan's voice implied Sam needed him. "She's a little spooked," he told Patrick when he and Joe finally arrived. They were all now crammed into the small space, staring at the thick black ink sprawled across the wall next to the paper towel dispenser.

I am the dark knight.
As I avenge a history that I cannot change,
I seek hope for a tomorrow of silence
From the bats inside my head.

A flash bulb illuminated the wall as the forensics tech took photographs of the seemingly harmless graffiti. Then the technician put his camera away and removed a small handsaw from his bag. "I'll get one of our experts on this right away, but the handwriting looks pretty similar to me," Dan noted.

Sam shuddered at the thought that she could be standing in the same room as the monster who had killed all those women. "I… I need to get some air," she muttered, and then slipped quietly from the cramped room. None of the officers seemed to notice.

Grateful to be outside, Sam took a long, deep breath then closed her eyes. She needed to relax. She must have looked silly, standing on the street corner with her eyes closed and her arms tightly wrapped around her chest, because she heard a familiar voice behind her laughing.

"I give you the afternoon off, and what do you do? You hang out on a street corner three blocks from work? You're a strange duck Sam." She turned around and saw Tony smiling at her.

"An afternoon off would be nice. Hell, even an uninterrupted lunch would cut it," Sam quipped, "but I'm still working." She caught the puzzled look on her editor's face. "I may have stumbled onto some evidence," she explained.

"Here?" Sam nodded. "What kind of evidence could you possibly find in this rat trap?" Tony asked.

"The good kind," Patrick cut in as he stepped through the front door of the café. "You must be Tony?" he asked, extending his hand.

Tony took it and smiled. "And you must be Patrick? Nice to finally meet you."

"Likewise."

"So," Sam asked, "they almost done in there?"

"Yeah. The tech just finished cutting out the wall and he's got our piece bagged. Joe and Dan are heading back to the station with it soon. They want to start analyzing it ASAP." Patrick paused and looked at Tony. "I hope you don't mind, but I have direct orders to take Sam home."

"I did promise her some time off," Tony smiled, then added, "but Sam, I still need your story."

Just then Dan, Joe, and the crime scene tech emerged from the café. The technician carried a large, clear bag containing a section of the lavatory drywall. Tony's eyes grew wide when he saw it. "What's that?" he inquired, half whispering.

"Nothing," Dan answered. He looked directly at Tony, knowing Sam already understood what he was about to say. "It's critical this information stays between those of us present here. I *will not* read about this in the paper. Sam, run your story, but this information stays out. My investigation is not to be jeopardized in any way, do you understand?" Sam nodded and then nudged her editor to do the same.

"Good." Dan then turned to Patrick. "Take her home."

Chapter Ten

The following morning every newspaper, radio station, and local television news program was green with envy when they saw the headline story in the morning edition of the Tribune. Sam's story was front page and many newsstands around Portland sold out of copies. Everyone was talking about the killer in their midst.

As for Sam, she called Tony and told him she wouldn't be in. After yesterday's events there was little he could say in protest. Grudgingly, he told her to "Take it easy," but his tone let her know he fully expected to see her at work the next day, no excuses.

Detective Johnston called her shortly after eight, just after his press conference finished, to let her know the analysis of the handwriting was almost complete. "Looks like we've got a pretty good match. Your graffiti is a close match to the handwriting in all the murder scene notes."

"My God!" Sam had felt yesterday that this would be the result, but she was still shocked to hear it. "So, what's next?"

"Lots of legwork," came the detective's pragmatic reply. "We'll obtain copies of customer receipts from the café and cross check them with known associates of our victims and maybe we'll get lucky and find a match. Look, I'll have Patrick keep you updated." Then he added, "Updated as much as possible, you understand? I'll be in touch."

"Thanks, Detective." Sam hung up the phone and curled up in the recliner in her living room.

As she sipped a cup of hot tea, her mind wandered to the latest murder. Sam's ever active imagination took her back to the vision she'd seen two nights ago. The comfort, the familiarity with which the woman, Tracy, had reacted to her killer unnerved her. Sam wondered how it was that this man was able to win over his victim so quickly. If the roommate's story was to be believed, Tracy had met a man, a customer who'd come into the bookstore where she worked. According to the roommate, they'd only met two days before Tracy was killed, and that night had been their first date. How, in such a short a time, had he been able to gain her trust? Sam stifled an uneasy laugh. She thought back to how her own relationship had started with Patrick. Perhaps she shouldn't judge. Their start had been almost as fast.

Sam glanced at the clock and saw it was already almost ten. She had promised Patrick she would meet him and Joe downtown for lunch. She headed into her bedroom to take a shower and change out of her pajamas.

As she waited for the shower to warm, Sam laid out her clothes. Then she sat down at her vanity table to take out the pair of simple braids she had put in her hair the night before. Staring at her reflection in the mirror, Sam whispered, "Just show me who he is." She sat quietly for a while then, when nothing happened, she climbed into the shower.

~ ~ ~

Sam sat in her car outside the apartment of Tracy Randolph and her roommate, Rebecca. Well, now it was Tracy's *former* apartment, Sam reminded herself. She had made up her mind to come here, to speak with the roommate, Rebecca, and to see the apartment if she'd allow it. Sam needed to see where it happened, to know she wasn't making things up. Part of her was scared to death to set foot in that apartment, to see and touch things she otherwise could dismiss as a hallucination. Screwing her courage up, Sam pushed open her car door and trudged across the street.

Making her way up to the third floor, Sam steeled herself for a possible confrontation. She had no idea how Rebecca would react when she saw a reporter at her door. Now, knocking lightly at the apartment door, Sam had no idea what she was going to say. When the door opened, Sam was met by a gaunt, tired face.

"Hello," Sam began, "Are you Rebecca Bray?"

The girl nodded slightly. "Who's asking?"

"Well, my name is Samantha Williams. I work for the Tribune." At this, the door started to close, so Sam quickly interjected, "I'm here because he killed my cousin too." The door opened fully and the girl waved Sam in.

"Have a seat. Miss Williams, didn't you say?"

"Please, call me Sam. Listen, Rebecca, I know this must be hard for you and I'll understand if you don't want to talk to me right now. But I want to assure you, I'm not here to work. My reasons for being here are strictly personal."

Rebecca's weary face forced a smile. "Can I get you a cup of coffee?"

"That would be nice."

As Sam waited for Rebecca to return with coffee, a picture on the entertainment center caught Sam's eye. She stood to examine it more closely. It was a picture of Rebecca and Tracy, taken on a summer hiking trip. Sam recognized it as one of the waterfalls in the Columbia Gorge, not far from Portland. "Oneonta Gorge?" Sam asked when Rebecca reentered the room.

"Yeah. You been there?"

"It's one of my favorites."

"Ours too." Rebecca set the coffee cups down and joined Sam. "We would go every summer, at least once."

There was a mournful tone in Rebecca's voice and Sam was compelled to express her condolences. "I know it doesn't mean much coming from a total stranger, but I'm sorry."

"Yeah... Well, me too. You said this man killed your cousin?"

Sam nodded. "It was a long time ago. I was only ten years old. They think Emily was his first victim." The two women sat down and sipped at their coffee. Sam let Rebecca ask most of the questions at first. She wanted her to feel comfortable, for the request she planned to make was an unusual one.

When the story of Emily's murder was completed, Sam felt compelled to add, "My cousin's murder isn't my only connection to this case. My boyfriend, Patrick Logan, is a police officer. He was here the other night with one of the detectives. Detective Johnston?"

"I remember the detective, but Patrick? Can't say I remember him," Rebecca said with a weak smile.

"Didn't expect you would. I'm sure you've talked to enough cops in the past couple days to last a lifetime."

"You've got that right." Rebecca's smile widened genuinely. "I have to say, for a reporter, you sure don't ask many questions."

"I told you, I'm not here to work. But I do have one request. I'm just not sure how you'll take it."

"Only one way to find out," was her frank response.

"I'd like to see Tracy's room. See where it happened."

Rebecca was silent for a moment, her face blank and impossible to read. "Why?" she finally asked.

Sam wished she could tell the truth, but it was just too unbelievable. Instead, she lied. "I'm looking for anything similar to my cousin's murder. Something the police might have missed. The detectives working this case, they weren't there during my cousin's investigation. I was."

"I haven't been back in there since I found her. I can't even bring myself to open the door," Rebecca's voice began to catch and she turned her head to try and hide the tears welling up in her eyes.

"I understand." Sam stood to leave.

"Please, don't go."

"I'm sorry. I thought…"

"That I was telling you no? I probably should, but… go ahead. I'll be in the kitchen when you're done."

"Thank you," Sam said as Rebecca stood and trudged wearily out of the living room.

~ ~ ~

Standing outside Tracy's bedroom, Sam balked. Did she really want to go in there? She took a deep, cleansing breath and turned the doorknob.

The bed stood against the left wall, its mattress bare, likely stripped of its linens by some pale-faced forensics technician. Beside the bed stood the nightstand with its digital alarm clock and little stuffed dog. Sam stepped into the room and over to the bed. Turning, she sat down and was confronted by her own reflection.

Sam was startled for a moment, and then realized she was looking into a mirror which had been mounted above a low dresser next to the door. Leaning forward intently, Sam realized this was where she had watched from. Somehow, from her room, she had looked through this mirror as if it were a window. As unbelievable as it seemed, this was the only explanation that made any sense.

Moving over by the dresser, Sam slid her hand along the wall behind the mirror. She wasn't sure what she expected to find and she was surprised when her fingers brushed the edge of a piece of paper. "What the…?" she mumbled as she grasped at it, but the paper wouldn't budge. Sam reached up and removed the mirror from its hanger on the wall and set it face down on the bed. She stared a moment at the note taped to the mirror's backing, then pulled her cell phone out of her pocket.

Patrick picked up on the second ring. He heard the words Sam was saying but he didn't comprehend them fully. "Sam, we know he left a note. It's already in evidence."

"Not *that* note," came her exasperated reply. "There's another one. And it's addressed to me."

Chapter Eleven

Sam stared at the wall in silence awaiting Patrick's arrival. It seemed like hours had passed since she'd called, but in reality she knew it had only been a matter of minutes. As she read the note again, her skin crawled.

Dearest Samantha,
Emily was my treasure. My secret.
D.K.

Just then, Sam heard a faint knock at the front door. She stepped out into the living room as Rebecca walked to the door muttering, "Now who could that be?"

"It's the police," Sam answered. "I found something in Tracy's room."

Rebecca opened the door, a bit shocked, and was greeted by Patrick. "Miss Bray? I'm Sergeant Patrick Logan and this is my partner Joe Torrance. We received a call from..." Patrick cut off abruptly when he saw Sam standing across the room. He hurried over to her and took her hands in his. "Are you all right?"

"Yeah," Sam nodded. "The note's in here. Come on."

Sam led Patrick and Joe into Tracy's room. Rebecca followed as far as the doorway, and then froze. "I... I can't," she started. Joe turned and took her under his fatherly wing.

"Come with me dear. We'll go back to the kitchen and have us some coffee while we wait for Detective Johnston to arrive. How's that sound?" Rebecca nodded numbly as she let Joe lead her away.

When they were alone, Patrick knelt down next to the bed and inspected the note closely. "Did you touch it?"

"Right there," Sam pointed to one of the corners. "I was sitting here on her bed and looking into the mirror. For some reason, I thought to check the back. I reached behind and felt something. I tried to pull it free and that's when I touched it. When it wouldn't budge, I took the entire mirror off the wall and put it here. That's when I called you."

"What do you think it means?"

"You're asking me?" Sam scoffed, forcing a smile. "You're the cop!"

"Sorry. I'm stumped." Patrick flashed her a winning grin. "*D.K.,*" he muttered under his breath. "What's that supposed to mean?"

"Dark Knight," Sam replied flatly. "Remember his poem? '*I am the dark knight.*'" Sam paused and shuddered visibly. "He knows who I am... How could he know who I am?"

"It seems simple to me." Sam was startled to hear the sound of Detective Johnston's voice behind her and she actually jumped a little. "Edgy are we?" the detective quipped.

"Oh, I think I can be forgiven for being a bit jumpy right now. I have a serial killer leaving me love notes at his murder scene."

"Love notes, eh?"

"It's addressed to me! Look!" Sam exclaimed, pointing, "How does he know me?"

"I don't think he knows you, per se. I think he saw your name in the paper, maybe on one of your stories. Perhaps he figured out you were related to Emily? What better way to get publicity? That's all these guys really want. In the end, it all boils down to notoriety... to fame."

"Somehow, that doesn't make me feel any better."

"Me either." Patrick looked up at Sam, genuine concern in his eyes.

"Listen," the detective addressed them both, "I'm not going to take this lightly. Sam, I don't think you're in any direct danger, but I'm going to have some extra patrols assigned to your neighborhood. We'll be keeping an eye on things... Just in case."

"Thank you."

~ ~ ~

Sam drove straight home. Her skin was crawling with goose bumps, but she knew it wasn't from the cold. She couldn't shake the feeling, despite Detective Johnston's assurances, that this man knew more about her than just her name. As she pulled into her garage and watched the automatic door lower itself behind her, Sam exhaled in relief.

Somewhere out there in the cold and cloudy world an evil man was waiting, maybe even watching her. Sam shivered involuntarily at the thought. *But I'm safe*, she reminded herself, *this is my sanctuary.*

Stepping through the door and into the hall, Sam felt relief ebb through her weary mind. She tossed her purse onto the hall table and hung her keys on the hook by the door. Walking into the darkened living room, Sam was startled by a noise over by the sofa. Turning, she was surprised to see a dark figure sitting on the couch, silhouetted against the window, his face shrouded by shadow.

As she fumbled quickly to turn on a light, the stranger across the room began to stand. Sam's heart beat so fast in her chest she could barely hear as the man spoke her name.

When the lamp beside her flashed to life Sam exclaimed, "Tony?" Shock and relief flooded over her. "What are you doing here?"

"Well," he explained, a sheepish grin on his face, "Jen was supposed to meet me here tonight, but when I got here there was no sign of her. Your front door was unlocked and... well, it's freezing outside. I hope you don't mind."

In reality, Sam *did* mind and was about to tell him as much when she heard the front door open. "Lucy, I'm home!" came Jen's voice.

Then, when she entered the living room and discovered Tony standing there with her roommate, Jen flushed with embarrassment. "Tony!" she gasped, "You're early. I wasn't expecting you until six."

"Six? Are you sure?" Tony glanced at his watch doubtfully. "I thought we agreed on five thirty?"

"Well, you're here now, that's what matters. Listen, why don't you have a seat and give me a couple minutes to change? I'll be right back down." Jen started to walk out of the room, then stopped to look back at her friend. "Sam? Could you help me with something in the kitchen for a second?"

Sam nodded. "Sure. Tony, excuse me." Sam's anger at discovering Tony in her house had dissipated completely in the past minute. As soon as she and Jen were behind the closed kitchen door, Sam asked, "Why is my editor, *my boss*, sitting in our living room waiting to meet you?"

Jen smiled. "It's just coffee. He called me at work today and asked if we could get together to talk." The excitement in Jen's voice faded a bit as she continued. "He's worried about you. He thinks this serial killer thing may be too much for you. I mean, this is more than just a story Sam... you're involved."

Sam thought it best not to mention the afternoon's developments to her friend right now. "I'm fine," she insisted.

"And that's exactly what I plan to tell Tony," Jen assured her. Heading out of the room and toward the stairs, Jen shot a wink back to Sam and added, "Don't wait up."

Sam smiled knowingly. Jen had always harbored a secret crush on Tony. Sam recalled her office holiday party last year. She'd taken Jen as her date and had laughed heartily as she watched Jen down a quick shot of tequila and then catch Tony beneath the mistletoe for a quick kiss. Sam had offered to try and set them up on a date, but Jen always refused. Now it looked like she was getting her chance.

As she busied herself with getting ready to prepare dinner, she heard Jen descend the stairs again and heard Tony say, "You look beautiful." Sam laughed out loud. *Just coffee, indeed.*

When she heard them leave, Sam turned on the small stereo mounted to the underside of one of the cabinets. She tuned in a station and cranked the volume up so she could sing along. She removed some potatoes from the pantry, dropped them into the sink, and then pulled a Styrofoam tray containing two steaks from the fridge. As she set about peeling the potatoes, singing along with the song on the radio, she didn't hear the front door open again.

From the hall, he could hear her singing, loudly, enthusiastically, and a bit off-key. He stifled a grin as he proceeded silently toward the kitchen. When he reached the door, he quietly swung it open to find her with her back to him, tapping a foot and swaying her hips in rhythm to the beat.

He continued to move forward, his shoes making no noise on the tile floor. Finally he was standing right behind her. He reached out silently and quickly, wrapping his arms around her chest, pinning her arms to her side.

Sam screamed and dropped the spud she was peeling into the sink. Her scream was met by laughter as the arms around her loosened their grip. Turning, Sam was met by Patrick's face. "That's not funny!" she yelled, smacking him hard in the chest with a wet hand. But even as she reprimanded him, she was fighting back a smile.

"I'm sorry," he began, "but I just couldn't help it. Can I have a chance to apologize?" She smiled faintly at him as he pressed his lips to hers.

"Apology accepted," Sam said, turning back to the sink. As she resumed peeling potatoes, Patrick reached out and took the potato and peeler from her hands.

"Leave it." She watched as he placed the steaks, still in their plastic wrapper, back into the refrigerator.

"What are you doing?" She moved to push past him and retrieve the steaks again, but he stopped her.

"I said, leave it. Now come with me." Patrick reached out and took her hand and pulled her gently from the room.

She allowed him to lead her across the living room before inquiring, "What about dinner?"

He didn't answer her. Patrick reached into the coat closet in the hall. He removed his and Sam's coats and then pulled his keys from the wall. "I said, come with me."

"Where are we going?"

"It's a surprise," Patrick grinned. He led her out into the cold evening and to his truck. Climbing inside, he glanced at her and saw that she was staring intently at him. "What?"

"Where are we going?" she repeated.

"You really don't understand the concept of a surprise, do you?" he laughed.

Sam shook her head defiantly. "So are you going to tell me?"

"No." He started his truck and backed out of the driveway. Sam pouted silently beside him, but made no further inquiries. They drove in silence for several minutes until Patrick pulled his truck into the parking lot of a Chinese restaurant. Sam looked at him curiously. "I thought you might like to get out of the house," Patrick explained as he pushed open his door. "Come on."

Sam didn't want to sound ungrateful, so she didn't say anything, but all she really wanted was to be safe in her house. She felt so vulnerable outside. *He* might be watching. Sam tried to tell herself she was safe. Her fears were ridiculous. And, Patrick was with her. She forced a smile and stepped out into the crisp air. "A night out sounds nice," she forced herself to say, then followed him into the restaurant.

~ ~ ~

Sam laughed heartily as Patrick read his fortune cookie to her. She had relaxed quite significantly since their arrival. The hot tea, plentiful food, and Patrick's company all helped greatly.

Patrick had sensed on their arrival that Sam was tense. He was sure it had to do with the note she'd discovered that afternoon. It unnerved him to know some lunatic was leaving notes behind for her, so he could only imagine how it affected her. Patrick did the best he could to provide diversion for her as their evening progressed and he was pleased to see his efforts were paying off.

However, as he paid the tab and they stepped out into the dark night, Patrick could see his hard-earned progress slipping away. As he looked at her in the glow of the dome light of his truck cab, Patrick could see the worry and preoccupation creeping back into her face. Patrick sighed to himself as he shifted his truck into drive and pulled out of the parking lot.

"Sam?" he inquired, glancing at her across the cab, "Do you mind if we make one more stop before we go home?" Sam wordlessly nodded her assent. Patrick concentrated on the road, attempting to make small talk, but gave up after only a few minutes. Sam was in her own world.

Glancing her direction, he saw her staring fixedly out the window. Her eyes darted about nervously. She seemed so wary of her surroundings; she reminded Patrick of a scared animal. It pained him to see her so anxious. He hoped after their next stop some of her anxiety would be alleviated.

As for Sam, she paid little attention to where Patrick was taking her, so she was surprised to find them in the parking lot of his apartment complex. Sam had only been here a handful of times, as they both preferred to spend their time at Sam's house. She looked at him curiously and he smiled slyly in return. "What are we doing here?" she inquired.

"Come on. I just needed to pick something up."

Sam sighed wearily as she stepped from the cab, but followed him to his upstairs apartment. She could hear music coming from the unit directly below his, loud rock and roll, accompanied by the sounds of many voices. Clearly they were having a good time. Sam was a little envious that they could be so carefree. She longed for the ignorance within which she had lived up until a few hours ago. What she would give to go back to a time before she realized there was a madman out there, possibly watching her every move.

She was lost in her thoughts as Patrick unlocked his front door. It took her several moments before she noticed the boxes piled in a stack in the middle of the living room floor. As realization dawned on her, Sam looked to Patrick incredulously.

Patrick smiled at her knowingly. "I've been giving things a lot of thought and… well, I spent some time packing this afternoon and I thought… if you still wanted me to move in…"

Sam didn't let him finish. She flung her arms around his neck and smothered his words with a kiss. "Do you mean it?" she asked disbelievingly, her eyes beginning to cloud with tears.

Patrick nodded. "I love you," he said. Sam sat down in the middle of the living room because she felt her legs were too weak to hold her steady. Patrick followed suit and pulled her to him. "I hope this means you're happy?"

"You have no idea."

"Good." Patrick paused for a moment to collect himself. "Sam," he began, "I love you so much. I want to be there for you. For everything. Always." Sam's beaming smile gave him the daring to continue.

Reaching into his coat pocket, he pulled out a small box. Sam saw it but couldn't believe her eyes. Nor did she believe her ears when he spoke next. "Samantha, will you marry me?"

For once, Sam was incapable of speech. Her heart was pounding so hard in her chest, she felt sure Patrick could hear it. Warm tears cascaded down her cheeks. She simply nodded. He placed the ring on her finger then she sprang forward to kiss him.

They spent the night there on the living room floor. Patrick brought a blanket and some pillows from the bedroom. They made love. Twice. Sam could still hear the music from downstairs, the bass thumping against the floor. They talked most of the night away, warm and comfortable in one another's arms.

When morning came, they got up early and grudgingly left their makeshift bed to take a shower together. As Sam turned the water on, she caught sight of the ring on her left hand and smiled widely. She turned around and pressed her body against Patrick's. "I love you, so much."

"And I love you."

They showered and then dressed again in yesterday's clothes. They had a couple hours before they were each supposed to be at work, so they took boxes downstairs and loaded the bed of Patrick's truck. With the truck loaded, they headed back to Sam's house.

Once there, they unloaded the boxes into a corner of Sam's garage. "We'll move them into the house tonight," Patrick said. "Now we need to get ready for work."

They bumped into Jen as they walked through the living room. "Where have you two been? Sam, I wanted to tell you about my evening." Jen paused when she saw the smiles on Patrick and Sam's faces. "What?"

"Well," Sam glanced at Patrick, "we have something to tell you, too." Sam held up her hand and Jen jumped up to hug her friend as soon as she caught sight of the ring.

"Oh my God! You guys, this is incredible! I'm so happy for you!"

They both muttered their thanks, then excused themselves so they could get dressed for work. What Sam really wanted to do was spend the entire day with Patrick. She might be able to get out of work again today, but she shuddered at the hell Tony would give her if she tried. After a few minutes, they emerged from Sam's room ready to go.

Sam was all smiles and, she was pleased to see, so was Patrick. They sat at the kitchen island and sipped at their coffee in silence. Sam glanced at her watch and sighed reluctantly, "I've got to get going."

Patrick nodded, "Yeah, me too." He stood up and walked with her to the front door. Sam reached automatically for her keys off the wall hook and stared blankly when her fingers grasped only air. "What's wrong?" Patrick asked.

"My keys. I could have sworn I left them here last night?"

"Are they in your purse?"

Sam checked, and then shook her head. "I don't have time for this!" she lamented.

"Don't worry about it honey. We'll find them tonight," Patrick offered. "Why don't you let me give you a ride? I'll pick you up after work and we can swing by my apartment, pick up a few more boxes? What do you say?"

Sam smiled. "Sounds good to me."

Chapter Twelve

The workday passed uneventfully and before Sam knew it, the day was almost over. Sam hadn't told anyone about her engagement. She didn't really have anyone at work she considered a close friend with whom she would share the information. Her editor, Tony, had noticed her ring and only smiled knowingly at her. He made no mention of it as the day progressed, but she caught him staring at her hand each time he came to her desk.

Finally, Sam pulled her left hand up in front of her face and asked, "Why do you keep staring at this?"

He was silent for a moment. "Sorry," he finally said. "I'm just surprised. I didn't realize you two were that serious."

"Yeah, well, we are," Sam smiled.

"Why didn't you say something about it to me this morning?"

"Oh, yeah! So you could make a formal announcement to the entire staff?" Sam laughed. "Sorry Tony, I felt like keeping this to myself for a little while."

Tony smiled. "You're right, I probably would have done something to embarrass you." He paused for a moment, and then added, "I'm happy for you guys."

"Thanks." As Tony turned to leave, Sam inquired, "Hey, what about your little outing with my roommate last night?" She was delighted to see a quick smile spread over Tony' face as he turned around.

"It was just coffee," Tony stated.

"So I've been told."

Tony took a seat beside Sam's desk. "Can you keep a secret?" he asked. Sam nodded. "Well, I like her. I mean, I asked her out on the pretext that I needed to talk to her about you. I figured it was a guaranteed 'yes.' But I just don't know if she'd want to go out with me again. What do you think?"

Sam laughed so loudly that several people turned their heads to look at her. "Sorry," she managed, pursing her lips closed against another chuckle.

Tony looked at her questioningly. "What's so funny?"

When she felt she could continue again without erupting in laughter, Sam said, "Tony, just call her and ask her out. No pretexts, no tricks. Just tell her you'd like to see her again." Tony stared at her skeptically. "Just trust me, okay."

"Are you sure?"

"Positive." As he walked away, Sam muttered to herself, "Clueless."

Glancing at the clock on the wall across the room, Sam realized it was almost time to go home. She dialed Patrick's cell phone number and confirmed he would be by to pick her up soon. Sam shut down her computer and then proceeded to the front lobby to wait for Patrick. Passing by Tony's office, she saw him on the phone and he gave her a quick wave and a wink. Sam thought he must have called Jen. She smiled to herself as she took a seat on a bench in the lobby to wait for Patrick.

~ ~ ~

They made their stop by Patrick's apartment and loaded the truck bed with more boxes. They picked up a U-bake pizza on their way back to Sam's house. Patrick loved the glow he saw on Sam's face. He was pleased he could make her so happy and he told her exactly that. Sam smiled at him and planted a quick kiss on his cheek. As they pulled into her driveway, Sam was only slightly surprised to see Tony's car parked across the street.

"Good thing we got the big pizza," Sam commented jovially. As they walked through the front door, Sam could hear the murmur of voices from her living room and smiled knowingly at Tony when he caught her gaze.

Jen stood up from her seat beside Tony on the sofa. "Hey guys!" She caught site of the flat cardboard disk in Patrick's hands and beamed, "Pizza?"

Sam nodded. "I think there's enough for everyone. Are you hungry, Tony?" she inquired.

"Famished," came his reply.

They all stepped into the kitchen where Patrick and Tony took seats at the kitchen island while the girls popped the pizza in the oven. Sam reached into the refrigerator and removed a head of lettuce and set about making a salad. Jen noticed they were low on beer and offered to make a quick run to the corner store. Tony watched wordlessly as she swept out of the kitchen. They all heard the jingle of her keys as she pulled them from their hook, then the unmistakable sound of the front door.

Once she was gone, Sam piped up. "So, you took my advice?"

Tony grinned sheepishly. "Actually, no." He laughed a little at Sam's bewildered expression, and then added, "She called me."

"Okay then," Sam nodded, continuing to chop lettuce, carrot, and tomato for the salad.

Patrick turned an accusatory glance upon Sam, "Playing match-maker, were you?"

"Just helping out a little. I gave him a nudge." She smiled warmly in her own defense.

"Turns out I didn't need it," Tony added, and the three of them had a good laugh.

When Jen returned, they each held a crisp, cold beer and enjoyed their simple meal. After dinner, they retired to the living room and settled in comfortably to watch a movie Jen had rented. Tony stayed late, sitting up with Jen long after the movie had ended.

Sam and Patrick excused themselves for the night around ten, and didn't hear Tony leave until almost midnight. Sam drifted off to sleep as Jen's soft footsteps faded up the stairs.

~ ~ ~

The next morning, Jen was all smiles. Sam didn't have time to question her about it over their coffee, but she enjoyed seeing the glow upon her friend's face. Patrick joined them a minute or two later, running a hand through his sleep-rumpled hair. He yawned and asked the time, eagerly pulling an empty mug from the cabinet.

"Six thirty," Jen replied.

"Shit," he muttered as he spilled a bit of the hot coffee on his hand. "Well, we'd better get moving."

Sam looked at him curiously. "We've got plenty of time."

"Not if I'm dropping you off at work again. We didn't find your keys last night, remember?"

"We didn't exactly look," Sam sighed.

"Your keys?" Jen inquired.

"Yeah, I've lost them," Sam explained.

Jen smiled broadly. "They're hanging on the hook in the hall. I found them in the living room when I got home yesterday and put them away for you."

"In the living room?"

"Yeah. Tony had come over and we were chatting and I found them in the sofa cushions. I figured you'd misplaced them, so I put them away. I forgot to tell you last night."

"Well, thanks," Sam said.

"No problem."

Patrick took a gulp of his coffee and announced he was heading for the shower. Sam smiled at her best friend, winked conspiratorially, and then followed him to her room without a word.

Behind the closed bedroom door, Sam stepped behind him and slid her hands beneath the fabric of the T-shirt he had slept in. She ran her hands around his waist to the flat muscles of his stomach, delighting in his sharp intake of breath as she dropped her hands under the waistband of his pants. He turned around abruptly and kissed her hungrily. "I want you," he growled.

"Then come get me." She smiled wickedly as she stepped away from him and into the bathroom. She turned the shower tap on to allow the water to warm, then turned back to Patrick. He approached her slowly, his eyes bright with hunger for her. When he reached her side, Sam slowly removed her nightclothes, then helped him to remove his own. She allowed her hands to wander, her fingers to linger in all the right places. As soon as he noted the steam above the shower curtain, he moved eagerly under the hot jets, pulling her in after him. He pressed her body against the shower wall, lifting her powerfully to a height at which he could enter her. It was fast and needy. Sam had never seen Patrick so forceful and it excited her.

When it was over, they soberly went about the mundane business of dressing for work, said their good-byes in the hall, and went their separate ways.

~ ~ ~

"Come on, Jen! Get a move on," Sam called up the stairs that night. She and Patrick were waiting impatiently in the living room for Jen to get off the phone. They had been planning this trip to pick out a Christmas tree for days.

As Jen bounded down the steps, taking two at a time, she grinned sheepishly down at them. "Sorry. I had to finish talking to Tony." Sam rolled her eyes in mock exasperation. Tony had called just as they were all arriving home from work.

"You've been talking to him this whole time?" Patrick queried. Jen just nodded.

"Well, let's get going," Sam huffed, starting toward the door.

"Yes," Patrick intoned with slight sarcasm, "we wouldn't want all the good trees to find homes before we get there."

Minutes later, they stepped out of Patrick's truck into the cold night air. Sam had suggested they visit the Boy Scout's tree lot first. She found it much less irritating to pay for a tree that would end up in the garbage heap in a few weeks if the money was going to a good cause. As they approached the small, fenced area where the trees were kept, two young boys, rose-cheeked from the cold and smiling broadly, met them. Sam returned their smiles.

It only took them a short while to decide on their tree. Sam was delighted. It was the biggest Christmas tree she had ever purchased. Sam was really looking forward to the first Christmas in her house and all the fun she would have decorating.

"Sure puts our little Charlie Brown trees to shame, doesn't it?" Jen joked, referring to the short and scrawny trees they had always had to choose in their small apartment.

They paid for the tree, Patrick slipping the Scout leader an extra $20 to put in the troop's coffer, and then piled back into the truck to head home. On their way, Sam insisted on putting in a CD of Christmas music and singing along. "To get in the mood," she explained. Patrick and Jen rolled their eyes, but they were enjoying it none-the-less.

The rest of their evening was spent stringing lights and putting various other decorations on the tree. Hot chocolate and laughter abounded. Sam couldn't recall many other times when she had been as happy as this, simply spending time with two people whom she dearly loved.

When they were done, Sam made a big show of turning off all the lights in the living room, then ceremoniously plugging in the tree, the big gold star shining brightly atop the boughs. It was all done up in silver, gold, and blue with white twinkling lights.

"It's beautiful," Jen sighed.

"Yes, it is." Sam smiled to herself in the dim light, moving closer to Patrick and soon finding herself wrapped in his strong arms.

He bent his head close to her ear and whispered, "I've never seen a prettier tree."

Jen excused herself a few minutes later, amid accusations she was just going upstairs so she could call Tony. She smiled sheepishly at them, but did not deny it. Alone, Sam and Patrick curled up together on the sofa, just looking at the twinkling white lights on the tree. They sat there in silence for quite some time, until both their eyes began to droop with sleep. Wordlessly, they turned out the lights and went to bed.

~ ~ ~

His heart raced furiously and his hands shook with excitement. He had been so close tonight. Right there and she didn't even know it.

He sat at his desk, computer screen glowing in the otherwise darkened room, digital camera at his side. His printer hummed rhythmically, churning out two color photographs he soon held in his trembling fingers.

She's so beautiful, he thought, tracing a finger across the image before him. Diligently, he turned to his camera, erased the images, and then turned off the computer. He turned on a small desk lamp so he could see them better, set the photographs on the desk before him, and began to undress.

As the last piece of clothing fell to the floor, he placed a hand upon himself, and then whispered into the dark, "You'll be mine soon."

~ ~ ~

It was late. Sam had been sleeping soundly, curled safely in Patrick's embrace, when something woke her from a dead sleep. Rubbing her eyes tiredly, she scanned the room. All was as it should be. She breathed a sigh of relief when her eyes passed over the small mirror and vanity table and noted nothing was amiss there either.

She slid from the warmth of the bed and tiptoed to the bathroom for a glass of water. Closing the door behind her, so as not to disturb Patrick, she turned on a light. She got her drink then proceeded back to the bedroom. It took her eyes a moment to adjust back to the darkness. While she waited for her vision to return, Sam stood stock still in the bathroom doorway, staring across the room at the vague form of Patrick lying on the bed. She reflected back on the short months she'd known him and was amazed at how quickly and completely they'd fallen into each other's lives. She was grateful to whatever power held sway in the heavens that had seen fit to bring them together.

As engrossed as she was in her reverie, it took Sam a moment or two to realize the room was not exactly as she had left it. A small beam of light cut right up the middle of the bed. Sam's warm thoughts evaporated and a cold shiver wormed its way down her spine. The light was originating from the mirror.

Slowly, hesitantly Sam approached. The nearer she came the brighter the light grew. By the time she reached the foot of her bed, a vision had formed in the surface of the glass. It was hazy, blurry, like a picture out of focus. Sam had learned from prior experience not to call out, else the scene should disappear. She held her breath as the image before her sharpened.

It was the same small office space she had seen before. There was a desk and a chair, and in that chair a man sat. He was mostly in shadow, but Sam could make out his naked shoulders and an indistinct tattoo on the middle of his back. His upper body rocked back and forth in a frantic motion.

One small lamp illuminated a disk of space upon the surface of the desk. As Sam stared silently at the scene, the image swept up and forward, over the man's shoulders, allowing her to see what was on the surface of the desk. That was when she screamed.

In a blink, the room went dark, the mirror blank. Patrick had his arms around her in an instant, stroking her hair, whispering soothing words in her ear. Sam was lost in the darkness, sobbing quietly. Patrick's strong embrace was her only anchor. She gasped when he pulled his arms away from her to lean back across the bed and turn on a lamp.

When it seemed she was calm enough to talk Patrick asked, "What was it? What did you see?"

"I saw him."

"Him?" Patrick was pretty sure he knew who she was talking about, but he just couldn't believe it.

"Yes, *him*," Sam looked meaningfully into Patrick's eyes, "and he had a picture of me."

~ ~ ~

It was a sleepless night. Patrick made a pot of coffee and Sam brought a couple blankets from their room out to the sofa. Holding a steaming mug apiece, Sam attempted to recount what she had seen.

"It was a picture of us," she began, closing her eyes momentarily to let the image replay on the back of her eyelids. "He was sitting at a desk looking at a picture. It was tonight, at the tree lot... It was a picture of you, me, and Jen."

"Honey, are you sure?"

"He must have followed us," she stated hollowly. Then she shuddered as she realized, "He knows where I live!"

"Sam, no. Come on... No one was following us! That's just crazy."

"How can you not believe me? Do you think I'm making this up?" Sam was hurt, the tears beginning to flow again. "After everything that's happened, after everything I've *seen*... Why won't you believe

123

me?"

"Well, are you sure you weren't dreaming? Couldn't you have just imagined it?" Patrick was doing his best to be supportive, but he just could not fathom how Sam could have seen what she claimed. In his mind, he had long ago dismissed Sam's vision of Tracy Randolph's murder. He had written it off as Sam's imagination and a very bizarre coincidence. He could not bring himself to believe, fully, what Sam had claimed.

His disbelief hurt Sam more than she could bear. "Why won't you believe me?"

"Honey, I trust you, you know that. But... this is just... Well, it's," Patrick trailed off.

"Unbelievable," Sam finished for him. Then her voice took on a sharper, angrier tone. "You're acting like I don't know how crazy this sounds. But I know what I saw! And I didn't imagine it! It wasn't a dream, it was real!"

Feeling dejected, Sam pulled a blanket tight up under her chin and turned her back to Patrick. She laid down and placed her head on one of the small pillows. She stared silently across the room, waiting for Patrick to say something, to offer an apology. But no apology came. Patrick looked at her quietly for a minute or two, and then he too lay down, placing his head at the other end of the sofa.

Chapter Thirteen

It was Saturday morning and Patrick had slipped away early. Sam wasn't sure where he'd gone, but she assumed he'd gone into work. She had spent the past several minutes recounting the night's events to Jen. Sam knew Jen didn't believe her either, but Jen at least was a willing and compassionate ear.

"So, you think he's following you?" Jen asked as she and Sam sat in the living room sipping coffee.

"I don't know what to think," Sam sighed. She was relived Jen had not dismissed her story outright. "I know what I'm seeing is real. I mean, it's just too much to be mere coincidence." Jen silently nodded her assent. "But," Sam consented with a rueful laugh, "I would rather it just be my imagination. It's better than having a killer tracking me."

"Now, don't be selfish," Jen said with a smile, "You said the picture was of all of us. Maybe he finds *me* irresistible?"

"That's not funny, Jen!" Sam chided, despite a small laugh welling up in her throat.

"I know, I know... But I had to try and get a smile out of you."

"Thanks for listening, Jen. It's nice to know someone will listen to me, even if they don't fully believe me."

Jen grinned knowingly then stood up. "Come on," she stated, "It's time to get you outta this funk. Go get dressed and we'll head downtown for the day. What do you think?"

"I think that sounds fabulous."

~ ~ ~

Within the hour, they had left the house and hopped the Max train into the downtown Portland shopping district. Bundled against the crisp winter breeze, they wandered the sidewalks and occasionally ducked into the warm, inviting stores.

Laden with purchases they settled comfortably into a booth at one of the many local breweries to order lunch. Sam was glad Jen had gotten her out of the house. The further away she was from her bedroom and the vanity mirror, the more and more far-fetched her visions seemed to be. Drawing in a deep, cleansing breath, Sam finally felt herself relax.

By the time their waitress returned with their meals, Sam had almost forgotten about her midnight vision. She was laughing at Jen's jokes, thoroughly enjoying herself. She almost didn't notice when someone approached their table and started talking to them. When she looked up she was surprised to see Joe Torrance smiling down at her.

"Doing some Christmas shopping, eh ladies?"

"Hi Joe," Sam said. "What are you doing here?"

"I was just passing by outside, saw you two through the window and decided to pop in and say hello."

"It's good to see you, Joe," Jen said. "Would you like to sit down?"

"No, I can't. I'm on my way to meet Lisa. We're going to take the girls to see Santa."

Sam smiled widely. "That sounds nice."

"Yep. Well, I better get going. You girls behave," he said as he turned and started to walk away.

"Behave?" Jen quipped, "Now, why would we want to do that?" Joe laughed loudly and waved back at them from over his shoulder.

When they got home they found Patrick in the kitchen attempting, it appeared, to cook dinner.

"What are you doing?" Jen asked.

Patrick turned and grinned sheepishly at them. "Trying to apologize."

"Let me get out of your way then," Jen quickly said, heading back to the living room, shopping bags in tow.

Patrick stopped what he was doing and moved toward Sam. "Listen, Sam," he started, "I know I wasn't... Last night... Well, I..."

"Apology accepted." Sam quietly smiled at him, but it was a tight smile. One that told him he was forgiven, but she was still hurting. They stood in silence for several moments, before she queried, "What's for dinner?"

Patrick laughed. "Hopefully, it will be taco salad. Figured that was a safe bet. I don't have to do much actual cooking." The smile in his eyes was contagious.

"Well, I'll leave you to it." Sam held up her package-laden arms and said, "I'll be in the living room wrapping presents. No peeking!" She planted a quick kiss on his cheek then left the room.

Patrick was pleased things had gone so well. When he had left for work that morning, he'd known he had screwed up and that Sam was hurting because of him. He had spent the whole day worried about her. Whatever Sam thought she'd seen had upset her, but it was nothing compared to how upset she was by his response. Patrick had expected to have to work much harder at his apology. He smiled to himself and went about his work preparing dinner.

He called to the girls through the closed door some time later, "Is it safe to come in?"

Sam laughed a little as she replied, "Yes, it's safe."

"You two have been busy," he commented as he noted the pile of wrapped and beribboned packages now stowed safely beneath the tree.

"I've only just gotten started," Sam quipped.

"We saw Joe downtown today," Jen stated, "while we were eating lunch. He said he and his wife were taking the girls to see Santa."

"Really? That's funny. I thought he was working today." Patrick looked perplexed, then added, "But now that you mention it, I didn't see him around the station."

"Maybe he took the day off," Jen proffered.

"Maybe. Anyway, dinner is ready when you are."

"Good. I'm famished," Sam stated.

"All that shopping worked up an appetite?" Patrick asked jovially. Sam punched him lightly on the shoulder as she passed into the kitchen.

Jen was happy as she watched Patrick and Sam over dinner. Things seemed to have been smoothed over between them. Jen thought back incredulously to the story Sam had told her. She couldn't blame Patrick for reacting as he had. Jen thought that if she had been the first to hear Sam's story, she would have acted the same.

She didn't know what to make of her best friend's assertions that she was seeing these visions. Jen just didn't believe that kind of stuff. Still, the conviction with which Sam held to her story made Jen a bit uneasy. It was as Sam herself had stated; either these things were real, or she was losing her mind.

~ ~ ~

It was the same nightmare all over again. Sam sat transfixed staring into the glowing surface of the small mirror set against her bedroom wall. She had awoken from a dead sleep to see a pinpoint of light originating from the glass, just like before. She vowed that no matter what she saw this time, she would not cry out. She would not tell Patrick or Jen, for, although Jen had listened patiently the previous morning, both of them would likely be more incredulous than ever.

As she stared, spellbound, she saw more pictures of herself spread across the killer's desk. They were from her shopping trip downtown with Jen. Sam shivered uncontrollably as she gazed at the photographs of herself. He had followed them all day, counting on the anonymity of the crowds of shoppers. He had snapped pictures of them through shop windows, as they ate lunch, and even as they boarded the Max train to come home.

Her breath coming in ragged gasps, Sam tried to steady herself. She was biting into the inside of her cheek to keep herself from crying out with the panic she felt. As the manifestation before her blinked out, Sam got numbly to her feet and left her bedroom. She no longer felt safe, even in her own house.

She tiptoed across the living room to the large picture window overlooking the street. As she pulled back one of the drapes, she prepared herself to see someone standing right outside, gazing back at her. But there was no one there. She looked furtively up and down the street, searching for a vehicle she didn't recognize. All appeared to be as it should.

Berating herself for her paranoia, Sam moved to the kitchen. Turning on the lights, she put a kettle of water on the stove to boil. As she rummaged in the pantry for the hot chocolate mix, Sam tried to clear her head and think what she ought to do next.

She'd never felt as vulnerable as she did at this moment. He had followed her twice. Well, twice that she was aware of. How many other times had he been there, in the background, in the shadows, watching her as she went about her day unaware? When the kettle began to whistle, the sound actually made her jump. Taking a deep, steadying breath she pulled a coffee cup from the cabinet. The glowing green numerals of the clock on the microwave read 3:35am.

She knew she'd get no more sleep, so she curled up on the sofa in the living room with her cup of cocoa. She turned on the television so she'd have something to distract her thoughts, but it didn't help as much as she would have liked. In her mind she kept going back through her day with Jen downtown. She thought hard and tried to remember if there was anyone in the crowds that looked out of place. She shivered involuntarily as she thought about how vulnerable she was. He had been right there, following her, watching her, and she'd had no idea. For all she knew, he could have been one of the many people she smiled at, or said "Merry Christmas" to.

Sam didn't want to set foot outside her own home, the mere thought made her heart rate quicken. How could she face the world outside, knowing he could be anywhere? Yet in a couple hours, Patrick and Jen would arise and she would have to put on a brave face. She could not let on to either of them that she'd had another of her nighttime visions. If they found out, they might just suppose she'd gone off around the bend and lost her mind completely. At least it was Sunday and she wouldn't have to go to work. That meant she had one more day to try to make sense of the chaos around her and to screw up her courage to venture out of her safe haven.

~ ~ ~

Patrick stretched his arms out to find Sam in the dark and was startled into consciousness as he found only the empty bed. Lazily, he turned his eyes toward the bathroom door, looking for light beyond but he saw none. For a moment, his mind jumped in panic, recalling how certain Sam seemed that this man, this killer, was following her, and he worried something had happened to her. But in an instant he had calmed his fear into nothingness. Her paranoia was infectious. Patrick couldn't help but worry about her, he loved her, but he knew the fears Sam harbored were irrational. Looking at the clock, he saw it was almost six o'clock, so he reached over and turned off the alarm, then swung out of bed.

Walking into the living room, he saw her curled in a ball on the sofa. Her eyes were closed, as if she was asleep, but as he drew nearer she opened her eyes and looked directly at him. "Good morning," he stated.

Sam forced a smile. "Good morning to you too," she replied.

"What are you doing out here?"

"Couldn't sleep. I didn't want to wake you, so I came out here for a little while."

Although Sam's face and voice conveyed nothing unusual, there was a dull look in her eyes that unsettled Patrick. "What's wrong?" he asked.

"Nothing. I just couldn't sleep, that's all," Sam insisted.

"Are you sure?"

"Yes," she lied. She patted the sofa next to her and invited him to sit down. He did, and she was grateful for his strength as she snuggled in against his side. He helped make her feel safe, even though somewhere deep inside she thought she'd never really be safe again.

~ ~ ~

"Sam? Sam, are you listening?"

"Huh?" Sam grunted in reply.

"You haven't heard a word I've been saying, have you?" Patrick sighed in exasperation.

"I'm sorry," she stated.

"Sam, what's wrong?"

"Nothing," she reassured him. She hoped she sounded convincing, because she felt as though the whole world was falling in on her.

Despite Sam's efforts, Patrick had known something was wrong from the moment he found her on the sofa that morning. All day, she had become more and more guarded, the vacant look in her eyes becoming increasingly pronounced with each passing hour. Her face had become a blank mask.

As he reached across the dinner table to retrieve the salt he'd asked for, he continued, "I was trying to figure out how you'd like to handle Christmas? I know my parents would love to have us over. And your grandma called this afternoon, while you were in the shower, to see if we wanted to come over for Christmas dinner."

"Oh?" Sam nodded feebly. She just couldn't think straight; her mind was a jumbled mess of nerves. She'd been trying her best to pull things together all day and she knew she was failing miserably. She forced a smile and managed to say, "What would you like to do?"

"Well, I thought we could swing by my parents' house on Christmas Eve, have dinner there. We could do Christmas dinner with your grandma. That would leave us on our own for Christmas morning." Patrick paused and looked meaningfully at Sam, "I thought it would be nice to spend Christmas morning alone... just the two of us. What do you think?"

"Sounds great," came Jen's voice. She had just walked into the room and sat down at the table to join them for dinner. "And it's feasible too," she explained, "since I'm staying over at my folks' house for Christmas Eve and Christmas morning."

Patrick smiled his wicked smile and dropped a wink at Sam, "Hmm... Jen will be away overnight. Whatever shall we do with ourselves?" Sam laughed, but Patrick was disappointed at how forced it sounded. He pushed his plate aside, even though he wasn't quite finished. "Jen, would you excuse Sam and I for a minute or two?" Jen nodded and started to stand up from the table. "No, that's not what I meant. You can stay here. Sam, can I talk to you in here for a minute?" He nodded his head over toward the door into the living room.

Sam stood woodenly from the table. She knew exactly where this was going. She followed Patrick out into the living room, but she was surprised when he continued straight into their bedroom. Her legs felt numb as she stepped through the doorway. He motioned to the bed and, as she sat down, he knelt on the floor in front of her.

"Honey, I don't know what's going on, but something is not right with you today." He placed a comforting hand on each of her legs. "I can't help you if I don't know what is wrong." He watched her carefully for a reaction. Her face remained a mask, but her eyes flicked to her right for a fraction of a second, toward the vanity table against the wall. He had almost expected it.

He moved a hand away and pointed to the vanity mirror. "What did you see?" Sam closed her eyes and turned her head away without answering. "Sam," his voice was firm, "I need you to tell me. I promise, I won't question you."

Sam's frame started to shake, a silent sob welling up inside her. It broke Patrick's heart to see her like that, but he didn't know what else to do. "Honey, I need you to talk to me. Tell me what you saw."

Finally, Sam opened her eyes and looked up at him. Tears had begun to stream down her face. Her voice was hollow, eerily devoid of emotion, despite the obvious distress etched on her face. "He followed me again."

"When?"

"Yesterday. When Jen and I were downtown. He had photographs of us."

"And you saw the photographs in there?" He gestured at the mirror again. She nodded. "Did you see anything else? Did you see him? The room? Anything?"

Sam shook her head. "I couldn't see anything but the photographs." Finally, she let out an audible sob. "God, Patrick, I'm so scared!"

Quickly, he moved to sit next to her on the bed and wrapped his arms tightly around her trembling body. "It's going to be okay. I won't let anything happen to you, I promise." She seemed to sink into him, her whole body relaxing against his as she quietly cried. "Sam," he said after a few minutes, "I want to talk to Detective Johnston about what you've been seeing. I think he needs to know."

Sam went rigid and pulled quickly away from him. "No," she said, conviction and emotion leaping into her voice with a passion, "You can't do that. He'll think I'm crazy. I mean, you and Jen already think I'm nuts. You can't tell anyone! Not Joe, not Dan, not anyone."

"But..." he began.

"No!" Sam shook her head defiantly. "You have to promise me.

You can't tell anyone!"

"Okay," Patrick sighed in defeat. "I won't tell anyone. But," he raised a hand to silence her as she started to interrupt, "I still think we need to let Dan know you at least *think* you're being followed. We don't have to tell him anything more than that, but maybe he can keep a closer eye on things around here?"

Sam nodded weakly. "Maybe. Let me think about it, okay?"

"That's reasonable."

They sat in silence for several more minutes before Sam spoke up again. "I'm afraid to leave the house. I don't think I can do it. I mean, what if he's out there waiting for me?"

"He's not," Patrick assured her. "And even if he is, he's not stupid enough to try anything." Patrick pulled an arm away from her, flexing it to show his bicep. A jovial smiled danced on his face. "You've got your bodyguard right here. Nobody's going to mess with you." Sam released a small, snort of a laugh and Patrick smiled. "That's more like it. Feeling better?"

"A little."

"Good. Listen, you don't have to go anywhere tomorrow if you don't want. But, I don't think sitting around the house like a paranoid shut-in is going to do you any good."

Sam laughed a little more. "Oh, so now I'm paranoid?"

Patrick met her jovial tone, "Only a little." She punched him lightly on the shoulder. "But," he offered, "paranoid or not, you have a right to be. If you want, I'll drive you to work. I could probably make arrangements to meet you for lunch. You won't have to be alone. What do you think?"

"Hmm... My very own chauffeur *and* a lunch date? I might be able to face the world after all."

"Good. That's what I wanted to hear." Patrick kissed her gently on the top of the forehead. "Now, can we go finish dinner?"

Chapter Fourteen

Sam was only mildly surprised when Tony sat down across from her desk the following morning. "I spoke with Patrick," he started, "He told me you think this killer is following you and asked if I could keep you here at the office today." Tony stared hard at her for a moment. "Do you really think that?" Sam nodded silently. "Wow."

There was something in Tony's voice that left Sam in wonder. Tony was normally all business, yet just now he seemed genuinely upset. "What makes you think that?" Tony queried.

"Are you serious?" Sam scoffed. "Tony, he left a note for me in the last victim's room. It was addressed to me. He talked about Emily. And," she added cautiously, "I've just gotten this feeling lately that I'm being followed. That I'm being watched."

"Well," Tony said somewhat dismissively, the tone of concern leaving his voice swiftly, "that can come with the territory. I mean, you write a high profile story like this and people are bound to take notice. I'm not trying to reject your concerns, but maybe it's just someone who took an interest in you. Your stories on this case have been high profile; your name and picture have been everywhere. I wouldn't be surprised if you didn't have your own fan club by now."

Sam laughed. "Gee, I don't know if I should be flattered or worried."

Tony did not join in her laughter. "Maybe you should be both." The concern was back in his voice. "I don't really know what to make of all this, but Patrick seemed genuinely worried about you. So, today at least, we'll keep you here, okay?"

Sam nodded gratefully. "Thanks Tony. It's not like you to be so accommodating, but I appreciate it." Then Sam added with a rueful laugh, "To tell you the truth, the whole idea of setting foot out there scares me silly."

Tony glanced nervously over his shoulder, an uncharacteristic anxiety evident in his eyes. He moved forward in his chair until he was sitting on the very edge of the seat. "Can you come to my office for a minute? I need to talk to you in private."

Sam was perplexed, but nodded her assent. She stood and followed him silently to his office. He sat down on the couch across from his desk and motioned for her to sit next to him.

He moved a hand nervously over his mouth and then began. "Sam, I haven't been entirely honest with you about something and, well, I don't know how you're going to take this." He sighed loudly.

"Just spit it out. I don't think anything would surprise me right about now."

He took courage from her words, but his hands still wrung nervously in his lap. "I knew Emily," he finally whispered.

Sam was shocked in spite of herself. "What do you mean, you 'knew' her?"

"God," Tony sighed, "I was so shocked that day, when you told me you were looking into her murder... and that she was your cousin. I didn't know what to say, so I told you I'd only heard about it, but that wasn't entirely true."

The hair at the back of her neck began to prickle as realization dawned on her. "You're Anthony," she breathed.

"We went to different schools, but we had been dating for about three months. When she died, everyone thought it was me. It was terrible." Tony closed his eyes, as if he couldn't bear to look at Sam's reaction as he spoke. "I moved away for a while, went to live with my aunt in Montana, finished school there. After college, I moved back. It seemed enough time had passed, no one would remember me. All this time you've worked here, I had no idea you were her cousin."

Tony finally opened his eyes and looked directly at Sam. He tried to speak, but only managed to choke back a sob. Finally he mastered himself. "I didn't hurt her. I loved her." His eyes were moist, but he seemed able to prevent the tears from falling.

Sam was shocked. She couldn't find any words. Tony seemed to implore to her with his eyes as he added, "I lied to you Sam, I'm sorry." She still couldn't bring words to her lips, so instead she reached out and pulled Tony into a hug. A sob finally wrenched its way free of his control. He rested his head on her shoulder gratefully as she stroked his hair.

They sat like that in silence for a minute until Sam finally found her voice. "I'm sorry too," she finally managed.

Tony released a shocked "Humph" against her shoulder.

"I mean it," she assured him. He pulled away in order to look at her and Sam placed a hand gently on each side of his face. She put her lips to his forehead, but pulled away suddenly at the sound of Tony's office door opening.

"Oh, excuse me," interjected a startled voice. "I'll… I'll just come back." The office door closed again.

The interruption was precisely what they needed to break the tension and bring them back to the present. They both laughed, despite the gravity of their preceding conversation. Tony wiped at his eyes with a fist, like a child, then smiled awkwardly.

"So, we're okay?" he asked.

"We're okay," Sam nodded. "I'd like to talk about this some more. Not right now," she added quickly, "but later. Is that okay?"

"Of course." Tony had expected as much. "Could you do me a favor though?" Sam cocked her head to the side inquisitively. "Can you not mention this to Jen right now? I'd like to be the one to tell her, I just…" He left his words unfinished.

"I understand," Sam said. She knew it must have been difficult for Tony to relive his past when he'd tried so hard to outrun it.

"I'll tell her soon," he assured her, forcing a weak smile.

Sam returned the smile. "Listen," she offered, "Patrick is supposed to come meet me for lunch. Would you like to join us?"

"Thanks, but not today."

"I'll give you a rain check," Sam said as she stood. "I'll, uh, get back to work." She smiled back at him as she headed to the door, "And you'd better go talk to Tammy and make sure she's not spreading rumors about us and our little tryst." Tony groaned but nodded his understanding. He followed close behind her as they left his office.

Back at her desk, Sam stared blankly at her computer screen. She couldn't concentrate. Although she had disguised her surprise during Tony's confession, now that she was alone her emotions were getting the better of her. She just couldn't believe Tony had known her cousin, that he had been close to Emily. She felt she could believe him, of course, when he'd said he had not been the one who hurt Emily, but somewhere in the back of her mind something dark and distrustful gnawed at her.

Why had he kept quiet about this for so long? She could understand his initial secrecy, but once Sam had uncovered the fact that Emily's death was only the first in a string of murders, she was shocked Tony had continued to remain quiet.

Then there was his insistence that she not mention it to Jen. Why? Was it shame? Was he worried she would think he had done it, just as everyone he'd known at the time had? Or was it, as Sam had initially supposed, just a difficult part of his life to relive?

She glanced at the small digital clock display on her phone and was relieved to see it was almost lunchtime. Patrick should be arriving soon. Sam felt guilty about it, but she knew she would tell Patrick everything. She'd never promised Tony she wouldn't tell Patrick, only that she'd keep it quiet from Jen. It was a loophole, one she felt slightly dirty slipping through, but she couldn't help herself. She had to know what Patrick thought of everything. The intersection of so many people and so many events was too coincidental for Sam to fathom. She needed a fresh perspective and hoped Patrick could provide it.

~ ~ ~

"So. What do you think?" Sam queried. They sat at a small table at a nearby diner, empty plates before them. When they had first arrived, Sam had felt incredibly vulnerable. There were so many people around. Anywhere, a madman could be watching her, snapping pictures of her. But looking across the table at Patrick sitting there in his blues had helped to calm her. She realized if the killer saw her sitting with a uniformed police officer he would probably pass right on by. It would be too risky to linger.

Patrick had listened to her story quietly as they ate. Now he sat back and folded his arms across his chest. "It's a big coincidence," he admitted. He tried to keep his voice calm and not convey the shock he really felt. "But it's probably nothing."

Sam smiled as she sipped at her Pepsi. It was apparently the reaction he'd been looking for so he pressed on. "I mean... it's Tony. You don't think he had anything to do with what happened to Emily, do you?" Sam shook her head and smiled.

Patrick was pretty sure Tony was a good guy, in fact he'd begun to think of him as a friend, but he wasn't willing to take any chances. Especially when it came to Sam's safety. As soon as he got back to the station he'd have to find Dan and tell him about Tony. That is, if the detective didn't already know. That was why Patrick was so upset. If Dan knew about Tony's connection to Emily's murder, he certainly had not shared the information.

"What time will you be back to pick me up?" San inquired.

"Shouldn't be any later than 5:30, but if I get held up I'll give you a call."

Sam nodded. "Will you walk me back to work?"

They stood and paid the tab, then left the diner. They walked up the sidewalk toward the newspaper office in silence. When they reached the front door Patrick told Sam he'd be back in a few hours to pick her up, kissed her goodbye, then watched as she wove her way through the crowd in the lobby. Once she'd disappeared into an elevator Patrick turned and headed toward the parking garage and his car.

Joe was sitting at his desk, surrounded by paperwork when Patrick got back. He stood eagerly, anxious to leave his paperwork behind. "Ready to go?" he asked.

"Not yet. I need to find Detective Johnston and ask him a few questions."

Patrick walked past Joe and headed across the station to the Robbery/Homicide offices, Joe close on his heels. They found Dan in one of the conference rooms. It had been turned into a central command area for the investigation. Patrick let his eyes scan the walls. Along one wall, directly opposite the door, was a timeline of the murders. Photographs, maps, and other pieces of paper were tacked along a line. At the start of the timeline, Emily smiled back at him.

Dan glanced up from the desk at which he sat. Before he had a chance to greet them, Patrick fired off his first question. "Did you know Sam's boss was the primary suspect in Emily Vance's murder?"

"What?" Joe exclaimed in surprise. Dan just nodded.

"You knew?" Patrick fumed. He crossed the room in a few quick strides and stopped just inches from Dan. He glared into his face and said, "You knew and you didn't bother to tell me? How long have you known?"

"Wait a minute," Joe interjected, stepping up to Patrick and pulling him back a few steps. "What is going on? What the hell are you so upset about?"

"Please Patrick, sit down." Dan gestured to one of the nearby chairs.

Reluctantly, Patrick moved to one of the chairs, jostling it in irritation before finally sitting down upon it.

"Will someone please tell me what is going on?" Joe pleaded.

"Sam's editor was the primary suspect in Emily's murder. Tony was her boyfriend at the time, and *he* knew about it," Patrick explained. He turned to Dan again and demanded once more, "How long have you known?"

"Since the day Sam found the graffiti," Dan admitted. "Tony showed up outside and he seemed to recognize the motto when he saw it. I did some checking on him and made the connection."

"And you never bothered to tell us?"

"I'm heading up a major murder investigation here Patrick. I can't tell just anybody…"

"Just anybody?" Patrick interrupted. "*Just anybody?* For Christ's sake Dan, you wouldn't even be onto this guy if it weren't for Sam. This is my fiancé you're talking about. You should have told us. He's dating our roommate. He's been in our house."

Dan sighed wearily. "Listen, Patrick I can appreciate where you're coming from. Honestly. But if I thought this guy posed any threat to Sam, I would have told you." Dan turned around and pointed to the wall behind him. Patrick noted a small map on the wall with color-coded pins stuck into it. "I've cross checked all the murders with his known locations. I've got nothing that puts this guy close to any of the victims but Emily."

Patrick's face flushed a little in embarrassment. He should have known Dan would've done his homework. Plus, he felt bad that he was judging Tony for events he had no control over. "You should have told *me*, at least," Patrick pushed.

Dan sighed again. "Look, I'm sorry Patrick, but I really didn't feel it was something you needed to worry about."

"Have you talked to him?" Joe asked. Dan looked to Joe inquiringly. "Have you interrogated him about any of the other cases?"

"No. I haven't," Dan admitted, "and I don't plan to unless something new turns up. I think this guy got tangled up in things as a kid. He went through hell because word got around about him being questioned about her murder. I don't want to put him through that again unless I have to."

Patrick was silently relieved. Despite his anger with the detective for not sharing his knowledge of Tony's past, he didn't want to put Tony through that kind of ordeal again either. Patrick smiled tightly at Dan. "Listen," he began, "I'm sorry if I overreacted. This whole thing's got me worried. And now Sam's convinced this guy is following her. I guess her paranoia is wearing off on me."

The detective smiled warmly at him. "It's okay. If it was my wife or my daughter, I'd have done the same thing."

"We'll let you get back to work," Joe stated, heading out of the conference room.

Patrick followed, tipping his head to Dan as he left. Dan settled back into his chair as he watched them leave. He really liked the young man and he hated to lie to him. The truth was, he'd been watching Sam's editor rather closely. And, although he'd told Patrick he had nothing to link Tony to any of the other murders, he still felt it was possible he could be involved.

Dan turned and looked at the map on the wall, at all the red pins. Each of those pins represented a woman, her life cut short. He'd told Patrick and Joe he couldn't connect Tony to any of the other murders, but that wasn't entirely the truth.

Tony had left Portland as soon as he could after Emily was murdered, moved away to live with an aunt, then off to college. Dan had been busy these past weeks trying to run down Tony's whereabouts at the times of the other murders. While he didn't have anything that proved Tony was in any of those cities when the women were killed, he hadn't found anything to prove he was elsewhere either. He'd found nothing that could exclude him as a suspect, which meant there was still a possibility he could have been near these women. The truth was, he was getting close to bringing him in for an interview.

He cringed as he thought about the lie he'd just told Patrick. He'd been truthful when he said he'd react the same way if it was a woman he cared about who was involved, but he couldn't let on to Patrick where his thoughts were really leading him. As much as he hated it, he needed to use Sam. This killer had singled her out once already and, Dan hoped, he might do it again. If it was her editor, he couldn't have Patrick pulling her away from him and cutting off his contact with Sam. He hoped this creep would slip up, do something to reveal himself, and Sam seemed to be a likely temptation. "God forgive me," he whispered.

~ ~ ~

Patrick was late. He had called, promising to meet her soon, but Sam was still sitting on a bench in the lobby. She was starting to get anxious. Almost everyone else had gone home. She'd managed to get through her day by remembering she was surrounded by familiar faces. But most of those faces had now vacated the building.

She actually jumped when the elevator bell chimed, announcing its arrival in the lobby. Sam turned to see who was there and was only mildly relieved to see Tony step forward. Sam wasn't sure she was ready for another conversation with her editor just yet. He made a beeline for the bench upon which she sat.

"Waiting for Patrick?" he asked. Sam nodded. "Would you like me to stick around? Looks like most everyone's gone."

Sam was half tempted to accept his offer. It had grown dark outside and rain had started to fall just on the other side of the lobby windows. "Thanks, but I'll be all right. He should be here any minute."

"You sure?" Sam nodded again. "Okay. I'll probably see you in a while. Jen called and asked if I'd stop by." Tony shifted anxiously on his feet. "I want to thank you for listening this morning. I wish I'd told you a long time ago. It would've been easier."

"I'm glad you told me," Sam assured him.

"Yeah," he scoffed, "sure you are." He smiled weakly at her. "Promise you won't say anything to Jen?" He seemed so earnest.

"It's your past Tony. You'll tell her when you're ready."

"Thank you." He glanced toward the door. "You sure you don't want me to wait with you?"

Sam smiled widely. "No need," she said, for Patrick had just appeared from the dark, jogging toward the door.

"All right. Looks like you're in good hands." Tony walked to the door, passing Patrick as he entered. The men nodded to each other in acknowledgment before Tony disappeared into the night.

"Sorry I'm late," Patrick panted, shaking his head and sweeping damp hair back off his forehead.

"You're worth waiting for," Sam quipped. She stood, slipping an arm around Patrick's waist and giving him a quick kiss.

As she started to move back, Patrick pulled himself tighter against her, hungrily pressing his lips against hers. "Let's go home," he growled when he finally pulled away. Sam nodded silently and let Patrick lead her to the door.

~ ~ ~

From the shadows, he watched her leave and then stepped bravely through the doors of the Tribune. He made his way surely past the elevators and directly to the stairs. It was a quick climb. He found himself standing before her desk more quickly than he'd anticipated.

There were a few people still milling around the newspaper offices, but none seemed to take note of him. He placed a gloved hand into his pocket and withdrew a plain, white envelope. He placed it in the middle of her desk, where he knew it would not be missed, then retraced his steps back out into the rainy night.

~ ~ ~

"So," Patrick climbed into the cab of his truck, "how was the rest of your day?"

"It was fine," she answered, and then added with a laugh, "It was uneventful."

"That's what I wanted to hear," Patrick smiled.

Sam slid across the bench seat and sat right next to Patrick as he started the truck's engine. It felt good to snuggle against him; it made her feel as if the dark and the rain were miles away. She watched through rain-streaked windows as the lights of buildings and other cars slid by. She was surprised when Patrick pulled off the street about halfway home.

"Why are we stopping?"

"I ordered take-out," he explained. "Do you want to wait here while I run in and pick it up?"

"Not really," she sighed, "but I will."

Patrick smiled knowingly, pulled into a parking place, and then stepped out of the truck. "I'll only be a minute," he reassured her. Sam noticed he'd locked the truck doors as he left.

Sam looked around and saw the brightly lit neon sign above the parking lot. "Chinese food," she muttered in approval, as she studied the patterns of reflected red neon in the rain puddles. She had apparently lost herself in thought because, when Patrick tapped gently on the glass, she shrieked in surprise.

Patrick stifled a laugh as he climbed back into the truck. He reached across Sam to put the food on the seat next to her. "I'd better get you home before you scare yourself to death."

"Very funny," she sniffed, but even as she said this the corners of her mouth twisted up into a small smile.

They were home a few minutes later. Sam sighed with relief when the front door closed securely behind her. She paused a moment in the hall as Patrick struggled to balance the food he carried so he could lock the door. As she heard the lock slide home, a tension Sam had been unaware of all day slipped away from her. She could feel herself let go as the muscles in her shoulders and neck relaxed.

"That's better," she sighed.

"Glad to be home?" Jen asked, poking her head into the hallway. Sam nodded. Jen stepped forward and took the bag of food Sam carried. "Here, let me help."

"Tony's not here yet?" Sam asked, realizing she hadn't seen his car outside.

"No," Jen answered, a note of wonder in her voice. "How'd you know he was coming over?"

Sam laughed. "Name a night he hasn't been over!" Jen rolled her eyes. "Besides," Sam explained, "I saw him as he was leaving work. He mentioned he might see me later, that's all."

"He left when you did? Then he should have been here a while ago," Jen sounded worried, "I hope he's okay."

"He's fine," Patrick reassured her, "I'm sure he'll get here any minute." He turned and removed a couple plates from a cabinet. "Listen Jen," he said, "Sam and I are going to grab some food and eat in our room."

"Trying to avoid me?" Jen quipped.

Patrick smiled. "Not at all. You and Tony can help yourselves to the food and you can have the run of the place." He dropped a wink toward Sam, "I just need some time alone with my girl, that's all."

Jen smiled and nodded knowingly, "Understood." Jen started to leave the kitchen, undoubtedly to sit in the living room and await Tony's arrival, then turned back to her friends, "Enjoy yourselves."

Chapter Fifteen

Sam stared in disbelief. She had just arrived at work to find something waiting for her. Her name was scrawled in blue ink on a white envelope sitting in the middle of her desk. Her entire body had erupted in gooseflesh the moment she'd laid eyes on it. She would recognize the handwriting anywhere... She'd seen it often enough in her nightmares.

Numbly, she reached for the phone and dialed Patrick's cell. As soon as he picked up she said, "He was here."

"What? Sam, is that you? What are you talking about?" Her voice sounded wooden and hollow, he hadn't recognized it at first.

"Please, just turn around and come back. I need you," she said, and then she repeated, "He was here."

"Okay," he assured her, "I'll be right there. But honey, don't hang up okay? I want you to keep talking to me." He was met with silence, but he knew she was still on the line. "What happened?"

"There's a note on my desk."

"Did you read it?"

"No. I haven't touched it."

"Good girl. Now, I want you to just stay right there and don't let anybody touch anything, do you understand?"

"Yes."

"I'm going to hang up because I need to call Detective Johnston, but I'll be there in just a minute or two, okay?"

"Okay." Sam shivered uncontrollably as she listened to the line disconnect and then she put the phone back in its cradle.

She couldn't take her eyes off the envelope. When had he put it there? Could he have done it this morning? Perhaps she'd even passed him, one of the people getting off the elevator as she stepped into it this morning? She jumped when she heard someone say her name.

"Whoa," Tony laughed as he stepped to her side. "Didn't mean to startle you. I missed you last night," he began, but then he realized Sam had not yet looked at him. "Sam, are you okay?"

"No," came her simple reply. She pointed toward the desk, "He left me something."

Tony's eyes traveled to where she pointed and then grew wide. "Oh my God," he muttered. He put an arm around Sam's shoulders protectively. Sam was shocked by his behavior, but was grateful for his concern.

"Patrick's on his way back," she told him.

"Let's wait in my office. Come on, you don't need to be here," Tony offered.

Sam shook her head. "I have to make sure nobody touches anything," she explained.

"I'll wait here with you then."

"Thanks."

True to his word, Patrick strode up a few minutes later. He was panting slightly, as he'd been too anxious to wait for the elevator and ran up the stairs instead. "Are you okay?" he asked.

Tony let his arm fall away from Sam as Patrick stepped in to hug her. Patrick looked at Tony for a moment, a hard glint coming to his eyes, but it faded away a moment later. "Thanks for staying with her Tony."

"No problem man," Tony waved his hands dismissively. "You'd

have done the same."

Patrick's gaze fell onto the desktop, to the envelope sitting harmlessly there. It looked so innocent. He wondered silently if Sam had overreacted. She'd called him before reading it. It could be a note from a co-worker for all they knew, but Patrick had already alerted the detective. Undoubtedly, Detective Johnston would be arriving soon, forensics team in tow. On one hand, as a cop, he hoped the note was from the killer. On the other, as Sam's fiancé, he prayed it was a mistake.

"Look," Tony offered, "Sam doesn't need to be here right now, does she?"

Patrick understood the offer immediately. "No, she doesn't." He looked at Sam, "Honey, why don't you go with Tony and have a seat in his office for a while? I'll come in there as soon as I can, okay?"

Sam nodded numbly, then turned as Tony took her by the hand and led her away. Patrick's mind was running a mile a minute. He hoped the detective would get there soon. He needed to know what the note said. He needed to know if Sam was in danger.

~ ~ ~

The entire newspaper office came to a standstill when Detective Johnston arrived. He had several other men and women with him, and they immediately set to work the moment they stepped off the elevators. Several broke away and started interviewing those who sat at nearby desks. Patrick stepped forward and shook the detective's hand.

"Hell of a morning," the detective grumbled.

"You're telling me," Patrick sighed, then led the way toward Sam's desk.

"Where is it?"

"Right there." Patrick followed the detective's gaze as it fell on the small envelope, then felt compelled to add, "I don't know if it's really from him. Sam didn't touch it. She sounded so sure on the phone, so I called you. But when I got here, I found out she hadn't read it." Patrick looked to Dan apologetically, "It could be from anyone."

"Don't worry about that," Dan assured him. He stared at the envelope, drinking it in. He, like Sam, felt sure he knew who this note was from. He'd spent so many hours staring at the crime scene notes, the graffiti sample, and the other note to Sam, that he knew this handwriting.

Dan turned to a nearby forensics tech and signaled her over. "I want photographs before we touch anything." The tech nodded and started to work. As her flashbulb flared behind them, Dan said, "Let's go talk to Sam, okay?"

To Sam, it seemed like hours had passed. She and Tony had sat wordlessly on the couch. Occasionally, Tony would stand and pace back and forth across the room a few times. Sam just stared blankly at the wall across the office.

"What's taking so long?" Tony asked. He slumped back into his seat beside her as his office door opened.

Sam stood eagerly at the sight of Patrick and Detective Johnston. "What did it say?" she asked.

The detective smiled at her. "We've only just started," he explained, "It will be a while before we get to the note itself." Sam looked disappointed.

Dan turned and addressed Tony. "What kind of security do you have set up here? Any video surveillance? Cameras?"

Tony nodded. "There is a video system set up in the elevators, set to record on the lobby level. It records who enters."

"I'll need access to it."

"Of course," Tony conceded. "We can go check them now if you'd like." Dan nodded and Tony led him from the room. Sam started to follow after them, but Patrick held her back.

"Honey, are you okay?" he asked.

Sam nodded. "I'll be fine," she assured him, "Now, can we go look at the security tapes?"

Patrick sighed deeply. He knew he could not deter Sam, so he followed her reluctantly as she left Tony's office. They wove their way through the desks toward another office at the back. Tony and Dan had already settled themselves in front of a pair of dark video monitors.

Tony leaned forward as Sam and Patrick entered. "What time did we all leave last night?" he asked.

Patrick scowled, trying to remember. He shrugged, "I was running late, so it was probably around 6:15, I'd guess."

"That's what I thought," Tony replied. "See, I can cue up these tapes by time, so I can start the tapes right before we left and we'll see anyone who got on or off the elevators after that."

Dan nodded at Tony to proceed. Tony reached forward and pulled a keyboard closer. He entered a series of commands and a moment later the pair of monitors before them blinked to life. Each monitor provided a view of one of the two elevators.

They all settled in as the videos flashed before them. Sam noted a time stamp across the bottom of the feeds. Tony had set the videos to play back starting at 5pm the night before. They ran at double speed for now, and Sam watched as her co-workers quickly filed out of the elevators. Since the recordings were only activated each time the elevator reached the lobby, they quickly reached the point at which Sam left last night.

She watched herself exit the elevator alone. On the other monitor, a few moments later, Tony exited to join Sam in the lobby while she waited for Patrick. After that, it showed a few more employees leaving for the night, then the time stamp on the feed skipped forward to 6:30 that very morning.

"Well, he didn't get in last night," Detective Johnston stated. As the video showed the influx of newspaper staff, Tony slowed the video to regular speed so they could more easily assess each person entering. "Point out anyone you don't recognize," the detective prompted.

Sam and Tony obliged, pointing out a small handful of people, several of them women. Dan made note of each of the men, jotting down a quick entry of the time stamp in his notebook so he could more easily review the video later.

As they continued to watch the video feeds, Sam felt her heart beat faster and realized her palms were sweaty. She was eager to see him, to put a face to her nightmares, but at the same time, she was frightened. She glanced over at Patrick to find him looking, not at the monitors, but directly at her. He gave her a small smile of encouragement and she turned back to the videos.

Sam and Tony persisted, trying to pick out strange faces from among their co-workers. Sam was so engrossed in the search that she didn't notice how quickly they were approaching her own arrival. As she watched herself step into the elevator, Sam sighed in disappointment. Although they had pointed out several strange faces, Sam felt certain none of them were responsible for leaving her the note, she could feel it in her gut.

Tony allowed the video feeds to continue to play out. The detective continued to watch. His eyes widened in astonishment as he watched his team enter one of the elevators. He turned quickly to Patrick. "Hold up. Why didn't we see you?" he asked.

Patrick's hand moved to his forehead, a deep sigh of frustration escaping before he replied, "That's because I took the stairs. I was in such a hurry to get to Sam, I didn't wait for the elevator."

Dan flicked his notebook closed in disgust. "Damn it! You can bet our guy did the same thing." Dan sat back in his chair and began to tap his notebook angrily against his knee. "Who knows about your security?"

Tony scoffed, "The staff knows, of course. And we consulted with a local security company when we were installing the system. Anybody who wanted to find out about it probably could..."

"Shit!" Dan mumbled.

"I'm sorry," Tony apologized feebly.

Sam laughed in spite of herself. "What are you apologizing for, Tony?" Her editor only shrugged. Sam glanced at Patrick again and saw him and the detective exchanging what appeared to be a meaningful look. When they realized she was looking, both men averted their gaze.

"Why don't you and Tony head back to his office," Dan suggested quickly. "Patrick and I can check on the progress, see if we're ready to get to that note yet."

"We'll let you know as soon as we open it," Patrick assured her.

Sam knew they wanted her out of the way so they could talk openly. It annoyed her slightly, yet she consented. Quietly, she and Tony left the room and moved back to his office.

As soon as the door had shut behind them Patrick turned to Dan. "What do you think?"

Dan considered his words before answering the young man. "I think I'll question Tony once we're done here. Something isn't adding up. Either our guy knew about the video layout, which I find unlikely, or he's someone close to Sam."

Patrick's face fell. After watching the security tapes, he was afraid Dan would feel the need to question Tony. Misreading his expression, Dan was quick to add, "Listen, I know you're worried about her. That's why I'm going to question him. I want to make sure he doesn't have anything to do with this."

Patrick sighed. He knew it was inevitable that Tony would be interrogated, but he'd hoped he would be spared the experience for at least a while longer.

"Let's go see about that note, shall we?"

The technician Dan had assigned to photograph the area had apparently finished her work. She stood casually several desks away, chatting with a few other technicians. When she saw the detective approaching she moved forward. "We're ready when you are sir."

"Let's do it," Dan instructed. The tech quickly donned a pair of gloves, then seated herself at Sam's desk. Patrick held his breath as he watched her carefully remove a piece of paper from the envelope. Patrick noticed the envelope had not been sealed. He watched silently as Detective Johnston and the technician bent over the paper.

When he couldn't stand it any longer he breathed, "What's it say?"

~ ~ ~

Detective Johnston had taken Tony back to the station with him for questioning. He'd spent what was left of the morning and part of the early afternoon interrogating him. When he was finished, he was no closer to excluding him as a suspect than he had been before, but his instincts told him Tony wasn't the killer.

After he'd allowed Tony to leave, he called Sam and instructed her to run her story, complete with a copy of the letter and a photo of herself. He didn't share this with her, but he hoped that by pushing her farther into the public eye he could help protect her. He was counting on the people of the city to take an interest in her and to keep an eye out for her. It was a long shot, but Dan feared Sam would need all the help she could get.

Patrick had not gone back to the precinct. Rather, at Dan's insistence, he had remained at the newspaper offices with Sam. He was never more than five feet from her, his piercing eyes taking in everything around them. Sam still felt edgy, but it helped to have him nearby.

As she proofed her story one last time, her eyes fell to the photograph of the note she would run with her story. She shuddered as she reread the menacing words:

My dearest Sam,
The beauty I see around you is such that my heart races.
I cannot wait for our special time alone.
D.K.

Sam looked up again just in time to see Tony return. She noticed Patrick had seen him too. Patrick's face was filled with a mix of pity, sorrow, and suspicion as his eyes followed Tony's progress toward his office. Patrick must have sensed Sam looking at him for he pulled his gaze away from Tony and forced a smile for her. Wordlessly, Sam stood from her desk and walked to Tony's office, Patrick on her heels.

Sam had never seen Tony look so exhausted. Although they entered the office only a few steps behind him, he seemed not to notice them. He walked straight to his desk, opened the bottom drawer and reached all the way to the back in order to remove a small bottle and a glass. He poured out some whiskey then slumped into his chair. Sam moved to his side as he drained the amber liquid.

"Care for some?" he asked. Sam shook her head slowly then sank into a crouch beside his chair. Silently, she reached out and pulled Tony into her arms. As Patrick watched from just inside the door, he was astounded to hear quiet sobs filter through the air. Sam gently pulled Tony from his chair and moved to the couch where she could sit beside him. Quietly, she held on to him, stroking his hair as he cried.

Patrick felt as though he were intruding so he left the office, pulling the door closed behind him as he left. He wondered if either of them had even noticed he'd gone. He sat down on the floor, resting his back against the door. He'd give them some time alone... for now.

Sam's heart was breaking as she listened to Tony sob. It must have been so painful for him to have to answer those questions about his past, about Emily. She could feel him tremble as he tried to force his tears under control.

Finally, he seemed to master himself and, to prove it, he let forth a strained laugh. He pulled away from Sam and said, "What a day, huh?"

"Well, I can think of at least one good thing that came out of it." A warm smile played at Sam's mouth.

"What's that?"

"We've got one hell of a story to publish." Sam knew her words would do the trick. Tony let lose a genuine peal of laughter. He rubbed at his face with his hands as if trying to wipe away any last vestige of his tears.

Patrick had heard their laughter and thought it safe to reenter the room. Tony glanced up as he did so and nodded to him in thanks. He was grateful Patrick had given him some privacy. It was one thing to cry, but it was a whole other thing to do so with an audience.

"Are you all right?" Patrick asked. He was genuinely concerned. He knew what it must have been like for Tony to sit there in a small, gray interrogation room with Detective Johnston firing questions at him.

"I'll be fine," Tony assured them. "But I don't think I can put off telling Jen any longer." He looked meaningfully at Sam before continuing, "I don't know if I can do it alone."

"We'll do it together," she assured him and Tony smiled in thanks.

"Why don't we get outta here?" Patrick suggested.

Tony and Sam exchanged a meaningful look, suddenly all business. "First things first," Tony said.

Patrick looked befuddled and Sam explained, "I have a story to submit."

~ ~ ~

It took Sam quite a while to present her final copy for printing. She convinced Tony to leave with them, but by the time they all managed to leave it was only a little before five. At Sam's insistence, Tony rode with them. She assured him they would give him a ride to work in the morning and suggested he stay at their house that night. "You don't

158

need to be alone right now," she insisted.

"I don't know… After Jen hears what I have to say, she might not want me around."

"Well," Sam laughed, "it's a good thing we have a guest room then, isn't it?"

Following Tony's instructions, Patrick drove first to his apartment. Tony quickly went inside to retrieve a change of clothes for the morning. Their next stop was the grocery store. Sam was intent on making Tony comfortable.

"You name it, I'll cook it," she said. Tony assured her he wasn't likely to be hungry and she didn't need to go to any trouble for him. Sam just laughed, pulling him along behind her as she wove her way up and down the aisles. He never did make a suggestion, so Sam decided herself what she would prepare.

As the three of them stood in the line for the checkout, Sam saw a panel-sided van with the Tribune's logo emblazoned on it pull up to the curb. The driver hopped out and delivered a large stack of their latest edition. Despite herself, Sam's eyes darted about, searching for a reaction to her story.

Finally, a middle-aged man picked up a copy to purchase. Sam watched as he stopped in his tracks to read it. He glanced up, noting an acquaintance several paces away and waved him over to come read with him. Several people nearby took note of this and picked up copies for themselves.

By the time they reached the checker, she too had taken a moment to skim the headlines. "Can you believe this?" she asked.

"Yes," Sam replied, as Patrick and Tony laughed loudly behind her, "Yes I can." The checker glanced back down at her copy of the Tribune and noted Sam's picture, realizing who Sam was. Her eyes widened, but she made no further comment.

When they finally piled back into Patrick's truck, they shared a round of laughter. Sam and Tony were talking about calling the printers so Tony could order another run. Patrick smiled for another reason; he knew Detective Johnston had instructed Sam to write the story for a particular reason. The more people who were invested in Sam's story, the less likely it was she would be in danger. As Patrick watched each person leaving the store, he was glad to note those who had a copy of the Tribune tucked under their arm.

~ ~ ~

Jen met them at the front door. She'd apparently heard Patrick's truck as they pulled into the driveway. She wore a worried expression and pulled Sam into a hug as soon as she was within arm's reach.

"My God! Are you okay? Why didn't you call me? I saw the paper on my way home and I've been so worried!"

Sam laughed it off. "I'm fine," she assured her. "I've been in good hands." Sam indicated the two men standing behind her.

Jen noted Tony and a smile cracked the worry etched on her face. "Hey you!" She approached Tony, still standing in the open doorway, and gave him a hug. She glanced behind him and, when she didn't see his car outside, asked "Did you ride over with them?" Tony nodded.

"I wasn't the only one who had a bad day," Sam explained, "so Tony's going to stay with us tonight." Jen cast her friend a covert, questioning look. Sam offered a tight smile in answer, reaching past her to take the two bags of groceries Tony carried.

"Patrick and I are going to go get dinner started," Sam stated. "Tony, why don't you fill Jen in, let her know what happened today? We'll be in the kitchen if you need us." Tony nodded. Sam could sense him steeling himself for what lay ahead as he led Jen away and into the living room. Sam wanted to give Tony a chance to talk to Jen alone, to tell her about his history with Emily by himself if he was able. Sam hoped Jen would keep her head and not make things more difficult for Tony than they already were.

Patrick placed a reassuring hand on her shoulder as soon as they were alone. "He'll be fine," Patrick said.

"I hope so."

She and Patrick set about making dinner. The more time that passed, the more relaxed Sam became. She hadn't heard anything from the living room to make her suspect things had gone badly. As soon as she had things to a point where Patrick could proceed without burning anything, she stepped to the kitchen door.

Quietly, she pushed it open and stepped out into the dimly lit living room. "Am I interrupting?" she asked, knowing full well she probably was. She was greeted with a small, sniff of a sob from Jen. "Are you two okay?"

Tony answered, his voice sounding strong, "I think we will be." Jen nodded her agreement.

Sam smiled. "I'm glad. When you're ready, why don't you join us in the kitchen? We can all have a drink, try and relax."

Jen laughed nervously. "Sounds good to me."

"We'll be there in a few minutes."

"Good." With that, Sam retreated back to the kitchen.

As soon as the door swung shut behind her, Patrick asked, "How are they doing?"

"Okay, I think."

When they were finally joined by Jen and Tony a while later, Jen's eyes were slightly red from crying, but her tears seemed to have passed. Tony smiled weakly to both Sam and Patrick, and Patrick stepped forward to clap him supportively on the shoulder.

Jen looked to them all, realization dawning on their faces. "You guys know?" Sam nodded slowly. "How long have you known?"

"Not long," Sam stated, feeling the half-truth would make things easier for Jen.

Things were quiet for a while. Patrick pulled a few beers from the fridge and handed them around while Sam put the finishing touches on dinner. They ate in a strained silence, but as the evening continued to wear on, Jen seemed to warm slightly. She wasn't her normal, chipper self, but she was getting there.

Jen excused herself for a moment and Sam pounced on the opportunity. "Are you okay?" she asked.

Tony nodded. "She took it better than I'd expected." He smiled at both Sam and Patrick. "Thank you both for everything today. Really."

They smiled warmly at him, assuring him it was nothing, then Sam stood. "I'm going to just check on Jen."

She found her upstairs, sitting on her bed. She knocked lightly on the open door. "Jen, sweetie? Can I come in?" Jen nodded wordlessly so Sam entered.

"Are you all right?" Jen only nodded again. "I'm sorry I didn't say anything to you. I only found out a couple days ago. Tony asked me not to tell you…"

"I understand," Jen sniffed, "It's okay. It's just a lot to take in, you know?"

Sam laughed, "Yes, I do."

Jen smiled finally herself. "Yes, I suppose you do." Jen sighed deeply. "Tony said a detective took him in for questioning today." Now it was Sam's turn to nod. "What do you think? Does he have anything to do with all this?"

Sam was shocked by the question, but she could understand Jen's need to ask. Sam had asked herself many times in the past days.

"No," she stated firmly, "I don't think Tony has hurt anyone." Sam sat down on the bed next to Jen before continuing, "I know he doesn't want to hurt you. It was really hard for him to even think about telling you about his past. He was so worried about you this whole time."

Jen smiled. "I guess I should get back downstairs then, huh?"

"When you're ready," Sam assured her. "I just wanted to check on you, make sure you were okay. We'll just be down in the living room when you're ready to join us."

"Soon," Jen said.

Chapter Sixteen

Sam and Patrick rose early the next morning. As they sat in the kitchen sipping coffee, Jen entered.

"How are you?" Patrick asked.

"I'm good." Then, seeing the concern on Sam's face, she added, "We're *both* good."

Sam smiled warmly at her best friend. "I'm glad."

"Me too." Tony had just walked in the room and stepped up behind Jen, slipping his arms around her waist and pulling her back into him. He planted a quick kiss on Jen's cheek and she blushed.

As they all sat around the kitchen with their coffee, Sam was pleased to see the strain of the previous day had lifted. Abundant laughter filled the room. They talked about their plans for the upcoming holiday, marveling that Christmas was only a little over a week away.

When it was time for them to depart, Jen pulled Tony to the side. Sam could hear her whisper something to him, but couldn't quite make out what it was. Then Jen stepped out the front door and headed for her car.

"What was that about?" Sam asked.

"None of your business," Patrick stated, rolling his eyes at Sam's brazen inquiry.

Tony just laughed. "Just making some plans for later," he admitted. Sam raised her eyebrows in interest, but Patrick interjected.

"Let's go. You can interrogate him some more *after* I drop you off at work."

~ ~ ~

Tony became a regular fixture around their house over the next week. Sam was seldom surprised to find Tony sitting in her living room chatting with Jen or, at times, Patrick. They had become an unconventional family unit, sitting around the dinner table each night talking about their day. Sam looked forward to coming home each night and enjoying the comfort and safety of the group.

Patrick was pleased too, as he watched each day pass. Every day separating them from that note found Sam acting more and more cheerful, more like her old self. It also helped that Tony was around the house so much. Sam had taken him up on his offer these past few days and had ridden to and from work with him, as she still felt too uncomfortable to venture out alone. Patrick had initially been uneasy about this, but the more time he spent around Tony the more foolish he felt for his earlier suspicions about him.

By the time the weekend arrived, Sam had relaxed to a point where she felt she might be able to actually enjoy Christmas, which was the following Tuesday. She spent most of Saturday doing some last minute shopping with Jen. Sam's nerves took a backseat as she and Jen hurried about town.

Jen laughed as occasionally they were stopped by strangers in the street inquiring if Sam was "the one from the newspapers." Sam always nodded politely before moving on. She was amazed how many people recognized her. Patrick had spoken to her, a few days after her story ran, about why Detective Johnston had insisted she print her own photograph next to the story. She had initially been upset and a little angry, however the more she thought about it, the more she understood and appreciated his advice. It did help make her feel safer.

Sam and Jen arrived home late that afternoon. They tried to shake most of the water off their umbrellas before propping them up against the wall just inside the front door. The house was quiet. Patrick was still at work and Tony had returned to his apartment that morning, promising to be back in time for dinner. The girls took the opportunity to spread their purchases around the living room, laughing and joking as they wrapped each one. Festive paper, bows, and ribbons soon covered the new packages which were then placed beneath the tree. Christmas was in two days, and Sam was happier than she had been in weeks.

~ ~ ~

They spent Christmas Eve with Patrick's parents, as planned. Sam enjoyed herself, spending a good portion of the evening chatting with his sister, Heather. Sam found her to be a very likable young lady. His parents made her feel like part of the family, which, thought Sam with a smile, she soon would be. Dinner was fantastic and the evening passed too quickly. Before she knew it, they were standing in the foyer exchanging hugs and saying good night.

They returned home, the house dark, quiet, and empty. Jen was staying with her parents and Tony, despite Jen's invitation to spend the holiday with her, was back at his apartment. His parents had moved away years ago and he didn't have any other family in the area. Sam felt bad that he was spending the holiday alone, but he kept insisting he didn't want to intrude. He did agree, however, to meet them all at Sally's for dinner Christmas night. Sam was looking forward to it.

It seemed strange to Sam for her house to be so quiet. She turned to face Patrick as he locked the front door behind them. "All alone," she said. "Whatever shall we do?"

Patrick grinned. "I can think of a couple things." He took her by the hand and led her into the living room. "Wait here," he instructed, then kissed her quickly on the lips before striding purposefully into their bedroom. Sam stepped to the fireplace and flipped the switch. Warm orange flames sprang to life. Sam sat down on the couch to watch them while she waited for Patrick.

He returned a few moments later with a couple pillows from the bed and a blanket.

"What are those for?" Sam asked.

Patrick didn't answer. He spread the blanket down on the floor, then placed the pillows. "Come here," he said, settling himself comfortably on the makeshift bed.

"We can't sleep out here," Sam protested, even as she lay down next to him, "Santa won't come."

Patrick laughed heartily, then stretched himself out on the blanket. "I love you," he said, a hint of laughter clinging to his voice. Sam leaned over him and, pressing her body against his, tenderly kissed him.

"I love you too."

When she awoke Christmas morning, Sam found her limbs entwined with Patrick's, a blanket lightly covering them. If not for the fire, Sam would've been quite cold, as her clothes lay in a small pile near the sofa. She blushed slightly, glad Old Saint Nick wasn't real, considering they both lay there in their birthday suits.

She nuzzled against Patrick's neck as she settled back down next to him. It felt good to lay there with him, to feel the warmth radiating off his muscular body. She let her arm rest across his chest and breathed deep, reveling in the smell of him. She allowed her eyes to close and drifted back to sleep.

They were both awakened suddenly by the ringing of Patrick's cell phone about forty-five minutes later. "Ignore it," Sam pleaded, tightening her arms around Patrick's torso.

"I can't," he grunted, "it's probably work." Sam sighed in displeasure as Patrick rolled away, pulling his cell phone from their jumbled pile of clothing. After a quick glance at the incoming number he look apologetically to Sam.

"This is Logan," he said, answering. He listened for a moment. Then, "Now? Yeah, sure. Give me about 20 minutes."

As he ended the call, Patrick turned to Sam. "Who was it?"

"Detective Johnston. I'm sorry. This shouldn't take long." Sam smiled weakly. She couldn't pretend not to be disappointed, this was the first time they had been truly alone in a while. "I'll hurry," he assured her, placing a quick kiss on the tip of her nose before leaving her side.

A few minutes later he was ready to leave. He assured her he would call soon, and that he would be back with plenty of time to exchange presents before they left for her grandmother's house that afternoon. Sam wrapped the blanket around herself and went to the living room window to watch him leave.

It took a few minutes for her to realize she was alone, but as soon as she did, she stood and drew the blinds. She then went around the house double checking the doors and windows were all locked. Confident that she was safely locked inside, Sam went to take a shower.

She spent a while under the hot water. Her back ached slightly from sleeping on the floor, but the warm spray helped soothe away some of the discomfort. She had turned the stereo on in her room and she sang along with the music as she showered. She didn't hear the front door open and then close quietly again.

Sam was busy wondering how long Patrick would be, wondering what had happened that necessitated his going in to the station. Wrapped in thought as she was, she didn't hear the boot steps moving slowly from the hall into the living room. When she finally turned off the taps and stepped out of the shower, Sam heard the faintest of sounds but dismissed it out of hand. She pulled her hair up atop her head, wrapped it neatly in a towel, and started to get dressed.

She'd gotten as far as putting on socks and underwear when another unexpected noise drifted to her. She had been humming along to one of her favorite songs, but stopped abruptly. She stepped to her stereo and turned it off, listening hard. She didn't hear anything else.

Quickly pulling a sweater over her head, Sam moved to her bedroom door. She opened it, half expecting to see that Patrick had returned, but was surprised to see Tony standing across the living room staring back at her.

The room was cold, which made Sam realize she was standing there in a sweater and her underwear. Shocked and embarrassed, Sam immediately excused herself and backed into her room to throw on a pair of pants.

When she emerged again, fully dressed this time, Tony immediately began to apologize. "I'm sorry. The door was open. I called out, but you must not have heard me."

"What are you doing here Tony?" Sam asked.

Tony shifted uncomfortably on his feet, staring sheepishly at the ground. "I was lonely," he finally stated.

Sam was unable to suppress a small laugh. "Tony, how many times did Jen offer to have you go with her today?"

"Apparently not enough," he smiled. "Anyway, I went for a drive and wound up here. The front door was open when I got here, so I decided to check in."

"Hold up," Sam interrupted. "What do you mean 'the door was open?'" The skin on her arms began to prickle, despite the thick, warm sweater she wore.

Tony gestured over his shoulder. "It was open," he repeated.

"Unlocked?"

"No, open. As in wide-open." Tony shrugged. "I thought it was strange, so I figured I'd better check on you guys."

"There's no way," Sam muttered, "I locked it. That's impossible." But as she again noted the chill in the room, Sam realized Tony must have been telling the truth.

"How long have you been here?" she asked.

"I'd just walked in when you saw me. Like I said, I called out, but you had music on. I guess I should have yelled louder?"

"Yes, louder would have been good," Sam quipped. She tried to sound jovial, but she was deeply upset by Tony's account.

How had her front door gone from being securely locked to standing wide open? A horrible thought came to her; *he* had been there. Sam's eyes searched the room wildly, looking for anything amiss, anything to indicate his presence.

Tony noticed the sudden trapped and terrified look that came to Sam's eyes and reacted immediately. "What's wrong Sam?" Sam was lost, her mind whirling in panic, and she didn't answer Tony immediately. "Sam?" he repeated, "Tell me what's wrong."

She brushed past him, moving blindly to the front door. "He was here," she breathed. Tony followed her into the hall and watched as she frantically wrenched the door open. She stepped out onto the small porch and looked wildly up and down the street.

"Sam," Tony said gently, putting a hand on her arm, "come inside." He could feel her shudder beneath his hand. She turned and Tony started to lead her inside, but instead she began to fiddle with the lock, as if ensuring it worked properly.

"I don't understand," Sam mumbled.

Tony took her arm and gently pulled her inside, closing the door carefully behind them. "Come sit down," he said. "Where's Patrick?"

"Gone," she replied. Sam ignored Tony's instruction to sit and instead began to move around the living room, her eyes scanning every surface. Tony observed her carefully, watching as she moved toward the door leading to the kitchen.

He stepped in behind her as she reached the door. "Sam," he offered, "let me go first." Sam was glad he was there and appreciated his offer, however she ignored him and pushed the door open before her.

Sam's hands flew to her mouth, stifling the cry that burst forth.

There, sitting in the middle of the kitchen island sat a single red rose…
and a note. Fingers trembling, Sam stepped forward, reaching out for
the scrap of paper. Tony stopped her before she could touch it. But she
didn't have to, she could read what was written without picking it up.

For you, my love.
D.K.

Tony was only just able to catch her as Sam swooned and fell.

Chapter Seventeen

Patrick had been at the station for only a short while when Joe arrived. "Bummer huh?" Joe grunted as he sat down across from Patrick in the conference room.

"Do you know why he called *us*?" Patrick asked. As he gazed around the room, he was not surprised to see most of the homicide division present, but he and Joe were two of only a few other officers there.

Joe shook his head, "No idea."

They were sitting in the conference room Detective Johnston had converted to house the bulk of his investigation. The room was filling up fast. Dan stood in the front of the room, waiting for everyone to settle down. Patrick felt apprehensive, worried about why Dan had called so many people in. When Dan finally spoke, Patrick's fears were confirmed.

"We've received a communication from the killer," Dan announced and the room fell completely silent. Dan raised his hand in signal and the lights were dimmed. A projector beamed an image of a handwritten note up on the wall.

"This arrived this morning," he explained. As Patrick read he felt as though the bottom dropped out of his stomach. "As you can see," the detective continued, "he's altering his routine. He has basically named his target and he's telling us when he will strike." Detective Johnston read the note aloud:

My love shall know me soon.
On New Year's Eve, we will be one.
D.K.

Dan's gaze fell heavily to Patrick before he continued. "He's also provided us with these photographs." Dan pushed a button and the projection changed. On the wall flashed a photo of two women. Then he pushed the button again. This time the image showed the same two women and one man surrounded by trees.

Detective Johnston sighed, "He's taunting us, ladies and gentlemen."

Patrick's hands were trembling with a mixture of fear and rage. His vision was blurred by hot, angry tears. Someone in the room called out, "Do we know who these people are?"

Detective Johnston nodded, but it was Patrick who said, "Yes." He pointed at the screen before them, "That's me."

Every head in the room turned to take in Patrick, then back again at the projection screen. Realization dawned on the room as many present recognized Sam from her press photograph.

"I'm sure you can all forgive me for calling you in today, now that you've seen this," Dan said. "The women in the photos are Patrick's fiancé and their roommate. The fucker is targeting one of our own! I will not take this!" The detective's voice rose with anger and he slammed his fist down on the desk before him.

Patrick wanted to leave right away, to go home and never leave Sam's side until this maniac was captured. He stood, intending to excuse himself, just as his phone rang. Glancing down, he saw it was Sam. "Honey," he began, but was interrupted.

"No Patrick, it's Tony. You'd better get home quick. He was here."

"Where's Sam?" Patrick asked, his voice loud with panic. Once again everyone in the room looked to him.

"Sam's fine, she's here with me. But you'd better get over here quick. He left her another note."

"How?" Patrick couldn't believe what he was hearing.

173

"He had to have broken in. Sam swears she locked the door after you left. But when I got here it was standing wide open. There's a rose and a note sitting in the kitchen for her."

"I'll be right there. Don't leave her side," Patrick instructed.

"You have my word."

Patrick hung up the phone numbly. Turning to face the expectant gaze of Detective Johnston he stated, "He broke into our house." If Patrick thought the room was quiet before, the silence that fell after he spoke those words rang throughout the conference room.

Joe stood behind Patrick, placing a hand on his shoulder. "Is Sam all right?" he asked.

Patrick nodded. "Tony's with her now," he explained to Joe, then turned back to the detective. "He left her another note. In our kitchen."

Dan turned to the room in general, pointing to a small handful of people, indicating he wanted them to come with him. "Sergeant Torrance, I'd like you to stay here and help coordinate a watch schedule. I want a unit posted outside her home, her office, and anywhere else she goes. You can help figure out her schedule and make sure we have someone on duty at all times." As he spoke, Dan gathered up a small pile of papers from the desk before him, and stuffed them into an attaché case, then moved toward the door.

Joe nodded his understanding. Before Patrick stepped from the room, Joe reassured him, "We'll keep her safe Patrick."

Patrick was glad the detective asked him to ride with him, he knew he couldn't concentrate and it would've been stupid for him to drive. His mind was elsewhere as he sat silently in the backseat of the unmarked sedan. He couldn't believe what was happening to them. He glanced up at Dan to find him looking at him from the front passenger seat.

"Look," he began, "I know you're worried. I understand. But you have to know we won't let him get to her."

Patrick nodded numbly. He appreciated everything Dan had said, but it barely registered at the moment. He gazed out the window, eagerly watching for their arrival at Sam's house. As they pulled into the drive, Patrick swung open the car door and stepped out before his astonished driver had fully stopped. He strode quickly to the front door, barely able to restrain himself from running.

Tony had locked the door, which Patrick appreciated, but he was still angry at the delay as he fished around in his pockets for his keys. Tony must have been listening for their arrival; just as Patrick started to insert his key into the lock, the door swung open.

Stepping through the doorway, Patrick clapped Tony on the shoulder in silent thanks, then moved to the living room where Sam sat, wide-eyed and trembling, on the sofa. Rushing to her side, Patrick pulled her tightly to him.

"Are you all right?" he asked.

Sam laughed weakly. "No." She noted Detective Johnston standing silently behind Patrick and forced a smile.

"Where is it?" the detective asked.

Patrick started to stand so he could show Dan to the kitchen, but Tony pressed him back down to Sam's side, "Stay with her. I can handle this." Tony turned to Detective Johnston and said, "He left a note in the kitchen, right through here."

Patrick was immensely grateful for Tony's presence. He was torn between his responsibilities as a police officer and his duty to Sam. Tony had allowed him to avoid having to make the choice.

As he held Sam close, he could feel her entire frame trembling. He turned and placed a kiss on her forehead and stroked her hair. He couldn't imagine how she must be feeling, and it was only going to get worse. She didn't know anything yet about the note and photographs the maniac had sent to Detective Johnston. He dreaded having to tell her about that as well.

They sat in silence for a while, until Tony and the detective returned. Tony knelt down on the floor before them both, placing his hands warmly on Sam's knees. He glanced furtively up at Detective Johnston, then turned and addressed Sam slowly and deliberately, almost as if talking to a child.

"I'm going to leave for a little while. I talked with the detective and he thinks it would be a good idea to change the locks, just in case. I'm going to go get that taken care of, then I'll come back, okay?"

"Thanks Tony," Patrick said while Sam nodded numbly. Tony turned quickly and left. Patrick felt, deep down, that Tony was eager to get away from the prying, accusatory eyes of Detective Johnston.

As soon as Tony left, Dan turned to Patrick. "Have you told her?" Patrick shook his head.

"Told me what?" Sam asked, her voice still tremulous.

Dan took a deep, steadying breath before beginning. "Okay," he started, "the first thing you have to know is that we're already all over this. I don't want you to worry, although I know you will. I'm going to make some arrangements at work and Patrick will be on a paid leave of absence for a while, until everything gets straightened out." Patrick was surprised by this bit of news.

Sam looked between the two men, realizing something big must have happened. She steeled herself, and her new-found resolve was apparent in her voice when she said, "Just tell me what's happened."

"Okay." Detective Johnston retrieved his attaché case and pulled several items out. "This arrived at the station this morning." He handed Sam a facsimile of the note and watched as her eyes quickly scanned the menacing words. He was relived to see how well she held herself together.

Then he produced copies of the photographs, handing them to Sam. "These arrived with it," he explained.

Sam's hands began to tremble violently as she took in the images before her. She looked pointedly at Patrick. She'd seen these pictures before. She'd seen them in Emily's mirror.

As her fingers continued to shake, Sam returned the pages back to the detective. "Why is he doing this?" she asked. "Why me?" Sam knew there was no answer to her questions, but she had to ask.

Dan's face betrayed his frustration as he said, "He can't get to you. We're making sure of that." He sat down on the sofa next to her, Patrick still holding her in his arms from the other side. "Sergeant Torrance is back at the station working out a watch schedule. We're going to have a car posted outside the house whenever you're here. At your office too, if you want to continue working."

He placed a fatherly hand upon her cheek and his voice became soft and soothing. "Don't let him in Sam. Don't let him ruin everything for you. Trust us. We'll keep you safe. Patrick will be with you, 'on the job' so to speak, but I want you to try to keep things as normal as possible. Do you understand?" Sam looked at him blankly.

"He wants you to be afraid," Dan explained, "Fear is what drives him, makes him powerful, and motivates everything he does. Don't let him have the satisfaction."

Quietly, tears began to slide down Sam's cheeks. "But I *am* afraid," she whispered.

Detective Johnston smiled, "I know you are. But try not to let *him* know that."

He turned to Patrick. "What did you have planned for today?"

Patrick looked astonished. "Umm, well… We were supposed to go to Sam's grandmother's house for Christmas dinner."

"Good!" The detective clapped his hands once in enthusiasm. "I want you to go. Why don't you stay the night? Give me the address later and I'll be sure to send a unit to stay on watch. We have a lot of work to do here, and it might do you some good to be elsewhere. As soon as Tony gets back with the locks, we'll get that taken care of, then send him to meet you."

"All right." Patrick nodded. He understood what Dan was doing. Their home was now, essentially, a crime scene. There was, as he had stated, a lot of work to do, and he didn't want to ruin their holiday any more than it already had been. "Give us a little bit?" Patrick asked.

"Of course."

Patrick guided Sam quietly to their room. While she sat on the bed, he dialed up Sally's phone number on his cell phone. When she answered, he briefly explained the situation and asked if she'd mind having a few overnight guests.

"You're always welcome. You should know that," she assured him. Patrick thanked her and told her they would be arriving soon.

Next, he called Jen. Tony had apparently already spoken to her; she already knew everything. "Sam and I are going to stay with Sally tonight. Detective Johnston suggested it. Maybe it would be a good idea for you to stay too?"

"Tony and I talked about that. We're going to meet you there for dinner, but we'll stay at Tony's apartment tonight."

"Do you need us to bring you anything from the house?" Patrick offered.

"No, I'm fine. How's Sam?" she asked.

Patrick chanced a glance in her direction. She stared silently ahead of her. Patrick turned away and dropped his voice, "I don't really know yet. She's upset, obviously, but she seems to be doing okay."

"All right," Jen said, "Give her a hug for me, okay? I'll see you both soon."

With his calls complete, Patrick turned and moved to the closet. He removed a small duffel bag and placed a few articles of clothing into it. Then he pulled Sam up by the arm and led her quietly out of the house. As Sam passed, she looked forlornly at the wrapped packages still sitting beneath the tree.

~ ~ ~

Sam's recollection of Christmas night was that everyone tried to act as if nothing were wrong. Everything seemed too bright and too cheerful to Sam.

Tony showed up about twenty minutes after Sam and Patrick arrived. He had returned to Sam's house to install the new door locks, but promptly left. He said Detective Johnston and his team were still combing through the house and had assured him they would install the new locks before leaving.

"Your partner was there," Tony told Patrick. "Said he'd take care of things."

Patrick nodded his acknowledgment. "I'll have to call him later and check in, tell him thanks," he muttered.

Jen arrived in a flurry of noise a few moments later. She rushed straight to Sam, throwing her arms around her in a fierce hug. "My God! Sam, are you okay?" Without waiting for Sam to reply she said, "I just can't believe this. You must be so scared!"

"Nothing like stating the obvious Jen," Tony scoffed. This elicited a small smile from Sam. Everyone in the room seemed to notice her weak smiled and was encouraged by it.

Sally offered her granddaughter a glass of wine and Sam accepted it quickly. As she reached for the bottle only minutes later to refill the glass, Patrick stayed her hand. Sam looked up into his eyes, the look of fear that had been evident on her face briefly giving way to a quiet rage. She shrugged of his hand and pulled the bottle from the table, filling her glass to the brim.

Dinner was a falsely cheery affair. Sam smiled for the sake of the others, laughing as if on cue, but she didn't really feel any of the emotions she showed. She felt scared, more scared than she had ever been in her entire life. She was chilled to the bone, the type of chill that couldn't be removed despite the warmth everyone in the room was trying to infuse into her.

By the time dinner was over, Sally had convinced Jen and Tony they must stay the night "for safety." She wouldn't take no for an answer and Jen, knowing better than to argue, nudged Tony's side meaningfully, accepting Sally's offer with a smile.

Sam watched numbly as her grandmother stood, excusing herself from the table. A few moments later she was seen heading toward the front door with two plates of food.

"Where are you going Sally?" Patrick called after her.

Sally smiled warmly, "Just taking something out to our guardians."

Patrick laughed. "I'll go with you. I want to see who's out there anyway." He stood, giving Sam a quick squeeze on the shoulder before heading out the door with Sally.

Sam watched him go, shuddering as she caught a glimpse of the dark night outside. Floating serenely down from the sky were snowflakes, starkly white in the glow from the porch lights.

Despite the beauty of the snowy Christmas night, Sam was repulsed by the what she saw outside. It wasn't so much the dark, but what was out there. Regardless of the police officers on guard, Sam knew she was being watched and that she was not safe. Detective Johnston could assure her safety all he wanted, but Sam knew the truth. He would find her… and he would get her.

~ ~ ~

Patrick sat up most of the night watching Sam toss and turn in her sleep. She had taken two sleeping pills and had drifted off into an uneasy slumber. He watched her occasionally move her arms as if pushing someone or something away. He wondered what she was dreaming about, but knew it wasn't likely a pleasant dream.

Glancing out the small window, he was thankful for the two officers outside, although he did not envy them the cold, lonely watch they kept. He knew the men by name only, nothing more about them, but they were of the same brotherhood and he knew he could count on them. Despite that, he still recognized he would not sleep. Sam meant the world to him and, as long as she was in danger, he knew he would not be able to rest.

Moving quietly so as not to wake Sam, Patrick left the room. He went downstairs to the kitchen for something to drink. He was surprised to see Sally sitting there, as if waiting for him. She looked small and frail sitting there in her dressing gown. But when she spoke, her voice was strong.

"You should be sleeping young man," she scolded.

"Can't."

"Doesn't change the fact that you should be." Patrick smiled at her. There was really no arguing with the woman. Then she offered, "I'll make you some cocoa, how's that sound?"

"Sounds wonderful."

Patrick watched as she filled a kettle and set it upon the stovetop. They sat in the hushed kitchen while the water heated. After a while, Sally reached out and took one of Patrick's hands in her own.

"She's going to need you to be strong," she stated simply, "This will be so hard for you both, but you must be strong for her."

Patrick nodded. "I understand."

"Good." The old woman smiled and winked at him, "But you know, you don't have to be strong for me. If you need anything, you know my door is open." She patted the back of his hand lightly in reassurance.

As the kettle began to sing, Sally retrieved two mugs and the cocoa mix from the cupboards, then removed the water before the noise awoke the rest of the house. She quickly and deftly mixed up the cocoa, topping each with a few marshmallows, then handed Patrick his. They sipped their drinks, enjoying the warmth. When Patrick

181

finished Sally took his mug back, placing it in the sink.

"We'll wash these up in the morning. Now, you get up to bed and get some sleep." She hugged him tightly before letting him leave the room.

Back in the bedroom, Sam was sitting up in bed. Although Patrick had tried not to disturb her, Sam had sensed his absence and awoken moments after he left. Pulling the blankets close, she rocked back and forth uneasily. She wondered why Patrick had left her side. She understood he could not be with her always, but she felt so vulnerable. She chanced a glance to the window and saw, with mild relief, the faintest hint of the rising sun. It would be daylight soon and, she hoped, the sun would provide her a modicum of sanctuary.

Caught up in watching the sun rise, she didn't hear Patrick's footsteps as he approached the bedroom door. When the door opened, she shrank back in fear until she realized who it was.

"Good morning," she muttered, forcing a smile for Patrick. "Where were you?"

"Down in the kitchen with your grandma," he explained. "Want some company?"

Sam shifted in the small bed, allowing room for Patrick to climb in beside her. "I'd love some."

As he climbed beneath the blankets he wrapped his arms protectively about her shoulders. Sam willingly sank against him, grateful for his warmth and shelter. In the safety of his arms, she found her eyes closing again, heavy from the sleeping pills she'd taken earlier. When she finally drifted back into her medicated sleep, Patrick closed his eyes and joined her.

Jen's knocking awoke them a couple hours later. Considering how little sleep he'd had, Patrick was amazed to discover he still felt like a human being. He credited Sally's hot cocoa for that miracle.

When they made their way into the dining room for breakfast,

Patrick was only mildly surprised to find they were joined by the two officers supposedly on watch. He'd suspected Sally would try something like that, but he was amazed the men would have consented to leave their post. *Wait*, he thought with a laugh, *on second thought I'm not surprised at all. Sally can be quite persuasive.*

As if sensing his initial reproach both officers looked at him, a guilty expression in their eyes. Patrick smiled understandingly to them both and they smiled back in relief. "So, she managed to pull you from your cold, cramped car?" he asked.

"It's just not right," Sally clucked, bustling into the room with a large platter of scrambled eggs, "expecting these poor men to sit out there all night. And it wouldn't have been decent of me to leave them out there in the cold while we enjoyed a hot breakfast."

She smiled warmly to each of them, handing out plates and inviting the officers to help themselves first. "You let me know if you gentlemen need anything else."

They tucked in, enjoying the food Sally had prepared. She was an excellent cook and, as always, even a simple breakfast was a delicious experience. Sam noticed the two officers glancing up at her occasionally over their food. At least, she thought ruefully, they're doing their jobs.

Despite joining the family for breakfast, both officers were taking their job very seriously. As soon as they'd been briefed by Sergeant Torrance, one of the two, Kyle, volunteered for this first watch shift. He was outraged this killer was mocking them. Not only was he sending correspondence directly to them, he was now targeting someone with direct ties to their precinct. It was a slap in the face he was unwilling to take. Even as he enjoyed his home-cooked meal, Kyle's eyes and ears were on lookout for anything unusual.

Sam couldn't understand what all the fuss was about. She felt certain she was safe for the time being. She knew he would be watching her, but she also knew he wouldn't make a move for another few days. He'd told them precisely when he would strike, and Sam believed he would keep his word.

Chapter Eighteen

Sam didn't leave the house over the next few days. Tony was more than understanding. He told her not to worry about a thing, that when this was all over she'd have one hell of a story to write. He alluded that she would, of course, write it for publication as a serial installment for the paper, and Sam smiled at this. She sincerely hoped she'd be around to write such a story.

The days passed slowly into the weekend. Jen and Tony had stuck around all day Saturday, keeping Sam and Patrick company, but today they had bundled up against the winter cold and announced they were going out to the Columbia Gorge. Jen and Sam had taken a hike that summer around Ellowah Falls and Jen was eager to see it again in the winter. There were two trails, the first leading down into the bowl of the falls, the second hugging a cliff wall high above and ending at a second, upper waterfall. Sam was envious. She knew Jen and Tony were in for a beautiful sight. The cold December air ensured the moist cliff walls would be glistening with icicles and frost.

Joe had been a frequent visitor, stopping by several times each day. He came to check on the officers assigned to watch duty, but turned at least one visit daily into an opportunity to chat with Sam and Patrick. It was on his visit Sunday that Joe broached the subject of New Year's Eve.

"What are you guys going to do?"

Patrick looked to Sam, a worried expression on his face. They hadn't spoken about New Year's Eve at all. Each time Patrick had tried to bring it up, Sam had retreated into a reticent silence that worried him.

Joe had anticipated some resistance from Sam and pressed on, heedless of the expression of trapped fear in her eyes. "I was thinking it would do you both some good to get out of the house and," he paused, "well, if this guy's threat is real, I think it would be best to keep Sam somewhere he wouldn't dare set foot."

Patrick's attention was piqued. "What do you suggest?"

"The Policeman's Ball. It's in two nights, New Year's Eve to be specific." Joe placed a supportive hand on Sam's shoulder. "You'll be safe there, Angel. There'll be no need to worry."

Sam shook her head. Joe, again, was expecting such a response. "Just think about it," he said, "for me?" Sam gave a wan smile and Joe returned it warmly. "That's my Angel." Then he excused himself and left the house.

"It's not a bad idea," Patrick proffered. "It would do us both some good to get out of this house. And, Joe's right, there isn't anywhere you'd be safer. He'd have to be crazy to try anything with you surrounded by cops like that."

Sam's laugh surprised him. "Don't you get it? He *is* crazy."

Patrick was glad to hear laughter once again coming from the woman he loved. "You know what I mean," he laughed back. She nodded, a true smile flirting with the corners of her mouth.

"Will you think about it?" he pressed. She nodded her assent, which was good enough for Patrick. He settled back down on the sofa, pulling Sam against him to rest, then grabbed the remote. He'd never spent so much time watching television before, but with little else to occupy their time, he'd become quiet the aficionado.

As she reclined next to Patrick, Sam kept her word. She thought about the Policeman's Ball. Or, more precisely, she thought about New Year's Eve. With each passing hour, the looming threat of that night grew larger in her mind. She had to admit, although going to a party was the last thing she really wanted to do, she would feel safer there than just about anywhere else.

"Patrick," she murmured, turning slightly in her seat to look at him, "I think Joe's right. We should go."

Patrick smiled, squeezing her lightly in his arms. "Good decision," he assured her.

They were surprised when Detective Johnston stopped by later in the afternoon. They hadn't spoken to him directly since Christmas day. Every time Patrick had called to speak to him, he was told the detective was unavailable. So, when Patrick answered the doorbell, he was a little shocked to see Dan standing there.

"Come in," Patrick offered, but Dan had already started to push past him into the hall. "Is something wrong?" Patrick asked, for there was a worried expression on the detective's face.

Dan scoffed. "Wrong?" He peeked his head around the corner to see Sam sitting on the couch, expectantly waiting for Patrick's return. The detective dropped his voice so Sam wouldn't hear and then said, "He's sent us more photographs."

"What? Of Sam? How?" Patrick was incredulous.

Dan ran a hand through his already disheveled hair. "Not of Sam, per se," he sighed, "but of the house, our watch units… He's mocking us!"

Patrick raised his eyes toward the heavens. "Please don't say anything to Sam."

"I don't intend to." Taking a second to compose himself, Detective Johnston led the way, striding into the living room. He beamed a smile at Sam who returned it weakly. "How are you doing young lady?"

"Well, for a girl who's become a total and complete recluse, I think I'm doing okay. You? How's the investigation?"

"Knew it would come to that," Dan grinned, casting a conspiratorial look in Patrick's direction. "We're not really any further along than before," he admitted. "We didn't find anything out of place when we searched here. The prints were all from people we'd expect:

you guys, your roommate, Tony... we even found a few prints from your grandmother and Sergeant Torrance. But nothing else."

"Well, regardless, we appreciate all you're doing to keep Sam safe," Patrick assured him.

"Yes, that's why I'm here," Dan explained. "We need to talk about New Year's Eve." He looked pointedly at Patrick when he spoke next. "I don't think it will be safe for you to be here."

"Joe already talked to us about this," Sam stated wearily, "We're going."

"Going where?" Dan was confused.

"The Policeman's Ball," she replied.

When Dan continued to look perplexed, Patrick added, "Joe thought it would be a good idea to get Sam out of the house. He figured the ball would be a safe place."

Dan nodded his understanding. "It's an excellent idea, but it only covers the evening." He gave an apologetic laugh, "Forgive me, but this guy didn't exactly specify a particular time New Year's Eve, so I think we've got a bit more planning to do."

Sam slumped against the back of the sofa. "What do you suggest we do?" she asked. She was so tired of feeling hunted. She just wanted it to be over. Patrick and Dan both sensed the weariness in her voice.

"Well," Dan began, "I've thought about this a lot. You're going to come to my house. I don't want you to tell anyone. Certainly your roommate will have to know, but otherwise I want this to be hush-hush. Do you understand?"

Patrick certainly understood. He squeezed Sam's hand reassuringly. She didn't answer the detective, but allowed her head to nod feebly.

"Why don't you pack a few things and I'll be back in a couple hours to pick you up," Dan instructed. "My family is looking forward to having you around," he added, "My wife's become quite a fan of yours. And my daughter has decided she wants to be a reporter."

Normally, such statements would have done wonders for Sam's self-esteem, but not today. She sat on the couch, emotionally drained, as Patrick walked the detective to the door. When he returned, he knelt before her on the floor.

"Sam, honey, it's going to be okay. I promise." He pulled her hands to his lips, lightly kissing her knuckles, then pulled her to her feet. "Now, we need to pack."

True to his word, Detective Johnston was back precisely two hours later. Jen and Tony returned from their hike, their faces red from the biting winter wind. They kicked their damp shoes off in the hall then stepped into the living room to find Sam and Patrick standing with the detective. Jen eyed the duffel bags in Patrick's hands inquisitively.

Sam noted her appraisal. "We're going away for a little while," she explained before Jen could even pose the question. "Detective Johnston thinks I'll be safer…" she paused thoughtfully, "*elsewhere* for the next few days." She couldn't explain why she didn't tell Jen and Tony where she was going, but she stepped forward, hugged her friend and said, "I'll see you in a few days. If you need me, you can call my cell phone."

Jen nodded understandingly. Tony, for his part, couldn't help but wonder if the detective had told Sam not to let him know where she was going. Each time the detective looked his direction, Tony felt as if he was accusing him with his eyes. He had become adept at recognizing that expression all those years ago when Emily was killed. He'd seen it often enough. He watched, somewhat dejectedly, as Detective Johnston shuttled Sam and Patrick out the front door to his waiting car.

~ ~ ~

Sam was glad to finally be settled in the guest room Dan's wife, Connie, had prepared for Patrick and herself. The past hour, since their arrival at Dan's home, had been more grueling than she had anticipated.

First, Connie had insisted on giving her a tour of the house, assuring Sam every few minutes she should consider herself family and help herself to anything she needed. Sam sensed Connie was sincere in her statements, but at the moment, it was hard for Sam to hear.

After the tour was complete Sam had hoped for some quiet time, but her hopes were dashed when Detective Johnston's daughter cornered her in the kitchen. Leslie was an energetic thirteen year-old who had, as Dan had already warned Sam, set her sights at becoming a reporter. She had come to view Sam as something of an ideal role-model for her aspirations and, having her under the same roof, took the opportunity to question Sam endlessly.

Finally, wearied, Sam made her way to the guest bedroom. Patrick was already there, unpacking their two duffel bags into the empty dresser. He smiled warmly at her entrance.

Sam returned the smile weakly. "I'm exhausted," she stated.

"Leslie talked your ear off, eh?" he sympathized, "Dan warned me she might do that."

Sam groaned as she slumped onto the bed. "She's a sweet girl, but my goodness! I've never been asked so many questions in my life!"

"I suppose not, normally you're the one asking the questions."

Sam smiled and then laid back on the bed, closing her eyes. Before she knew it, she was fast asleep.

She didn't wake up again until late in the afternoon. She awoke with a start in a strange room, momentarily forgetting where she was. It took several minutes for her to remember, but as soon as she did she felt the racing gallop of her heart slow perceptively.

She'd thought she'd been taken, that he had come for her in the middle of the night and spirited her away. She berated herself for such foolish thoughts. Despite the turmoil surrounding her, she did feel relatively certain she was safe. She scoffed out loud, then muttered to herself, "Until tomorrow."

Sam swung out of bed, pulling on her jeans and sweater, then headed down to the kitchen to round up something to eat. She had skipped lunch and was now starving. Patrick was already in the kitchen, sitting at the small corner table with a bowl of cereal. He looked up and smiled when Sam came in the room.

"Hey sunshine. You slept well."

Sam stretched her arms above her head as she yawned. "I can't believe I slept so long," she marveled.

"You needed it. You were wiped out," Patrick observed, "But this will all be over soon and then we can get back to normal."

Normal? Sam could barely remember what that was. "Patrick?" she asked suddenly, "What happens after New Year's eve? I mean, we're nowhere close to catching this guy. I can't stay in hiding my entire life."

Patrick motioned to the empty spot at the table beside him and Sam sat down. He pulled her hands into his and spoke honestly. "I don't know what we're going to do honey. My first priority is just to keep you safe, for however long it takes." He paused, considering his next words carefully. He hated to speak when he was unsure it was true but, remembering Sally's words about strength, he spoke anyway. "We're going to get him Sam, I promise."

She could sense the uncertainty in him, but was bolstered by his reassurances regardless. She smiled her appreciation, then stood to help herself to some cereal.

The time passed faster than Sam could have imagined, slipping quickly into night. With the passing hours Sam became preoccupied. She couldn't help but wonder what tomorrow would bring. Could it be possible that, despite Detective Johnston's efforts at secrecy, the killer knew where she was? She looked longingly out the front window, actually missing the guards who had been posted outside her house.

She felt vulnerable here.

Scolding herself for harboring such foolish anxiety, she joined Connie and Leslie in the kitchen to help prepare dinner. As she entered the room, Leslie greeted her enthusiastically.

"Hey Sam! Wanna help me set the table? Mom just asked me to do it, but I'm sure she wouldn't mind if you helped me."

Connie cast a sympathetic grin in Sam's direction as she hoisted a stack of plates that stood ready and followed Leslie into the dining room. The young girl chattered nonstop as she proceeded to set the table. Sam didn't even realized she'd been asked a question until Leslie repeated it.

"Aren't you scared?" There was a genuine note of concern in Leslie's voice that touched Sam deeply.

She smiled at her and said, "I have Patrick and your father looking out for me. That helps."

Leslie beamed. "I'm glad Daddy brought you here. I don't want anything to happen to you." Before Sam could stop her, Leslie had wrapped her arms around Sam's waist in a fierce hug.

Her innocent and childish sincerity brought silent tears to Sam's eyes. She wrapped her arms around the girl and hugged her tightly. She held her for a moment before releasing her, then quickly wiped at her eyes so Leslie wouldn't notice their moist sheen.

Patrick had been standing unnoticed in the doorway and had observed their exchange. He stepped from the shadowy hall and into the brightly lit dining room just as Sam was swiping hastily at her eyes.

"Hello beautiful," he stated.

Sam looked up and smiled. "Hello," she answered.

Patrick winked at Sam before saying, "I was talking to Leslie."

The young girl glanced up at Patrick, a wistful look barely

concealed in her blue eyes, and started to blush. "Hi Patrick," she managed to mutter. She fiddled with the place setting before her and then hastily excused herself from the room.

"I think someone has a crush on you," Sam giggled.

"What?" Patrick was incredulous.

"Just like a guy to not notice," Sam scolded. "Haven't you seen how embarrassed she gets whenever you talk to her?" Patrick just shook his head. "Well," Sam continued, "she does. And when you're not looking she just stares at you with this dreamy look on her face."

"No way," Patrick shrugged. "She's just a kid."

"That doesn't change the fact she has a crush on you." Sam was silent for a moment, then added with a laugh, "The poor girl. She probably doesn't know what to do with herself."

"What do you mean?"

"She's got both of us under the same roof: her career mentor and her first crush. Must be overwhelming."

Patrick smiled. "Well, lets go to the kitchen and see if we can torment her a little more." Sam hit him playfully upon the shoulder, but followed him into the kitchen anyway.

Dinner was fun. Sam watched as Patrick pointedly asked Leslie questions about school, her friends, hobbies, and anything else he could think of in order to keep her talking. While he continued to ask her questions, Sam watched as Leslie's face progressed from slightly pink to a deep crimson.

Dan and Connie noticed too and smiled quietly to each other. After a while, Dan joined in the fun. He teasingly asked Leslie if there were any boys at school she liked. When she replied that there weren't, everyone at the table laughed out loud.

"What's so funny?" Leslie asked defensively.

"Nothing," her mother assured her, resting a hand lovingly on her daughter's arm. "Your father is just teasing you."

"Well, stop," she pouted. This brought another small round of laughter to the table.

As Connie stood to clear away some empty plates, she once again put a doting hand on her daughter's arm. "Have you decided what you're going to wear tomorrow?" she asked.

Leslie's countenance brightened and she looked to Sam. "Not yet, but maybe Sam can help me decide?" She raised her eyebrows excitedly, awaiting Sam's answer. When she nodded her assent, Leslie grinned widely and made to get up from the table.

"After dinner young lady," her father scolded with a smile. Leslie sank back into her chair with an audible sigh and waited impatiently for her mother to return with desert.

For Leslie's benefit, Sam ate her desert quickly and then excused herself in order to follow Leslie upstairs to her room. Stepping into Leslie's room was like stepping back in time. Sam looked around her thinking that, as a younger girl, she would have probably been quite good friends with Leslie. Her walls were adorned with what appeared to be her own artwork: black and white pencil sketches were posted on almost every available surface. There was little in the room to indicate you were in a girl's bedroom. There were no ruffles, no dolls. Sam could imagine that, as an only child and with a cop for a father, Leslie had been raised as a bit of a tomboy. But even tomboys like the idea of dressing up, and Leslie emerged from her closet with three dresses in tow.

"When Daddy asked me to go to the Policeman's Ball with him, I was so excited. Mom didn't want to go, so she suggested I go instead. She said I was old enough." Leslie picked up one of the dresses, holding it beneath her chin and stepping in front of the mirror. She made a little face that caused Sam to laugh, then turned and retrieved another dress from the bed.

While she examined this next choice, Sam picked up the third dress. "I like this one," she told Leslie. She held up the green dress for Leslie who took it, a smile upon her face.

"I was hoping you'd pick this one," she grinned, holding the dress to herself and spinning in a small circle. "Green's my favorite color," she explained, suddenly becoming a bit shy and embarrassed by her excitement.

Sam smiled as a memory surfaced from a long time ago. The recollection was fuzzy, she'd been so young at the time, but her memory flickered with a scene from Emily's room some years ago. Emily had been planning for a school dance and Sam sat on the edge of her bed watching as she tried on dresses. Emily had always been nice to her younger cousin and had asked her which dress she preferred.

Thinking hard, Sam recalled selecting a dress for her cousin. She wasn't sure if her current selection was clouding her memory, but Sam was almost certain she'd chosen a green dress for Emily back then as well. Sam's eyes began to fill with tears as she realized it was the last time she'd seen her cousin.

Leslie could tell something was wrong. She set the dress aside and moved next to Sam. "What is it?" she asked.

Sam shrugged. "I was just remembering my cousin."

Leslie's eyes took on a wise and understanding look well beyond her years. "Daddy told me about her. Emily? The man that's threatening you is the one who killed her."

Sam was shocked. Leslie smiled when she saw the surprise in her face. "Daddy talks to me about his work a lot," she explained, "He says it is important for me to know that there are bad people out there. He says it will make me smarter and safer. But I think it's sad people hurt each other like that." Her brow furrowed in concentration for a moment before she continued. When she spoke next, her voice had a quality as if reciting a well rehearsed speech, "Daddy says that the more people are aware of the evil in our society, the better equipped we will be to change it." She nodded her head curtly when she finished, as if punctuating her conclusion. This made Sam smile again.

"You remind me of myself when I was young," Sam admitted. She was pleased by the grin that spread unchecked across Leslie's face. She wanted desperately to watch this young girl grow into the strong woman she was destined to become and, regardless of the circumstances leading to their acquaintance, Sam was glad to have met her.

Chapter Nineteen

New Year's Eve had finally arrived. Sam had never known a day to pass so slowly. As the day dragged on, Sam could sense the mounting anxiety throughout the house. Although virtually no one knew exactly where she was, Sam caught Connie staring anxiously out the front windows, as if waiting for some unwanted visitor to arrive.

Dan and Patrick were also to be found prowling the house, on the alert for anything out of place. Sam tried her best to lay low and stay out of everyone's way. She wanted nothing more than to go to bed, fall asleep, and wake up several days later to find this was all just one, long, horrible dream.

Leslie was the only one who seemed remotely excited about the day. She buzzed about the house continually asking the adults around her, "What time is it? Should we start getting ready? When are we leaving?" It was hard for Sam to suppress her laughter as she watched Detective Johnston grimace each time his daughter entered the room. Leslie was immune to her father's ill humor. She was looking forward to attending the Policeman's Ball with her father and nothing was going to spoil her time.

Everyone was relieved when Connie finally announced it was time to get ready. Leslie eagerly bounded up the stairs with her mother while Sam, Patrick, and Dan lingered in the living room for a moment's peace. Dan wanted to talk.

He looked at Sam and Patrick solemnly. "This is it. We've just got to get you through the next few hours."

Sam looked to Patrick, a weary smile on her face. As much as she wanted to believe what Dan was saying, she knew there was a much longer road ahead. She wouldn't be safe until this maniac was captured. She listened to Dan's pep talk halfheartedly, then excused herself to go get changed.

In the guestroom, Sam pulled her cell phone off the dresser and turned it on. She hadn't spoken to Jen since she left the house and thought she'd better call and check in. As she dialed her own home phone number, Patrick entered the room. He looked at her inquisitively.

"Calling Jen," she announced. "I'm sure she's worried about me. I'll just be a minute." The phone had just begun to ring. "Want to start the shower? I'll join you in a minute."

Patrick grinned mischievously, dropped Sam a wink, and then said, "See you soon."

Jen answered on the fourth ring. She sounded truly relieved to hear Sam's voice on the other end of the line. "How are you?" she asked.

"I'm fine," Sam assured her. "What about you? How are you doing?"

"Good. Tony's been worried about me staying here at the house alone, so I've been spending a lot of time over at his apartment. You're lucky you caught me," Jen explained.

Sam too had been worried about her friend staying at their house alone. She thought the killer may still try to get into the house, looking for clues to Sam's current location, and she hated the thought of Jen being there if he showed up. "Are you going to be at Tony's tonight?" she asked.

Jen laughed. "Wouldn't you like to know!" she teased.

Sam matched her jovial tone, "Oh, it's like that is it?"

They laughed together for a moment before Jen said, "Be careful tonight, okay? Stay safe."

"You too." They exchanged farewells, Sam assuring her friend she'd see her soon, then hung up. Sam sat quietly on the bed for a minute, listening to the sound of running water from the adjoining bathroom, a nagging feeling in the pit of her stomach.

Something felt wrong. Something was coming, and Sam knew that before the night was concluded things were going to spiral wildly out of control.

~ ~ ~

Every head in the room turned to watch their arrival at City Hall. The main chamber had been cleared to accommodate the ball and the room was already quite full of officers and their guests. Sam tried to tell herself they were looking at Leslie. Sam thought she looked stunning in her dress, her hair swept into a loose pile atop her head, her freckles muted by a light sheen of makeup.

Sam knew the real reason they stared, however. Every officer in attendance knew who she was and, while she was in their presence, they were charged with ensuring her safety. A dull murmur arose as many of the officers pointed her out to their companions. Sam felt her face flush with warmth. She'd always dreamed of being recognized, just not like this.

Patrick placed a strong hand reassuringly in the small of her back and Leslie grabbed one of her hands. The young girl was quite perceptive. She looked up into Sam's eyes and smiled.

"Come on Sam, let's go get something to drink." Leslie pulled her into the crowd and toward the buffet table along the far wall. Once they were amid the throng of people, it was less noticeable to Sam that she was being stared at. Soon, the novelty of her arrival wore off and Sam found she was only occasionally stared at.

As the evening progressed, Sam found herself relaxing and slowly starting to enjoy herself. When Patrick asked her to dance, Sam joined him cheerfully. She no longer was bothered by the occasional, surreptitious stares in her direction. They were joined on the dance floor a short while later by Dan and his daughter.

Sam smiled as she watched Leslie dancing with her father. She nudged Patrick and whispered something in his ear. He smiled broadly at her, flashing his white teeth, then moved away. She watched as he stepped in and asked Leslie if she'd dance with him. A beaming smile spread across Leslie's face as she nodded.

Dan walked to Sam's side and stood along the edge of the dance floor. "She's a special girl," he whispered proudly.

Sam picked up the detective's hand, holding it in her own. "Well, she's got a special father." She looked into Dan's eyes. "I want you to know I appreciate all you're doing for me. You and your family have been so wonderful to Patrick and I these past couple days."

Dan waved his free hand dismissively. Sam pressed on. "No matter what you say, I know it was a risk bringing me to your home. I wouldn't want anything to happen to your family because of me."

"It's nothing Sam," Dan assured her. "There's not an officer here who wouldn't do the same."

"I doubt that," Sam laughed, thinking back to some of her more frosty receptions by officers at the various crime scenes she'd responded to as a reporter. Dan understood her joke and laughed with her.

He pulled his hand from her grasp and laid his arm over her shoulder paternally. "Would you do me the honor?" he asked, gesturing to the dance floor. Sam nodded and allowed Dan to lead her to an empty space near Patrick and Leslie.

They had a wonderful evening. Sam took little notice of the time as it swept past on her wristwatch and was surprised when someone stepped to the microphone and announced it was 11:45. The woman at the microphone suggested everyone get a glass of champagne, or in Leslie's case sparkling cider, and get ready for the New Year countdown.

Sam and Leslie returned to their table to sit down while the men filled their glasses. When they settled into their chairs, Sam kicked her shoes off beneath the table. Her feet were sore from all the dancing. She reached for her purse, wanting to touch up her lipstick, and noticed her cell phone's display was flashing. She had a voicemail.

Disinterestedly, she pulled the phone from her clutch and checked the call log. She was surprised to see the call had come from her house. She'd assumed, from her talk with Jen earlier, that she and Tony were going to spend the evening at Tony's place.

"Excuse me for a second?" Sam asked Leslie. The girl nodded and Sam put the phone to her ear. Why was Jen calling? She knew where Sam was going to be tonight and that she wasn't likely to answer her phone. Sam distractedly punched in her access code and listened impatiently for the message.

When she finally heard the message, Sam's heart felt as if it had stopped. Her hands began to shake uncontrollably. She could barely hold the phone. Leslie saw this and reached out to Sam.

"What is it?" she asked.

Sam could barely find words. When she finally was able to make her mouth work, she uttered shakily, "Get your father."

She watched Leslie hurry through the crowd, trying to reach Patrick and Dan. Sam could feel a scream building inside her. It took all her effort to suppress that scream as Jen's frightened, tearful words echoed inside her head.

"Sam, help me."

~ ~ ~

They sat in an antechamber off the hallway at City Hall. Leslie had her arms wrapped protectively around Sam, stroking at her hair while Sam cried. The officers standing just outside the open door made an effort to look the other way, trying to offer Sam some illusion of privacy in her grief.

They, along with all the others in attendance, had been in shock when, minutes before midnight Detective Johnston had stepped to the microphone and announced that they had work to do. He had explained that Sam had received what seemed to be a message from her roommate. He had assigned these two men to escort Sam and his daughter to another room and stand watch while they mobilized several other officers to various tasks. Dan and Patrick joined them in the antechamber a short while later.

"We're sending some people over to Tony's apartment, to check there too," Dan explained. He looked to Patrick for a moment before saying, "We can't seem to reach either of them. There's no answer at Tony's, at your house, or on either of their cell phones."

"You're going to stay here for a while," Patrick told Sam. He knew she would want to come with them, but Patrick feared what might await them at home. He didn't want to admit it to himself or to Sam, but he was afraid they were going to find something horribly wrong.

Dan leaned in and kissed his daughter on the forehead. "Your mom's on her way to pick you up. You're going to go home and wait for us there, okay?"

Leslie pulled back and looked at her dad indignantly. "What about Sam?"

"She's going to stay here and wait for us to get back."

"I'm not going to leave her alone," Leslie stated. "Mom and I will wait here with her until you get back." The force in Leslie's voice took everyone, even Sam, by surprise.

Dan could only nod reluctantly, then kissed his daughter again. "We'll be back soon." Then he pulled Sam into his arms and, like a father, told her, "Everything's going to be fine, you'll see." Then Dan stepped from the room.

Patrick lingered a moment longer. He didn't dare look Sam in the eyes, afraid she'd read the truth of his fears in his own. Instead, he kissed her on the forehead and said, "I'll call you as soon as we get there, let you know what's going on." With that, he left.

It seemed an insufferable amount of time passed. Connie had arrived and swept into the room, overflowing with matronly concern. She went to her daughter first, of course, ensuring Leslie was okay. But moments later she was sitting on Sam's other side, supporting her, holding her, and reassuring her.

When finally her cell phone rang, Sam retrieved it from her lap and answered before it could complete its first ring. "What's going on Patrick?" she asked, her voice tremulous with worry.

Sam could hear Patrick take a deep, steadying breath on the other end of the line. "Nobody's here," he explained, "The front door was open. Jen's car is still here. Her cell phone is laying in the middle of the living room."

He was leaving something out, Sam could tell. "What else?" she demanded, her voice stronger than she felt.

Patrick began to cry. That sound alone unnerved Sam more than anything else all night. "Jen's gone," he managed, "he took her." Patrick couldn't manage to say any more and he certainly did not want to tell Sam about what else they had found. In the past months, Jen had become like family to him, like a sister, and the thought of her in danger was almost as bad as if it had been Sam herself.

Dan saw Patrick's distress and took the phone from him. "Sam?" he said, "Is Connie there yet?" Sam muttered an affirmative. "Let me talk to her."

Sam gratefully passed the phone to Connie who listed to the instructions her husband gave, then hung up the phone. Sam sat there numbly as Connie excused herself and spoke to the two officers outside, then returned to shepherd Sam and Leslie out of the room.

When Dan hung up the phone on his end, he turned back to Patrick. "Why don't you step outside for a bit," he suggested.

Patrick took the phone back numbly, shaking his head at Dan's proposal. "I'll be all right," he insisted.

Dan suspected otherwise, but he didn't press the matter. Instead, he pulled his own cell phone out of his jacket and called one of the officers he'd sent over to Tony's apartment. With a few quick exchanges he learned that Tony's apartment was empty and nothing was amiss.

"The complex manager was glad to see us. There's a raging party going on in the apartment directly below Mr. Goodwin's," the officer explained. "He thought we'd come about the party. Seems Mr. Goodwin placed a call to the manager and complained about the noise about two and a half hours ago. The manager unlocked the apartment for us and we looked around, but didn't find anything unusual." Dan had heard all he needed to. He imagined Tony and Jen had been fed up with the noise and had decided to come back here, where it was quiet.

For some reason, however, suspicion gnawed at Dan's insides. How had Jen managed to disappear if she was with Tony, unless Tony was somehow responsible? This was the doubt that plagued him. He'd always held a kernel of suspicion when it came to Tony, given his history, but he had felt in his gut that Tony was innocent. Now, Detective Johnston was forced to admit his gut may have been wrong.

He strode purposefully over to the crew processing the note they had found alongside Jen's cell phone. Similar to the note at Sam's office, this one was tucked inside a plain, white envelope. Sam's name was scrawled across the front in blue ink.

"How are we doing?" Dan asked, anxious to read what was written inside.

"Almost there," grunted one of the technicians. He had the envelope gripped firmly in a pair of metal forceps and was gingerly extracting the paper from inside. Dan watched, holding his breath, as the paper slowly emerged.

Patrick approached and stood behind the detective. He too found that he was holding his breath as he watched the piece of paper slide into sight. He dreaded to read what was written, fearful that it spelled disaster for his friend. Agonizingly slow, the technician finally extracted the paper and held it for them to examine.

She is mine.
D.K.

Patrick shuddered as he imagined the implications of those few, simple words. He feared Jen was lost to them forever. He felt a wave of nausea spread its way out from the pit of his stomach and turned away. He now understood why Dan had suggested he go outside.

Dan sensed, rather than saw, Patrick leave. He was busy giving instructions to the technicians around him. "Get this back to the lab and process it for prints. Now." He caught the skeptical looks from those who surrounded him. He sighed wearily. He knew there was a snowball's chance in hell that there were any prints to be found. "Just run it," he persisted, and then turned to join Patrick outside.

"You doing okay?" Dan asked, taking Patrick by surprise. Patrick turned to face Dan, struggling to keep his face composed. Dan could read the despair and grief in his eyes. He couldn't imagine how Patrick must feel. He knew Patrick would be worried about his friend, but he also suspected he would feel guilty as well. Dan worried that Jen had been taken only because Sam was out of reach. If that was the case, then Dan held as much blame as anyone, for he was the one who insisted Sam go into hiding.

Dan considered telling Patrick as much, but held his tongue. He knew nothing he could say would change how Patrick felt. Instead, he placed a hand on the younger officer's shoulder. "Connie and Leslie are taking Sam to the station. We're going to meet them there, so let's get going."

"What about…," Patrick gestured feebly back toward the house.

"They can manage from here. Let's go see Sam."

The men moved toward Dan's car out in the street. As they climbed inside, Patrick looked once more toward his house and was chilled to see fellow officers stringing yellow tape across the front yard.

He sped through the dark night, giddy with euphoria at his success. He chanced a glance onto the floorboard of the back seat, to the draped form of his love. She moaned quietly, the drugs he'd administered keeping her docile, almost unconscious. His pulse quickened as he imagined the days to come, how she would be his and his alone. His foot fell harder onto the gas pedal in his eagerness.

He had prepared a quiet spot for them to enjoy, a small cabin off the beaten track. He'd found it months ago, deserted and derelict, and had been preparing it for his needs. It was nestled between two small foothills, isolated, despite being only a short half-hour drive from the outskirts of Portland. As he negotiated the rain and snow-slicked roads, his car's headlights illuminating the midnight darkness, he counted down the minutes until he reached their destination.

~ ~ ~

Sam sat anxiously awaiting Patrick and Dan's arrival at the police station. She had only been there a short while, but it seemed forever. Connie had delivered her safely into the hands of a detective who was a friend of Dan's. Then, much to Leslie's dismay, Connie and her daughter left for home. She assured Sam her husband and Patrick would be back soon and that they'd asked for her to wait for them there.

Sam had been led into the conference room and immediately found herself unable to breathe. Gazing around the room at the victims' photographs, Sam couldn't believe she'd ever thought herself a target. Each face that stared back at her seemed to mock her. She now knew Jen had been his target from the start.

She sank wearily into the nearest chair, unable to pull her gaze away from the series of photographs. Sam could have kicked herself, but she'd never gotten a good look at all his victims. The only two she'd seen clearly had been Emily, then Tracy Randolph. She'd had no reason to connect the similarity before now, but seeing their pictures posted among the other women, Sam could clearly see the killer had a preferred type. She could imagine Jen's image on the wall, at the end of the timeline, her beautiful red hair no longer unique among her fellow victims.

Sam's eyes began to cloud with tears. She blamed herself, although she'd had no way of knowing. *Hell*, she reminded herself, *the entire police department thought the threat was directed at me, so why would I question it?* Still, she felt responsible. She prayed they could find Jen before something terrible happened.

A noise in the hall outside roused Sam from her musings. She looked up with relief to see Patrick and Dan stride into the room. She stood from her seat and rushed into Patrick's arms. She broke into tears immediately. Dan stood silently by as he watched them try to comfort one another.

"Where is she?" Sam sobbed.

"We don't know," Dan answered, using her question as an opportunity to usher Sam back to her chair.

"Well, what *do* you know?" Her question was not meant to be angry, but she couldn't help keeping her frustration and fear from showing.

Dan did not seemed phased. He coolly recounted the events as they knew, or hypothesized, they occurred. "As far as we know, Jen and Tony left his apartment and drove to your house. That's where she was taken. There's no sign of either of them. Tony's car is missing. We found Jen's phone in your living room next to another note. It was addressed to you."

Sam was afraid to ask. "What did it say?" she whispered tensely.

Patrick answered, his voice shaking a bit still, but strong and under his command once more. "It said 'She is mine.' That's all."

Sam buried her face in her hands. "This is my fault."

"Don't say that," Dan said. "This is in no way your fault."

"I was never his target," Sam scoffed. She swept her hand toward the pictures lining the walls. "Look at them," she said, half yelling in her frustration, "Look at them and then tell me if you still think I was his target." She was met with silence.

Finally, Dan spoke. "He tricked us Sam. All of us. This is not your fault." He reached out to put a hand on Sam's shoulder for reassurance but stopped short when a uniformed officer came running into the room.

"We've found Mr. Goodwin's vehicle," the man announced.

"Where?"

"Abandoned about two miles from the scene." Dan cleared his voice significantly and the officer amended himself, "I mean, about two miles from her house." He looked apologetically at Sam as he said this.

"I'll be right out, wait for me at the car." Dan turned to face Patrick and Sam. "Take her back to my house," he instructed Patrick. "Connie will be waiting for you. I want you both to stay there. I've got a lot to do, but I'll be back as soon as possible." He started to stride purposefully from the room, but stopped and turned back to face Sam one last time. "We're going to find her."

Chapter Twenty

Jen awoke in darkness, her head throbbing. She tried to sit up and found she couldn't. She was bound hand and foot and was lying on something soft, a bed she supposed. Her eyelids brushed against a cloth blindfold as she blinked desperately trying to clear her head of its fog. She could feel cool air against the skin of her belly and something sticky and slightly wet on the back of her head. She realized her shirt was off and she felt exposed and vulnerable.

She struggled to remember what had happened, to figure out where she was. She remembered a loud party, leaving Tony's apartment and going back to her house. But that was where things got muddy.

She was able to recall entering the house while Tony grabbed their bags out of the car. Then there was pain and confusion. She thought the sticky feeling at the back of her head must be her own blood, where she'd been struck. She thought she must've lost consciousness. When she next woke, she found she'd been blindfolded. A phone was pressed to her ear. An eerily familiar, vicious voice told her to leave a message for her friend. She had been scared and couldn't think straight. Reflecting back, she scolded herself for not trying to convey a message to Sam, tell her something important, but in the fog left by the drugs she'd been given, Jen could not recall what that important thing was.

In the darkness, Jen heard a faint noise coming from across the room. She turned her head, straining to hear the noise again. A soft moan reached her attentive ears. "Who's there?" she called. There was no answer. She feared being alone, but she feared the thought of her captor's return even more.

~ ~ ~

Sam lay in bed, sleep eluding her. Patrick had long since fallen into a restless slumber, tossing back and forth on the bed beside her. Dan had come home late that morning and had filled them in as best he could.

Tony's car had been found not far from the house, keys in the ignition. There was a torn shirt in the backseat with a small amount of blood on it. Detective Johnston had known immediately it was Jen's shirt, he'd seen her wear it on one of the few occasions he'd seen her, but they didn't know yet if it was Jen's blood or not.

"We're looking into places he could've taken her," Dan had explained.

"Wait," Sam asked, "you're not talking about Tony, are you?"

"At this point, we have to assume he's involved," Dan sighed.

"No," Sam and Patrick had said vehemently, Sam shaking her head strongly for emphasis. "There's no way," Patrick added.

Dan looked to Patrick meaningfully. "You know as well as I do, we have to include him as a possibility. I don't want to believe it either, but…"

"But what?" Patrick asked.

Dan sighed heavily again. "We found a fingerprint on the letter. It was Tony's."

"No," Sam said again. "Maybe… maybe he left for a while, went to the store or something, came back and found Jen gone? Maybe he touched the envelope then? He's probably out looking for her right now." Sam knew her words were far fetched, but she could not believe Tony had anything to do with Jen's disappearance.

"I'm sorry Sam, but no. The print was on the letter, not the envelope. It was sealed until my techs opened it. There's no way his print could've gotten there unless he wrote the note." Dan saw the weary look of defeat upon both their faces. "Listen, go to bed, try and get some sleep. You can't do anything now, so you might as well try to get some rest. Everyone's working as hard as they can to find her Sam, I promise."

They had followed Dan's instructions and had come up to their room where Patrick had then fallen promptly to sleep. Sam kept telling herself Patrick was used to things like this, it was the only way she could justify his ability to sleep, regardless of how fitfully, with their friend missing.

She stared at the ceiling as she tried to will herself to sleep. It was to no avail, so she sat up on the edge of the bed, staring at her reflection in the mirror across the room. The sun had risen several hours ago and the room was filled with gray winter sunlight. Her image was haggard and rundown. Dark circles had taken up residence beneath her eyes.

She gazed into the mirror for a while, her eyes losing focus. Then a thought hit her: the mirror. If she could get back to her house, maybe Emily's mirror would show her something. Something that could lead them to Jen. A nagging voice in the back of her mind squeaked something awful she tried to ignore, but it kept repeating, like a broken record: maybe Jen was already dead.

Doing her best to suppress that thought, Sam turned and shook Patrick purposefully. "Patrick," she urged as he slowly opened his eyes, "Wake up. I need to talk to you."

"What it is? Has something happened?" He was fully alert now, his body reacting out of instinct.

"No, it's nothing really, but…" Sam paused, wondering how best to proceed. Finally, she spit it out. "I need to go back to our house. I need the mirror."

Patrick looked at her with a bemused expression on his face. "The mirror? You mean Emily's mirror?" Sam nodded. Patrick groaned. "Honey, no. Now, you know I believe you about what you say you've seen, but if you think I'm going to let you sit in front of that mirror hoping it will show you Jennifer, you're wrong. What if it showed you

211

something like before? Like when it showed you what happened to Emily, or to Tracy Randolph? Would you want to see that? Would you want to see Jen like that?" Patrick ached for her. He understood her compulsion to do something, anything at all, to help her friend, but at the same time, he could not allow her to subject herself to that kind of torment.

Sam looked at him with a steely expression. "I have to try. I can't just sit here. Maybe he hasn't hurt her yet? Maybe there's still time?" She stood and began to pace the room anxiously. "I have to try," she repeated.

"Sam, you know as well as I do there is no way Dan will let you go. I think you need to stay here, where it's safe. I know you think he was after Jen all along, but what if you're wrong about that? It's just not safe." Sam didn't seem to be paying him any heed. "Please, Sam, just think about this for a minute."

She turned her head to gaze at him for a moment. "I have thought about it Patrick. I have to try and I need you to help me. Please?"

Patrick nodded reluctantly. He knew he could not deny her his help, but at the same time, he knew it was folly. Sam smiled at him, her first smile since she received Jen's message. "Thank you Patrick."

"I don't see how we are going to get back into the house, though," Patrick sighed.

Sam wrung her hands before her. "Do you think I should tell him everything?" Sam asked. Patrick nodded an affirmative, but then shrugged his shoulders noncommittally. Sam sighed, understanding his indecision, but figured she had little to lose at this point. She resolved to tell Dan, and to try to enlist his help. "Will you come with me? I think I'm going to need your help trying to explain it all." Patrick stood and followed her from the room as they went to find Dan.

He was sitting quietly in his small study, the curtains drawn closed and all but one lamp dark. Sam knocked softly from the doorway and Dan looked up, surprised to see them.

"What is it?" he asked, a look of concern blooming on his already worried face.

"Can we come in?" Sam asked. "I need to talk to you… explain a few things."

"Of course." He motioned to a couple chairs nearby and Patrick swung them around closer to where Dan sat. "What's up?"

Sam looked to Patrick for encouragement and he smiled reassuringly to her. "I need to tell you some things, and I'm afraid you'll think I'm crazy," she started.

Dan scoffed aloud. "You're not crazy."

"I know I'm not, but honestly, you may change your mind after you hear what I have to say."

"I didn't believe her for a long time," Patrick confessed. "She gave me plenty of reasons to, but I just couldn't wrap my mind around it."

"What are you two going on about?"

Sam took a deep, steadying breath. "Okay, you know about my cousin Emily, how she was killed in her own bedroom?" Dan nodded. "After she died, my grandmother held on to a piece of furniture from her room: a vanity table and mirror. When I moved into my house, my grandmother gave that table to me."

"I don't follow."

"I started looking into Emily's murder. I asked Patrick to see what info he could get for me."

"Remember when you got the file for me?" Patrick prompted and Dan nodded.

"Patrick, Jen, and I looked through her files: at the interrogations, the photographs, everything. I was upset and I went back to my room to be alone for a little while and I… well, I saw something in the mirror."

Dan was staring at her fixedly, but betrayed no hint of skepticism. Patrick patted her on the arm reassuringly as she went on. "I saw what happened to Emily on the night she died. I saw everything."

"Everything?" Dan sat up excitedly.

"Well, almost everything," Sam admitted. "I never saw his face. But she knew him. I watched him kill her." Sam took a moment to collect herself. "I saw other things too. The time with Emily, it was like I was watching an old recording, but the other times, it always seemed like it was happening right then."

"Once, I saw him sitting at a desk. It was like I was looking over his shoulder. He had photographs of them all spread out on the desktop in front of him. I saw Emily's picture, but I really couldn't make out any of the others. I just knew they were women, and that he'd killed them all."

Dan leaned forward eagerly. "Do you remember anything specific about the room? About him? Any distinctive marks? Anything unique on the desk?"

Sam shook her head. "The next time I saw anything was the night Tracy Randolph was killed."

Dan raised his eyebrows excitedly. "Do you mean to tell me you saw that too?"

Sam nodded. "It was terrible. I saw her bedroom. I could see the clock on her nightstand. It was like I was looking through a window right into her room. I watched the whole thing happen. I saw him a little better, but still nothing specific. His hair was dark, he had an average build, that's all I could really make out."

"This is unreal," Dan breathed, but it was said more out of amazement than disbelief.

"Remember when you and I were heading out to Tracy's apartment and Sam called?" Patrick asked. Dan nodded. "Sam told me what had happened. I didn't believe her. She told me that he'd killed someone and that we'd find her laying on a red floral bedspread."

"I remember," Dan breathed. "Your face went completely white when you saw her." Patrick nodded. "Is there more?" Dan asked Sam.

"Yes. The photographs he sent you, the ones of Jen, Patrick, and I... I'd seen them before. We'd gone out to buy our Christmas tree and I saw him again, at his desk, looking at the pictures. Then again when Jen and I went shopping downtown, I saw him with the pictures later that night."

"In the mirror?"

"Yes. Do you think I'm crazy?"

Dan shook his head. "I know you better than that young lady. It's...," he chose his next words carefully, "amazing. But I believe you. Why didn't you tell me before?"

"I was afraid you wouldn't believe me."

"It's my fault," Patrick stated. "I didn't believe her until I saw the photographs he'd sent. I kept telling myself she was imagining it, or dreaming, or something. All of a sudden, everything clicked and I realized Sam was right."

"Jen didn't believe me either," Sam stated, hanging her head.

"Why are you telling me now?" Dan asked, sensing there was a motive behind Sam's story.

"I need to get back to my house, to the mirror."

"She hopes it will show her where Jen is," Patrick added.

Dan stared at Sam for a long moment then, turning to Patrick, he asked, "Can I talk to Sam alone for a minute?" Patrick looked uneasily to Sam, but when she nodded, he stood and left the room.

When they were alone, Dan stood and moved to the chair in which Patrick had sat, closer to Sam. "First off, please understand that I'm not upset, but you should have told me this a long time ago."

"I know," Sam sighed, staring at her lap shamefully. "I'm sorry."

Dan pursed his lips together thoughtfully. "It's spilt milk," he assured her, "that's all. Now, we have to figure out what to do."

"I know what I have to do," Sam said. "I need to get back to my house and…"

"And what?" Dan interrupted. "Can you summon these visions at will? Can you make that mirror show things whenever you want?" Sam shook her head slowly. "I didn't think so. So what were you going to do? Just sit there waiting for something to happen?"

"I don't know. I hadn't thought about that," Sam admitted.

"Listen, I'll let you go. Hell, I'll even take you back there, but I need to ask you a few things first, okay?"

"Okay."

Dan settled back in his chair. "Now, this office you saw? Did it look like it was in a house or was it maybe his work?" Sam shrugged. "Did you see a telephone?"

"Yes!" Sam brightened as she remembered. "It was cordless, like a home phone."

"Good. Did you see anything else? Framed photos, sports trophies?" Sam shook her head. "What color was the desk?"

Sam closed her eyes and took a deep breath. She'd pushed the vision to the back of her mind, hoping never to see it again, but as Dan questioned her she willed the image into being once again. Her eyes remained closed and she spoke in a faraway voice. "It's a dark wood, like mahogany. The last drawer has a hidden compartment in the bottom. He keeps the trophy photos there. He used a digital camera when he took the photographs of us, and he printed them at home. Then he deleted the pictures from the camera's memory. There wasn't anything else on the desk." She stopped for a minute, then corrected herself, "No, there was a map." Her voice became excited.

"A map?"

"Yes. There was a map on the desk." Her eyebrows furrowed in concentration, trying to recall what the map had shown. She could almost see the map on the back of her eyelids. A red circle was marked on it, but she couldn't distinguish much else. Her eyes popped open. "I'm sorry. I don't know what the map showed."

"It's okay," he assured her. "Can you remember anything else?"

Sam closed her eyes again. "The night I saw him with the pictures of Emily and the others," she started, "he seemed nervous. I remember he acted like he heard a noise. It seemed to worry him and he swept the pictures up quickly and put them into the secret compartment in the bottom drawer." Sam looked meaningfully at the detective. "He must have been at home, heard someone else in the house."

Dan sat in silent contemplation for a moment. There were several things she had said that gave him pause, especially the last. He tried to tell himself he had to look at things analytically, but he was amazed by what she'd told him. Any other time, he would have dismissed her story as too fantastical. He didn't put much stock into the supernatural, but he'd come to know Sam well and knew she was telling him the truth. He only wished she was able to recall what was on that map, it might lead them somewhere.

"Okay," Dan said after a moment's contemplation, "I want you to promise me a few things."

"What?"

"First, I want you to tell me anything and everything else you can remember about the things you saw before."

"Yes, of course."

"Second, you're to tell me about anything new you see immediately. I don't care where or how you come across this stuff, as long as it helps us catch this guy in time."

Sam smiled apologetically. "Is there more?" she asked.

"Yes." Dan sat straight in his chair once more. "I want you to write a story for the Tribune… about Jennifer."

"What?"

"We need help Sam. I want as many people to know about this as possible. We're holding a press conference in a few hours, but the public seemed really drawn to you before. I want them to know Jen is your roommate, that we all thought you were his target, but that we were wrong. I need everyone on our side and looking for her and Tony."

"I won't write anything against Tony," she stated adamantly.

"No, not at all. You write what you want, you've got free rein. But I want it to be personal, and I want everyone who reads it to feel involved. Do you think you can do that?"

Sam nodded her assent. She understood why he was asking and it would feel good to do something that may help. She looked around the office. "Do you have a computer I can use?" She noticed his office was conspicuously bare of almost any electronic devices.

"Hate the damn things," he muttered, "but I'm sure Leslie will let you use hers."

Thankfully, Leslie's computer turned out to be a laptop. Sam was able to bring it into Dan's office and set herself up at his desk. She made a quick call to the paper and alerted the assistant editor of Tony and Jen's disappearance. Paulette was all too happy to hear from Sam and, Sam noted, seemed very enthusiastic when she told her some of the details and that she'd be submitting a special report.

"You e-mail me as soon as it's done. I'll get it on the front page," Paulette assured her. Sam thanked her and set to work.

Everyone left her alone while she worked. Connie popped in once to bring her something to drink, but otherwise she wrote without interruptions. She cried at times. Writing about two of her friends and begging the public for help was difficult. She finished fairly quickly, tears blurring her vision as she tried to proof her work.

"Patrick? Dan?" she called, "Could you come here?"

The men entered the room moments later. She supposed they had been sitting nearby, waiting for her to finish. "I want you both to read it. Make sure it's what we need."

"I told you, I'm hands off on this one," Dan said.

"Yes, I know, but I want you to read it. I need to make sure you think it'll help."

She turned the laptop to face them as they sat down across the desk. Patrick scrolled down the page as necessary while they both read in silence. When they finished, Dan sat back, exhaling heavily.

"That'll do," he assured her.

Sam looked to Patrick. "If anyone can read this without wanting to go out and start searching for her themselves, I'll be amazed."

Within moments, the file was on its way to the Tribune. "I hope this works," Sam sighed.

"Now," Dan offered, "let's see about that mirror."

~ ~ ~

A noise startled her. She called out to the darkness but got no response. She thought she heard more soft moaning from the corner, like before, but she couldn't figure out what it might be. She listened intently, closing her eyes behind the blindfold. A footstep crunched outside, she was sure of it. The sound was followed by another, and another, growing closer. Her heart began to race in panic. Someone was coming.

Jen struggled against the bonds holding her hands fast, working desperately to try to free herself. Cold metal bit into her skin and she could feel the blood, dried from her earlier efforts, beginning to coat her wrists again. Suddenly, she heard the sound of a door dragging open and she was able to see brightness around the edges of the blindfold. She swallowed the scream that tried to burst forth, turning it into a stifled whimper.

The man laughed at her. "I thought you'd be happy to see me." His voice was angry, menacing. Something familiar tugged at her, but Jen could not understand what it was.

"What do you want?" she managed.

"Oh, you're a smart girl. I think you can figure it out." She felt a hand brush up against the outside of her thigh and she flinched. Hot tears soaked into the fabric of her blindfold.

"Please..." she sobbed.

"You look so much like her."

"Like who?"

A peal of laughter echoed in the small room. The whimpering from the corner started again. "Like my Emily," he explained. "I see why *he* chose you."

"I don't understand." Jen forced herself to speak, hoping she could buy herself time. "Who chose me?"

"Anthony," the voice spat. Jen flinched again, this time merely at the venom in his voice.

"Where is he? Where's Tony?" She began to struggle harder against her restraints, heedless of the pain it caused. "Where is he?" she asked again. Her question was answered with more whimpers from the corner of the room. Suddenly, she realized Tony was there, captive just as she was.

"Tony? Is that you?" The plaintive moans from the corner became more agitated at her question and she sobbed in terror and relief as she realized she was not alone.

A hard thud sounded from that part of the room and Jen realized their captor had kicked him. "Quit it!" he spat. In a flash, he was back at the bed next to Jen. She felt his weight press down on both sides of her, over her, as he straddled her and put his hands upon her abdomen.

"He can't have you too! Emily was mine and he tried to take her. Then I found you and he's tried to claim you too."

The feel of his hands on her skin made her sick. She struggled beneath him to no avail. "Please, let us go," she begged.

At her words, he struck her hard across the face. "You bitch!" His fists pummeled into her body and Jen thought she felt her ribs crack. He sprang from the bed, screams and curses pouring forth in a tirade. Jen had never been so frightened in her life. Little did she know, worse was yet to come.

"You'll want me," he said, calming slightly, "you'll see. I'll make you want me." He stood still for a while, Jen could no longer tell where he was in the room. Then, the muffled sounds in the corner changed as Tony's gag was pulled free. "Say something to her," he demanded.

Tony coughed and it was a wet sound, then Jen heard him spit up what she thought was probably blood. "Don't hurt her," he groaned.

"I said, say something to her!" There was another thick thud, the sound of boot leather on skin.

Tony was seized by another coughing fit, then said, "I love you Jennifer."

"I love you too," she managed.

"Wrong answer."

She heard the unmistakable sound of a pistol hammer locking and screamed, the sound drowned by the resounding crack of the gun as it fired.

~ ~ ~

It was starting to get dark. Sam's hands were splayed flat against the top of the vanity table. She stared purposefully into the mirror, trying to will something, anything, to happen. Of course, nothing did.

She'd been there almost an hour. Dan and Patrick sat patiently in the living room, waiting for her to emerge. She knew it was futile, but every time she stood to leave, she found herself sitting down again on the small stool. She couldn't explain why, but she was compelled to stay. Frustrated tears began to pool in her eyes. With each passing minute she felt more and more certain they would be too late to help Jen.

"Please," she whispered, "help me." She sat in silence for a few more minutes, then stood resolving she would really leave this time.

As she took her first step toward the bedroom door, she heard it: a familiar static-like crackling. Turning back to face the vanity she felt gooseflesh erupt over her entire body.

She saw a small room, rustic and stark. There were three people there. Sam stifled a cry when she saw Jen, bound to the bed, her shirt missing. Slick, wet blood trailed slowly down her forearms where the handcuffs at her wrists had caused her to bleed.

There was a man standing in the corner, in shadows. He held a gun, pointing it maliciously at another man tightly bound in a wooden chair, his hands cuffed behind him. Although the chair had obviously once stood upright it, and the man tied into it, now lay sideways on the floor.

Sam couldn't hear anything, but she saw the gun fire, saw the man jerk painfully against his bonds, and saw Jen screaming and thrashing on the bed. Sam could hardly bear to watch, but she forced her gaze to remain steady. She couldn't fathom how she'd been lucky enough to be present to see this, but she didn't want to miss anything.

She tried to study the man with the gun, but he was too well concealed in the gloom for her to make anything out. When her eyes fell to the man at his feet, Sam recognized him and lost it. She couldn't contain the scream that surged forth.

As Patrick and Dan burst into the room, the image in the mirror disappeared. "What is it? What did you see?" Patrick asked, kneeling at her side. Sam was panting so hard she couldn't speak. She started to hyperventilate.

"Easy… Take it easy," Dan urged. He placed a hand against her back and began to rub up and down her spine, pressing hard, speaking to her in a calm and soothing voice. "Slow it down," he instructed.

After a minute which felt like an eternity, Sam got her breathing back under control. "Now, take a deep breath and tell us what you saw."

Chapter Twenty-One

Jen was sick with worry. Behind her blindfold, she could almost envision Tony lying there, bleeding copiously, crying in agony. She didn't want to believe what she'd heard, but she knew it was real. She had heard him howling in pain for some time, then, quite abruptly, the sounds stopped. She worried what it might mean.

She didn't know where he'd been shot and she feared he was dead. She began mumbling a prayer, repeating in like a mantra, her words barely audible. She sensed her captor nearby, watching her. After a long while, his voice filled the room.

"He's not dead. Not yet."

Jen sobbed loudly in relief at these words. "Please, don't hurt him."

"That's up to you," he told her. Then, his footsteps moved to the heavy door. She heard it grind open and then shut again.

She sank into the bed in relief at his departure. Her whole body ached from her struggles, but she barely noticed. "Tony?" she whispered, afraid their tormentor would hear her from outside. "Tony? Please answer me?" There was no response. She strained her ears to listen for retreating footsteps, and only spoke again when the sound had faded away in the distance.

"Tony? Please, you need to answer me. I'm scared." She was too drained to cry any more. She simply called his name periodically, until the sounds of night time surrounded them. Finally, she heard a faint moan from Tony. Relief washed over her. Her exhaustion caught up with her and she passed out, her dreams filled with the sound of malevolent laughter.

~ ~ ~

As soon as they had calmed her, Patrick and Dan ushered Sam back to the car and drove quickly back to Dan's home. Patrick had to practically carry Sam into the house where he then sat with her upon the sofa. Connie saw them coming, a worried look on her face.

"What's happened?" she asked. Dan put his arm around his wife's waist before she could ask any more and led her out of the room toward the kitchen. "What's going on?" Connie asked once they reached their destination.

"I don't know how to explain it," Dan sighed, running his hands through his thinning hair.

"Did they find her roommate?"

"No, no we haven't found her." Dan began to pace across the kitchen tiles. "Listen, you know I don't hold much stock with psychics, the supernatural, or any of that stuff, right?" Connie nodded. "And you know Sam's a smart girl, normal…"

"What are you getting at?" Connie interrupted.

"Sam… Sam believes she's seen things. Visions, I guess, in this old mirror that belonged to her cousin. Things to do with this serial killer."

Connie was startled. Her husband was one of the most practical, logical people she'd ever known, and to hear him talking about visions was a shock. "And you believe her?"

"I think so." Dan took in the expression of surprise on his wife's face and laughed. "I know it sounds crazy, but Patrick can corroborate some of the things she says she saw." He thought about how earnest she'd been when she had come to him earlier to confess her previous visions. Then, there was they way she had acted a short while ago, after she claimed to have seen her friends.

"Honey, you didn't see her just now," Dan continued, feeling the need to justify his belief in Sam. "I… I agreed to take her over to her house. She had this idea she might be able to see something in the mirror again, something that will help us find Jennifer. Honestly, I didn't think it would work, but I figured, 'What the hell,' you know?"

"Well, what happened?" Connie prompted.

"She saw something, I guess. We haven't been able to get her to tell us what it was yet, but it must've been bad. When we got to her she was screaming and she could hardly breathe. We got her calmed down and brought her back here." Dan halted his pacing and looked imploringly at his wife. "I've got to find this guy."

Connie stepped alongside her husband, wrapping her arms tightly around his waist. "And you will," she assured him. "I think you'll have plenty of help, too," she added, stepping away to retrieve the evening edition of the Tribune from a nearby counter. "Was this your idea?" she asked, indicating Sam's story prominently featured on the front page.

Dan nodded. "It's good," Connie stated, "I read it and I couldn't stop crying. I wouldn't be surprised if half the city started going door to door looking for her."

He forced a smile. "That's what I was hoping for." He turned and looked back toward the living room. "I'd better go check on her. Could you get some coffee going?" Connie nodded.

Dan scooped up the Tribune and went back to the front room. "How's she doing?" he asked Patrick.

"She still won't tell me what she saw." There was worry in Patrick's eyes. He feared Sam had seen Jen raped or killed... or both. He turned and ran a hand gently through her hair. He prayed she hadn't seen that.

"Connie's making us some coffee," Dan stated, kneeling on the floor in front of Sam. "Would you like some?" he asked her. Sam nodded numbly. "Good," Dan smiled. "We'll all have some hot coffee, then we'll see if you want to tell us about what you saw, okay?"

Sam shuddered involuntarily. She couldn't stop the scene from playing out in her mind. Every time she closed her eyes, she saw the flash of the gun, saw Tony's body buckle, and the blood begin to flow. She saw the expectant and concerned eyes of the two men before her and wanted to tell them, but she couldn't find words.

Patrick watched her mouth open and close again soundlessly. "It's okay, honey."

Dan produced the copy of the Tribune he'd brought back from the kitchen. "Looks like they got your story printed tonight. Connie read it. She says you did good."

Sam's eyes drifted wearily to the paper held before her. It was somewhat of a shock to see her friends' faces in print like that. Both of them smiled out at her. She started to cry again, praying they would find them quickly.

"We have to find them," she whispered. These were some of the first words she'd spoken since they found her. Patrick and Dan sat in rapt attention, waiting for her to say more. Once she'd started talking, she found it easier, the words starting to pour forth.

"I saw them," she breathed. "I saw them both."

Dan was hesitant to interrupt, fearful she would stop talking again, but he had questions he had to ask. "Where were they Sam?"

"In a room."

"Were there windows?"

"I don't know. I couldn't see any."

"What did the walls look like?"

"Wooden."

"Wooden? You mean, like a cabin?" Sam nodded hesitantly. "Where was Jennifer?"

"On a bed. She was tied up." As Patrick listened to her, he shivered. Sam's voice sounded hollow even though her body shook and tears

227

fell from her eyes.

Dan pressed on with his questions. "How was she tied? With rope?"

"No," Sam said, shaking her head, "not her hands. There were handcuffs. She had rope on her feet."

"Was she hurt?"

"Her wrists were bleeding." Sam's eyes closed tightly in concentration as she called the images back into her mind. "She had a blindfold on. I don't think she was hurt, but Tony…"

Her voice trailed away. Dan wanted to ask about Tony, but Connie entered the room then carrying a tray with three cups of coffee. She handed a cup each to her husband, who still knelt on the floor in front of Sam, and to Patrick. Then she sat down next to Sam. "Here you go honey." Sam gripped the hot cup between her hands like a lifeline. Connie wrapped her arms around Sam, the protective wings of a mother bird, and Sam sank gratefully against her. Under the protective shelter of Connie's arms, Sam spoke more freely.

"Tony was there, too." She looked directly at Dan, knowing her next words would interest him. "He was tied and bound to a chair. I watched him shoot Tony."

"What?" Patrick blurted. She had stated it so matter-of-factly that her words hadn't sunk in for a moment, but when they did questions began to tumble forth. "Tony's been shot? Is he okay?"

Sam hung her head shamefully. "I don't know," she whimpered. "When I saw it, that's when I lost it and started screaming."

Dan looked to Patrick in confusion. "Any time someone else is around, the mirror stops working," Patrick explained.

Standing, Dan gestured for Patrick to come with him. He walked out into the hallway where Sam wouldn't hear them. Looking down at his watch Dan asked, "It's been almost an hour since we left, right?" Patrick consulted his watch then nodded in agreement. "Okay, so if this is like what she explained before, we can assume Tony was shot and hour ago. She says she always saw things as they were happening, right?"

"Except the first times, when the mirror showed her cousin."

"Okay. Time's against us here." Dan felt guilty for his earlier suspicions of Tony and felt it his personal obligation to find and help him. "If Sam's right, Tony was shot about one hour ago. If he wasn't hit bad, he should be fine, otherwise…" Dan paused, waving his hands in a frustrated gesture. "I feel like I need to be doing something," Dan admitted.

"I know what you mean," Patrick commiserated.

"I'm going to get back to the station, check on things," Dan stated, starting to step back into the living room.

"Mind if I tag along?" Patrick asked. He was torn between staying at Sam's side and performing his duty as a cop. His instinct for action was winning however, and despite the guilt he felt, he knew he would be unable to just sit by the sideline and not do something to help find Jen and Tony. Dan glanced back at him and recognized the tormented look on his face.

"It's okay," he assured him. "Connie and Leslie will take good care of her." Patrick nodded gratefully, then followed Dan back into the room.

"Sam, I need Patrick to come with me for a while, okay? I need his help on a few things back at the station. We won't be gone long." Sam nodded. She had known it would only be a matter of time before Dan and Patrick left, that they'd be wanting to get back to work.

Connie tightened her arms around Sam. "You'll stay here with Leslie and I, okay?"

Patrick leaned in and gave Sam a quick, strong hug. He kissed her on the cheek and whispered, "We're going to find them." She hoped he was right. She stood and walked to the front windows, watching as they pulled out of the drive and out of sight.

Connie stood silently behind her, observing. She didn't quite know what to make of what Dan had said about Sam seeing things in her mirror, but Sam seemed truly shaken, regardless of what had transpired, and Connie's maternal instincts were on overdrive trying to ensure Sam was cared for. "Are you hungry?" Connie asked.

Sam turned to look at her and shrugged her shoulders. "I don't think so."

"When was the last time you ate?"

"Last night," Sam admitted.

"Come on." Connie held her arm out to Sam warmly. "You'll feel better with some food in your stomach, I'd bet." She followed Connie into the kitchen and sat listlessly to the side as she watched her prepare a snack.

Leslie wandered in a short while later. Connie cast her a warning look, but Leslie ignored her mother. She walked straight to Sam's side and threw her arms around her, trapping her in a tight hug. "Are you okay?" Leslie asked, her eyes searching Sam's.

She forced a smile for Leslie. "I'll be fine," Sam assured her. "I'm just worried about my friends."

"Of course you are," Leslie said. She looked sheepishly at her mom, then dropped her voice so Connie couldn't hear. "I heard some of what you told my dad before, in his study," she admitted. "Did you really mean it? Did you see that other woman get killed?"

Sam was too exhausted to be angry with Leslie. "Didn't your parents teach you it was impolite to eavesdrop?" Sam teased, the hint of a real smile playing on her lips.

Leslie smiled sheepishly. "I didn't mean to," she asserted, "but I was walking by and I heard the three of you talking. I couldn't really help it."

"It's okay," Sam sighed. She really didn't want to talk about it anymore, but Leslie continued to gaze at her expectantly. Sam took a deep breath, trying to decide what to say to the girl, when the front doorbell rang.

"Who could that be?" Connie wondered aloud, stepping past Sam and Leslie. "I'll be right back."

Sam felt suddenly edgy and nervous. She stood and followed Connie, several paces behind. When she reached the hall, Connie was pulling open the front door. Sam froze as a wave of terror washed over her. She started to open her mouth to call out to Connie, to tell her not to open the door, but her words froze in her throat. She watched as the door swung open and Connie greeted their visitor.

~ ~ ~

Dan and Patrick were disappointed when they returned to the police station. There had been little change in the state of things during their absence. Detectives and other officers streamed in and out of the conference room in a steady stream. Virtually every officer in the department, along with some pulled from neighboring precincts, were working diligently trying to find Jennifer. Everyone still thought they were searching for Tony only as a suspect, a person of interest, but Patrick knew better.

He also knew there was no way he and Dan could convey this to their fellow officers without looking foolish. Patrick had been worried when Sam insisted on telling Dan about her visions in the mirror, but they had been lucky and were not met with skepticism. Patrick knew they would not be met with such understanding again. It was difficult to stand by and watch the officers working. Patrick wanted to shout out to them to hurry up. Tony was wounded, possibly dying, and they had to hurry. But his better judgment called for caution so Patrick held his tongue.

Dan was having an equally difficult time, but for different reasons. Now that he was away from Sam's haunted eyes, he started to doubt what he had believed wholeheartedly only a short while ago. He knew, deep down, Sam was telling the truth, but doubt had begun to ooze into his mind. The urgency to find Jen and Tony was still there, but he couldn't see Tony as a victim any more. His suspicions of the man had taken root again.

As Dan moved throughout the room talking to other officers and obtaining updates, Patrick sat quietly in a corner observing the organized chaos around him. He found himself staring at the timeline and photographs tacked to the wall. Emily's face smiled back at him. As he continued to stare at the old photo, his eyes glassing over slightly and he was struck by a sudden realization. Although all the women killed had red hair, like Emily's, Jen herself bore a striking semblance to the killer's first victim. It was subtle and one had to take into account the years that separated them, but the similarities were there.

Until now, Patrick hadn't understood why the killer had altered his routine so suddenly. Kidnapping had never been part of his program, choosing instead to befriend and then ensnare his victims. But this time, he had taken Jen away, hidden her somewhere. Why? Patrick thought he understood now.

He wanted time alone with her, to bond with her. He saw Emily in Jen and was eager to recreate some aspect of his past. It would also explain Tony's kidnap as well. Perhaps this killer had known of Tony's past with Emily. He might view Tony as competition, of sorts, and would want to make him suffer for his closeness to first Emily and now Jen.

Patrick had no real basis for his speculations, but his intuition told him he was probably onto something. If he was right, it might buy them more time.

"Dan?" Patrick called, motioning the detective over. "Did you guys go back and interview Emily's parents again?"

Dan nodded. "Yes, why?"

"Can I see the tapes?"

"Sure. But why?"

"Just give me a minute, okay? I'll explain later… if I'm right."

Dan could sense the younger man's eagerness and submitted without further question. He left to retrieve the tapes Patrick would need, then set him up in an adjacent room to watch the interviews. He left Patrick to himself.

On the video monitor, Carmen and Phil sat stiffly in their chairs, a detective seated directly across the table. The years had dulled the pain of their daughter's murder, but being back and questioned about it all over again was obviously hard on them. They had left years ago, moving north into Washington. Being back had stirred many memories. Patrick sat through the entire interview, listening to their recollections of that night, but he heard nothing that struck him. Disappointed, he sat back in his chair. He had hit a dead end. The thought of Tony somehow as competition nagged at him, but he could find no basis for his feelings. Then he had another thought.

Pulling his cell phone from his pocket, he quickly dialed. The phone rang only once before it was pounced upon, the woman's quavering, worried voice saying, "Sam? Is that you?"

"No Sally, it's Patrick."

"Where's Sam? Is she all right? I saw the article about Jen. I've been so worried. Have you found her?" Sally's normally chipper voice was heavy with concern.

"No, I'm afraid we're still searching for them." Although she said nothing, Patrick could sense her disappointment on the other end of the line.

"Listen Sally," Patrick explained, "I've thought of something and I don't know if you can help me, but…"

"Spit it out," she urged.

"Well, it's about Emily and Tony. Anthony," he corrected. "I don't know if Sam told you, but her editor, Tony, is the same man who was seeing Emily. He went by Anthony back then."

"Oh my," Sally breathed. "I didn't know. I always felt sorry for that boy. I met him once. Very nice kid. I always thought they came down on him too hard after Emily died." Sally paused for a moment and then asked, "You don't think he has anything to do with this, do you? He seemed like such a nice man."

"No," Patrick assured her. "Actually, I think he's in just as much trouble as Jen. That's why I called you."

"I don't follow."

"Before Emily started dating Tony, do you know if she was seeing anybody else? Or was there someone who had asked her out and she refused?"

Sally sighed. "That was a long time ago, Patrick. I really don't recall."

"I understand. But I really need help on this. I hate to ask, but could you…" Patrick paused, hesitant to ask.

"You'd like me to call Carmen and Phil? See if they remember anything?"

"Would you?" Patrick said eagerly. "I know they came back down for another interview, I watched the tapes, but there was nothing mentioned about Emily possibly seeing anybody else."

"I think Carmen and Phil both blamed that poor boy." Sally sighed. "As soon as they heard the police were questioning him, I don't think they gave anything else a second look. In their mind, he was responsible. It's a shame really, I raised Phil better than that."

Patrick thanked Sally and she assured him she'd call them right away. She'd let him know if she found anything out. With his call complete, Patrick went back to the conference room with Dan and the others.

"Are you going to tell me what you were looking for?" Dan asked.

Patrick shrugged. "I don't think it's anything."

"We don't have much of anything anyway," Dan assured him, "so I'd like to hear what you're thinking."

Patrick gestured to the wall and Emily's picture. "Why did he change his routine?" Patrick started. Dan shrugged. "Well, we know all his victims were similar, but look at Emily." He stepped briskly to the other end of the room and tore Jen's recently added picture from the wall. He held it up right next to Emily's and said, "Now look at Jen."

With the two pictures side by side it was easier to identify their similarities. They had the same eyes; the colors were different, but their shape was identical. Although their mouths were different, they both wore the same easy grin. Emily wore her hair longer, but the straight red locks were the same shade.

"I think he sees Jen as a substitute for Emily. Emily was special to him. She was his first and I'm sure he knew her more closely than any of his other victims. It's why he's treating Jen different. It's why he took her. He wants to spend more time with her, maybe capture something from his past."

Dan stood rapt. Several others nearby had stopped what they were doing to listen too. "But," Dan questioned, "if Sam's right, why did he take Tony too? Wouldn't he just be a distraction? Get in the way?"

"Not necessarily," Patrick sighed. "I think Emily was seeing someone else, besides Tony, back then. What if this guy harbors some grudge against Tony? Now he sees Tony and Jen together. Maybe he wants to hurt Tony for coming between them. First him and Emily, and now with Jen."

"My God," Dan breathed, sinking into a nearby chair.

"That's why I wanted to see the tapes," Patrick explained, "to see if her parents mentioned anyone else Emily might've been seeing or hanging out with."

"Did they?"

Patrick shook his head. "But I called Sam's grandmother. She's going to make some calls for me, ask around, see if she can dig anything up."

Dan's head was spinning. Sure, Patrick's ideas were only conjecture, but they made a certain kind of sense. He looked at the young man across from him and said, "Good thinking."

Patrick shrugged his shoulders modestly. He began to pace the room impatiently, holding his cell phone eagerly in his hand, waiting for it to ring. Each minute that passed seemed an eternity. He kept imagining Tony lying somewhere, bleeding, maybe dying. Finally, his phone rang and he answered.

"This is Patrick."

"Patrick, it's Sally. I'm sorry, but I couldn't reach them. I left a message, but I don't know when they'll call me back."

Patrick was crestfallen. "That's okay," he lied. "Just call me as soon as you get to talk to them."

"I will."

Chapter Twenty-Two

"Joe?" Sam said, stepping closer to the open door. She was just able to see him over Connie's shoulder.

Before Connie could invite him in, Joe Torrance swept past her, stepping quickly to Sam and wrapping his arms around her in a bear hug. "I've been so worried about you, Angel. How are you holding up?"

"I'm okay," Sam assured him. "I'm just really worried about Jen and Tony."

"Of course you are. She's your best friend." Joe turned apologetically to Connie. "I'm sorry, I didn't mean to intrude. I'm Sergeant Torrance." He held his hand out and she shook it. "You must be Dan's wife, Connie?"

"Yes, yes I am."

"Joe is Patrick's partner," Sam explained. "We've known each other for a long time."

"Would you like to join us in the kitchen?" Connie offered. "I was just fixing Sam something to eat."

"I don't want to intrude."

"Nonsense. Come on." Connie closed and locked the door, then led the way back into the kitchen.

Leslie was still sitting at the small table, waiting for Sam to explain about what she'd overheard earlier, and was surprised to see they had a guest.

"Joe," Sam said, "this is Dan's daughter, Leslie. Leslie, this is Joe Torrance. He works with Patrick and your dad."

"Pleased to meet you," Leslie said.

Joe pressed Sam down into a chair, then pulled one up next to her. "Have you heard anything?"

Sam shook her head. "Dan and Patrick went back to the station a little while ago, but I haven't heard from them yet." Sam's eyes darted around the room, an anxious fear building behind them. "What if we don't find them Joe?"

"Don't talk like that, Sugar. Everything's going to turn out fine, you'll see. I just can't believe Tony would do something like this."

Sam didn't have the energy to contradict him, so she just smiled weakly at his reassurances. His words were spoken from the heart, she knew, but she couldn't believe things were going to work out like everyone kept telling her. She wanted to believe Jen and Tony would be found safely, but a nagging voice in her head kept telling her it couldn't happen. The image of Tony, shot and wounded, hounded at her.

"Listen Sugar," Joe said, standing again, "I only wanted to check in on you and I don't want to impose. I'm going to get back to work." He leaned in and kissed Sam on the forehead, then said farewell to Connie and Leslie. Connie walked him to the front door and saw him on his way.

Sam was thankful for his visit, but his sudden appearance seemed odd and out of place. She was amazed he'd gone so far out of his way to stop by and see her when he could just have easily called her or checked in with Patrick. She was glad to have seen him though, and his departure left her feeling more alone than ever.

As Connie escorted Joe to the door, Leslie resumed her expectant appraisal of Sam. Questions burned at her, yet she held her tongue, knowing Sam would tell her if and when she felt ready. She was patient, like her father. Sam could see the questions behind Leslie's eyes, but she tried to ignore them. Instead, she turned to look out the kitchen window. She caught a fleeting glimpse of Joe's car as he pulled away into the growing darkness.

"I'm sorry," Sam said, as Connie re-entered the room, "I'm going to go upstairs and try to get some sleep. I'm sorry you went to any trouble." She indicated the items Connie had removed from the refrigerator.

"Don't worry about that," Connie assured her, "it was no trouble. You just let me know if you need anything."

Sam nodded her thanks and left the kitchen. It felt oddly comforting to be alone with her worry and grief. She'd been surrounded by people since this whole thing began to unravel, but she'd felt alone none-the-less. Now, to be on her own felt appropriate. She could cry freely, wail, pound her fists in rage, exhibiting her tumultuous emotions in any way she desired.

It was amidst one of these fits that she was startled by the vibration of her cell phone in her back pocket. Pulling it free quickly, hoping it was Patrick calling with news, she was surprised to hear her grandmother's voice on the other end of the line.

"Sam, darling, how are you holding up?" Sally inquired.

Sam knew better than to try to lie to her grandma. "Not well," was her frank admission. "I feel so helpless."

"I do too," Sally commiserated. There was a moment's silence while both women reflected on their shared impotence. When Sally spoke next, it was with forced enthusiasm. "I spoke to Patrick a little while ago," she admitted.

"You did?"

"He wanted me to ask a few questions of Phil and Carmen."

"What?" Sam couldn't fathom what information Patrick could be seeking from her aunt and uncle.

"He had some questions about Emily's past. He wanted to know if she might have been seeing someone other than Tony back then."

"Really?" Sam was intrigued, her imagination piqued. "What did you find out?"

"Nothing yet. I couldn't reach them," Sally explained. "I promised Patrick I'd ask them when they call me back."

Sam was quietly disappointed. She didn't really know the reasons behind Patrick's query, but she was hopeful the information he gleaned would help find their friends. She spoke to her grandmother for a few more minutes. It felt good to share her worries and fears with someone else who knew and loved Jen almost as much as she did. Finally, assuring Sally she was safe, Sam said her farewell.

Next, she called Patrick, curious about his sudden interest in Emily's past. She waited impatiently for him to answer his phone. When he did pick up, his voice was tinged with both worry and fatigue.

"Is something wrong?" he asked quickly.

"No," she assured him, "but I just talked to Sally. She mentioned you'd called her with more questions about Emily. What's that about?"

Patrick hesitated. "It's probably nothing," he sighed dismissively.

"She said you were asking if Emily might have been seeing someone else. What are you thinking?"

"Well," he began, "why did this guy suddenly change his routine and kidnap Jen? And not just her, but Tony as well?"

"I don't know," Sam admitted.

"Neither do I, but I started thinking if this were someone that Emily had a past with, someone that she perhaps passed over for Tony back then… It would explain why he took them both, why he's spending time with both of them."

"My God!" Sam breathed.

"Don't get excited," Patrick warned. "I'm probably way off base."

"But it makes sense, doesn't it?" Sam pressed.

"I think we just *want* it to make sense," Patrick said half-heartedly. "Even if I'm right, who's to say anyone would even know who this guy is." His voice was filled with doubt.

"Will you call me if you find anything out?" Sam asked.

"Of course. Listen, I'd better go. Try and get some rest, okay?"

"Yeah, I'll try." She started to say goodbye to Patrick, then added, "I almost forgot, Joe stopped by to check on me. He should be on his way to the station now."

"Good. It'll be nice to have him here." He dropped his voice a little before continuing, "Everyone here thinks Tony's behind this. We've tried suggesting to a few people that Tony's a victim as well, but there's too much evidence pointing directly to him. Dan and I don't really know how to convince anybody otherwise."

Sam laughed a little ruefully. "No, I imagine they'd think you're crazy."

Patrick understood her jest and let it go without comment. "At least Joe knows Tony a little. Maybe he'll believe us?"

Sam told him she loved him, wished him luck, and then hung up the phone. She curled forlornly on the bed, intending only to lay down for a few minutes. She closed her eyes wearily and, within moments, drifted off into a restless sleep.

~ ~ ~

Jen knew they were alone. She had heard no noises from outside for many hours. It sounded like night time in the forest to her. She heard the forlorn cries of night birds calling. There were none of the sounds she was accustomed to in the city.

Tony was conscious again, but unable to actually speak to Jen. With her blindfold in place, she knew very little about their situation, however they had been able to work out a rudimentary means of communicating with one another.

Although he'd apparently been gagged again before their captor left, it didn't prevent him from answering questions as Jen posed them. She had to ask questions that could be answered with a yes or a no. If he did not respond, the answer was no. A grunt or other noise indicated a yes. This way, Jen was able to learn much about what had transpired.

"Are you hurt badly?" Tony's response to this was mixed. Jen was met with a long silence followed by a faint grunt.

"Where were you hit?" she asked. Then, remembering he couldn't answer that, she started to list body parts.

"The arm?" Silence.

"The chest?" Thankfully, more silence.

"The leg?" Tony groaned. Jen was quietly relieved. It could have been much worse.

"Are you still bleeding?" A small grunt.

"A lot?" Silence.

"Do you know where we are?" Tony was mute.

"We're not in the city, are we?" More silence from Tony.

"We're in the woods somewhere?" This time, she got another mixed response: a long silence followed by a quiet groan. She gathered that he was unsure, but she thought she was right.

Jen struggled a minute with her bonds before speaking again. "He really killed Emily, didn't he?" This time, Tony's grunt sounded more like a sob.

"I'm so sorry," Jen whispered.

It was a long time before she spoke again. "He's going to kill us too, isn't he?" Jen could hear the quiet creaking of the ropes binding Tony as he shifted uncomfortably, but he made no other noise, refusing to acknowledge the inevitable.

"I love you," she stated.

He answered her, his series of groans clearly translating to, "I love you too."

They both lay in silence until Tony could just make out the faint glow of sunlight building outside the room in which they were captive. He feared this day would be their last and only hoped, more for Jen's sake than his own, that it would end quickly.

~ ~ ~

Sam's dreams were filled with memories of what she'd seen in her cousin's mirror. Repeatedly, her mind returned to the night she saw him looking at the pictures of herself, Patrick, and Jen at the Christmas tree lot. She tossed feverishly, trying to rid herself of the image, but her mind persisted. She couldn't dispel the sight.

Once again she saw the office, dark except for the small desk lamp. She saw his bare shoulders, a shadowy blotch visible between his shoulder blades. Sam bolted awake and upright in bed, her eyes popping open in shock and surprise.

Dan had asked her if she'd seen anything distinctive about the man. She'd said no. Now, panting heavily, she realized she was wrong. She had seen something unique. She struggled to remember what the image, the tattoo, was. Tears of frustration began to build in her eyes as she struggled with the hazy memory.

She began to pace the small room, laboring with the effort of recalling the memory again. Try as she might, she couldn't pull anything recognizable from the memory. She was gripped with an intense feeling of helplessness and the tears started to fall again.

She laid down again, curling into a ball. Slowly, her sobs faded and she drifted back into her restless sleep.

~ ~ ~

The sun had fully risen. Jen could feel the change in temperature and worried what the day would bring for herself and Tony. Despite their limited exchange overnight, she was still worried about his wound. She remained hopeful one of them could slip their bonds, but with each passing hour they remained captive her hopes were continually diminished. More than anything, she feared the return of their abductor and what that would mean for Tony.

His animosity toward Tony unnerved her in ways she could not explain. Their situation was terrifying, but when Jen thought about the danger they were in, her own fears were dwarfed by her fears for Tony. She was terrorized by thoughts of what this man intended for both of them, but she knew Tony would be subjected to more before it was over. She was snapped out of her reverie by a sound outside. There were footsteps approaching.

"Tony," she hissed, her voice a harsh whisper, "He's come back." He didn't respond, but she could hear him struggling against his ropes in a last, frantic effort.

When the door groaned open, Tony immediately halted his efforts, closing his eyes and feigning unconsciousness. As yet, he'd been unable to see the face of their tormentor, he'd been wearing a mask during his last visit to their prison. Tony hoped by pretending to sleep, he may be able to glimpse who this man was. He clung to the hope that, before he died, he could find some way to help Jen, tell her who was responsible, and she could put an end to all this. It was a faint, futile hope, but he clung to it desperately.

Beneath his eyelashes, he watched as thick, black work boots made their way across the room over to the bed upon which Jen lay. Tony could hear Jen's breath coming in terrified, ragged gasps. She tried to remain calm, but she was losing her grip in the thick silence. She knew he was standing there, watching her, and it unnerved her. Finally, she spoke out, her voice tremulous with fear.

"What do you want from us?"

She was met with silence, but could hear his breathing quicken. She shuddered as she thought about what he imagined doing to her. "You're going to love me," was all he finally said.

Then, in absolute silence, he reached forward and ran his hand across the flat of her stomach, down to the waistband of her jeans. She bucked beneath his touch, trying in vain to throw his hand off of her. But try as she might, his hand always returned, never straying inappropriately, but menacing with its steady touch.

After a long while he stopped and she heard his footsteps move back across the room, to where Tony lay. He kicked out heavily, connecting with Tony's midsection causing him to grunt and cough thickly behind his gag.

"Are you awake, Anthony?" He spat Tony's name like it was poison. Reaching down and pulling the gag away forcefully, he repeated, "Are you awake?"

Tony rolled his head to the side to look up at him. As before, he could not see his face. Piercing eyes glared at him from behind the mask. Tony watched, unable to stop him, as a heavy boot fell upon the wound in his thigh, pressing forcefully down. Tony howled as ribbons of pain snaked up his body.

"Stop it!" Jen screamed. "Please stop it!" Her protests were met with jeering laughter, but she continued to scream, pleading with him to leave Tony alone.

"Do you hear her?" he spat at Tony. "She wants me to stop. Should I stop?"

Tony didn't want to give him the satisfaction of an answer, but his head nodded despite himself and he breathed, "Yes."

Removing his boot, he knelt down at Tony's side. Warmth was spreading across his leg again and Tony knew he was bleeding heavily once more. His captor leaned in close and Tony could smell a faint hint of liquor on his breath.

"Tell her you love her," he hissed into Tony's ear. When he didn't immediately respond, Tony was rewarded with a heavy fist planted in his stomach. "Say you love her," he was instructed again.

"Jen," Tony called, trying to calm her. "Jen, it's going to be okay."

"That's not what I told you to say," he hissed.

Quickly, before another blow could fall Tony said, "I love you Jen."

Their captor stood, waiting anxiously for her response. Jen fought back her tears until she could find her voice. "I love you too Tony."

Jen barely had time to realize her mistake. In an instant, she heard a commotion, the metallic click of the gun, and her captor spat, "You didn't learn last time?"

"No! I love *you*! I love *you*!" she screamed, but it was too late. Gunfire rang out inside the small room.

Jen continued to scream "I love *you*!" over and over again, as the echoes of the gunshot faded away. These were the words he had been waiting to hear. Tony writhed and cried in pain at his feet. As much as he enjoyed the other man's pain, he yearned to revel in Jennifer's admissions of love. Reaching into his pocket, he withdrew a needle and syringe. Swiftly, he sank the needle into Tony's neck, pushing the plunger steadily inward. As the medication began to course through Tony's system, his vision faded to black, his pain disappeared, and he sank into a drug-induced oblivion.

Tony's sudden silence brought a new round of wails from Jen. "Oh my God! Oh my God!" she repeated, her breathing out of control. "Tony? Tony? Oh my God! What have you done?"

Moving to her side, he spoke tenderly to her. "I haven't killed him. Yet. But displease me and that may change."

Jen shuddered at the new tenderness in his voice. She felt his weight settle onto the bed beside her. His hand returned to the bare flesh of her belly, resting there lightly. "I want you to love me," he whispered.

Hot tears poured from Jen's eyes as her mind raced, trying to understand what was going on. She needed desperately to keep him happy, to prevent him from hurting Tony any more. Screwing up her courage she said, "I do love you."

Abruptly, his lips were on hers, pressing down with a tenderness that surprised her. The feeling of his lips upon hers brought bile to the back of her throat, but she forced it back, marshaling herself to remain calm.

Withdrawing his mouth from hers, he whispered, "I'm so glad you chose me."

Jen was grateful for the blindfold then, as it helped to hide her tears. She had never hated anyone in her life, not really, yet now the feeling filled her entirely. She wanted nothing more than to hurt this monster, to take revenge for the brutalities he had visited upon herself, upon Tony, and upon all those other women. She prayed God would grant her the opportunity to make this man suffer.

A sudden sound startled her, a soft metallic click. She shivered when she felt cold metal slip against her skin, beneath the fabric and elastic of her bra. Realization dawned on her as the knife blade cut through the fabric and it fell away leaving her completely exposed. She could tell he was staring at her, despite the blindfold. His eyes seemed to bore into her as he stared.

Relief washed over her as he lifted his weight from the bed. "Wait here," he instructed, laughing quietly at his own sick joke. She heard him retreat to the door, then away. She assumed he must have a car nearby, but at a considerable distance as she never heard the sounds of an engine.

As soon as he was gone, she began her useless struggles against the ropes at her feet. With her hands, she continued to feel along the wooden headboard her handcuffs were attached to, testing the rough wood for weaknesses. She had to free herself and get help. No one would find her. Nobody was coming to save her. She was utterly alone.

~ ~ ~

He moved swiftly along his makeshift forest trail, back toward his hidden car. It was parked just off the road, about a half mile from the cabin, obscured from passerby by dense brush. He'd left his camera behind and he needed a record of his time with Jennifer. He wanted something to remember this special time once it was over.

His hurried footsteps halted not far from the road when he heard voices nearby. Frozen, he ducked behind a large fir tree, straining his ears to hear.

"It was that way," a man said, "I'm sure of it."

"Yeah, I heard it too," his companion, a woman, agreed. "Let's get back to the car."

"But someone could be hurt," the man persisted. "That was a gunshot."

"I know. Let's just go back to the car and call someone. Please?"

"What if it's that woman everyone is looking for?"

"I know! But if it was a gunshot, we need to call the police. Let's just go, *please*?" He listened as they moved away from him, back toward the road, to an area further up the blacktop where a trailhead for a hike through the forest began.

Cursing his poor luck, he crept quietly toward his car. He hadn't expected anyone to be out here in the dead of winter. If these strangers called the police, it would be unwise to linger. He would be prevented any further time with Jennifer and his revenge and torment of Tony would not be completed. He could only flee, in the hope of saving himself for another opportunity.

~ ~ ~

Patrick and Dan came home late the following morning. Nothing new had come about overnight, and Patrick was frustrated he hadn't heard back from Sally. He'd known Sally wouldn't be able to get in touch with Emily's parents in the dead of night, but he was impatient for their response. Both men were exhausted beyond words.

Connie and Leslie were in the kitchen, cleaning up after a quiet breakfast, when they arrived. Dan ushered Patrick upstairs, instructing him to get some rest, then went to join his family.

Trudging upstairs, Patrick pushed open the door to their guestroom quietly, hoping Sam was asleep and that he wouldn't disturb her. As much as he longed to see her and wrap her protectively in his arms, he couldn't bear the thought of looking into her expectant eyes and trying to explain that they were nowhere closer to finding Jen and Tony than before.

To his chagrin, she was sitting on the edge of the bed, facing the door as if waiting for him. Wordlessly, he sat down at her side and put one of his arms over her shoulder, pulling her close to him. He buried his face against her hair, breathing deep, taking comfort from the smell of her. He didn't want to talk, he was exhausted both physically and mentally. Sam understood and she let him hold her tightly as occasionally his frame shook with the effort of holding back his own tears.

Long minutes passed in silence before they were roused by the sound of heavy footsteps pounding down the hallway toward their door. Dan burst in, his face a jumble of emotions Sam couldn't decipher.

"What's wrong?" she and Patrick asked together, standing up in shock at his sudden appearance.

"We may have a lead."

Sam's legs gave way at his words. She struggled to breathe. Her mouth moved, trying to form the questions that pounded feverishly to the rhythm of her heart.

Dan looked meaningfully at Patrick. "Couple heading out for a hike to Ramona Falls heard a gunshot, called the police. It's not that far from here. There's a unit heading out there already, but we're not far, so I was going to go check it out. You coming?"

Patrick moved for the door but stopped when he noted Sam close at his heels. "You should stay here," he instructed.

"Like hell," Sam insisted, "I'm coming with you."

Patrick looked to Dan for reinforcement, but Dan nodded wearily. "Come on."

The car ride from Dan's home in Sandy was intolerably long. Sam tried to keep her hopefulness in check, knowing she was likely to be disappointed when their lead turned out to be nothing. Yet she could not help but feel excitement that, at last, she was doing something, not just sitting around moping while others searched for her friends. As they wound their way up the twisting, turning roads, Sam watched the landscape around them pass by in a blur. She barely noted the beautiful, wet landscape around her.

"How much farther?" Patrick asked, voicing Sam's own impatience.

"Shouldn't be too far," Dan assured them, slowing to negotiate a steep curve. As they rounded the bend, Sam could see a car parked in a nearby turnout. Dan pulled off the road, stopped behind the other vehicle, and climbed out quickly.

"Are you the ones who called?" Dan inquired of the worried looking man and woman who stood out of the first car.

"Yes," the man stated.

"Do you mind if we ask to see your badge?" the woman asked, fear and nervousness etching her simple features.

"Not at all," Dan assured them, removing his badge and showing it to them freely. Sam and Patrick had climbed out of the car and walked up a few paces behind Dan. Sam was surprised they had made it out there before the other unit.

When the couple saw Sam, their eyes widened in surprise. "You're that reporter, aren't you?" the woman stated.

"Yes." Sam smiled weakly.

"I'm Detective Johnston," Dan told the couple, "this is Sergeant Logan, and this, as you know, is Samantha Williams."

"Sam, please," she interjected.

"Sam," Dan conceded. "What are your names?" Dan removed a small notepad from his coat pocket and took down some notes.

"Taylor Walden," the man said, "and this is my girlfriend Abigail."

"I was told you heard gunshots?" Dan asked.

"Just one," Taylor stated, waving his arm to the west, "in that direction."

"Okay. I'd like to ask you two to wait here. There should be another unit on the way. I'd like you to let them know where we are and what you've heard." Both Taylor and Abigail nodded their understanding. Neither wanted to go into the forest looking for trouble.

Dan turned to Sam next. "You're going to wait here too," he stated in a tone that told Sam there would be no arguing the point.

She tried anyway. "What if Jen's out there? I need to be there."

"No," Dan stated. "You will wait right here, understand?"

Sam didn't respond right away, so Patrick said, "Please Sam, just wait here."

"All right," she sighed in dejection.

She stood in the cold watching Dan and Patrick disappear into the darkness of the trees. She stood stock still in the frigid air long after she had lost sight of them through the underbrush. She barely noticed her companions shivering in the cold.

"If you don't mind," Taylor stated, "we're going to get back in the car... to stay warm." Sam only nodded numbly.

"Would you like to join us?" Abigail asked.

"No, but thank you."

Alone now, she began to pace along the fog line, walking back and forth between the two cars. She strained her ears to hear any sound from the forest depths which might cue her in to what Dan and Patrick may find. The woods were quiet. Her hypersensitive ears did, however, pick up the drone of a car engine in the distance. She turned her gaze expectantly down the road in anticipation of the approaching car.

It wasn't a marked police cruiser, like she expected. Instead, she saw a navy blue sedan pull off the road behind Dan's SUV, from which Joe Torrance emerged.

"Joe?" Sam exclaimed in surprise. "What are you doing out here?"

"I heard about the call. I wasn't too far away, so I figured I'd come check it out."

Sam hugged Joe thankfully. "I'm glad you came."

"Where're Dan and Patrick?"

"They went into the woods, told me to stay here and wait for the other officers."

Joe nodded toward the car where Taylor and Abigail sat. "Are they the ones that called it in?" Sam nodded. "Come on, let's go ask them a few questions."

Joe approached the car with Sam at his side. He tapped lightly on the glass, causing Abigail to jump. When Taylor dropped the window, Joe apologized. "I didn't mean to scare you."

"That's okay," Taylor assured Joe.

"Guys," Sam interjected, "this is Sergeant Joe Torrance. Joe, this is Taylor and Abigail."

"What did you guys see?"

"We didn't see anything," Taylor said, "but we heard a gunshot."

"We were going to go snow shoeing," Abigail explained. "We'd heard the falls are really pretty in the winter. When we got to the trailhead, we were climbing out of the car and heard a gunshot."

"I wanted to go check it out," Taylor assured them, looking pointedly at Sam when he said this, "but Abigail was scared."

"I was not," she protested.

"It was smart to wait here," Joe said seriously, almost berating Taylor with his words. "You don't know what you might've stumbled into out there. You could've gotten yourselves hurt. Better to let us check it out." Abigail smiled warmly at Joe at these words.

"Now, Sugar," Joe said, turning to face Sam, "let's go see if there's anything to get excited about."

Sam hesitated for a moment. She wanted to go, but Dan had been so adamant she remain behind. She pushed her indecision aside and strode purposefully into the forest beside Joe.

"Which direction did they go?" Joe asked. Sam pointed vaguely to the west, the same direction Taylor had indicated earlier. She could just pick out a rudimentary trail through the brush. It could've been a game trail for all she knew, but they followed it in silence for quite some time, Joe leading a few paces ahead. Sam was beginning to wonder if they were on the right track when, suddenly, the trees began to thin around them and she could just make out the shape of a building ahead.

"Joe," she breathed, her voice barely audible above the hammering of her heart. "There's a cabin up there."

"I see it," he replied. He pointed to a large fir tree. "You wait here, you understand?" Sam nodded and followed his instructions. She held her breath as she watched him approach the small, dark structure.

Her knees were quaking as she stood there waiting. It seemed an eternity as Joe crossed the small clearing and approached the single door. He made a pass around the outside of the cabin first, keeping his back to the exterior wall, scanning the surrounding forest for anything unusual. When he completed his circuit of the building, he looked meaningfully toward the spot where he'd left Sam, making a silent gesture with his hand, reminding her to stay put. Then he shouldered the door open quickly.

Chapter Twenty-Three

Time stood still. Sam kept waiting to hear something, anything from the tiny building. Finally, Joe's face emerged from the darkness and he called, "Get in here Sam. Quick!"

Immediately she ran from her position against the tree, worry beginning to infuse her again. "What it is?" she called.

"They're here."

"Patrick! Dan!" she screamed as she ran, "We've found them!" She hoped wherever they were they could hear her and would come. Her legs pounding, she closed the final twenty yards to the cabin and burst into the gloom.

She tripped on something just inside the door and called out in fear when she realized it was Tony's prone form. He looked dead. He was too quiet, way too still. In her panic, she screamed, but the sound of Jen's voice in the room brought her back to the moment. She swallowed hard, standing again, and made her way to the small bed. Joe was busy trying to unlock the cuffs that held her fast.

"Jen!" Sam cried, falling onto the bed beside her and tearing wildly at the ropes on her feet. "Thank God! Are you okay?"

Joe had removed her blindfold already and Sam ached at the sight of her friend's face. Her lip was split and she had a bruise building below her left eye. Tears streamed from Jen's eyes. They were a mixture of fear and relief, as well as worry for Tony. Her gaze continued to dart his direction while they worked at freeing her. Sam cursed in frustration as she fumbled with the tight knots.

"Is he okay?" Jen croaked, staring in shock at Tony.

"I don't know," Sam admitted.

"Please," she begged, "take care of him. I'm fine."

"I'll take care of her," Joe assured Sam as he finally released the metal cuffs from Jen's battered wrists. Torn, Sam left her best friend's side and knelt on the floor beside Tony.

He looked terrible. His breathing was shallow and he lay in a pool of his own blood. From the way the blood soaked his clothes, Sam knew he'd been shot at least twice. His left leg was soaked, his denim jeans now rust colored from blood. She knew he was hurt bad, but this wasn't the wound that worried her. It was the red puddle growing beneath is abdomen that had her heart racing in panic.

Sam turned to Joe. She'd never seen anyone wounded like this. She didn't know what to do. "Joe?"

Joe looked her general direction, but didn't really seem to take in the gravity of Tony's situation. "What do I do?" Sam asked.

Before Joe could answer, Jen asked, "Is he okay?" She too could see the blood, even though Sam was trying to block her view of it.

"He's going to be fine." Sam choked on the lie, but she told it anyway. She reached a hand out and stroked Tony tenderly on the side of the face. *Please God*, she thought, *let him be okay.*

A noise outside caught Sam's attention. Patrick was calling frantically somewhere outside. She looked back to Joe, who was still working on the ropes binding Jen. "Joe, can you please? I don't want to leave him," Sam explained.

Joe nodded his assent. "I'll be right back," he assured Jen, then closed the distance to the door in a few hurried steps. Sam could hear him outside, his loud voice guiding Patrick and Dan to their location.

When Patrick and Dan pushed their way into the small room, Sam sighed in relief. Dan seemed to realize the urgency of Tony's state immediately. More roughly than he intended, he pushed Sam aside and removed a small pocket knife from his belt. He cut quickly through the ropes binding Tony to the chair, then started to cut and rip at the clothing covering his wounds. He sliced straight up the leg of Tony's jeans, exposing the angry bullet wound to sight, then ripped through his tee-shirt.

"I need something clean," Dan instructed. Patrick understood and quickly removed his coat, then the shirt he wore beneath it. "There's a jug of water and a first aid kit in the back of my rig," he told Patrick as he pulled his jacket back on and zipped it closed. "While you're out there, try to call an ambulance. If you can't get cell reception, send those other two down toward town and have them call for help as soon as they can, then tell them to get back up here to guide them in." Wordlessly, Patrick nodded his understanding, then turned and began to run back through the woods to where their cars were parked.

Dan used his knife to deftly cut Patrick's shirt in two then placed one of the pieces on Tony's leg. "Sam, hold this here, firm." She did as she was told, gingerly at first, but when Dan repeated, "Firm," she pressed harder. Tony groaned a little but did not wake.

"Is he going to be okay?" Sam asked, keeping her voice low, trying to prevent Jen from hearing her.

"He's hurt pretty bad," Dan admitted. He had begun to swab gently at the wound on Tony's midsection. The bullet had entered right below his ribcage and, from the way he was breathing, Dan feared his lung was punctured. He had no way of knowing how extensive the injury was, but he knew it wasn't good. He wished Patrick would hurry with the water and that they wouldn't have to wait too long for an ambulance.

Holding steady pressure to the wound on Tony's leg, Sam turned to look back at Jen. Her feet were still bound, but she was sitting up on the dirty bed, staring in worry while Dan continued to tend to Tony as best he could. Joe had removed his jacket and, as Sam watched, he guided Jen's arms into the sleeves providing her with some cover. Jen didn't even seem aware she'd been laying there half clothed, but the moment the warmth of the jacket enveloped her, she began to shake and shudder with the memory of her exposure. She mumbled her thanks to Joe and he reciprocated by wrapping his arms protectively around her.

"I'd like to take her back to the cars," Joe stated simply.

"I think that's a good idea," Dan agreed. He tossed his knife the short distance to the bed so Joe could cut the stubborn knots and free Jen. His task complete, Joe stood and faced her, blocking her view of Tony.

"Come on honey," Joe coaxed. "Do you think you can stand up for me?"

"I can't leave him here," she protested.

"It's okay Jen," Sam assured her, forcing her voice to sound strong, "Dan and I are going to be here and Patrick will be back any minute. We'll take care of him, I promise."

"But," Jen cried, "I can't."

"Sure you can," Joe soothed, his voice calm and gentle. "You just stand up for me now, okay?" He leaned forward and helped her lift her weight from the bed. Sam saw her legs looked shaky, weak, but she held herself upright.

"Good girl," Joe pronounced. He kept himself solidly in the way of Jen's line of sight so she couldn't see Tony as Dan and Sam continued to minister to his wounds.

"Get her in a car and get her warmed up," Dan instructed. Joe nodded and ushered Jen as quickly as possible out the door. Sam imagined it would take him a while to get Jen back to the road as slowly as she was moving, but she was glad Jen was away from this nightmare place.

While Sam watched them go, Dan was busy scanning the room for something to put beneath Tony's head. Since they'd arrived, his breathing had continued to become more and more erratic, more labored. He didn't see anything which would be of use, so he put his hand to Sam's, indicating he would take over holding pressure on the wound.

"I need you to hold his head," Dan instructed.

Sam quickly followed his instructions and sat down hear Tony's head, placing it tenderly in her lap. She stroked at his hair and muttered soothing words to him. She wasn't sure he could hear her, but she felt better saying something to him. The way he was breathing worried her. It sounded wet, and it rattled. She didn't know what it meant, but felt instinctively it wasn't a good sign.

When Patrick returned, he was short of breath, but continued to move quickly. As he spoke, he removed the cap from the jug he carried and sparingly poured water when and where Dan instructed. For his part, Dan mopped at the wounds gently with gauze from the first aid kit, trying to clean them as best he could. Then he removed a roll of silver duct tape and began wrapping it around and over the gauze-packed wound on Tony's thigh.

"Our unit arrived," Patrick explained while they worked, his voice coming in quick pants as he struggled to catch his breath. "They radioed for an ambulance. They're posted along the trail to guide the paramedics in when they get here."

"Should we move him?" Sam asked uncertainly. "Won't he get help faster if we meet them halfway?"

"No," Dan stated adamantly. "You hear how he's breathing?" Sam nodded. "I think the bullet punctured his lung. We don't know what else could be wrong. I don't want to risk moving him. We might hurt him worse."

Patrick reached up and lifted one of Tony's eyelids. "His pupils are dilated," he remarked in wonder. "That's strange."

"You think he's drugged?" Dan asked.

"I don't know," Patrick admitted, "but you'd think with everything you've done to him, if he was just unconscious he'd have come around by now."

"Yeah," Dan agreed.

Sam felt helpless again and hated the feeling. Tony was badly hurt and there was nothing she could do for him. He'd lost so much blood. She stared at his wounds and at his starkly white skin while her tears splashed onto his pallid forehead.

~ ~ ~

The wait for the paramedics had been interminably long. When the medics had finally covered the half-mile distance from the road and entered the small cabin with their backboard, Sam breathed a deep sigh of relief. She watched helplessly as they transferred Tony to the bright orange board and strapped him down, then followed as they tried to quickly maneuver through the woods.

Once they got him loaded in the ambulance, Sam caught a quick glance of Tony being strapped to monitors and one of the medics trying to start an IV line. Then the doors slammed shut and the ambulance rumbled down the twisting road.

With Tony safely in the hands of the paramedics, Dan turned back to the business of securing his crime scene. He gave explicit orders to the uniformed officers, who in turn radioed back to the station with Dan's instructions. Within the hour, the area would be crawling with technicians and forensics specialists, scouring the woods and the small cabin for evidence.

Meanwhile, Jen sat cowering in Dan's SUV. Joe had not left her side since bringing her back out of the woods. He sat with her in the backseat, his thick arms wrapped tightly and protectively around her. Jen had never felt so grateful in her life. She could still hear the sound of Joe's voice when he entered the cabin and called out her name, just as she could still feel relief continuing to wash over her.

Once, Joe released her from his arms and she began to quake again in fear. "Don't leave me," she pleaded.

Joe smiled and willingly wrapped his arms around her once more. "I'm not going anywhere, Doll."

Sam opened the door and climbed inside the cab with them. "How are you?" she asked.

Jen nodded weakly. "I'll be fine. How's Tony?"

Joe quickly interjected, before Sam could answer. "Don't worry about him right now."

"He'll be fine, I'm sure," Sam reassured her. "But what about you? We need to get you to a hospital."

"I'm fine," Jen insisted.

"No, you're not," Sam started, but Dan opened the door just then, interrupting them. Once more, Joe started to release his hold on Jen and she whimpered fearfully until his arms gripped her tight again.

"Sam," Dan instructed, "I'm going to have Patrick take you and Jen to the hospital so Jen can get checked out and you guys can check on Tony. I need to talk to him as soon as he comes around, you understand? You guys need to call me the minute he wakes up." Sam nodded her understanding.

"I'm going to stay out here for a while," Dan continued. "When I finish here, if I haven't already heard from you, I'll come out to the hospital." Dan looked expectantly to Joe for a moment, and then said, "I could use your help here, if you don't mind."

Joe looked significantly at Jen and then let his arms fall from their protective circle. He started to slide toward the open door, but when Jen started to cry hysterically, he hesitated. Sam quickly tried to take up Joe's station, but it didn't seem to help.

"I think I'd better stay with Jennifer," Joe stated, slipping his arms back around her. Within seconds, Jen started to calm.

Dan consented grudgingly. "All right. You go with them."

Joe reached into one of the pockets of his jacket, which Jen still wore, and fished out his car keys. "You can use my car, bring it to the hospital when you're done." Dan nodded gratefully, then left without another word to await the arrival of his investigative team.

"I'll go get Patrick and we'll get going," Sam explained, leaving the warmth of the cab behind.

Patrick was standing beside Taylor and Abigail's car, thanking them for their help. "You guys have no idea how grateful we all are," he was saying as Sam approached. "If you two hadn't been here, hadn't heard the gunshot…"

Abigail shuddered visibly. "I can't believe they were out there." Taylor draped an arm over her shoulders and pulled his girlfriend close to his side.

"You two may very well have saved our friends' lives," Patrick continued. "We're in your debt." Abigail began to blush and Taylor looked quickly at his feet.

Sam, unable to express her gratitude in words, stepped forward and hugged Abigail briefly, then placed a quick kiss on Taylor's cheek. "When this is all over," Sam said, "I'd like you both to join us for dinner or something. It's the least we can do." She fished one of her business cards from her purse and handed it to Abigail. "Promise me you'll be in touch?"

Abigail smiled warmly. "Of course."

"Now, go take care of your friends," Taylor added.

Patrick smiled, turning to lead Sam back toward Dan's SUV. He stopped to get the keys from Dan, promised to call him as soon as Tony was lucid, then climbed into the driver's seat and headed back toward town.

~ ~ ~

At the hospital, Jen still couldn't seem to tolerate Joe's absence from her side. He was patient and stayed with her the entire time her wounds were dressed. Eventually, she was sent for an x-ray, which confirmed she had two broken ribs. Joe stood supportively by her, holding her hand, never out of contact. Knowing Jen was in good hands, Sam and Patrick went in search of an update on Tony.

It took a while before they found someone who could tell them what was going on. The nurse was very calm as she explained to them Tony had been taken to surgery. The bullets, she explained, had done some damage, but nothing they couldn't repair. Sam glanced at her hospital I.D. badge, taking note of the woman's name: Laurel Reis.

"One of his lungs is punctured," Laurel confirmed.

"When will we be able to talk to him?" Patrick asked.

"Not for a long time, I'm afraid. He's lost a lot of blood and the surgery will leave him very weak. He's going to need rest. We don't even know when he may regain consciousness."

"Can we see him?" Sam asked eagerly.

"As soon as he's out of recovery, we'll move him into the ICU. I think we can make arrangements for you to see him, one at a time."

"Thank you," Sam said.

"Why don't you go get something to eat, I'll have you paged when Mr. Goodwin comes out of surgery, okay?"

"Thank you," they muttered, then wandered off to check on Jen once more.

She had been assigned to a private room for the time being, and when they entered, they saw Joe dutifully at his post, holding her hand. A rape advocacy counselor was there posing her delicate questions.

"Why aren't you *listening* to me?" Jen said desperately, "I wasn't raped! He didn't touch me!"

"Jennifer," the woman soothed, "it's very important we run these tests as soon as possible. This is for your safety and it may help us find the man who did this to you."

"I wasn't raped!" she screamed.

Patrick stepped up behind the counselor, placing his hand heavily on her shoulder, surprising her. "I think you should leave," Patrick stated, his voice calm and level.

"But…" she began.

"Now," Patrick asserted. She continued to hesitate, so he actually guided the woman from the room

Stepping up to Jen's other side Sam said, "You're sure you're all right?"

"Yes," Jen managed, taking a deep, calming breath, "now that that woman is gone." A nervous titter of laughter escaped from Jen's mouth.

"She kept telling her she was fine, but that woman kept pestering her," Joe explained. "She kept saying Jen was in denial."

"He really didn't… do anything to you?" Sam asked tentatively, as Patrick came back into the room, shutting the door behind him.

Jen shuddered as memories of her imprisonment washed over her. "I think he would have, eventually," she stated, "but all he did was touch me." Her voice rose to a shrill pitch as she started to recount her harrowing hours in the cabin.

"I woke up on the bed, tied up, blindfolded." She paused and looked meaningfully at Patrick and Joe. "I never saw him. I'm sorry."

"Don't apologize," Patrick reassured her. "You have done nothing to be sorry for."

Jen gave him a weak smile. "When I woke up, I tried to remember what happened, but everything was fuzzy. I couldn't get things straight in my head. I felt like I'd had too much to drink, you know what I mean? It was a long time before he came back. I didn't know Tony was there with me, until then."

Tears started to fall from her eyes again. Sam scanned the room and located a box of tissues sitting on a nearby counter, then handed the box to Jen.

"Thanks." She wiped furiously at her eyes before continuing. "He told me I was going to love him. He was going to make me want him." A tremendous shiver ran itself through her frame.

"I can still feel his hands." One of her own hands, trembling uncontrollably, moved gingerly across her abdomen, as if trying to rub away the feel of him. Sam had begun to cry herself and Patrick wrapped her in his arms.

"What happened then?" Joe prompted. Patrick understood what he was doing. Jen's memory of events would only deteriorate with time. They needed to gather as much information from her now as they could. He tried to remember everything Jen told them, knowing somewhere in her recollections might be a detail crucial to their manhunt.

Her hands still trembling, Jen looked pleadingly at Joe. "I can't," she whispered.

"Did he do something to Tony?" Jen nodded. "Did he hurt him?"

"He kicked him, I think. Tony was coughing and it sounded bad."

Joe tried to guide her though things, asking, "What did he do next?"

"He had Tony gagged, but he took it out and told Tony to talk to me."

"What did he say."

"He said he loved me." Jen started to sob heavily, her words difficult to discern. "I told him I loved him too. It's my fault!" Jen was positively wailing now, repeating, "It's my fault! It's my fault!"

Realization dawned on Sam just as Joe spoke the words. "That's when he shot him, didn't he?" Jen was crying so hard she could only answer with a nod.

"Shh," Joe soothed, stroking gently at Jen's hair, pulling her head comfortingly against his chest.

"It's not your fault," Patrick stated, his voice strong with conviction. Sam was too shocked for words. It was what the mirror had shown her, the aftermath of what Jen just described.

Sam turned to Patrick and said, "That's what I saw. I saw them after Tony was shot."

Joe looked up suddenly, his eyes turning into tight slits as he stared intently at Sam. "What are you talking about?"

Jen had heard Sam's words too. She marshaled control over her tears long enough to ask, "You saw us?"

Sam looked apologetically at her friend and nodded. "I didn't know where you were. I was so frustrated. But I saw you and Tony in that room. I knew Tony was hurt. But we couldn't do anything."

Joe was still staring at Sam in disbelief. "Hold on, Angel. I'm missing something here."

"Sam's been… seeing things. In her cousin's old mirror," Patrick tried to explain.

"I don't want to explain it right now," Sam stated, waving her hand dismissively.

"But…" Joe started, an expectant look on his face.

"Not right now," Sam reiterated.

Joe's face fell. Patrick, taking note of his disappointment offered, "Let's take a break Joe. We can take a walk and I'll fill you in, okay? Sam can look after Jen for a while."

Joe's gaze fell to Jen appraisingly, taking in her situation and gauging if he should leave her. He did, however, seem eager to hear what Patrick could tell him about Sam's visions.

"I'll be okay," Jen assured him, although her hands trembled harder the moment he let go of her. She watched as he left the room, then

266

turned her frightened eyes toward Sam.

"Are you sure you're all right Jen?" Sam asked, her voice filled with concern.

Jen's eyes darted frantically between Sam's face and the door for several long moments. Sam waited patiently while Jen tried to put words to her raging emotions.

Jen wasn't sure her friend could understand the overwhelming flood of relief that had washed over her in the moment her blindfold was torn free and she saw Joe's familiar face. Deep down Jen knew Joe's role was hardly any different from Sam's, or Patrick's, or Dan's, or even the two anonymous hikers who'd heard the gunshot and started the process leading to her rescue. But, despite that knowledge, Jen felt an unusually strong link to Joe, almost a dependence on him for strength. She knew the reasons, her psych background rearing its head, but trying to put them into words Sam would fathom was proving difficult.

Finally, she stated simply, "I need Joe."

"You *need* him?" Sam's inquisitive tone proved she wasn't understanding what Jen was trying to convey.

She took a deep, cleansing breath before she spoke again. "Yes, I need him. I... I feel safe if he's around. I know it doesn't make much sense, but he found me, you know? I didn't think anyone was ever going to find me. I thought I was going to die there. Then Joe found me. Can you imagine how I felt?" Sam nodded, but Jen doubted she could fully grasp the enormity of it.

She felt a need to explain her feelings further. "This kind of reaction is normal," Jen continued, and Sam noted a return of Jen's normal tone and inflection as she spoke. "It'll get better with time, but right now, I just feel so vulnerable unless he's here."

"Okay," Sam said, soothingly. Jen's explanation made sense. She still thought it a bit strange how she was suddenly so attached and dependent on Joe, but she pushed the feeling aside. "I'm sure he'll be back soon anyway," Sam said, hoping Patrick would keep the explanation of what Sam had seen in Emily's mirror brief.

"How is Tony?" Jen asked suddenly, an eagerness springing forth in her voice as she realized she'd neglected to ask sooner.

"He's in surgery," Sam explained. "That's all we know right now, but there was a nurse who promised to come give us an update as soon as she had more news."

Jen sighed and sank deeply into the pillows of her narrow hospital bed. "Please God," she whispered, leaving her prayer hanging unfinished.

Sam reached up to stroke her friend's arm soothingly, her fingers brushing against the gauze wrapped securely around her lacerated and bruised wrists. "He's going to be fine," Sam assured her.

Sam and Jen both jumped slightly at the sound of the door swinging open. Turning, Sam was surprised to see Laurel, the nurse, striding into the room. A feeling of dread washed over her as she asked, "What's happened?"

Chapter Twenty-Four

"So, let me get this straight," Joe said, "Sam's been able to see what this guy's been doing?" His voice carried an air of amazement, but he seemed to believe what Patrick had told him.

"Yeah," Patrick sighed. "Crazy, isn't it?"

Joe stared hard at Patrick. "You said she actually saw the Randolph murder?"

"She sure did," Patrick nodded. "I didn't believe her at the time. I wish I had. Maybe we could've stopped all this long ago."

"Did she see the guy?"

"Not really. She said it was like he was always in the shadows and she could never see his face."

"What about the times she saw the photos he'd taken? In his office, or wherever that was? Did she see him then?"

"No."

Joe whistled softly in amazement. "This is unreal," he murmured.

"Yeah. Well, after Jen was taken, Sam really wanted to get back over to the house and see if she would be able to learn anything about where Jen was. We really didn't expect anything to happen. But Sam saw them. She saw Tony get shot. But we didn't know where they were or how to find them. It was so frustrating. I don't know what we would've done if those hikers hadn't heard that gunshot."

Joe shrugged, as if he didn't want to contemplate the thought either. "This is unreal," he repeated. "Sam could have seen something that could ID this guy."

"Yeah, it's possible," Patrick admitted, "but I don't think she's seen anything useful or she'd have told us by now." Patrick sank back against the hard plastic of the chair upon which he sat, closing his eyes wearily.

"You okay man?" Joe asked him, noting the way Patrick's breathing had quickened.

Patrick didn't answer him right away. When he opened his eyes to look at Joe, they were glazed with tears. Relief washed over him like a tidal wave and he let himself ride the crest of the emotion for a while. Joe simply reached out and patted him reassuringly on the shoulder.

Feeling a need to explain himself, Patrick said, "All this time I thought Sam was in danger. Then, when Jen was taken, I felt like it was my fault… Like I should have known better. You know what I mean?" Joe nodded understandingly. "I'm just so glad we got her back safe." Patrick sighed deeply, trying to fight back the worry creeping in upon his thoughts. "Now we just have to get Tony through this."

He was silent for a long moment, then thought he should give Dan some type of an update. He reached into his coat pocket for his cell phone and instead removed a small wad of keys. He handed them absently to Joe saying, "Hold these a moment would you?"

Joe didn't respond, although he didn't get much of an opportunity. As he glanced up, Patrick noticed the nurse he and Sam had spoken to earlier at the end of the hallway stepping through the doorway into Jen's room.

"Something's wrong," Patrick said abruptly, abandoning the search for his phone. "Come on," he instructed Joe, as he stood and walked rapidly back toward Jen's room.

~ ~ ~

They entered moments after the nurse had shut the door behind herself. "What's happened?" Sam was asking. Hearing a sound behind her, Laurel turned and saw the two men who'd followed her.

Sam seemed agitated, her voice rising in a slight panic as she repeated, "What's happened?"

Laurel noted her anxiety and smiled. "It's okay. Your friend is going to be fine," she told them. "I wanted to come tell you in person. I'm sorry if I scared you."

Sam seemed to sink into herself as relief overtook her. Jen's relief was more noticeable as she actually began to sob. "Thank God," Jen managed to mutter through her tears.

Patrick stepped further into the room. "Is he awake?" he asked.

"I'm sorry, but no," Laurel said, shaking her head. "He's going to be asleep for quite a while I'm afraid. He's on several medications to control swelling and pain… we will need to keep him unconscious for a while."

"Can I see him?" Jen's whispered question cut through the room, drawing everyone's attention.

Laurel's eyes turned to Jen, drinking in her worry and anxiety. She seemed to understand what Jen and Tony had been through, although she knew very little of the real details. "Give me some time to make arrangements," she said. "We usually don't allow visitors this soon after surgery, but," she glanced back at Patrick then to Sam, "I'm sure we can make some accommodations under the circumstances."

"Thank you Laurel," Sam said, rising from her seat next to Jen. She took the nurse's hands in hers. "We really appreciate your help."

"I'll be back to get you as soon as I can," Laurel assured Jen before leaving the room. As soon as the door closed, Sam and Patrick moved reassuringly to Jen's side. Only Joe remained where he was, standing solemnly aside.

Patrick reached out and stroked Jen's arm lightly. "He's going to be fine," he stated, as much for his own reassurance as for Jen's.

Jen looked up at him and smiled warmly. "We're only safe now because of you guys. I can't tell you how grateful I am." Her bandaged arms were suddenly thrown wide, encompassing both Sam and Patrick in her hungry embrace.

None of them noticed Joe slip silently from the room. They were too relieved to take in much of their surroundings. Sam did note, however, how Jen's arms shook as she held them to her. They stayed like that for several quiet minutes before Patrick finally withdrew.

"I should call Dan and let him know what's going on," he stated simply. The girls nodded understandingly as he stepped away and out into the hallway.

"Maybe you should try to get a quick nap? Before you go see Tony?" Sam suggested, thinking of the way Jen's arms trembled. "I'm sure you're exhausted."

"I am tired," Jen admitted.

"Then lay down. We'll wake you as soon as they say it's okay to see Tony."

"Promise?"

Sam smiled. "I promise."

Jen nodded, sinking down onto the bed. Sam sat at her side, a hand resting reassuringly on Jen's arm. Within moments she was fast asleep. Sam smiled to herself, then quietly withdrew to join Patrick in the hall. She left the door open slightly so she could hear Jen quickly should she awake.

Joe sat a short distance down the hall, lost in his own quiet contemplation. Sam left him to his thoughts and moved to Patrick's side.

"Yeah, I'll let you know," he was saying, his conversation with Dan nearing its completion. After a few more brief exchanges, Patrick returned his cell phone to his coat pocket.

Sam wrapped her arms around his waist and hugged him tightly. "I didn't think we were going to find them," she admitted, her voice tremulous.

"Neither did I," he admitted. "We got lucky. Very lucky." He planted a kiss on her forehead, his lips lingering there for a long moment.

Sam released a shuddering sigh as she allowed herself to finally admit this was almost over. Tony and Jen were safe. The killer was still out there, but perhaps Tony knew something or had seen something that would help them. Sam also held out hope Dan and his technicians would find something out in the woods, some vital clue. The nightmare would end.

~ ~ ~

It was over an hour before Laurel returned. Jen, thankfully, slept the entire time. Sam woke her gently and, as she sat up in bed, Sam was relieved to see only the faintest hint of fear lingering in Jen's troubled eyes.

"I can take two of you over to see him," Laurel explained. "You'll have to keep it brief. Ten, fifteen minutes at most."

Jen swung her legs over the side of her hospital bed without hesitation. Everyone there understood Jen would, of course, be one of those who would see Tony.

As to the other visitor, Sam and Patrick looked at each other. Sam wanted to see her boss and friend. She also wanted to be there to support Jen. But she understood Patrick had a job to do. She reminded herself Patrick and Tony had also become friends. The visit wouldn't be all work for Patrick. Reluctantly, she told Patrick to go with Jen.

"Are you sure?" he asked.

"Yeah. You go ahead," she assured him. Then, turning to Jen, "You tell him I'm here and that I love him too."

"He probably won't hear you," Laurel stated matter-of-factly.

273

Sam looked quickly in the nurse's direction and then repeated, "Tell him I'm here and that I love him too."

"I will." Jen squeezed her roommate's hand as she passed. Sam watched as Laurel led Jen and Patrick down the hallway. Sam smiled as she watched Patrick wrap a protective arm around Jen's shoulders.

Looking around, Sam realized she was alone. Joe had remained quietly in his chair down the hall the whole time. Striding down the hallway, Sam sat in the neighboring chair.

"Can you believe this?" she asked her old friend.

Joe seemed startled by her sudden presence. He looked up at her, a blank expression on his normally animated face. "Patrick told me about the mirror," he stated simply.

"Oh, that," Sam sighed.

Joe sat rigid in his chair. "He told me you saw the killer."

"Not exactly."

"Then what did you see?"

Sam sighed again. "I've been over it again and again in my mind so many times, trying to remember things…" Her voice trailed off, thinking back to the visions she'd revisited and the indistinct tattoo she'd been able to recall.

"But you do remember something, don't you?"

"Dan had asked me before, but I didn't remember then," she admitted, "I saw a tattoo. He has a tattoo in the middle of his back."

"Could you describe it?"

"I don't know. Not yet, but I've been trying to remember it more clearly."

Joe looked up and down the hallway for a moment and then stood. "Let's get outta here for a few minutes," he suggested. "We can get some fresh air, maybe some food, and see what you can remember."

"That sounds good," she agreed. Sam looked up, expecting to see Joe's familiar, warm smile, but it wasn't there. Hesitantly she stood and followed him toward the exit.

~ ~ ~

Jen began to sob the instant she saw Tony. Patrick had known, deep down, what to expect, but he was still shocked by how pale, drawn, and fragile Tony appeared. Jen rushed from beneath Patrick's sheltering arm and quickly enveloped one of Tony's still hands in her own.

As he watched, Patrick could feel quiet tears tracing down his cheeks. He shuddered as he thought what might have occurred had they been even an hour later in their discovery of the cabin in the woods. He pushed the thought aside quickly.

Standing silently out of the way, Patrick felt like an intruder as he watched Jen sob quietly and lovingly over Tony's still frame. Her sobs quieted with time. Eventually, she looked up at Patrick apologetically.

"He wanted to hurt him," Jen stated suddenly. Patrick didn't have to ask who "he" was. Jen continued, her voice thick with suppressed emotion. "He was going to use me to hurt him."

"This isn't your fault," Patrick assured her, but she didn't seem to hear.

"He always called him Anthony."

"What?" Her words drew his attention like a magnet.

"He never called him Tony. Only Anthony."

Patrick shuddered. "There's more, isn't there?" Patrick asked, knowingly.

Jen nodded, but it took a while before she spoke further. "He talked about Emily. He said I looked like her, said it was why Tony had picked me, and…"

"And what?"

"He said Tony had taken Emily from him and he wouldn't get to have me too."

Patrick was nearly breathless as he whispered, "I was right."

Jen looked expectantly up at him. "Right about what?"

"It's just a theory I had." Patrick waved her off.

"I'd like to hear it."

Patrick nodded, pulled a chair alongside Tony's bed and began to tell Jen his thoughts.

~ ~ ~

"Thanks for listening Joe," Sam said. They had walked across the small park nearby the hospital. Sitting on a bench, they had watched the sun set as Sam relayed her visions to Joe yet again. He was eager to hear any details she could provide.

He had been a patient listener as Sam struggled to put her recollections into a coherent chronology. She had told him all she could remember. He stared back at her, his eyes dark pools full of questions.

"You're sure that's all?" he asked.

"Yes, I think so," Sam nodded. "Of course," she added with a small smile, "I didn't remember about the tattoo until a short while ago, so you never know. I may be able to remember more later." She sounded hopeful. She truly wanted to be able to provide information that would lead to the capture of the monster, and she told Joe as much.

He smiled at her. "Of course you do, Angel."

"I'd like to get back and check on Tony," Sam said, standing. She looked back expectantly and was surprised to see Joe was still seated.

"You go ahead Sugar. I'll be along in a little bit."

"You sure?"

Joe nodded silently.

Sam set out across the park, her path lit by incandescent lamps which had sprung to life with the setting of the sun. The shadows made her nervous, but she pushed her fear down deep inside.

A faint noise behind her brought the fear up again in an instant. Wheeling around, her eyes searched the shadows. She could no longer see the bench where she and Joe had sat.

"Joe?" she called out, "Is that you?"

There was no answer and she heard no other noises, so she struck out again toward the hospital. After about five more paces, she heard it again; the distinctive sound of a footstep in the grass just off the path behind her.

Sam quickened her pace, eager to get back to the relative light and safety of the hospital. Chancing a quick glance over her shoulder, Sam still saw no one trailing her. She sighed and scolded herself for having such an overactive imagination. Allowing her pace to slow slightly, she wrapped her arms around herself.

"There's nobody back there," she whispered to herself.

She took two more steps before she was proved wrong. She heard the loud, unmistakable sound of running behind her. She knew she should run but she was overwhelmed by the need to see him, to put a face to the nightmare. As she turned, she was blinded by a bright light; the concentrated beam of a flashlight shone right into her eyes. She could see nothing as she was wrested to the ground. In an instant, she felt the sharp sting of a needle and the blinding light faded to black.

Chapter Twenty-Five

Dan was frustrated. Their search of the cabin and the surrounding woods had yielded precious little. They were able to locate some boot prints in the forest loam a short distance from the cabin, but that was about it.

Dan knew, in their efforts to free Jen and help Tony, they may have contaminated the scene and destroyed some vital clues. As a detective, he was furious, but as a man he wouldn't change anything. He wouldn't have done anything different. Jen was safe and Tony was, he'd just learned, going to be okay.

He was lucky to have gotten Patrick's call. Discouraged by how little they were turning up back at the cabin, Dan had set off down the now well-worn trail back to the road. His cell phone had started ringing before he'd quite reached the end of the path.

Now that he'd spoken to Patrick his exasperation had dissipated some, but he was still angry about the way this man had taunted them. Like Patrick, Dan partially blamed himself for not realizing Jen was his target all along. Second guessing himself wasn't going to get him anywhere, but it didn't stop him from doing it anyway.

Taking a deep breath of the cold night air, Dan tried to calm himself. There was nothing more he could do here. The technicians knew their job and didn't need him around to oversee things. He thought about heading to the hospital to check in. Patrick had told him Tony was unconscious, but he wanted to be there when he woke up. He had questions to ask and wanted answers as soon as possible.

His mind made up, he put his hand in his pocket and removed his keys then scanned the area for his rig. It took him a moment to remember he'd had Patrick take his SUV when he drove Jen to the hospital. The keys he held were Joe's, not his own. There were so many vehicles there now and it took him a while to find Joe's car; it looked so similar to many of the other dark sedans parked along the roadside.

Stepping up to the door, Dan fit the key into the lock and started to climb inside, then hesitated. The dirt track from the cabin had been traveled so extensively in the past hours that it had become thick with sticky mud. Dan's shoes were now caked with it. Had he been in his own vehicle, he wouldn't have thought twice about it, but as this was not his car he figured he should try not to make a mess of things.

A quick scan of the car's interior yielded nothing helpful; no stray grocery bag he could put his shoes into. He checked the trunk next. It contained nothing besides a black duffel bag. The night was dark and the trunk poorly lit. He thought about checking the bag for a spare pair of shoes, or something he could wrap his into, but hesitated. Anxious to get going and not wanting to pry, Dan ignored the bag and simply deposited his shoes into the trunk, mud and all, then walked back to the driver's seat in his bare feet.

~ ~ ~

"So you think Tony may know who this other guy is?" Jen breathed. She had sat transfixed as Patrick told her what he suspected.

"I don't know, but it's definitely possible."

"It makes sense." Jen looked up into Patrick's eyes and he was amazed how hardened they'd become, the fear so evident before now locked behind a wall of steel resolve. "The whole time we were there, it was like I was just a bonus, an added perk." Jen's voice dripped with anger as she spoke. "It was like his real agenda had been to hurt Tony, to break him, and to use me to do it. Does that make sense?"

Patrick nodded. "Yes, I think it does."

They sat quietly beside Tony for several minutes, just watching him breathe and listening to the steady beeping of all the monitors surrounding him. When Patrick's cell phone rang they both jumped, startled by the noise.

"This is Logan," he said, answering.

"Patrick, it's Sally. You found Jen? How is she? I heard it on the news. Is she all right? What about Tony?"

The bottom dropped out of Patrick's stomach guiltily. How had he and Sam forgotten to call her? She'd been just as worried as the rest of them. "Sally, I'm so sorry, we should have called you," he began, but she cut him off.

"Don't be ridiculous. You've been busy, I'm sure. Don't even bother yourself about that. I'm just glad you found them. Are you with them now?"

"Yes. Tony just came out of surgery."

"Surgery?"

"He'd been shot," Patrick explained, trying to figure out how best to condense the tale for her. "They say he's going to be okay, but he's still unconscious. Jen and I are here with him now." Patrick glanced at Jen and she smiled conspiratorially at him. Jen knew what a spit-fire Sally was and could only imagine the barrage of questions being tossed at Patrick.

"How is Jen? Was she hurt?"

"No, not really. She's fine." Patrick hated to change the subject, as he knew how worried Sally must be, but he had to know if she'd spoken to Carmen or Phil. "Sally, did you get hold of them? Phil and Carmen, I mean."

"Oh, that dear. Yes, I did." Sally sounded vague, as if she didn't want to tell him what she had found out.

"And?" he prompted.

"Well, they recall Emily was seeing someone before Tony. He was a few years older and they broke it off when he left for college."

Patrick stood from his seat, his limbs tingling with excitement. But Sally's next words brought him crashing back into his chair. "They can't remember his name Patrick. I'm sorry."

Jen saw the sudden shift in Patrick's demeanor and reached a comforting hand out to his shoulder. "What is it?" she asked.

Patrick didn't answer her. Instead, he spoke incredulously to Sally. "What do you mean they can't remember? This is important!" He didn't mean for his voice to sound so irritated, but he couldn't help it.

"Patrick, I'm sorry, I really am. Listen, I've asked them to look through some of Emily's old things: letters, yearbooks, that kind of thing. They're going to try, but I don't know if they can do it. It's been years and it was so hard for them to even talk to me about this. Put yourself in their shoes. Would you want to dig this all up again? They promised they'd call me back after a bit, to let me know if they could remember anything else, but I wouldn't hold out hope."

"I understand," Patrick muttered, "and I'm sorry for how I reacted. This isn't your fault."

"Don't apologize young man. I understand, believe me." Sally paused a moment, as if debating whether she should inquire further about the day's events. Instead, she said, "Give the girls a hug for me, and tell one of them to kiss Tony from me. I'll be praying for him."

"I will," Patrick said, then hung up the phone.

Jen knew what had transpired without asking. "No luck, huh?"

"None." Patrick hung his head in defeat.

"Something will turn up, Patrick. I know it. I can feel it."

Patrick smiled to himself. Jen was acting more like her normal, eternally optimistic self. The smile still lingering, he said, "Sally wants to deliver a kiss to Tony and, seeing as how I'm not going to do it..."

Jen smiled back at him. "It would be my pleasure." She stood and gently placed a kiss on Tony's forehead, a single tear splashing the site as she pulled away.

~ ~ ~

Driving through the nighttime streets, Dan struggled to keep his eyes open. He hadn't realized how tired he was, but now the fatigue caught up with him. He pressed his bare foot hard on the accelerator, the grooved plastic biting back at him. He was anxious to get to the hospital and hoped the bright lights and sterile atmosphere would help enliven him. He still had lots of work to do.

Nearing the off-ramp which would lead him to the hospital, he fished his cell phone from his pocket and punched in Patrick's number.

"It's me," he said, when Patrick picked up. "I'm almost at the hospital. Where are you?"

"I'm in Tony's room. A nurse made arrangements for Jen and I to visit."

"He's awake?" Dan asked hopefully.

"No, he's still out. We're just sitting here."

"What room?"

"412."

"Okay. I'll be there in a few minutes." Dan hung up.

Winding his way up the multi-level parking structure, Dan finally found a parking place and pulled the sedan into it. The garish lights of the garage reflected off all the surrounding metal, chrome, and concrete and gave everything a green tint. Moving toward the trunk, Dan opened it to retrieve his shoes, then stepped back for a moment in shock.

The glaring lights illuminated the contents of the trunk and several of the items which had spilled from the black duffel bag. Leaving his muddy shoes where they lay, Dan quickly closed the trunk and sprinted barefoot toward the bank of elevators and the hospital's entrance.

~ ~ ~

Patrick and Jen were sitting quietly at Tony's bedside, awaiting Dan's arrival, when loud noises from the hall caught their attention.

"Sir! Sir, you can't go in there."

"The hell I can't." Patrick recognized Dan's voice and thought, though he couldn't be certain, the other voice belonged to the nurse, Laurel.

"Sir, if you don't leave, I will have to call security."

"Please do," Dan's voice rumbled, as he shouldered open the door to Tony's room and pressed his way past the nurse.

"What's going on?" Patrick asked.

"Do you know him?" Laurel inquired.

"Yes. He's with us, it's okay."

"No, it isn't," Dan stated, his eyes scanning the room. "Where's Sam?"

"I'm not sure. With Joe somewhere, I guess."

"Shit!"

"Dan, what's wrong?"

The detective ignored the question, turning instead to Laurel, who stood stonily behind him. She was still determined to escort the intruder out of the ICU. Had he not been in such a hurry, Dan would've admired the woman's resolve, but at the moment, he simply needed her help.

"What's your name?" he asked.

"Laurel."

"Listen Laurel, I'm sorry I came barging in here, but this is important. Sergeant Logan and I have to leave for a while and I need you to stay here with Jen and Tony. No one is to come in here. No one.

Do you understand?"

"But I have patients to care for," she protested.

"I want you to call security and have them stand watch outside the door until I can get a couple officers up here. Once that's done, you can go about your business."

"I don't understand," Patrick interjected. "What's going on?"

Dan once again ignored Patrick. He stepped closer to Laurel, placing one of his fatherly hands upon her shoulder. He lowered his voice in hopes Patrick and Jen would not hear what he said next. "Did you see the other man who was here with them?" he asked. Laurel nodded. "If he comes back, don't let him in here. I want you to call 911. Give them my badge number," Dan pulled a scrap of paper from his wallet and pulled a pen from Laurel's pocket. He scribbled his badge number down and handed her the paper. "Tell them to contact me immediately."

Laurel looked up at Dan's face and saw the urgency in his eyes. Despite her better judgment she consented. "Just give me a moment to make a few arrangements?" Dan nodded and she quickly left the room.

"Will you tell me what the hell is going on?" Patrick demanded.

"We need to find Sam," Dan stated. He didn't want to say anything further until he and Patrick were away from Jen. He saw no reason to alarm her any more than his sudden appearance had already done.

Laurel returned moments later. Dan was grateful for her expedience. He felt as though he should at least acknowledge Jen before they left, so he hugged her quickly and said, "We'll be back soon."

Once out in the hallway, Patrick placed a strong hand on Dan's arm, spinning him to face him. "What was all that about?" he asked, determined to get an answer this time. Instead, he caught sight of Dan's bare feet and couldn't help interjecting another question. "Where are your shoes?"

284

Dan wasn't sure where to begin. He decided to simply show Patrick what he'd found, knowing words would be inadequate. "I'll explain in a minute. Just come with me."

Dan walked quickly, leading the way back to the parking garage. Patrick followed quietly, trusting Dan had reasons for his bizarre behavior. He had, of course, noted how Dan seemed concerned about Sam's whereabouts. And, despite Dan's efforts, he'd overheard his whispered exchange with Laurel, advising her to call 911 if Joe returned to the hospital. He couldn't even begin to fathom what Dan was thinking.

As Dan's bare feet padded across the parking garage toward the parked sedan, his feet made a soft slapping noise on the cold pavement. His mind raced behind his otherwise calm face. He just couldn't believe what he had seen and what it implicated. *On second thought*, he corrected himself, *I do believe it, I just don't want to.*

When they reached Joe's sedan, Dan handed the keys to Patrick. "Open it up," he instructed, waving his hand toward the trunk. Patrick was perplexed, but he followed Dan's instruction. He slipped the key into the lock and stepped back, unsure what to expect as the trunk's lid lifted open.

It took him a moment to appreciate what he was looking at. Initially, all he saw were Dan's muddy shoes, but then his gaze took in the black duffel bag and its spilled contents.

"Oh my God," he muttered, his skin erupting in gooseflesh. "We have to find Sam."

~ ~ ~

There were noises around her, strange sounds she couldn't place. Her head was swimming as if she'd imbibed too much alcohol, but she had a vague recollection that wasn't the case. Her limbs were numb and, as such, she really couldn't tell if she was sitting or lying down. She didn't know where she was, but it was dark. She opened her eyes weakly and strained against the darkness, trying to pick out any detail that might tell her where she was. She turned her head from side to side, able to discern a small amount of light generated from somewhere behind her.

With her movements, the noises ceased. Sam was unsure if she should consider it a good sign. "Hello?" she croaked, her voice thick and uncooperative. "Is anyone there?"

Her question was met with laughter. It was not a pleasant sound. Instead, it sent an involuntary shiver running down her spine. Sam tried to move and found she was unable. Fighting the rising tide of panic inside her, Sam tried to work each limb separately. She was gradually getting feeling back in her extremities. As far as she could tell, she was sitting in a chair, but she was still unable to move. She was unsure if it was because her limbs were asleep or if she was somehow restrained. Far back in her mind, she knew it was the latter.

Her mind still in a thick fog, she tried to recall where she had been before this, but she just couldn't seem to make her brain work right. "Where am I?" she inquired of the laughing man, although she suspected he would not answer her.

"Don't play stupid," his voice growled back at her. Once again his words brought a shiver to her frame. There was something familiar about the voice, yet it was foreign at the same time.

"Who are you?" she asked, unable to stifle the question.

There was the sound of sudden movement behind her as the man quickly approached her. Sam fought back a terrified yelp as his hands closed firmly atop her shoulders, menacingly close to her neck.

He whispered into her ear, his breath hot against her skin. "You don't know?"

Sam shook her head in confusion. None of this made any sense. "What do you want?"

He didn't answer. Instead, his grip moved upward slightly, onto her neck, tightening for a brief second, and then he released her. "You were going to ruin everything," he muttered, a genuine tone of sorrow and loss in his voice. Sam almost felt sorry for him.

"I don't know what you're talking about." Sam said.

"Oh, yes you do. Don't play coy with me Samantha."

"How do you know my name?"

He scoffed loudly. "I'll give you some time to think about it. How's that sound?" She could hear him moving away. Then he laughed menacingly again and added, "Don't go anywhere Sugar."

Chapter Twenty-Six

Patrick was frantic. Dan had closed the trunk, but he could still see its contents behind his closed eyelids. First, there were the handcuffs and rope. Patrick wouldn't have thought too much about those items on their own, especially in the car of a fellow officer. But beneath those items he'd seen photographs of Jen. Then there had been the four brown vials of sedative with spare syringes and needles. The reality of what he'd seen shook him to his core.

Now all Patrick could think was that he'd left Sam alone with him. Somewhere in the dark of night, she was alone with a man they had thought of as their friend. They couldn't have been more mistaken.

"How long ago did you leave her?" Dan asked, his words brisk, his voice full of concern. Patrick didn't hear him, he was so caught up in his own thoughts, so Dan repeated the question. "How long ago did you leave her Patrick?"

"I don't know. Maybe twenty minutes… a half hour at most."

"Okay. If he's tried anything, he can't have gone far. I have his car." Dan was doing his best to reassure Patrick, but his words hit Patrick hard. Patrick sank to his knees onto the garage floor, wailing in a mixture of agony and rage. "What is it?" Dan inquired, shocked by the younger man's sudden dismay.

It took a while before Patrick could find his voice, and it shook with rage as he spoke. "He has the keys to your rig!" Patrick thought back to sitting in the hallway with Joe, explaining about Sam's visions. He'd planned to call Dan, but was interrupted by the nurse's sudden appearance. "I was going to call you," Patrick explained, his voice cracking with emotion. "I pulled out the keys so I could get to my phone and just handed them to him. I never got them back." Patrick's eyes turned imploringly to Dan. "He could've taken her anywhere."

"Damn it," Dan sighed. He was so frustrated he could spit. When he'd first opened the trunk, he'd thought he might have Joe in handcuffs within a matter of minutes. Hope had glimmered at him from the end of a long tunnel. But instead, things had spiraled downhill fast. Not only did they not know where Joe was, he very likely had Sam with him. Now, to top it all off, he had access to a vehicle.

Dan punched a number into his cell phone and moved it up to his ear. When the other party answered, Dan was brisk, all business. He quickly rattled off his name and badge number, then demanded, "I need to talk to the Chief." There was a moment's silence while lines were transferred and then Dan spoke again.

"Paul? It's Dan. Listen, I think we've got a pin in our guy."

On the other end of the phone line, Paul Winstone, Chief of Police, was excited. "What's the news?"

"Well, you're not going to like it," Dan sighed.

"What?"

"I've come across some items in a vehicle belonging to one of our officers." Dan paused. Although his gut told him he was right, he was hesitant to throw Joe's name out there on the small chance he was innocent.

"Who is it?" Paul prompted, understanding instinctively the reason for Dan's hesitation.

"Sergeant Torrance has several interesting items in his trunk," Dan said, his words tumbling out in a jolting rush.

"Legal search?"

"He let me borrow his vehicle." A low whistle emanated from Paul. "I need you to send a unit down here to pick us up. Now," Dan said.

"Us?"

"I'm with Sergeant Logan. Listen, we have his car, but he's got another vehicle. And, that's not all... We also believe Miss Williams is with Torrance."

"You're sure?"

Dan glanced over at Patrick, who now paced angrily across the asphalt of the parking garage. "We're fairly certain. Listen, I know it's remote, but I'd like to have a unit drive by his house, scope it out."

"Shit," Paul mumbled, then, "Of course. I'll have someone get right on it. I'll send a car out for you and I'll get a team out there to go over the car. You're really sure about this?"

Dan took a deep breath. "Yeah, unfortunately."

"I was afraid you'd say that." Paul paused for a moment, allowing the gravity of the situation to sink in fully. "I'll make some calls and get a couple units rolling."

"Thanks Paul. I want someone posted outside Mr. Goodwin's hospital room too. Their security's on it for now, but I want two uniformed officers to replace them."

"No problem," Paul conceded.

"All right. We'll keep you posted."

"Damn right you will."

Dan put his cell phone back in his pocket, then turned his attention back to Patrick, still pacing the cold blacktop. "Come on," he said soothingly, pulling firmly at one of Patrick's arms to get his attention. "The Chief's sending a car. We need to get down to meet them."

Patrick was wordless as he followed Dan down to the garage entrance to wait. Dan understood his sullenness. If he spoke, his anger might erupt with a violence he could not control. They had all been betrayed and now Sam was in danger.

"She's going to be fine," he tried feebly, hoping to pull Patrick out of his gloom.

Patrick's eyes shifted and he gazed over at Dan, a faint glint of fear barely visible beneath a sheen of anger. "But what if she's not?" Patrick whispered.

"Don't even think it." Dan's words were strong and forceful, half for Patrick's benefit and half for his own. He had to believe they would find Sam and that she would be safe. As much as he wanted to catch this killer he still prayed, against the odds, that he was wrong about Joe.

The minutes passed interminably while they waited. Finally, Dan saw the cars approaching and he waved them toward the garage's entrance ramp. "Come on," he said to Patrick. "Let's show them where his car is, then we can go."

~ ~ ~

The shock of his last words had jolted Sam to her very core. Sugar? There was only one person who called her that, but her mind railed against the thought. It just wasn't possible. Suddenly, the fog in her brain lifted and memories came flooding back to her.

Finding Jen and Tony in the woods...

Joe, seemingly protective, refusing to leave Jen's side...

His sullenness whenever Jen spoke of Tony...

Sitting next to him on a park bench...

His eagerness as she recalled her visions...

Footsteps behind her...

Blinding light, pain, then nothing...

Was it possible?

Her eyes searched frantically through the dark room. She still did not know where she was. The cabin? No, certainly not. It would be foolish for him to return there. But then, where?

The darkness foiled her ability to see anything but dull shapes around her. There was some light coming from behind her, as if from underneath a door. A house? *His* house?

She tried wriggling her fingers and found them to be vaguely cooperative, but she could now feel the unmistakable bite of the metal handcuffs binding her arms behind her back. A panicked whimper escaped as the gravity of the situation hit, but she quickly stifled it. The panic was still there of course, galloping like the heart of a rabbit inside her chest, but it was overborne by hot, indignant rage.

Struggling now against her bonds, Sam's mind was awhirl with questions. How could he do this? How had he been able to fool her? Not only that, but she had trusted him, looked to him as a friend, and even considered him part of her family. But all this time, he'd been the monster from the shadows. He had crushed Emily, ripped her so savagely from the love and care of her family.

All those women… All those families…

She continued to struggle futilely against her bonds. Tears fell down Sam's cheeks, but she was unaware of them. She was so absorbed in her own thoughts she almost didn't notice the faint sound of the door behind her gliding open.

~ ~ ~

The patrol car sped through the night. He was eager to get to his destination. The call from Paul Winstone, Chief of Police, had been brief, but he'd learned all he needed to know in those quick exchanges.

Kyle Paulson was angry. As the streetlamps zipped past his window, he reflected back to a cold Christmas night, not long ago really, sitting in a cramped patrol car outside Samantha Williams' grandmother's house. He also recalled sitting across from her at the breakfast table the next morning. It was good food. She had a nice family.

That day, he'd invested himself in her welfare. He'd promised to himself he'd do whatever he could to help keep her safe. He had even volunteered for extra shifts keeping watch outside her house.

He remembered Sergeant Torrance dropping by to visit several times. He always stopped to talk to Kyle before entering the house and Kyle had always thought it was a nice gesture. Now, he cursed his foolishness.

When the call had come over the radio asking Kyle to call the Chief, he was perplexed. Dispatch would give him no further details. The secrecy of the whole thing had him on alert. But when he had hung up the phone, he understood why they had used such caution.

Chief Winstone wanted Kyle to drive by Sergeant Torrance's home and see if he might be there. He was also told to look for a blue Ford SUV. He was to report back immediately on his findings. It was merely a coincidence he'd been the one assigned to check things out, he understood that, but he was still honored he'd been given the responsibility and the trust it entailed.

Kyle knew Joe Torrance would not have taken Miss Williams back to his home, but he still had to check. He was angry Torrance had betrayed them. In his mind, he could no longer think of him as Sergeant Torrance. He had forfeited his title with his duplicity. The more he thought about it, the more he felt the rage building inside him.

He was close to his destination and he slowed the patrol car, searching for the right house. He found it and drove past slowly, gazing intently at the serene façade.

There were no cars parked in the driveway. But there was an attached garage and it's door was closed securely. No way to tell if there was anything inside. His eyes scanned the darkened windows. He thought he saw faint light from one of the upstairs windows but drapes hung heavily behind the glass and obscured his ability to discern with any certainty.

He drove on past the house, parking several blocks away. He

reached for the radio, ready to call in a report to the Chief, then hesitated. He didn't want to call in unless he had something solid to report.

Kyle started to get out of the car, then stopped. He should call for backup before he did anything else. His hand reached for the radio again, but stopped once more. He thought about Sam. What if she was in there? He had to find her.

He got out of the car and started up the street.

~ ~ ~

"Figured it out yet?" Joe's voice drifted in through the open door, mockingly sweet.

"Fuck you, you sick bastard," Sam spat. She struggled more frantically in the chair, but to no avail.

Her words and efforts were met with thick laughter. "Now, that's no way to talk to me, Sugar." Hearing him refer to her like that made her skin crawl.

"How could you?" she asked, twisting her head as far as she could in an effort to see him. She was able to discern his shadowy form in the doorway, but still could not see his face. "How could you hurt all those women?"

He didn't seem to hear her question, or if he did he simply chose to ignore her. Instead he stepped through the door, closer to her, putting one of his heavy hands on her shoulder.

"I didn't want you to get involved in this Sam." His thumb stroked against her shoulder gently, almost lovingly, and it made her shudder. She shrugged his hand off her as best she could and he laughed again.

He moved past her, deeper into the room. Suddenly, the room burst into view as he turned on a small desk lamp. She recognized the space immediately. She'd seen it often enough.

Joe gazed at her for a silent moment. "You know where we are, don't you?" he whispered.

Sam nodded numbly, unable to stop herself. "I've seen it before," she admitted.

Her eyes scanned the room. The large, wooden desk stood in the center of the room. A mirror hung on the wall behind it, facing the open door. She sat in a chair directly in front of the desk. There was little else in the room. A small filing cabinet, a floor lamp, another chair, and a bookcase containing a mixed collection of paperback novels. Some framed family photographs hung in a group above the bookcase. A solitary window interrupted the wall directly to her right, it's heavy drapes drawn.

She stopped her survey of the room and looked at Joe once more. "Patrick will be looking for me." She spoke the words strongly, with conviction, but inside her head she said a small prayer that her words were true.

Joe laughed loudly. "You think so?" Sam nodded vigorously. "Honey, don't kid yourself. Nobody knows where you are. How could they? Why would anyone think anything was wrong? You're with me, your old friend, Sergeant Torrance. No reason to worry." His words were thick with sarcasm.

Joe moved toward her. He moved quickly and it startled her. A scream escaped her mouth before she could stop it. The grin she saw spread across his face at the sound of her fear was sickening. He stopped just inches in front of her and she could feel his hot breath on her face as he spoke.

"You'll scream a lot more before I'm through with you."

His hands darted out and fastened a strip of fabric around her head and across her mouth, effectively muffling her protests. She struggled against it, but to no effect. He stepped back to inspect his work and muttered, "That's better, isn't it?"

Sam glared at the man before her. She no longer recognized him. Joe was gone. In his place stood a monster.

295

~ ~ ~

Kyle stood outside, near the garage. One small window interrupted the side wall and it was through this he endeavored to see. His eyes searched the gloom. He thought he could make out the outline of a vehicle, so he pulled his flashlight from his belt and directed its beam through the glass.

The light revealed a blue Ford Explorer. It was the vehicle he'd been told to look for. His heart beat rapidly. He couldn't believe his luck. There was a chance Sam was here and he could help her.

Kyle took a deep breath to steady himself. He needed to get back to his cruiser and call Chief Winstone. He put his flashlight back on his belt and started to step away, but something stopped him in his tracks.

He thought he heard a noise. It was faint, so faint he could have imagined it. But it sounded to him like a stifled scream. He envisioned the scream had come from Samantha and his plan to call for backup was forgotten. He pictured himself dashing to the rescue and plucking her from evil's grasp.

With determined steps, he set off around the house searching for a point of entry.

~ ~ ~

It seemed to take forever for Dan to direct the forensics team to Joe's car. In reality, it was only a few minutes, but they were the longest minutes of Patrick's life. He was eager to get going, to try to find Sam. He realized he had no idea where to start, but he felt he had to be doing something, no matter how futile it might be.

When they finally climbed into the cruiser, Patrick sank limply into the passenger seat. "What are we going to do?" Patrick asked, his voice full of emotion.

Dan didn't answer. Instead he pulled his cell phone from his pocket and dialed. "Chief Winstone please." Patrick watched silently while Dan waited to be connected with the Chief.

"This is Winstone."

"Paul, it's Dan."

"Good. Your car arrived?"

"Yes. Forensics has started on Torrance's car and we're just leaving."

"Good. I have a unit doing a drive-by on Torrance's house like you asked," Paul explained.

"And?"

"Haven't heard from him yet."

"Who'd you send?" Dan inquired.

"Let's see," Paul's voice trailed off as he shuffled some papers on his desk, looking for the name of the officer he'd sent. "Here we go… Kyle Paulson, car thirty-four."

"How long ago did you send him out?"

"Right after we spoke, so about thirty minutes I'd say."

"All right. Thanks."

"We put an ABP out on your rig. Haven't had any hits yet." Paul sighed quietly. "So what are you going to do now?"

"I'm not sure," Dan admitted. "But I'll think of something. You'll call me when you hear from Paulson?"

"Of course."

When Dan returned his phone to his pocket, he turned expectantly toward Patrick. "Okay, you know him best. Where would he take her?"

Patrick had been asking himself that very question, but hadn't come remotely close to an answer. "I thought I knew him," Patrick mumbled guiltily.

"We all thought that," Dan assured him.

Heavy silence hung in the air. Dan started the car and pulled out of the parking garage. He turned onto the road, choosing their direction at a whim. He had no idea where to begin. They drove in silence, crossing and turning through several intersections before Dan pulled the car to the curb and stopped. He banged his fists against the steering wheel in frustration.

"What are we doing?" he asked aloud, although the question was for his own benefit, not Patrick's. Dan took a few steadying breaths. He looked apologetically at his passenger. "I'm sorry."

"What are you apologizing for?" Patrick inquired, his voice still thick with worry.

A nervous laugh, half grunt and half sigh, escaped from Dan. Patrick smiled weakly at him and the tension in the car lifted somewhat.

"Okay," Dan said, a new air of enthusiasm in his voice. "Let's think about this logically."

"What do you mean?"

"Well, first off, does Joe have any reason to believe we're on to him?"

Patrick thought for a moment. "I don't know. He knows you have his car…"

"Yes, but he offered it to me. He was confident I wouldn't find anything, don't you think?"

"I guess so."

"So… if he doesn't think we know about him, where would he take Sam?"

"Someplace familiar," Patrick offered uncertainly.

"Exactly. So, where's familiar?"

Patrick rattled off locations, ticking them off on his fingers as he went. "His home... the cabin... the precinct... maybe my house?"

"Right. Okay. Your house... that's a bit iffy. But the station is obviously out of the question. And we know he can't take her back to the cabin. Forensics is still crawling all over it."

"So that leaves his house."

Dan nodded. He reached for the car's radio and contacted dispatch. His request was simple, "Get me car thirty-four."

There was a brief silence and then, "I'm sorry sir. That car's not responding."

Dan glanced meaningfully at Patrick. "You thinking what I'm thinking?"

Patrick nodded. "Let's check it out."

Chapter Twenty-Seven

Jen was nervous. She sat quietly at Tony's bedside, her hands wringing restlessly in her lap. Laurel had left only a short while before, once hospital security had arrived. They now stood posted outside the door, awaiting the arrival of the police officers Dan had promised to send.

She, like Patrick, had heard most of what Dan had said. Especially the part commanding Laurel not to let Joe in, and to contact him immediately should he arrive. Jen didn't know the details, but it didn't take a genius to deduce what Dan suspected. That thought alone was enough to make Jen nauseous.

She reached a trembling hand out toward Tony, resting it lightly on his forearm. As soon as her hand touched his cool skin, she stopped shaking. Just touching him calmed and soothed her raw nerves. She thought back to the way Joe had held her and touched her earlier, while on the way to the hospital and after they had arrived. He had been so protective and comforting. The memory of him touching her made her stomach flip again like a cold fish.

Jen chided herself for jumping to conclusions. She didn't have all the particulars. She reminded herself it was foolish to assume she knew what Dan was thinking. Perhaps he only needed to talk to Joe. He was, after all, the first one to enter the cabin. It was possible he just needed to speak with him about what he had seen. Yes, she convinced herself, that's all. Nothing to get excited about. She reined her imagination in and convinced herself she was overreacting.

Her hand slid slowly up and down against Tony's arm. She found comfort in the sound of her hand sliding against his skin. It created a soft rhythm. She stared at his quiet face. His eyelids were closed but they fluttered softly as if he were dreaming. She imagined he might be doing just that. She hoped it was a pleasant dream. She didn't want him reliving their nightmare from the cabin.

Jen leaned in close to his ear and whispered, "It's okay. We're safe. You're at the hospital."

She drew back quickly, startled. She'd thought she heard him murmur something in response to her words. She shook her head dismissively. It must have been her imagination. She remembered what Laurel had said about the medications Tony was on, how they would make him sleep for quite some time. She smiled a little to herself, then leaned forward to whisper one more thing to him. "I love you."

This time, when she drew away, she was genuinely surprised to find herself looking into Tony's eyes. His eyelids were heavy and he was still deeply medicated, but his eyes were open. Jen smiled widely for his benefit, unsure if he could see her, but when his lips twitched weakly in response, she stood and ran to the door.

Flinging the door aside, she spoke to the nearest security guard. "Please, get the nurse. Quick."

Laurel entered moments later. Her stride was quick and a look of concern spread across her thin face. "What's the matter?"

"He's awake!" Jen beamed, gesturing enthusiastically at Tony.

Laurel pushed her way alongside him, drawing her stethoscope from her pocket as she moved. She smiled warmly down at him as she pressed the head of the instrument against his chest and listened to his heartbeat. She then lifted one of his eyelids lightly, inspecting his pupils. Satisfied with her exam, she withdrew slightly and said, "Welcome back, Mr. Goodwin."

"Is he okay?" Jen asked, a hint of concern tainting the joy in her voice.

"Well, he's awake a bit sooner than I'd expected, but otherwise,"

301

she paused and scanned the monitors around the room, "I think he checks out just fine."

Jen smiled widely and gazed down at Tony's drowsy face. "Hi honey." A few joyful tears slipped from her eyes as she watched Tony's mouth work futilely. He tried to form words, but the only sound to escape was a quiet murmur. Watching him struggle to speak was hard. Jen tried to quiet him as best she could.

"It's okay," she soothed, "Don't talk. We're safe. It's over."

Despite her words, Tony's head shook feebly from side to side. His lips soundlessly formed the word, "No."

Those simple actions sent a shiver running down Jen's spine. "No?" she repeated. Tony continued to wag his head from side to side. She knew he could not answer, yet still she asked, "What do you mean no?" Tony only looked up at her pitifully.

"He needs his rest," Laurel interjected. She looked knowingly from Tony to Jen. "I'll leave you alone. You can try to talk to him for a moment, but you need to promise me you'll let him rest."

Jen looked up at her, distracted. "Okay. Yeah, sure." Her words were distant as her thoughts were elsewhere.

The door had scarcely closed behind Laurel as Jen repeated, "It's over." Again Tony's head wobbled back and forth against his pillow. She gazed deeply into his eyes and felt her stomach contract icily.

It wasn't over; that was what he was trying to tell her. "I understand," she said, her words hardly louder than a whisper. Her thoughts went back, reliving the day's events.

"I know you're tired, honey, so I'm going to talk. You just listen." His eyelids closed slowly as if in confirmation that he understood. "Patrick had a theory," she started. She explained what they had been able to learn from Sally, which wasn't much, and how Patrick thought it was possible Tony might know who Emily's older boyfriend may have been. Her voice was soft and soothing, but she noticed how Tony seemed to become more and more agitated the longer she spoke. She didn't mention her suspicions about Joe, or Dan's bizarre behavior earlier.

When she finished her narration, she reached out and picked up one of Tony's hands. It was trembling. "It's okay." She lifted his hand to her lips and kissed it tenderly. She watched as he struggled to speak once more. She leaned in close in an effort to hear him.

"You look... like her," he croaked. His throat was sore and raw and it hurt to speak, but there were things he felt he had to say. "But that's not.... that's not why... I love you."

Tears came to her eyes quickly. She couldn't stop them. Her lips brushed his ear as she whispered, "Hush. It doesn't matter." She laid her head on the pillow beside him and held him tenderly.

She struggled silently with her next question for several minutes before posing it. She didn't want to burden Tony with it right now, but she had to know. "Can you remember anything? From back then? About Emily?"

There was no response from Tony. She drew back and looked at him only to discover he'd closed his eyes and drifted off to sleep.

~ ~ ~

Kyle had circled the house. He had peeked through every ground floor window and had seen nothing out of the ordinary. No lights were on in any of the rooms as far as he could tell. He still thought, however, that he could see a faint glow from one of the upstairs windows.

Standing now at the back door, Kyle removed his wallet from his back pocket. He hesitated for a few moments, then removed his Costco card from it's slot. He slipped it between the weather stripping and the door and lifted quickly. He heard a faint grinding sound, pressed lightly on the door, and grinned widely as it popped open. He was lucky the deadbolt had not been engaged.

Again he hesitated. He debated going back to the car and radioing in. His actions to this point had been far from by the book and he knew the Chief would not approve, however he could not stop himself from proceeding. He was angry, he felt betrayed, and he wanted to take action.

The utility room beyond was dark and quiet. He stepped just inside the door, allowing it to swing closed loosely behind him. It took several long moments for his eyes to adjust to the gloom. While he waited, he listened carefully. His ears picked up very little. His own breathing was virtually all he could hear.

He edged forward slowly, careful not to make any noise. His heart beat rapidly within his chest and his skin tingled. He was excited and he had to remind himself to calm down.

He realized he was probably overreacting. The house was so quiet he could almost feel the emptiness. Yet he continued to slide his feet forward, one at a time, progressing steadily through the small room, past the washer and dryer, toward another door leading into the main body of the house. When he stopped at this next door, he pressed his ear against it, listening intently. He was met with continued silence. Satisfied, he edged the door open and slipped into the room.

The kitchen was pristine. White tile countertops and chrome appliances winked at him through the gloom. The place was so clean he doubted it had seen much use recently. He moved as quickly as possible through the room and into the next. The living room was equally tidy. The cushions of the sofa showed little signs of use. They revealed no sags, no wrinkles, or any other evidence of being sat upon.

Kyle was perplexed. From what he had heard about Joe Torrance, he had expected a warm, cozy home. Unless he was mistaken, he recalled being told Joe was married and had two young daughters. So far, none of the rooms he'd seen betrayed their presence. There were no toys in sight. No colorful crayon drawings adorning the fridge. The place felt sterile.

He pressed on. Stairs originated along the wall to his right. Kyle hugged the wall as best he could, avoiding furniture along the way, and edged around to the base of the stairs. From this new vantage point, Kyle received a thrill. His actions now felt justified. There was a soft glow from a light on somewhere upstairs.

~ ~ ~

Joe prowled back and forth in front of her. Sam had been unable to tear her gaze away, her eyes following him as his feet carried him quietly across the room. She was helpless to do anything, what with the bindings that held her to the chair and the gag that prevented her from calling out for help.

The clothes Joe had worn earlier, when they found Jen and Tony in the woods and then later at the hospital, had been removed. He now wore a pair of loose fitting black slacks and a dark green, short sleeved shirt. His feet were bare and silent on the carpeted floor.

He had apparently dressed in a hurry, as only the bottom three buttons of this shirt had been fastened. Those few that had been buttoned were misaligned. The skin of his chest, visible through the open top of his shirt, glistened lightly with sweat in the dim light and he breathed rapidly. His breathing was the only thing to betrayed his agitation. Otherwise, his demeanor was slow and methodical.

After several passes across the room and back, he began to speak. His voice was low, steady, only occasionally flecked with emotion. It was this last that chilled Sam to the core. He spoke hollowly of things that merited much more feeling than his flat tones conveyed. He only glanced at Sam occasionally, but when he did his gaze was that of a raptor evaluating his prey for a weakness. She strove to show him none, but it became increasingly difficult as his narration continued.

"I loved her," he began. It was difficult to believe, as his voice contained none of the emotion of which he spoke. "Emily was special. When I left for college she vowed she'd wait for me. I'd only been away a few months when she wrote me a letter. Told me she'd started seeing someone else, that it was too hard for her to sit around and wait for me to come home weekends or on break. She didn't have the guts to tell me herself, she just sent me a letter. A letter!" His voice rose in pitch slightly, but quickly returned to its monotone cadence.

"And that Anthony," Joe continued. "He would strut around with her on his arm like he'd won some trophy. It was disgusting." He paced in silence for a moment before continuing.

"She wouldn't talk to me at first. Then, when I came home for spring break, something seemed different. I tried calling her a few times. The first two, she just hung up on me, wouldn't let me talk at all. But that last time, she agreed to meet me."

"We met downtown, at Pioneer Square. She let me take her to coffee and we talked. You should know the place. It's different now, but back then it was one of our favorite hangouts. I still go back every once in a while, to remember her."

Sam's thoughts flicked to the café not far from the Tribune's office and the graffiti she had found scrawled on the bathroom wall. Her eyes must have lit up with the recollection, for Joe glanced at her briefly and said, "Yes, that's right." He paced in silence a few more steps before starting again. "She only mentioned *him* once, but I reminded her how much she meant to me and she stopped talking about him. I told her I still loved her. She started to cry and then left."

"I waited outside her house that night, and the next. It paid off when her parents finally left. I had to see her again, so I knocked on the front door. She answered it and let me in. She didn't seem to want to talk, so I just followed her as she moved from room to room."

"Eventually she went upstairs, and I followed. We sat on her bed. She admitted she missed me, but that we both needed to move on." He stopped talking again, and his pause lasted longer this time. He even stopped his restless pacing. Sam wasn't sure, but she thought she saw his eyes glistening.

He looked at Sam again, staring hard at her. "But you know what happened next, don't you?" Sam nodded weakly in answer. She had seen it. "She asked me to do it, you know? She told me she wanted me inside her one last time, but that when it was over I had to leave and that she didn't want to see me again. I told her I understood. But I didn't. How could I? I loved her and she was just throwing me away! She cooperated when I tied her up. She thought it was exciting, that our last fling was going to be different, something to remember." He huffed sarcastically. "I guess it was."

"I never expected to get away with it," he admitted, a faint chuckle rattling in his throat, "but I did. I left and went back to school."

"She haunted me. Everywhere I looked, I saw her. It wasn't really her, just women who looked like her. Usually it was the hair. I always loved Emily's hair."

"Sometimes I'd seek one of those women out. It became fun. Each time I thought of her. I'd see her face while I fucked them. I did things differently sometimes, but it always ended the same."

He turned suddenly, lunging toward the chair upon which Sam was tied. "Did you enjoy watching me?" he asked. "With that Randolph woman? Did you see how much she enjoyed me fucking her?" He seemed to gloat as he said this, his voice rising in another of his brief bouts of emotion. Then his elation quickly plummeted back to earth when he said, "Jennifer would have loved it too. I wanted him to watch while I made her scream, but those two fools out in the woods had to ruin everything!"

Sam said a silent prayer of gratitude for Taylor and Abigail. When they were missing, she had imagined all sorts of horrors befalling her friends, but now, hearing Joe speak of what he had intended, Sam realized her own imagination had not been sadistic enough.

Joe seemed done talking for now, and Sam took the opportunity to scan the sparse room for anything that might help her escape. She knew she would find no such item, yet it seemed too much like giving up to not at least look. As she allowed her eyes to travel across the top of the desk, the bookshelf, and the few other items in the room, her eyes lingered on one of the framed photographs.

The picture was of four people: Joe, his wife, and their two girls. Lisa and her two daughters smiled at her from beneath the glass of their frame. A horrible thought occurred to Sam. She looked furtively toward Joe and back at the pictures. Joe caught her glance and followed it. He laughed throatily.

"I wouldn't hurt them. In fact," his voice became soft, almost tender, "I stopped for a while after I met Lisa. I made a stab at a normal life."

"But we've been separated about two years now. Lisa left, moved down to Grants Pass to live near her mom. She blamed the job. She brings the girls back to visit for a weekend every month, stays in the guest room. It just seemed easier to let everyone at the station believe we were still together." He laughed again. "Not even Patrick knew," he added, an almost triumphant air in his voice.

"After she left, I needed to do something. I waited a few months and then took a drive down there, so I could see where she was living. I met a beautiful woman while I was there. She was just what the doctor ordered, what with that lovely red hair of hers. She lived a little further south, near the California border. We hit it off marvelously. She took me back to her place, I had a little fun, appeased myself for a while, and then came home."

"That seemed to do the trick," he admitted. "I didn't go out looking for anyone new for a long time. Not until I met Jennifer."

Sam could remember the moment as if it were yesterday. First, there was the shock of finding Jen out there at the accident site, introducing her to Joe, and then finding out her parents had perished. Tears spilled from her eyes at the memory. Fate had dealt them a bad hand that day, one they had been fighting, unwittingly, ever since.

"I had to have her. I had never felt a pull like that before. But how was I to get her? Other than Emily, the women I'd chosen had always been strangers, with no way to connect them to me. Jen presented a different challenge. But the fire had been lit, so to speak, and I had to do something. I bought myself some time with the Randolph woman.

It cleared my head a bit. I decided I could use you as my connection. Bring your relationship to Emily out into the open and use it as my springboard to Jen."

A hearty laugh escaped him. "It worked well, don't you..."

Joe cut off abruptly, cocking his head to the side, listening intently to a sound only he had heard. The seventh stair had a telltale creak and he was certain he had heard it. Someone was in the house. He reached behind his back, into the waistband of his trousers where he had a handgun stealthily tucked.

Sam watched him withdraw the weapon and approach her. He was careful to keep Sam's body between himself and the open doorway. He crouched low, holding the gun at the ready in front of him. It terrified Sam even more to have him this close to her, holding a weapon designed to kill.

She was vaguely aware that, positioned where he was, anyone coming through the door would not see him, and she would be unable to warn them. She recanted her earlier pleas that Patrick would find her. She couldn't bear the thought of him walking into this trap, with herself caught in the middle like bait.

Moments passed interminably slow. Joe had slowed his breathing to a silent crawl. He refused to look at Sam, yet she continued to shake her head from side to side, wordlessly pleading with him not to do what he was planning. She watched, helpless, as his fingers tightened around the gun's grip. A shadow had come into view from the hall, moving slowly toward the open door.

~ ~ ~

Kyle moved slowly. He had almost turned back at the base of the stairs, ready to return to his car and radio the Chief. But then he'd heard laughter, and it wasn't the jovial sound one usually associated with the word. Somewhere, in the depths of the sound, Kyle thought he recognized Joe Torrance's voice, so he pressed on. He had moved deliberately, climbing the stairs on the far left side, as close to the wall as possible so as to avoid any creaking. But, only a few stairs up he had lost his balance. Without the banister rail to steady himself, he had allowed his right foot to stray far out into the center of the stairwell and was met with a hollow groan. He stood still for several moments, but he heard no sudden, panicked movement from the second floor and so assumed his presence was still unknown.

Now, he shuffled slowly down the hall, toward the open door and the source of the light. His heart seemed to be beating high in his throat, instead of down in his chest where it belonged. Its galloping beat reminded him of horses' hooves on the hard dirt of a racetrack. Unsure what to expect, he had already removed his service pistol from its holster at his waist. He held it tightly in his hand, finger already resting lightly on the trigger, ready to swing down and take aim.

He was only a few feet from the door now and stopped to listen. He could hear a faint whimpering, but nothing more. No sound of movement could be heard. Screwing up his confidence, he closed the distance to the door in two quick steps. He swung his gun down in front of him, allowing it to lead the way into the room. Then he stopped.

Sam sat directly in front of him, her back toward him and her arms tied securely to a chair. Excitement washed over him. "Miss Williams, it's all right. I've come to…"

But he couldn't finish. A resounding crack slashed through the room, bringing him to his knees. He never saw Joe, crouched low in front of Sam, but he caught a brief glint of the gun as it fired. He fell forward onto the carpet, into a pool of his own blood.

Chapter Twenty-Eight

Patrick heard the gunshot before the car had come to a halt. As if from a distance he heard Dan murmur, "Holy shit," but by then Patrick had already flung himself from the moving car. He hit the pavement hard, but rolled to his feet fluidly, too worried to feel the pain of his landing. He knew Dan would be several paces behind him once he finally got the car stopped, and he refused to wait.

He ran full speed toward the front door, throwing his weight against it, not bothering to take the time to try the handle. The door was solid and didn't even budge against his momentum.

Cursing aloud, he regained his balance and set off around the house, his legs still pumping fast. He covered the ground in a few seconds. This time, he found the back door to be open. It had been closed just to the door frame, the handle still locked but not engaged. Someone had clearly been through before him. He hadn't seen Kyle Paulson's patrol car, however he had to admit he'd been a little too preoccupied to have looked thoroughly for it.

He prayed nothing had happened to Kyle, that the gunshot he'd heard had come from Kyle's gun, not Joe's. He couldn't escape the harrowing thought that perhaps it had been Sam on the receiving end of the bullet, and the thought propelled him forward with more speed than he'd thought he possessed.

Having been in Joe's house on one other occasion, he had a vague idea of the layout, although his visit had been several months ago. He burst out of the utility room into the kitchen and moved through it assuredly. He was certain he heard a commotion upstairs. He recalled the stairway leading from the living room up to the second floor and Joe's study. That was where they had spent most of their time during his visit, while Lisa and the girls ate their meal down in the kitchen.

As his muscular legs pounded to and up the stairs, he recalled Sam's brief description of the study and the desk she'd seen in Emily's mirror. He mentally kicked himself for not connecting the scant details she had provided with what he remembered of Joe's study. He pushed those thoughts from his mind. He needed a clear head if Joe was still free and able.

At the top of the stairs, he realized he held his gun in his hands. He had no memory of drawing it, but the feel of the solid metal against his palms had a steadying influence. He forced himself to slow down. It would do no good to rush headlong into trouble. He would be of no help to Sam if he didn't keep his head.

Keeping close to the wall, he crouched low and swung though, his gun held out before him. He recoiled in shock. The room was empty, except for a prone form in uniform just inside the doorway.

"Oh God! Kyle?" Patrick breathed loudly, his eyes continuing to scan the room as he moved forward. He was eager to check on his fellow officer, but the large desk in the center of the room made him nervous. He passed quickly by Kyle, one of his sneakers squelching through the puddle of blood that had spread from beneath him. He shifted his feet quickly, rotating around to inspect the large cavity beneath the desk's work space.

Relieved to find it empty, he returned to Kyle's side. Kneeling briefly he reached out and felt for the other man's pulse. A feeble throbbing could be felt beneath his fingers. Patrick sighed in relief. Kyle was unconscious but, for now, alive. Patrick could hear heavy footsteps pounding up the stairs and rushed back to the landing.

"Call an ambulance," he called down to Dan. "Paulson's been shot."

"Sam?" came his monosyllabic question.

Patrick had already turned and was moving cautiously back down the hallway. "I don't know," he admitted. Dan quickly caught up with him, then ducked into the study, his cell phone already at his ear relaying information to the 911 dispatcher. Patrick could vaguely hear Dan saying encouraging things to Kyle's unconscious form.

He wasn't sure what the other doors held, but felt certain Sam would be behind one of them. He didn't think Joe could have moved her far in the brief time it had taken him to get upstairs. He started with the door directly opposite the study. He kicked it open forcefully and then moved quickly aside. After a moment, when nothing occurred, he moved swiftly through the door into what had clearly been the room shared by Joe's daughters. Satisfied the room was clear, he moved on down the hall.

~ ~ ~

Sam could hear the commotion caused by Patrick's arrival. The mixture of fear and relief that washed over her was overwhelming. She wished she could cry out to him. As much as she longed for rescue, she wanted to yell for him to run, to get out of there, before something terrible happened.

After he shot Kyle, Joe had abruptly stood, grabbed the back of her chair and drug her bodily from the room and down the hall. He had started for the stairs initially, but the sound of Patrick throwing himself against the front door had changed his plans. He turned around and drug the chair along into the master suite instead and then shut the door. He had turned Sam to face the door then took up station behind her, crouching low and using her for cover just like before.

Sam knew instinctively Joe wanted her to watch. As the seconds ticked by interminably slow, she was able to imagine just how things would unfold, and hot, heavy tears fell from her eyes. She could almost see Patrick sweeping through the door. The look of relief that would wash over his face when he saw her sitting before him. That's when Joe would strike, shattering all their hopes and dreams in an instant.

She saw no way around it and could only sit there helplessly and wait for those terrible things to come to pass.

~ ~ ~

Patrick had progressed slowly down the hall, clearing rooms as he went. There was only one door left, directly in front of him at the end of the hall. It was a vulnerable place, he understood. There was precious little space for cover once he opened the door. His one consoling thought was that Dan was still in the study behind him and that, should something happen, Dan would be there to help Sam.

Screwing up his courage and taking a deep, steadying breath, Patrick turned the doorknob and pushed the door open quickly. In a single, fluid movement he flung himself through the door, onto the floor, and rolled left, trying to make himself a difficult target. The tough part was that Joe had been provided with the same training Patrick had received and would be anticipating such a move.

Although he couldn't see Joe, he heard the crack of the gun and felt the slug cut through the air just above his head, causing a shower of plaster to explode from the wall directly behind him. He lost no time in moving toward what little cover the room provided: a stout wooden dresser. He pressed himself as tightly against the piece of furniture as he could, surveying what little of the room he could still see.

In the fleeting glimpse he'd been able to get before he dove into the room, he had seen Sam seated in the chair, her eyes wide with horror. Once he saw her, his eyes were able to take in little else. He had no idea where Joe was and he feared the sound of the gunshot would bring Dan storming out of the study, into the hall, and directly into the line of fire.

"Stay there Dan!" Patrick yelled, as loudly as he could, praying the detective would heed him. He knew he was cornered. Without knowing where Joe was concealed and with Sam sitting out in the open like she was, Patrick didn't dare make a move.

He counted to three, building his nerve, and then swung his upper body away from the safety of the dresser, providing him with a split second view of the bedroom. He thought he saw movement directly behind Sam. As he pressed himself again into the cool wood of the dresser, he cursed his luck. Joe was crouched behind her, using Sam like a shield. Patrick considered taking a shot, but the debate only lasted a millisecond. He found himself thinking of the implications should he miss.

He said a silent prayer, asking God for some sort of assistance; some miracle that could bring Sam safely away from this place. He closed his eyes for a moment, trying to think of a way out. But then his eyes popped open in surprise.

An undulating sound filled the room suddenly. It seemed to originate from somewhere beside Patrick. He chanced another glance at Sam from around the edge of the dresser and saw her eyes fixed on a point somewhere above him and off to his left. He didn't know the layout of the room well, but thought there may have been a mirror attached to the wall above the dresser.

His suspicion was confirmed when the room was bathed in a bright, blue-white light. Even from his vantage point the light was mesmerizing. He heard movement coming from the center of the room. Steeling himself yet again, he prepared to move. He knew he would get only one shot.

Time slowed. Patrick could actually feel it happening. He pushed himself forcefully out into the room and saw several things all at once. Sam stared past him, her tearful eyes wide in amazement. Joe had stood from his station behind the chair and had stepped closer toward the dresser and Patrick's hiding place. He seemed to stare, transfixed, at the source of the light, at something Patrick did not see.

Leveling his gun before him, Patrick took aim. As he did, Joe saw him and raised his own weapon. Before Patrick could squeeze the trigger a single shot rang out.

Sam jumped against her bonds, a frantic scream escaping the gag in her mouth. Patrick fell back against the wall in shock. Then, eyes wide, he watched as Joe crumpled to the floor, a gaping red wound erupting from the back of his head.

Slowly, cautiously, Patrick moved from his safe haven and edged back toward the door. "Hold your fire," he called, presumptively to Dan. He crouched with his back to the wall, right beside the door.

Sam continued to scream through her gag and she was struggling so fiercely she tipped the chair over. He glanced her way, but she was staring at Joe's prone form. His eyes were wide, glassy, and seemed to stare right at her. She couldn't tear her gaze away.

"Dan?" Patrick called out.

"We're clear," Dan's voice rang back.

Sighing deeply, Patrick stood and stepped through the door, then stopped dead in his tracks, his knees buckling from shock.

At the end of the hall, arms trembling and tears streaming from her eyes, stood Jen. Her arms were held out in front of her, the gun gripped so tightly her knuckles were white. Patrick would later swear he had seen a faint wisp of smoke curling from the barrel.

Chapter Twenty-Nine

The official story was that Dan fired the fatal shot. Jen had used one of Patrick's revolvers, which she'd had access to at their home. Dan simply stated Patrick had tossed him his back-up weapon when they arrived and split up to search the house. His version of events was never disputed. Jen had protested but, as Dan had told her, she'd only done what he would have done anyway. He wrapped his fatherly arms around her for a while and then sent her outside to wait in the cruiser. He didn't want her in the house when the ambulance and the other officers arrived; it would require too much explaining.

Patrick had moved to free Sam quickly, then led her away from the nightmare. When Patrick tried to move her down the hallway, Sam tore free of his supportive arms and flung herself to the floor beside Kyle. Dan had rolled him onto his back and he lay there, clinging to consciousness, a dark, wet stain covering the front of his uniform.

She wanted him to know she was grateful. As Sam's face floated into his field of vision, he smiled. She was talking to him, but he couldn't hear the words. Then the medics were there and she left. It didn't matter. He understood. She was safe.

At Patrick's insistence, Sam joined Kyle in the ambulance for the ride to the hospital. He assured her they would send Jen as soon as they could, and that he would be along later. He wanted her as far away from that place as possible, plus he knew she'd want to be there for Kyle. They barely knew the man, but he'd risked his life to try to save her.

Long tedious hours passed while Dan and Patrick gave their statements. An officer was sent to the hospital to interview Sam and get her statement as well. Sam had already been cautioned by Dan to stick to minimum details about what happened after they arrived, and to stick to the story that Dan had fired from the hallway before Joe could shoot Patrick.

Using Sam's description from her visions in the mirror, Dan was able to guide the forensics team straight to the hidden cache of photographs in the false bottom of the desk drawer in Joe's study. All in all, things were expedited quickly, yet it still took hours.

When, finally, Dan and Patrick were given the go ahead, they made a bee-line for the cruiser where Jen still sat trembling. They had been unable to reclaim Dan's vehicle as it was being impounded as evidence for at least a short while.

Dan was pleased they had been able to keep Jen uninvolved. While a part of him knew what he had done was wrong and that it violated the very codes he swore to uphold, he refused to think twice on it. Jen was an innocent, a victim, and she had acted out of desperation. He would protect her to the last.

"Are you all right Jen?" Patrick asked, climbing into the backseat beside her.

Dan turned to face them from the driver's seat, gauging her expression. He was worried about her. He had fired his gun on the job many times, but only once had he killed anyone. Well, twice now, he reminded himself with a rueful half-smile. At the time he had torn himself up about it. He hadn't slept for weeks. He did not want the same for Jen.

She forced a weak smile and nodded. "I think so."

"What were you doing there?" Patrick asked, his arms enfolding her in a brotherly hug. "What happened?" The tears she'd managed to control all that time alone in the cruiser began to pour forth from her bloodshot eyes.

"Tony woke up," she explained, "right after you left. He tried to talk to me, but he was so tired." She sighed deeply, trying to steady her voice. "So I just talked to him, you know?" She paused and looked meaningfully at Patrick. "I told him your theory. He started to tell me something, but he was so tired. He couldn't stay awake."

"And then what?" Dan prompted. Patrick looked expectantly at her, although he thought he might know what she was going to say next.

"Well, he slept for just a few more minutes and then woke up screaming. I couldn't calm him down. He was trying so hard to speak to me but he just couldn't. He kept waving at me with his hands, like he wanted me to come closer." She broke down with a series of heavy sobs. Patrick stroked at her hair lightly, shushing her and trying to calm her. It seemed to do the trick.

"I'm sorry," she sniffed.

"It's all right," both men assured her. Dan asked her to continue. "What happened?"

"I... I leaned in so he could whisper to me. He said, 'Joseph.' Well, I lost it. I mean, after you came," she gestured toward Dan, "and I overheard what you told the nurse, I had wondered if you suspected him. Just thinking about it made me sick. But when Tony said that, I just *knew*." She took another deep, steadying breath.

"I left the hospital and took a cab back to our house. I asked the driver to wait while I went inside. I knew where you kept your guns and I... I took one." Her wet eyes looked apologetically to Patrick. "I'm sorry."

"Don't worry about that right now," he soothed.

"Well, I didn't know where else to go, so I had the cab take me to Joe's house. I remembered the address from helping Sam with her Christmas cards. I don't know what I was going to do. Just wait there in case he came around? But when I got there, I found the back door open. I must have followed right behind you both, but I never saw you."

Jen's eyes took on a distant sheen as she recalled what happened next. "I heard noises upstairs so I followed. Then I heard the gunshot."

Her sobbing intensified. "I thought for sure he'd hurt one of you. Like he hurt Tony… like he was going to hurt me. I thought about all those people." Her voice broke and it took a long while before she could continue. Dan and Patrick were patient. They knew better than to rush her.

"When I got to the top of the stairs, he was just standing there at the end of the hall. Sam was sitting right beside him and they were both staring off to the side. But Joe had a gun and I saw him raise it and I…" Jen shuddered with the memory. "I don't remember pulling the trigger. But I felt it go off and I saw him fall." She was sobbing so hard now that her next words were barely audible. "Oh my God, what did I do?"

Patrick pulled her tightly to him, pressing his lips reassuringly to her forehead. "What did you do? Jen, you saved my life."

Without another word, Dan turned around, fired the engine, and drove toward the hospital.

~ ~ ~

It was early afternoon. Almost two weeks had passed. Sam lay curled in the comfort of her own bed, wrapped in Patrick's strong arms. She couldn't believe the events that had come to pass. Nor could she believe she was still alive to reflect upon them. *I've got a few people to thank for that*, she thought. She closed her eyes and lost herself in memories.

When she had arrived at the hospital that night, she made it her first order of business to ensure Tony was still safe. She found him sitting up in bed, propped feebly against pillows, as if he was awaiting her arrival. She smiled at him and he forced a smile of his own.

"Where's Jen?" he croaked.

"She's safe."

"Is it over?"

"Yes, it's over."

Tony's smile spread wider, no longer forced. Although his voice was still thick with exhaustion, Sam could recognize his usual gruff but jovial tones. "You know, I'm going to expect a story on my desk tomorrow morning."

"Your desk? Don't you mean Paulette's? She's been keeping it warm for you while you were off gallivanting in the woods."

Tony groaned, rolling his eyes. "Oh, whatever! I'm still your boss and you promised me a story, remember? I expect you to deliver." Sam laughed and he joined in, but only for a moment until he realized how much it hurt. This, though, only caused Sam to laugh harder.

She stayed with him a little while longer and then excused herself to check on Kyle. She found Laurel a short distance down the hall and explained the situation and who she was looking for.

"You're just a magnet for trouble, aren't you? Remind me not to become your friend," she quipped, a hint of a smile playing at her eyes.

Sam just nodded. "Can you tell me how he is?"

"Give me a minute." Laurel turned and strode off to the nearby nurse's station, checked one of the computer screens, and then returned to Sam's side. "Come this way. He's just down the hall, I'll show you."

"Is he going to be okay?" Sam asked, genuinely worried.

"Looks like he got lucky. He won't even need surgery. Should be outta here in a few days."

"You're kidding?" Sam was incredulous.

Laurel stopped at a nearby door, pushing it open. "See for yourself."

As she stepped into the room, Sam was surprised to see she wasn't Kyle's only visitor. A bull of a man stood beside Kyle's bed. Sam pressed herself against the wall, trying to be inconspicuous. She didn't

321

want to interrupt.

"Off the record," the big man was saying, staring sternly down at Kyle's prone form, "what you did was irresponsible. You could have got yourself killed." The man paused, and then continued in a less reprimanding tone, "But, as far as the department is concerned, you'll receive a commendation for your actions."

Then Kyle spoke, and Sam was amazed. When she'd last seen him he had been barely conscious. But now his voice rang out clear and strong. "Thank you Chief."

The other man turned wordlessly to leave and then paused when he saw Sam standing silently beside the open door. "Miss Williams. I'd know your face anywhere. It's nice to finally meet you. I'm Paul Winstone."

"Chief Winstone," Sam nodded. "It's nice to meet you too."

"Please, call me Paul."

Sam smiled. "And I'm Sam."

"I want to thank you for all the help you provided."

Sam scoffed skeptically. By her reckoning she'd cost the department a lot of money in wasted surveillance and protection, possibly helped facilitate her own friends' abductions, and had more than a small stake in the fate of the officer lying wounded on the bed before her.

"Oh yeah, some help I've been," she sighed.

Paul shook his head dismissively. "I look forward to seeing more of you, Sam." He laughed, clapping one of his massive hands against her shoulder as he walked past. Sam staggered for balance and watched the Chief of Police saunter down the hall and out of sight.

Sam turned again to face Kyle. "You're all right?" she asked, and then laughed as Kyle asked her the same question simultaneously.

Sam extended her arm and took Kyle's hand into her own. "I

322

wanted to tell you thanks." Her words were inadequate, she knew, but it was the only thing she could think to say.

Kyle smiled warmly at her. "You're welcome."

Then she left Kyle to rest and went looking for Laurel. It was nice to have a familiar, friendly face around. She saw the nurse down the hall and walked quickly to where she stood.

"Laurel? I need to ask a favor."

"What's that?"

"I need some paper... and a pen." Laurel looked at her quizzically but Sam didn't elaborate further.

She nodded. "Wait here. I'll see what I can do." Sam watched as Laurel walked away to find what she needed and then sat down in a nearby chair. It wasn't ideal, she thought, smiling, but if Tony expected a story by morning she had better get to work.

"What are you thinking about?" Patrick asked. He had seen her smiling to herself in her reverie.

"Hmm?" Sam purred, nuzzling in deeper against his chest.

"What were you thinking about?"

"Things," she answered vaguely.

"Oh, things," Patrick mocked. She nudged her shoulder playfully against him. She was tired and she closed her eyes again.

~ ~ ~

Tony would be home soon. Jen had gone to pick him up at the hospital. They had decided, since he still had quite a bit of recovering left to do, that he would move in with them, at least temporarily. He had protested at first, but Sam's promise to cook him dinner every night was more temptation than he could resist.

Sam and Jen had turned the living room into a sort of convalescence room for him. With their work done, Jen had departed for the hospital and Sam and Patrick had retired to their room for a quick nap.

"Sam honey?" Patrick started, "I've been meaning to ask you something."

"What?" she mumbled.

"Well, it's…" He hesitated.

Sam propped herself up on an elbow to look at him, curious. "What is it?"

"What happened that night? With Joe? What was that light?"

"Oh, that." Sam smiled slightly.

"If you don't want to talk about it, I'll understand."

"No, no it's fine," she assured him. She smiled quietly to herself for a while, remaining silent.

"Well?" Patrick asked expectantly. "Are you going to share?"

"It was Emily." Sam's voice had a dreamy quality to it when she spoke.

"Emily?" he asked.

"Yes. She was there. In the mirror. She distracted him, bought you some time."

After everything that had happened, Patrick knew better than to doubt, however it was all too much. He was still incredulous. "Emily was there?" Sam just nodded.

As if on cue, a sound emanated from the corner of Sam's room. The sound was familiar to Sam now, but Patrick had heard it only once before: that night in the confines of Joe's house. It was quiet at first, building in intensity, a white noise that filled the room from corner to corner.

Patrick sat up, amazed. Sam just smiled. As they watched, a bright light began to emanate from the mirror and a picture formed on its surface. A girl, flowing red hair cascading down behind her shoulders, smiled out at them. She spoke, her mouth forming soundless words they didn't need to hear in order to understand: Thank you.

Then the image flashed. It seemed to disintegrate before them, and the mirror reflected only their startled faces. Sam knew it would be the last time she saw her cousin. The mirror was simply a mirror once more. She smiled sadly.

"Come on," she said, hearing the sound of a car in the driveway and standing from the bed. "Let's go welcome him home."

THE END

More titles from the author:

<u>From the Shadow:</u>

What makes a man a monster?

For too long Jacob has lived in isolation. Forsaken by God and cursed by a Shadow, he is doomed to a eternity of solitude with only the demons of his past for company. For nearly two hundred years, he has longed for that which he knows he can never have: forgiveness, love, and redemption.

A chance encounter could hold the key...

When Jacob meets Lynn, she shines a ray of hope across his bleak existence. But will she be strong enough to shoulder the truth of his past? Can she forgive the horrors he has wrought? Can she help him come to terms with his past and move with him into a brighter future?

An old nemesis threatens...

Confronted by an ancient enemy, Lynn and Jacob travel halfway around the world. There, they face the daunting task of sifting through ancient history for clues to their tormentor's weaknesses and a way to loose his grip on their future.

What good can come From the Shadow?

Desolation Gulch

Valerie knew fairytales weren't true... at least not the happily-ever-after kind. In her world, nothing ever worked out so neatly. Her life was full of dark secrets and deep hurt. Until she met Fallon. Somehow he could read her hidden chapters and he knew exactly how to turn her life into a dream.

But Fallon isn't everything he seems; he has dark secrets of his own.

When Valerie finds herself in a dangerous situation and must flee, it's a daunting task. With nowhere to run and no way to guarantee Fallon won't follow, Valerie finds herself stranded in a small Central Oregon town at the mercy of a handsome stranger. He promises to help her, but can anyone save her from desolation?

Made in the USA
Middletown, DE
06 June 2018